My *Beauty*
For Your *Ashes*

Traci Wooden-Carlisle

MY BEAUTY FOR YOUR ASHES

Dedication

This book is dedicated to my Heavenly Father, for without whom there would be no story and to my earthly Father, for without whom I wouldn't be confident enough to write it.

Acknowledgments

To Mimi, David, Kerri, and Daisia thank you for surrounding me with your love.

To Nicole, your friendship always makes me want to go higher

To Whitney, just because you trusted me enough to believe

To Dr. Newman, your strength bought me tomorrow

To Pastor Julien, thank you for not punishing me when I went MIA, but loving me back to work.

To Valerie and Sylvia, thank you for walking with me through this journey and pushing me to finish.

To Aziza, thank you for helping me bridge that communication gap.

Foreword

"My Beauty For Your Ashes" is a well-written novel with a clear message of God's grace overcoming human frailties and tragedies. The characters come to life as they struggle with betrayal, anger, accidents, sickness, death, hope and forgiveness. The author successfully portrays the family dynamics in relationships with the local church. While the characters struggle with issues like abortion, pornography, rape and unbelief the author is always clear in her emphasis that the Biblical values are true.

I strongly recommend this novel to teenagers and young adult readers who desperately need to have positive reinforcement of the Christian World View.

Bishop George D. McKinney,
Southern California 2ⁿᵈ Jurisdiction Prelate
General Board Member, Church Of God In Christ, Inc.

Preface

8If I go up to the heavens, you are there; if I make my bed in the depths, you are there. 9 If I rise on the wings of the dawn, if I settle on the far side of the sea, 10 even there your hand will guide me, your right hand will hold me fast. 11 If I say, "Surely the darkness will hide me and the light become night around me," 12 even the darkness will not be dark to you; the night will shine like the day, for darkness is as light to you. 13 For you created my inmost being; you knit me together in my mother's womb. 14 I praise you because I am fearfully and wonderfully made; your works are wonderful, I know that full well.

Psalm 139:9-14 NIV

Amongst the death of forgotten fields I sat, not knowing whether to go left or right, too angry to move on my own, too bitter to stir the words for help, but your heart heard my innermost cry and you picked me up and made me yours again. You wiped me off and peered into eyes gone dim, shining your rays of love, reviving and rejuvenating.

You caused the tears to come, rejoicing in the release and taking in the moisture. You caused the hardness to soften, even as the clay was being formed yet again.

You made me whole and branded me your own.

Lord, I live to worship You. You are the very being that stirs me. When I look up I promise that I see your love beholding me. My fame, my fortune mean nothing compared to your presence. I can't breathe, I can't think, I can't love and I can't hope without you.

I Live to worship You

CHAPTER 1

It all started with one lone tear.

It escaped unguarded, quickly falling from her high cheekbone, wetting the concrete below. It was closely followed by another. Soon there was a rain of tears splashing against the once warm, dry stone underneath her patent leather pumps.

As the pictures played in her mind, she fell deeper and deeper under the morose spell that continued to choke the pain and anger from her chest, spreading it to the very tip of her toes.

A warm, wayward wind pulled her out of her stupor, causing her to catch her breath. She sighed inwardly. *Mmmm, another dry, beautiful day and I am wasting it with dark memories.* She caught sight of the wet ground, wondering, even as she brought her hands to her face, where the moisture had come from. She straightened up, away from the railing she had been leaning over, and looked out over the brush and yellow grass of the old church's backyard. She straightened her simple, black dress, drying her hands on the soft cotton.

She didn't want to turn around. She had finally found a small place of peace and quiet in the midst of all the condolences, well-wishers, and those that wanted to share their feelings of celebration for the graduation of another 'saint'. She worked her shoulders back and forth in a vain attempt to ease some of the tension that had been building since she got off the plane three days ago.

Another gust lent itself in drying her cheeks and she cocked her head to the side wishing it was cool like the ones off of the coast, however, it would have been out of place here. This was not a place of refreshing; it wasn't a place for light breezes and even lighter cares. The heat was as heavy as her heart, and today it was welcomed. If it couldn't rain, then she would drink in the dry, Arizona sun.

She shrugged her shoulders, knowing someone would be looking for her soon, if not already. She turned, preparing herself for more awkward small talk, and walked back to the church to eulogize her cousin's funeral.

The small white church was too warm and the overhead fans failed to keep all the air circulating low near the pews. People were fiercely waving their fans back and forth in front of their faces, creating more heat than the small fans could contend with.

She walked along the side-aisle, aware of some of the encouraging looks and curious stares. She kept her head straight, concentrating on reaching her seat on the front row.

As the funeral progressed and the soloist resonantly sang 'The Lord's Prayer,' she kept her face blank of any emotion lest she give herself away before she reached the pulpit. Out of the corners of her eyes, she could see that no one from the immediate family was present. This didn't surprise her; Stone Winters was a hard one to love and almost as warm as his name most of the time. Actually, she was surprised by the amount of people in attendance.

As the last person stepped away from the pulpit she took a deep breath, releasing it slowly. As she was introduced as the speaker, she briefly wondered how many would believe her title of 'Elder' when she was done.

She walked up the short, shallow stairs to the pulpit, organized her notes, and requested that all present would bow their heads for her short prayer that would lead into the eulogy. Once she was finished she looked out over the sea of people dressed in black and began.

"Stone Winters was a lifetime disappointment to his family and anyone who dared to get close enough to call him 'friend'. He was a liar, a cheater, woman-beater, and the cause of much heartbreak to his mom until she died four years ago. He used everyone he met and left many children fatherless. When I went to visit him last Friday, he was headed to hell with a long-standing reservation to burn forever."

She paused as everyone's breath did at that moment and reached down to grab her glass of water. She took a sip, placing the glass back down with a wry smile tugging at the side of her mouth.

"But God. But God…."

2

CHAPTER 2

Mason waited with nervousness, causing his heart to beat double-time.

How long has it been? He quickly re-calculated the date and time in his mind, trying to preoccupy it with the figures while taking slower, deeper breaths. He shifted his weight from side to side, trying to see around the scores of people in front of him. He knew the first glimpse would tell him a lot.

Oh come on door, open up. The plane landed ten minutes ago. As if his thoughts conjured it up, the flight door opened. He stretched and strained as he peered over and around the heads crowded in the reception area. The first person who crossed the threshold was a well-dressed, businessman, the second, the same. The arches of his feet were starting to tingle now with the held strain of his stance. He ignored it, moving from side to side around the now moving heads of people who were also straining to see and greet their loved ones.

Then she was there. He saw the mop of soft, jet-black curls first. Taller than her twelve years could claim, she was easy to see. He could have sworn she had grown at least two inches since she had left at the beginning of the summer. He stepped forward, just barely mindful of the feet and shoulders blocking his passage.

"Viv!" He called out, waving his right hand like a flag. "Viv!" He called again as he saw the girl look up and around, searching every direction to find out where her name was being called from.

Mason mumbled excuses as he continued to make his way through the crowd. He lunged forward until he broke free of the bodies, ignoring the last glib remark from a person only a few feet from the aisle, forcing his way towards Vivian. He came up against the rope that created the aisle from the flight door, catching the attention of two perfectly wide-set, gray eyes.

"Hi, Daddy!" The squeal, melting his heart, he bent under the rope and scooped up his daughter's thin, gangly frame in a fierce hug. He took in her dusty smell as he buried his face in her curls. When he felt her arms slacken a little, he began to release her, only to have her cling harder to him as he walked to the edge of the carpeted area.

He let her down when they got to the edge of the seating area of her arrival gate. Vivian talked nonstop about her flight and how she met the pilot before boarding and how she had made friends with one of the flight attendants, who kept her cup full of Sprite throughout the plane ride. After retrieving her baggage, they walked to the airport parking lot. It wasn't until he placed the key in the ignition that she took a deep breath, allowing him to get in a question or two.

"So…? Tell me how you liked Oklahoma? How was Grandma? Did you have fun with your cousin, Asha?" It wasn't as if he didn't already know most of the answers, he just liked seeing the excitement on her face when she talked about his late wife's family.

Vivian shook her head, allowing her curls to move slightly, and giggled. "Daddy, you know everything. You talked to me every day and I sent you pictures…it was like you were there. Gram said if it were 15 years ago, you wouldn't have let me go 'cause they didn't have cell phones with cameras, and you couldn't go more than 24 hours without makin' sure I was alright."

He looked away from the road and into her smiling face, the expression akin to his wife's. He shrugged and pulled his attention back to the road that would take them to the Stevenson Expressway.

"I know, but you weren't able to tell me everything. What was your favorite part?"

"Mmmm…let me think."

As he pulled up to the red light, he glanced over to watch her drum her fingertips along her chin, posing as if in deep thought. He almost laughed.

She cocked her head to the side, looking at him out of the corner of her eye.

"Trisha, the cat Gram let me keep in the barn, had kittens. That…"

There was a terrible screeching sound, causing him to look in the rear-view mirror. He caught sight of a medium-size, sky-blue SUV racing towards them. He leaned over his daughter as best he could in that second, trying to shield her from the dashboard and the crushing blow that was no doubt about to happen.

The impact was fierce, propelling their SUV into the intersection. Mason's head hit the dashboard, sending off a ringing in his ears. He didn't know what was louder: the sound of metal crumbling and giving way, or his heartbeat. He could feel Viv's body rock forward and instinctively tightened his hold. Then everything began to slow. He felt her breath against his neck quick and erratic.

Then the car slowed and came to a stop. He opened his eyes only when he couldn't feel the car drifting anymore. He raised his head, peering into his daughter's eyes, examining her face for any sign of pain.

"Are you alright?" He tried to make his voice sound calm and controlled. She nodded. He pulled back, straightening his frame while trying to get a better look at her. He took a deep breath, sighing in relief at the fact that the crash wasn't worse.

He gave Viv a wry smile and then turned just in time to see a brown sedan come through the light at full speed towards them. Everything went black.

CHAPTER 3

Paige looked down at her notes, listening intently on what she was being prompted to say next. She felt a little uncomfortable. She wasn't given to drama in the pulpit; however, souls were at stake and she didn't want any of their blood on her hands.

"I came here at the request of my cousin, Stone. He placed it in his will that I give his eulogy; not because he thought me any better a speaker than any other minister, nor because I was part of his family. He and I shared a tumultuous past, at best, and before last month, the last time I'd spoken to him was over twelve years ago." She took another sip from her water, noticing that her hand shook slightly. She inhaled slowly, exhaling even slower, in hopes of quelling the tremble in her hands.

"I got a call from him late one night. His voice was hoarse and frail, not at all like the booming voice I remembered. I didn't even recognize it as being his, at first. It's funny where we leave people in our minds. I never would have thought he was capable of sounding frail or uncertain, but he did that night. He told me that he had been sick and wasn't going to get better. The doctors had given up on saving him and he wanted to know if I would speak on his behalf. I told him that I didn't eulogize funerals; they were too hard. I did, however, eulogize 'home-going' services. He asked me what the difference was. I told him a funeral was held to bury the dead; a home-going service was held to celebrate someone's graduation to everlasting life.

I told him that unless it was a 'home-going' service I could eulogize, he would have to find someone else. Last Monday I received a call from his caregiver who had been given a specific message for me. He was now unable to talk, but wanted to know if I would keep my word. I told her 'Yes.' He had also asked if I would forgive him. I told her to let him know that I had many years before, but I wanted to know if he had forgiven himself. She said he was still working on it."

She recalled the rest of the conversation with the caregiver in her mind.

Paige?

Yes.

He said he was very sorry. Paige realized that even though she had forgiven him for the past, she had never heard him say the words. A rush of tears left her, unbidden.

I will be on the next plane.

"When I arrived at his home three days later he was already gone but had left a letter of instructions that he wanted me to follow. The first part of the letter, regarding how I was to begin, is now done. This is a testament that God cannot fail.

Stone's mother was one of the most devout, Christian women I knew. She could easily be found praying or in church, attending services, or volunteering in an auxiliary. As strong as her relationship was with God, Stone fought his. I still remember his answer to why he was so angry with God.

'How could you love someone who took away the attention and love you felt should have been yours?' Though this line of thought was not new to me, I had heard it from quite a few children of preachers. It still saddened me to think of how lonely life must be to deny the ultimate request of love. Anger and resentment are cold bed-fellows that rob you of peace. The danger of not accepting God's love in life isn't just what happens in the afterlife."

Paige took a deep breath. She was preaching and this was not her cousin's or the path God was leading her on. She scanned the page in front of her and found her place, renewing her resolve to stick to his wishes.

"The Stone Winters I knew as a child was not a very nice man. Years of anger and searching for love so far from its source had made him bitter and determined; determined to prove that life without the acknowledgment of God was possible."

She looked out, allowing her eyes to rest upon one face after another, but never staying long enough on any one face to judge its expression. She spread her palms across the pages as if straightening them would allow for a straighter path to the main point of the eulogy.

"By the time he'd reached his mid-twenties, he had looked for love and acceptance from so many wrong places, he had given himself over to doing a lot of things he never thought he'd do. But when asked why he didn't stop, he said, 'It's hard to gain back self-control when you have surrendered it over.' The funny thing is, most people can't pinpoint the moment they lost control over the negative thoughts they'd constantly indulged in and are then controlled by those thoughts."

There were nods coming from some of the people, and whispers filled the air for a few seconds. "As I said before, my cousin and I had a strained relationship, at best, and if I had not forgiven him, not only would I not be here today, but I would not have been able to receive a great many gifts the Lord has bestowed upon me in this life. Most of all, I wouldn't have been able to witness God's unfailing grace and mercy in this situation."

A host of exultations to God went up in the sanctuary. Paige exchanged a couple of nods of agreement then opened her Bible to the story of the Prodigal Son and had the congregation follow along.

"Stone may not have been able to receive God's love earlier in life and save himself unnecessary pain and regret, but God's word is true. I am not here today to eulogize a funeral; I couldn't do it, even for him. I am here today to eulogize a home-going because the prayers of the righteous availeth much, and because he was trained up as a child in the way to go. He came back. Before Stone Winters took his last breath, he had not only accepted Jesus as his Lord and Savior, he asked God for forgiveness, accepted it, and forgave himself."

A cheer went up in the church. Paige let it die down before she continued.

"So today, I rejoice in celebrating with you the home-going of Stone Winters into the loving arms of God. Hallelujah!"

Words of praise went up in shouts and song in the chapel, filling the air with a warm thickness that filled eyes with tears and hearts with overwhelming emotion.

"I have one more request to fill." The chapel stayed full of words and praise but the volume lowered.

"For each person who has not accepted Jesus as their Lord and Savior or has once been in close communication with God but has allowed life, people, or situations to distract or take over the time you used to spend with God, I want to pray for you. For everyone who has done anything in their life that they are having a hard time forgiving themselves or someone else for, I want to pray for you. Life with God doesn't start once you leave your body here. Jesus came that you would have life and that it would be lived more abundantly; that means with peace, love and continued acknowledgment of God and the realization of His love. Now let us pray."

CHAPTER 4

Mason woke to the sound of a high-pitched noise coming to him in what seemed to be a foggy haze. As he tried to work his mind and research the sound, it seemed to get louder.

His mouth was dry and it was a strain to open his eyes. He wasn't in his bed and he wasn't at home. Besides the beeping, it was too quiet. He laid there taking inventory of his body while trying to shake off the sensation of sleep. A sharp pain went through his leg when he tried to work his left ankle, and then it came rushing back to him like a flood.

The accident, his daughter…

"Vivian!" his mind screamed, "Vivian!"

He tried to yell, but it only came out as a soft whisper. He worked his mouth, but it felt like he was speaking through cotton. If it weren't for the pain, he would have thought he was dreaming. He began to panic as he struggled again to open his eyes. He could hear the beeping become erratic, which only heightened his agitation. He worked harder to lift his lids and was finally victorious in prying his left eye open enough to make out a fuzzy dim light surrounded by shadows. He dared not blink, for he was afraid he wouldn't be able to get his eye open again. The room was dark, but it didn't help him judge the time.

To his left, a stream of light came through what he guessed to be a doorway, causing him to instantly squint his eyes against the onslaught of light. Squeaky shoes came towards him and he felt a hand on his wrist.

"Vivian?" he said as loud as he could.

"Ssshh," came the reply. "You need to rest."

He tried again, this time succeeding in a whisper. "Daughter, Vivian!"

The hand on his wrist gripped it firmly. "Okaaaay, alright. Calm down. Your daughter is alive. She is resting, she…"

He didn't hear anything else.

Vivian was alive. Vivian was *alive*.

Exhausted by the emotion and physical strain, he fell back to sleep, plagued by sedans and SUVs steering themselves towards him in a bizarre form of "Frogger."

The next time he woke, daylight was streaming through the window. He was surprised to find that his eyes opened with very little resistance.

Waiting for them to adjust, he squinted, turning his head slightly away from the light. He looked down, surveying his arms and legs, following the tubes leading from the inner-side of his elbow to a bag with clear liquid.

He looked up as the door opened, catching the eye of the nurse on duty. He wanted to be the first to speak, but the question of his daughter's whereabouts never got through his lips.

"So... you are awake. I am going to ask you a couple of questions. Do you know your name?"

Mason nodded, barely whispering, "Mason Jenson."

"Good. Mr. Jenson." The nurse spoke in a reassuring tone. "You are at Redford Memorial Hospital. How do you feel this afternoon?"

Afternoon? This sent off alarms in his head. It couldn't be afternoon already. "Vivian, daughter. Vivian." It hurt to talk; his lips felt cracked and so did his throat, for that matter. At least this time the words were more than a whisper.

The nurse, seeing his worried look, placed a hand on his arm. "Your daughter is alive and resting. The doctor will be in shortly to talk to you about her. Meanwhile, I need to know how you are feeling. Any pain, other than the head and ankle? Do you feel nauseous, dizzy, or light-headed in any way?"

Mason drug his thoughts from his daughter and answered the woman's questions to the negative as quickly as possible. He needed to find out more about his daughter. "I feel fine. Where is my daughter?"

"I will get the doctor for you," the nurse said checking off something on a nearby chart, "He will be able to answer those and any other questions you have."

Feeling his patience begin to wither, he whispered sternly, "Yes, please do that."

He laid there for what seemed like hours before he decided that getting up and going to find Viv by himself would be the best thing to do. He had his hand on his IV tube when the doctor walked in.

"I don't think you want to do that. It is just painful trying to get them back in...for everyone involved." The tall, sandy-haired man looked over the chart in his hand before he continued.

Mason was fed up. He wanted out of the bed, out of the room, and in the presence of his daughter. "My daughter."

The doctor looked up "Huh? Oh. Your little girl. She is resting. I will discuss her in a moment. First, do you know how you came to be here?"

10

Was he kidding? Who really cared? And why was it the only report he could get on his daughter was 'she is resting?'

"Car accident."

"Okay. Well, you have a broken ankle. It was a clean break, so it should heal fine. You are suffering from a concussion. You have a pretty hefty bruise on the left, front side of your head. We have been closely monitoring you. There was a little bit of swelling on the brain, but that started going down after the first couple of days."

"Days?! Days!?" Mason said incredulously, "How long have I been here?"

The doctor, now aware of what he said, gave him his full attention.

"When the EMT arrived at the scene of your car accident, you were unconscious. Your daughter was awake and quite frightened at the fact that she couldn't wake you. There was some swelling on your brain so we had to induce a coma to allow for faster healing. You have come out of it better than we expected." Mason sighed in frustration and through gritted teeth, tried to get his point across.

"I don't care about me. What has happened to my daughter? No more looking out for my health and not wanting to upset me. If you don't tell me, I will get more upset. I will get angrier. So you better tell me or I will walk around this hospital until I can find someone who will."

The doctor looked at him for a full minute, obviously judging whether this man was bluffing or not. He finally decided on not calling it and began to explain Vivian's situation.

Vivian also suffered a blow to the head, but nothing as severe as Mason's. What was concerning the doctors were her kidneys. With the trauma to the rest of her system: a ruptured sternum, one collapsed lung, and a liver threatening to shut down, her kidneys were the only organs that refused to react to treatment. She was young and the doctors believed she would pull through now, but she would have to go through dialysis for the rest of her life if she wasn't able to get a kidney.

It took a full 30 minutes after the doctor had left for it to sink in.

His daughter might have problems for the rest of her life if she didn't receive a kidney. Oh, how he wished his wife was still alive. She would wrap her arms around him and the world would right itself. She would probably network until she found someone that could donate a kidney and Vivian could have a normal life.

Why him? Why his beautiful daughter? She was so full of life; why did the being his wife called 'God' allow so many bad things to happen?

CHAPTER 5

The clouds looked grounded from this height. White, puffy pillows, lying against the spectrum of colors, squares, and circles outlining the towns, cities, and states, as the plane flew overhead. Paige looked away from the window and glanced over at the empty seat next to her. Twelve and a half years of empty seats, empty chairs, empty beds, emptiness...

Taking in a deep breath to keep away the tears, Paige signaled a passing stewardess and requested another apple juice. Today seemed harder than most to chase the memories away. Usually a peaceful song, a prompted scripture, or a prayer could help wipe away the cobweb of memories. But today, already spent from a weekend of saying 'good-bye' and helping to usher souls to Christ, she didn't have the strength to hide. She laid her head back, closed her eyes, and let the images play across her mind.

*   *   *

A small, green room reeking of dirty socks, underwear, and the faint smell of something not supposed to be present in a teenage boy's room; especially not one with a devout mother who claimed to know Jesus better than Matthew, John, or Paul. There it was, the demonic spirit, traipsing back and forth across the rug, waiting to use its host once again for this foul deed. Ugh, the stench was sickening. How could they not smell it? How could no one else know what was going on in that room? How could no one hear her quiet cries for help? How could they not see through the walls? Mothers were supposed to innately know when danger was coming for their children, weren't they? Weren't they?

She had stood there, trying to find the words that would give her freedom without losing his friendship; she didn't want to do that again. Even when she was requested to raise her hand towards him, she'd denied him that time, hoping that he might tire of her and send her back to her parents. He asked her again, threatening not to keep his end of the bargain if she denied him again. She averted her eyes and lifted her hand, and as is almost everything to an eight-year-old, he was huge.

A swirl of blacks and grays took her into a delivery room, where the pain was excruciating. She breathed in and out quickly, mimicking what she had seen on television – it wasn't working. She couldn't seem to get a cleansing breath that could bring enough relief for her to get any of her strength back; this was killing her and she was ready. She was looking forward to some quietness in the midst of the storm in her mind. She wanted the one thing that seemed to elude her since she was…she couldn't remember. Peace – she wanted peace. But before she could, she knew she had one last, awful task to finish. She pushed again with a nurse at her side, acting like a cheerleader for the Chicago Bears; Paige just wanted her to shut up. It was hard enough trying to hear the woman in front of her.

"Sweetie, come on and try to push a little harder next time okay? Push harder!"

Push harder? She didn't think she had it in her. She was much younger than most women having children these days.

A contraction cut off her breath and thoughts, her attention fully devoted to pushing and trying not to black out. It felt like her insides were coming out along with the child. The nurse beside her took her hand and Paige looked up into concerned eyes.

"Honey, you need to push harder. Your baby is almost here."

Her baby? No, not her baby. This was none of her. The baby was just a reminder of a sickness passed from one family member to the other. She had no breath to retort, so she stuck out her tongue in denial and used the anger burning inside to push harder. A searing pain ripped through her and then came a small release of tension. She laid there waiting for the next contraction to grip her, but the nurse next to her left her side for a second, then came back saying, "You did well, you did well. You can rest now, you did well." She heard whispering and wanted to lift her head to see what was going on, but lacked the strength to even open her eyes.

*   *   *

The "fasten seatbelt" signal alerting her to secure herself in her seat once again tore her from her haunting thoughts. Paige was grateful. She looked out of the window and was astonished to see that they were now amidst the clouds. The p.a. system announced the too-soon landing of the plane at LAX.

"Excuse me, I was wondering if you wouldn't mind? I normally don't do this, but I would really regret it if I didn't ask you."

13

Paige, slightly startled, looked up at the young woman with a very familiar book in her hand.

"Are you Paige Morganson?"

Paige nodded, looking around the woman in hopes that no one else was witnessing this embarrassing display. She tried to keep her voice to a whisper to hint to the woman to do the same.

"Yes."

Even though she refused to have her photograph on the back of the book, the best-sellers listing, a half-dozen book signings, and small, speaking circuits had cost her, her anonymity.

"Will you please autograph this book for me? I just finished it and I would be honored..."

Paige reached for the book, still in its perfectly-unscarred blue, mauve, and tan book cover. This woman must have taken it straight from the airport bookstore. Having learned to shorten her signature to keep long lines moving, after writing a friendly greeting, Paige scribbled the initials – almost illegibly – symbolizing her name.

She smiled at the young woman as she handed the book back.

"May I ask you one question?" The young woman, oblivious to the glances she was getting, continued standing in the middle of the aisle while the seatbelt sign was still lit. Paige nodded quickly, hoping the woman would get the clue and ask just as quickly. "I know it was fiction, but was any of it real?"

Paige's lip lifted at the corner. She would have been wealthy if she had a dime for each time she heard that question.

"What do you think?"

The woman mistakenly took this as an invitation and sat down next to Paige. Feeling her space threatened, she leaned back as far as she could, trying not to be rude, but let the woman know that she was invading something sacred. This went unnoticed.

"I think it was half fiction and half non-fiction. I think it was too close not to be real." Paige was amused by her enthusiasm.

"Isn't that what a good book is supposed to do? Isn't it supposed to take you on a trip and make you question whether it could have happened even though it has been dubbed 'fiction'?"

The woman blinked; she looked sheepish and a little embarrassed. Paige was a little ashamed of her behavior. She worked to clean up her faux pas.

"What did you find so 'believable'?"

The woman hesitated just a moment. "I just thought that the main character was a little too real. I related a great deal to her. I have been through some things, and I could see myself through her. I guess I was just hoping…"

Paige almost felt sorry for the woman. She seemed to be reaching out for anything, but as much as she wanted to give this person hope in her, she knew she couldn't save her. She could barely save herself.

"No honey, I am sorry. It was pure fiction," she lied, "but it doesn't mean that others aren't going through it. Besides, I think there is a better ending for you. However, you need to allow the one Being that the main character in this book wouldn't allow to help her with her wounds. You need to find the courage to call on Him yourself."

She leaned forward, intent upon her purpose to lead this woman in the right direction. "Do you believe in God? I mean, the One and only living God. The One who sent His only begotten Son, Jesus, down to this earth to save us?" The woman began to look uncomfortable, so Paige waited patiently for the answer.

"I was raised Catholic but I haven't been to a church since I left my parents' house. I felt like it was my mom and dad's religion. I just never seemed to be able to relate to the statues, reciting the prayers, and the incense. I couldn't seem to get any answers…" she trailed off, looking away.

"When you read my book, what were you looking for? Better yet, what are you looking for?"

"More… I don't know really…I just know there is more. I know it may sound crazy, but there has got to be more than just a successful career, a family, a boyfriend…" She trailed off again but then looked back at Paige with a pained look in her eyes. "Was I wrong? Is there more? Isn't there more to this life? Your book hinted to it. Was I wrong? Was I seeing something that wasn't there?"

Paige smiled inwardly. God was wonderful. He could pull you out of yourself if you listened.

"I'm sorry, I didn't ask you your name." Paige reached out her hand to shake the woman's hand.

"Margaret Soyer," replied the young woman.

Paige nodded, "Ms. Soyer," she began but was interrupted.

"Mrs. Soyer, but please call me Margaret."

Slightly surprised, Paige began again. The woman couldn't be more than 22 years old. "Margaret, what do you do for a living?"

The woman hesitated for only a second. "I am finishing my last year at UCLA, studying Psychology. I want to get into social work, but even though I feel I have studied and read almost everything I can get my hands on, I still can't seem to find out what causes people who don't have anything to still have hope. You know? That hope beyond strength, or what I would call a strong will to live, but I haven't found it. I mean, there has got to be more, right?"

Paige inhaled, wanting to catch her breath for both of them. "You don't seem to have a lot of faith in humans. Do you think we are so fragile?" Paige began baiting the hook.

"It's not that. I may have been a little clumsy in my expressions and thoughts…"

Paige interrupted her. "I believe you said just what you thought. Don't backtrack now! If this is the way you feel, be truthful. It is easier to get the answers you want if you are brave enough to ask the real questions."

Margaret sat back in the seat and nodded her head emphatically. "Okay, that is the way I feel, but what is the answer?"

"I can't tell you what they believe; I can only speculate. I do believe there is someone greater than anything I can go through. Someone greater than anyone I could meet on this earth that could open or close doors for me. What I believe is that the God I serve is not so high that He doesn't want to have an intimate relationship with me or so low that He doesn't see around my situation. He gives cause where I can't see any; He gives value to things we would be blind to or throw away. He loves me more than I love myself but isn't content to be the only one to see me as He does. He wants me to come into the full understanding of who I am in Him. He is the answer to the 'more' I was seeking and the underlying character in my book that you called 'true'. I believe the reason people live when you don't think they have anything to live for is because of God, and if you want to know more about Him, then you must first acknowledge that He goes beyond the edifice of a church building, a recited prayer, a statue, or a priest. He is not just your parents' God, no matter how many religious boundaries were placed between them. He could be yours, too."

Margaret sat still, soaking it in. Paige gave her time. She remembered when she came to the realization of what she had just said. A little mind-blowing, but strangely acceptable. After what seemed like minutes, Paige opened her mouth but it was Margaret that spoke.

"So if He is real, then why do people hurt as they do? Why is there so much death? Why are so many people left behind?"

Paige looked Margaret right in the eyes. "You sound like you have had this conversation before. Have you?"

Margaret never flinched. "I asked my mom's priest the same question, but he wouldn't answer me or couldn't answer me."

"Margaret, I believe you can have the answers you seek, but why don't you ask the very One you seem to be accusing?"

"Because I don't believe He would answer," Margaret replied heatedly.

"Why not? Have you asked Him, or are you just interested in being the judge of this 'mythical creature'?" Silence met her retort and she wondered if she was being too harsh. After all, wasn't she supposed to be loving and nurturing? She tried it from a different angle. "What if God was real – more real than anyone you knew? What if getting to know Him would answer your questions? Would you consider getting to know Him?"

"Why would He want to have a relationship with me? Why would He want to give me answers?" Margaret asked quietly, almost as if she was afraid to know.

"For the same reason you study to help people. He doesn't want to see you struggle if there is a better way. He wants you to be happy and see you fulfill your purpose. Most of all, He loves you."

Paige expected a long pause while Margaret soaked in what most people fought to receive.

"How does this relationship begin?"

"You receive a wonderful gift by acknowledging His son, Jesus Christ, who came down to earth, was born of a virgin, walked among us, but always united with the Father, and died for us so that we would not have to pay for our sins with eternal damnation. The gift is having eternal life with God in Heaven. That is the beginning."

Margaret nodded. "So how do I do that?"

"We pray and I lead you through a scripture; Romans 10:9 to be exact. I explain to you what you have accepted and received, and we rejoice that you are not only well on your way to receiving the answers you have been looking for, but also the start of a wonderful and beautiful relationship."

The tears that were glistening in both women's eyes when they began to pray were streaming unabashed by the time the prayer was over and Margaret accepted Jesus Christ in her heart.

Just before touching down, Margaret walked back to her seat and Paige tried hard to contain her joy, or at least the rest of her tears. "Thank you, God. You are amazing and continue to keep me in awe of your love for your children – those that acknowledge you and those who will. I so love you."

Suffice it to say, Paige felt much lighter getting off the plane than she did getting on. She was now looking forward to her quiet apartment.

Paige heard the last lock turn with a satisfying click. She pushed opened the door while clumsily trying to hold on to her luggage. She barely made it in the door before stumbling over a strap, dropping her luggage to the floor and following not too far behind it. Her laughter could be heard all the way down the hall.

*   *   *

Paige rolled over, groaning at the sound of her cell phone pealing in the early morning. Glimpsing at the name on the caller id, she answered, "Good morning, sunshine!"

"Wow! Sir, will you please put my sister on the phone? I need to tell her how her sinning is causing me to backslide."

Paige giggled at her sister's antics. "What's up? Why are you calling me so early?"

"Early? It is 8:30 am your time. You are usually up way before now. You call and wake me up. That's kind of why I called. You said you would call this morning and give me your answer about whether or not you would be able to come this way soon. Gladys would love to spend time with you, and I could use some alone time with Marc."

Paige sat up slightly, propping herself up against her oversized pillows. "Is everything alright with you and Marc?"

"Never better, just looking for some alone time."

"Mmmm, you don't play fair. I will come. Do you have any special day in mind?" Paige asked with a sneaking feeling she had just stepped into something.

"Yes, as a matter of fact, I do. Next Friday."

Paige laughed out loud. "Okay, I will check with my manager. If everything is clear, I will book a flight and call you back to tell you when you can pick me up."

"Fantastic. I will let Gladys know you are coming. Meanwhile, I will be making a few arrangements of my own."

"Now don't get too happy with those arrangements." Paige snapped. "You two have to be back by the third of September because I have a signing in New York on the sixth and I have to get ready for. Okay?"

"Eight days is more than I could ask. I will see you on Friday and I will hear from you sooner. Thank you, sis, I mean it. Thank you."

"You are welcome. Besides, I get to see my beauty. I still can't believe she is taller than me."

"I know, you watch them grow and you still can't believe it when they are old enough to do almost anything, independently of you. She recently told me she would like to get her ears pierced."

"And you said?"

"I would think about it. What do you think?"

"I'm not sure. Do you think she asked because she wants to, or because most of the young girls in her class already have their ears pierced?"

"I am pretty sure it is because she is ready. She was never really one to follow the crowd. I think her aunt's influence on her at an early age did that. I have to give it to you sis; the poems and letters you write her are wonderful. Even better is that she likes to read them."

"Mel, she is a one in a million. I love her."

"Too true. Paige?"

"Yep?"

"Marc and I have been talking." Mel paused briefly. Paige could imagine her biting her bottom lip. "Since Gladys is such a mature twelve-year-old, we think this would be a good year to tell her...about everything."

"Mel, it is awfully early. I am not sure I am ready to have this conversation." Paige cleared her throat noisily while she squirmed uncomfortably. She tried to think of anything that would waylay her sister. "I'm still a little jet-lagged, and the emotional strain of the weekend..."

"Paige. You and I agreed, and whether we talk about it now or tomorrow, I think it would be best if we told her sooner rather than later. Why are you so afraid?" Mel's voice began to climb.

"Mel. Why ruin a good thing? She is so happy." Paige began to feel desperation in the form of sweat trickle down her back. "No need to mess with the child's mind. She has the best of both worlds. A mother who can love on her better than anyone I know, and an aunt who can guide her from afar."

"Paige. She lives a lie and you are trying to go back on your word. I am prepared for many scenarios where Gladys is concerned, and I believe she will be just fine. You are the one who is running and honestly, I am to blame because I have given you too much space."

"Ugh. Mel. Please. I am just not ready. I just finished putting the nail in the coffin. I just need a little more time." Silence filled the line.

"Paige, I am sorry. I have given you years. It is time to face what you have so conveniently placed in my hands. You have had more than enough time to heal. You talked to God. You talk to others about your love, for the love of your life." Paige felt her resolve begin to wane.

Mel continued, her voice growing firm. "Gladys is precious. She is a beautiful gift from God. She is the love, redemption, and life-giving gift God gave you out of the snare the enemy used to destroy you. I have been to some of your conferences. It is hard to believe that you, who speaks so intimately about God and your relationship with Him to others, would purposely miss out on one of His most precious gifts to you."

"Please, Mel. I am begging you. I need you to understand how hard this is for me." Paige began sobbing. "I...I don't know if I have it in me to answer her questions. I don't know if I can answer them truthfully without doing her irreparable damage. I don't know if I am ready to look Gladys in the eye and tell her that she's the product of incest. That she lives because my plans for an abortion failed and she lives with you because when she was born, her grandmother wanted to pretend that she didn't exist. Why not the lie? Why not let her believe that she was the product of love and adoration?"

"Paige, you should know better than I. The reason is simple: she lives because God said so, and no matter the means by which she was conceived or the plans you had for her, God said she was going to live. That is the answer to her questions. She was meant to be; she is the miracle you speak to others about. She is the witness that we look for from day to day. She is God's love standing triumphantly through all of your storms, and it is time you came to realize that. No more running, Paige. I have to put my foot down. It's time for you and me to tell Gladys that you are her mother."

With a sigh of resignation, Paige asked how much time she had.

"Paige, I am not sending you to death row, so don't be so dramatic," Mel fumed on the other end of the line, "I am not giving you a deadline. I am just letting you know that I can't let this go on too much longer. Not for your sake or Gladys'."

"Understood. I will check with Carmen to make sure I'm clear and then email you the flight itinerary. Okay?"

"Okay."

Paige leaned over, placing the receiver down quietly. So the door wasn't closed yet...

"God. How do I get closure from the past with it staring me in the face?"

Not waiting to listen to the answer, Paige rolled out of bed, put on her robe, and walked to her office to call her manager.

Carmen was a great manager. She was not interested in micromanaging and when Paige told her no, she listened. She didn't always agree and, to her credit, had been able to convince Paige to change her mind twice in the five years they had been working together: she had changed her last name for a pen name and got her to finally stand in front of people and speak. Both changes were extremely beneficial. Carmen was matter-of-fact. Paige always knew where she stood with her and from the beginning, Carmen, an up and coming booking agent, pushed Paige behind the podium, especially after her second book reached the Best-Seller's list.

It was odd at first, taking vacation time from her job as a project coordinator for a nonprofit to drive or fly hundreds of miles to speak to women's groups, mostly Christian, about how to build or restructure ministries geared towards helping pregnant teens and single parents. She had never considered herself a speaker. She liked the thought of sitting at home, writing books, and getting paid. If it weren't for Carmen and God using her, Paige would still be doing just that.

She was so convinced that she needed help she even participated in a few local Toastmasters meetings. She was passionate about her subject and that was what Carmen had used to get her in front of her first audience.

She pulled up her latest itinerary on her computer. The dates between Friday the 29th and the following Friday were clear. She took a deep breath and dialed Carmen's number, all the while knowing she would be leaving a message on her voicemail. Carmen, for such a successful author's manager, did not answer her phone before 10 am.

"Carmen, this is Paige. I am going out of town next Friday. I will be back here for my flight to New York by the sixth." She hung up the phone and walked back to her bedroom, crawled into bed, curled up in a ball, and began praying until her words became sobs.

CHAPTER 6

Mason's heart was once again in his throat.

Only two weeks ago, he was looking forward to seeing his daughter and spending the remaining summer with her, and now he was on his way to her hospital room. Life had a way of turning your agenda upside down. Vivian was awake for a few hours at a time, the nurse had told him, so this was going to be a quick visit. He just couldn't wait any longer.

He took a deep breath as he pushed the door to her room open, steeling himself for the image of his daughter in a hospital bed. Nothing could have prepared him for the sight of his daughter lying in the bed with tubes running from her. He felt helpless. He rolled his wheelchair forward, drawing himself closer to her.

"Vivian, honey?" He took her small hand in his. "Vivian, are you awake?" He watched as her head turned and her eyes opened. The smile that lit her slightly pale, yellow skin, allowed him to hope. Only then did he notice that he had been holding his breath.

"You look tired, daddy. You have blue smudges under your eyes. Have you been crying?" His ever-perceptive daughter looked right through him.

He avoided the last question. "I have been worried. The doctors wouldn't let me see you until today, but all is well now that I can see for myself. How do you feel?"

She yawned, answering him with the single gesture before saying a word. "I am a little sleepy, which seems odd because it seems that all I do is sleep. I can't even get through a whole episode of any of my favorite shows. I start to read a book, and I am almost out before the end of one page. Is it always going to be like this?" She looked at him with those beautiful gray eyes and he wanted to move heaven and earth. He almost wanted to pray but he had not done that since his wife became ill. Look how successful that was.

"No, honey, it will get better. You are young and will get better day by day. When we find another kidney for you, you will be as fit as you were before the accident."

He watched as her features clouded. "I have been thinking about that day. I was so scared. You wouldn't wake up and I thought I would be all alone."

Mason squeezed her hand, trying to take her attention away from that day. "Vivian, there is no need to replay that day. I am fine. See?" He released her hand and set his wheelchair back so that he could turn around. Before he fully faced her, he heard her giggle and it was sunshine to his heart. He came back to her. "I have no intention of leaving you here alone. Your mother had to go and we both miss her deeply. I will not do that to you. Not if I have a say."

Vivian took her hand out of his and laid hers on his, with a supportive pat. "I know you miss Mommy very much, and I wouldn't be mad at you if you felt the need to go and be with her. I would miss you a lot and I don't know what I would do, but I know that God would take care of me, just like He is taking care of Mommy. He could take care of you if you would let Him." Her eyes were beseeching. He saw his wife's work in her. Even laying here in this bed she believed and waited on Him.

The fire in his chest that he had become accustomed to didn't disappoint; it was right there, ready to roar up. It had become his companion in place of the hope he had in his wife's healing. He didn't respond. He didn't believe as she did anymore, but he knew better than to talk against Him. She would find out soon enough on her own that God wasn't always listening and when she did, he would be there to help dry the tears.

"Daddy?"

"Yes, honey?"

"He saved us in the car. I know some angels kept the car from rolling."

Mason tried not to frown, but couldn't understand where she was getting this information. "Who told you this?"

"God did. I talk to Him a lot more now."

Mason was curious. "A lot more? A lot more than when?"

"Don't be angry, Daddy. I know you don't like Him much for taking Mommy away, but He loves you. He told me so."

He watched her face while she talked. The expressions reminded him of his sweet Rachael. He braced himself against what she was saying. "Honey, you say you know angels helped us in the car accident. Why didn't they keep me from hitting my head and keep your kidneys from getting sick?"

Her look became bleak. She looked down at her hands and whispered. "I don't know, Daddy, but I do know that He didn't cause Mommy's sickness. He just wanted her to be completely healed. She will never hurt anymore. I was hoping that would make you happy to know."

He gave up. He didn't want to agitate his daughter any further. "It's alright, baby. Your mother was such a beautiful person, I can't blame God for wanting her for Himself. Let's talk about something else, like what you would like to do when we get out of here?"

*   *   *

Mason rode back to his room slowly, deep in thought. He had almost lost his last reason for living. In one moment she could have been taken out of his hands. It was still touch-and-go; she still had quite a bit of recovery time left, not to mention the list she was now on for a kidney.

He worked his jaws to keep the tears back. Why couldn't it have been him? His daughter had her whole life ahead of her. Mason had another reason to hate the God his wife loved and now it seemed his daughter was finding comfort in Him as well. It made his stomach tighten. He couldn't understand why they would wish to devote any time to such a being that didn't seem to care at all. God had yet to prove to him that He was worthy of such time. He had been on his own most of his life and had done very well for himself. He had never thought of himself the father-type, but when he met Rachael, she made him feel and do a lot of things he never thought he would. Rachael showed him he was loveable. Her only flaw was her devotion and love for a being Mason could not understand.

At fifteen, Mason found himself going to school and working as a dishwasher to help pay the rent and debt that his father had left him and his mother after dying from a massive heart attack at 45. No one, least of all Mason, suspected his dad of having another family only 200 miles away.

He remembered his mom crying quietly when he got home from school a few days after his dad passed. He put his bag down and sat next to her on the couch. She wasn't the type to give in to fits, irrational behavior or deep emotion. She was the pillar of the family; the calm and cool one of his parents. So naturally, it shook him when her tears became sobs and he saw that she was visibly having a hard time containing herself. He thought she had just broken with the pain of losing his dad.

He placed his arm around her and she began to calm down until she was no longer crying. She just sat there; if the crying bothered him, this reaction scared him. It was as if in that moment, the mother he knew – the kind-hearted, quick to hug, slow to anger woman that he knew – was gone, and in her place was a ghost locked in living flesh.

He watched her for some time, stroking her hair and patting her hand. Finally, he whispered, "Mom, it will be okay. We have each other." His mom didn't make any move at first. He wouldn't have known she heard him if it weren't for a wry smile that crept up one side of her mouth. She got up from the couch; he thought she was just tired and was going to lie down.

Halfway across the living room, she turned around. "Baby, this time, having each other is not enough. I have no one, you have no one, and together we have even less." With that, she turned back around, walked into her room, and didn't make a sound for the rest of the evening. He couldn't even coax her out with dinner.

Two days later, he found out the reason for his mom's detachment. His dad had another family. A whole other family who he met at his father's funeral. He was now the youngest of four children by Michael Ronin. He had two half-sisters and one half-brother who he shared dark brown, slightly curly hair and a pointy chin with. All of whom he sat with during the reading of the will from which he and his mother received nothing. His dad had left them nothing. It was as if they hadn't even existed to him.

*   *   *

Mason shook himself out of the dark thought, pushing to climb back out of the hole of pity he felt himself sinking into. For his daughter, he was going to be strong. He was going to think of the brightness of tomorrow and spoiling his daughter with trips to anywhere she wanted to go whenever school was out. That was it. He would plan some trips for them to keep his mind off of the present. But first, he would have to use all of his attention maneuvering his body to cause as little pain as possible while getting back into bed.

Sweat was still on his brow when the nurse came in to give him his next dose of pain medicine.

"Are you alright? Do you need something stronger?" Mason shook his head, the pain taking his breath away. He could get through this pain, knowing that what his daughter was going through was much worse.

He thought to himself, *If you have an ounce of love for me and if you are real, please hear my daughter's prayers.*

CHAPTER 7

Paige sat at her desk staring out of her window. The computer screen in front of her was blank and had been for the last hour. The temptations to call one of her friends, go out shopping, or even to the gym were becoming a distraction. She was now on chapter three of her latest book, but couldn't seem to find a way to introduce the new character.

She had been working on a different piece at the beginning of the summer before Stone had called her. She set that work aside for a moment so that she could try to exorcise the emotions that erupted within her as she fought to close the door to that part of her life.

Two chapters into the book and she was working hard to distance herself enough to write from a more objective standpoint. The character she was introducing was a young genius whose family didn't have the time, knowledge, or discernment to recognize that all the trouble he was getting into was due to lack of focus instead of lack of morals. He wasn't mean-hearted, but hurt; he wasn't a womanizer but wanted to prove that he was a man, especially after being sexually abused. He was confused and misunderstood and after a few attempts to reach out to people, he decided to go at life on his own. This was as close as she could get to Stone Winters, a child who decided his way was better than his mother's because he saw no cause to make her god, his. From what he could see, his mom's god was selfish, judgmental, and unrealistic in his expectations. Her god, whom she would beat him with often, was just like her.

This book was pretty blatant in its description of what the author believed were causes for certain peoples' distance – no, hatred – and indifference to God, and if she wasn't careful it could easily become accusatory, judgmental and opinionated, without any room for redemption.

Stone Winters would be offered a chance in her book that he couldn't concede to taking in life.

She redeemed him in a way that she could understand; in a way that most people could see the sweet ending in. She looked up, wondering if she would get chastised for this. She decided to plead her case anyway.

I know You know my thoughts. I would like to understand why there was no one in his life he felt he could talk to in order to get to know the real You. I know You are bigger than any situation or person and that is even if we ourselves are the person in our way. I am open to Your wisdom but besides the wonderful eternity he was granted at the end, I don't see much benefit in his life here on earth. Could you show me? I would like answers on this.

CHAPTER 8

Victoria Branchett looked up at the skyscrapers through the window of the taxi. The scowl on her forehead and wry smile on her lips could have been mistaken for distaste of the fair city of Chicago, but in fact, it was the memories that turned her expression and her stomach, sour.

She stared out into space as the taxi waited for pedestrians to cross, her thoughts going back to the memory of a long-legged girl skipping and kicking up dirt to her hips. Her skip broke into a run as she tried to catch a chicken, squawking its irritation at being chased before breakfast. Around and around they went from one end of the fence outlining the coop to the other, with the child always close to the feathered creature, but too far to get a good grasp. Finally, huffing with shallow breaths, the child gave up her mission and let the chicken settle at the side of the coop. The little girl looked up and waved vigorously at Victoria who watched from a couch on the porch. She returned it with a lift of her arm. As the memory faded, she noticed that a wide smile was now pasted on her mouth. She quickly cleared it.

Though she fought it, that child had struck a chord in her heart. This young girl shared so many similarities with her daughter it was amazing that two people could be so much alike and not be related by blood. Vivian, named for the sister Victoria had lost during her freshman year of college, was even more energetic and light-hearted than her daughter, Rachael. At one time, she thought it would be impossible to find anyone with a more positive outlook on life than Rachael, especially after she "got saved." Victoria still remembered the day Rachael came home shouting for her with excitement in her voice. She had made Rachael calm down before she began by putting up one finger. It was very unladylike to huff and puff.

"Mom, I received Jesus Christ in my heart today and when I leave this world, I will spend eternity with Him, God, and the Holy Spirit. I have a purpose, a destiny, and I am fearfully made."

She stopped quickly to take a breath, but Victoria gave her a stern look, so she took another and slowed herself.

"Mom, I am so happy. I knew deep down that there was really a God and He loves me and cares about me. He wants me to be happy. I am not weird. I am… I am…"

Victoria could see that she was searching for a word, and even though she had a feeling she knew the same word, she would not offer help. A small frown came across Rachael's features as she tried to pull the phrase from her memory. After a moment she gave up, and the grin was back.

"Well anyway, I am special and God loves me and…could I go back? They have bible study on Tuesday night. I will make sure that all of my studying is done before I go. Samantha said she and her mom would pick me up."

Victoria couldn't think of an immediate reason for her not to. She knew of Margaret, Samantha's mom. They would run into each other in the supermarket or at a school event and, even though her head seemed to be in the clouds sometimes, she was a decent person.

"Give me some information on the church. The name, the pastor's name, what time this bible study is, as well as any events that are going on. I want to speak to one of the leaders and after that, I will decide." She thought this might lessen Rachael's resolve a little and show her that she needed to do research about everyone. No one should be taken at face value. It was just too dangerous.

The smile on Rachael's face didn't waver. She kissed her mom on the cheek, already thanking her and promising her the information before the end of the day. She started to dart out, but caught herself before Victoria could say anything, straightened her posture, and demurely walked out of the room.

Later that evening when her husband, Richard, was reclining in their sitting room, she broached the subject with him. Rachael had brought her the material she requested, and, if nothing else, the church had an excellent youth program. He listened thoughtfully to her pros and cons on the matter and after several minutes gave his approval.

"Vickie, Rachael will be going off to college soon. We can't be there with her every waking moment, and if she can develop a relationship with God now, He may keep her from getting into situations we can't foresee. Think of it as added insurance." Her pragmatic husband was excellent for thinking outside of the box.

"I just don't want her to get hurt. She has such a different outlook and she is so trusting."

"Well, she is going to get hurt, but don't you think she may have a better chance of bouncing back if she had a relationship with someone that couldn't fail her?"

Victoria shifted back and forth from one foot to the other, uncomfortable with where the conversation was going. She shrugged her shoulders, signaling the end of the discussion and went to the bathroom to begin her nightly beauty ritual.

From then on, Rachael's thirst for God and knowledge about Him seemed to take on a life of its own. There was scarcely a conversation in the house where God, Jesus, or the Holy Spirit wasn't mentioned. She had invited her parents on several occasions to come to church with her, but there was never a good time. By the time Rachael was ready to go to college, Victoria was almost relieved.

Almost.

"Ma'am. This is your stop. Do you need help?" The taxi driver's voice brought her out of her deep thought.

"Mmmm. No. No, I believe I can manage." She placed the fare into the receptacle, pushed in the drawer, and gathered her purse in one hand so that she could use her other to help her balance while she stepped out and away from the car.

She stood in front of the hospital entrance doors for a moment, desperate to see her granddaughter and just as determined not to see her son-in-law. She took a deep breath, moved her purse to her forearm, squared her shoulders and walked through the now open doors.

Once she reached the 5th floor, she followed the nurse's directions to Vivian's room, preparing herself for what she would find. She peered around the doorway – very out of character – and breathed a sigh of relief to see Vivian lying in bed, staring out of the window alone.

"Good morning, love." Victoria watched Vivian's head turn quickly towards her, and her eyes lit up. It was worth all the travel.

"Gram! You are the best ever! I didn't know if you would come!" Vivian said, a little breathless.

Victoria bent over the fragile-looking child to give her a kiss on both cheeks. "Well, now you have hurt my feelings. Why wouldn't I come if you called me?"

Vivian shrugged and smiled as Victoria straightened. She stood over her, taking her hand. "How do you feel, love?"

"I am feeling better every day. I am just a little tired. The nurses come in all the time, and sometimes they wake me up. It's not like I have any place to go, especially with Dad being here."

Victoria's stomach turned. "Does he come to visit you a lot? Has he come to see you today already?"

"I think he would stay in this room with me if the nurses let him. He was up here earlier, but I think his doctor was coming to see him or something soon, so you don't have to worry about seeing him."

Victoria made a mental effort to straighten her face and feign surprise. "What do you mean? I am not worried. Your father and I aren't enemies."

"Maybe, but you are not friends either." Vivian's eyes narrowed. "Otherwise you would want him to come with me when I visited you, and whenever you call for me you would speak to him longer on the phone." Vivian's face was stern her lips almost pressed into a line. Victoria placed her arms behind her and clutched her fingers together in an effort to straighten her back a little further. Where was this coming from?

"I am 12, Gram, not two. Besides, you are going to have to start talking to each other more because I need more help. The doctors said my life will be challenging and that is fine, but I will miss you a lot if you can't come and visit me more." With her color now slightly paler and her eyes looking stormy, she looked like a child that was determined to get her way or throw a tantrum. If Victoria didn't know her to be the sweet, beautiful girl she was, she would have reprimanded her for her tone. But this must have been really important to her, so Victoria would try to stomach being in the same room with the man that killed her daughter.

CHAPTER 9

"Pastor, I am checking in. I am sorry I missed you. I will be in town for a few days and will be in church on Sunday. This was a good trip. I would like to share it with you when you have some time. I will call and schedule with Pam. I love you. Thank you for all of your prayers. God bless you. Goodbye."

Paige hung up the phone slowly. She had hoped that her pastor would pick up the phone. She really needed to talk. She picked the receiver back up and dialed the number to the church office.

"Good afternoon, Pam. This is Elder Morganson." She always greeted Pam with professionalism first. She never knew if she had her on speaker-phone; the child moved around her friend's office more often than not. Sure enough, she heard the receiver come away from the desk phone right before she spoke.

"Hello, Paige. It's good to hear from you. I haven't seen you in a while. How was your tour?"

"Excellent. I was so busy I hardly had time to get your souvenirs, but I came away victorious. I'll drop them by when I come to see Pastor. How soon do you think that will be?"

"Paige you are a mess. You don't need to bribe me to see Pastor, but I am not complaining nor will I insult you by denying the gifts you have for me. Is tomorrow too soon? One of his appointments just canceled. You know he leaves for North Carolina on Friday."

A slow whistle came from Paige's lips.

"Wow. Has it been a year already?"

"Yes. In one week, your pastor will have been preaching at Skylight Temple for 12 years. Funny thing is, I think he is getting nervous about it. He has been getting a little forgetful lately and he has been more quiet than usual."

"Mmmm. Is he planning anything different for the church anniversary? Maybe he is trying to plan a surprise or something," Paige said, trying to console Pam who was in every aspect a very good, executive assistant.

She may have been a little controlling in the beginning, but Pastor was definitely not one to be controlled. The more she tried, the more he would go and "visit the sick" without telling her. Finally, Pam confided in Paige, telling her that she was thinking about quitting. When Paige understood the dilemma she tried to explain to Pam who, until this job, had not worked for a church let alone a pastor.

"Our pastor is not structured that way. He will keep his word and meet with people who have appointments. He will sometimes be the last to leave and the first to come in, but on the other end, if his phone rings in the middle of the night, he will pick it up. If someone walks in off of the street that needs help and doesn't have an appointment, he will welcome them as if he has all the time in the world. If he isn't overly concerned about time and how he feels God has structured his day, then do not go having a conniption over it either. Just roll with it and re-adjust his calendar so that people aren't waiting too long because their time is just as precious."

Pam thanked her for the words of wisdom, but it wasn't a one-speech fix. The dynamic of the church was one where each day was different from the last and one wouldn't think of starting the day without being prayed up.

"So what time is my appointment tomorrow?"

"Mmmm…How much time do you need?" Paige could hear typing on the other end while Pam scrolled through his calendar.

"I am checking in. It will take about an hour."

"Oh. No problem. Is two o'clock good?"

"Yes ma'am, that will be just fine. Does he have more of the congregation going with him this year?"

"Actually, just a few more. Are you going to be able to make it this year?"

"No, I have a little personal matter I need to give some attention to."

"Are you getting married?" Paige could hear the excitement in Pam's voice.

"Pam, you usually need a man for that. Stop playing."

"Well, remember what that preacher said eight months ago about God placing a man upon your path? A man He set aside just for you?" Pam's voice dropped low trying to match the one of the evangelist that had visited the church some months back.

"Don't do that. Either way, I don't know if I am ready for that complication in my life. I am still wondering how I am going to get my life outside of my business uncomplicated."

"Paige, are you okay? We never seem to talk about you, but you are always there for me. I would like to help if I can."

"This one will take a great deal of prayer because I need courage that I don't think I have, to see it through. So yes, you can help. Pray for me in general and specifically that I don't make fear an issue."

"You got it. I am taking notes right now." Paige heard the office phone ringing on Pam's end.

"So I will see you tomorrow at 2 pm. Just give me a heads up if anything happens okay?"

"Will do. God bless you."

Paige returned the sentiment and gave a hasty goodbye.

She sat at her desk going over the last of their conversation in her mind. She had been told a few times that God was going to gift her with a family and a man that He had set aside for her. The one Pam had been referring to was a friend of their pastor's, but she wouldn't insult her pastor nor the man in thinking that they had been talking about her. She had received her confirmation that they had and it made her nervous.

She had finally gotten to a place where she had a sense of normality in her life. She was very content. She loved what she did for a living: the challenge, meeting and helping people, traveling to different places. But what she loved most of all was being used by God and the wonderful relationship she had the opportunity to have with Him. It was satisfying, and there was such peace. A sense of security came with being in constant contact with Him, and a feeling of true purpose and humility in being used by Him to spread His word of holiness, love, compassion, forgiveness, mercy, and grace. To see the realization on a person's face that God, the Maker of the heavens and the earth, loved them enough to ordain a meeting where they could receive the gift of eternal life. With that gift would come the peace she most treasured: forgiveness of sins and the ability to step out of the bondage of guilt that blinded them from their true value and worth.

She knew she was a far cry from perfect. Sometimes she found herself watching couples walking into hotels she was staying in, holding hands. She missed the closeness and the touch of another person, a glance that spoke volumes, or coming home to someone. Then she was reminded that what she sometimes witnessed and wished for could be two different things. She was seeing what was on the surface, but in actuality, their lives could be completely different. There were still plenty of things she needed to understand about herself and her past was still an unwelcome memory.

Opening the refrigerator and moving idly from cabinet to cabinet, she moved around the open floor plan of her kitchen. Her stomach rumbled again in protest of its fast.

She smiled as she remembered a phrase frequently used by her father, who, for a slimly-built man, always seemed hungry. "I'm so hungry it feels like I have been cut at the throat," he'd say whenever more than a few hours went by before his next meal. Anyone within hearing range would groan in mock pain and try to leave before they were sent on a mission of finding or preparing something that would satiate him.

Paige grabbed some crackers (since she'd not yet gone shopping and had no bread in the house), found her favorite cheese, pepperjack, and a bunch of slightly too-ripe grapes in the fridge on her third pass. She promised herself she would go shopping a little later, just not on an empty stomach. She padded into the family room of her oversized apartment and sat on the floor in front of the couch. She spread out her meal before her and watched as cars drove by through her bay window.

The apartment was one of the last in the building to be leased. She had more than enough saved to buy herself a condo or a house, but she wasn't sure if she wanted to stay in this part of Los Angeles, or even if she wanted to stay in California at all. On one end, she loved the conveniences of a huge city. She enjoyed the diversity of people and their cultures, which gave way to different types of grocery, furniture and clothing stores. She also liked that you could walk down one block and find yourself in the middle of a busy intersection, with the dizzying activities of people walking back and forth to work amongst the industrial buildings. Then at the opposite end of the block, one would come face to face with antique shops and small-town charm. It was the best of both worlds.

She looked around her apartment at the craftsman-style fixtures, mixed with traditional-style, crown moldings and considered herself highly-favored for living in such a beautiful place. The two-bedroom, two-bath apartment was big enough for her to entertain 45 guests comfortably with its eat-in kitchen, complete with breakfast bar that doubled as an island. There was a living room, high-ceiling family room, office, and small patio. At 1,500 square feet, it was not so overwhelming that she couldn't clean it all herself if she got the urge – which she hadn't yet. That was where April came in.

The woman was an absolute sweetheart and at 5'3", she was a cleaning machine. From what Paige was able to surmise from the interview, April only cleaned a handful of apartments in the area. She was in school studying psychology and used the money from cleaning to pay for books and tuition. When Paige asked for references, she wouldn't give over anyone's name that she cleaned for in the apartment building; she did, however, render forth letters of recommendation from the current doorman, concierge and building owner. Paige, both impressed with the letters and the woman's professional business ethics, hired her on a trial basis. One look at her apartment after April's first cleaning made it very clear that Paige herself could use a lesson in cleaning. One thing April didn't do, though, was shop.

Paige lifted herself on to the couch, careful not to disturb the glass of half-consumed apple juice still on the floor. Picking it up along with the wrapping from her snack, she walked in the kitchen. Placing the glass in the refrigerator, she discarded the rest, picked up her keys and purse, and walked out the door.

*   *   *

Paige walked in the door, hands full of plastic bags, just in time to hear the beep of her answering machine. Closing the door with her foot and maneuvering her packages to be able to throw the bolt in place, she listened for the voice of the person leaving the message. On her way into the kitchen, the next sound she heard stopped her in her tracks.

She could barely make out the words let alone the voice, but the sobs were deep. "I was hoping (sniff) you might be there. I'm sorry." The sentence was interrupted by more sobs. "I just can't... (sniff)...I just can't do it anymore. I don't understand..." Letting go of her bags, Paige covered the length it took to get to her phone in record speed.

"Miranda?" she answered, picking up the wireless receiver.

"Oh, Elder Paige, you're there. Oh...I just needed...I mean...I can't...I am so tired..." The voice trailed off into sobs again. Paige's heart ached. She quietly waited for the woman to regain some composure.

"Miranda, beautiful...what's going on?" She waited patiently for an answer.

A voice almost void of emotion answered after a few sighs and a heavy nose-blowing into a tissue. "I am calling to let you know that I can't do it anymore. I am tired and I don't want to wait anymore."

Paige walked over to the couch in the living room as she began to pray to herself that the Lord would grant her the wisdom to speak to Miranda and reach her in the dark place she was in. It had been a long time since she'd had one of these calls from Miranda. She had progressed so far in her walk with God; Paige was hoping that this was not a setback.

Before she assumed too much she asked, "What is it you don't think you can wait for anymore, Miranda?"

"*Who,*" Miranda said emphatically.

"I am sorry. *Who* can't you wait for anymore?"

"God. I have tried and tried. I read and I believe I seek Him, but still nothing. I don't hear anything. Many days I hear the bottle calling me louder than I can even imagine Him loving me. I am so tired, so tired. I have lost so much since I turned my life over to Him. My friends don't want to be around me, my children don't believe I can change, I got a ticket the other day and I can barely pay my rent in this small piece of a place. I am miserable and I have no escape." The weeping came back, but she continued. "I don't feel His peace anymore...I don't feel Him anymore...you said-d He would never leave me nor forsake me, but what good is that if I don't feel H-Him near? I will tell you – it is no good because, without that feeling, the urge for a drink is too much to bear."

Paige could hear the anger in Miranda's voice and let her continue on her tirade, but when she began to blame God for her self-pity, Paige cut in.

"Miranda." She spoke with a stern voice to get her attention. The other end of the line went quiet. She softened her voice. "Miranda, have you been drinking?"

"No, but..."

"No 'but' Miranda. I am proud of you." *Where did that come from?* She wasn't going in that direction. She was going to be firm, but maybe it wasn't time for that. She thought quickly. "I am proud of you because you could have made another decision, no matter what you felt. You chose not to try to escape this time. I commend you on a victorious moment." She paused for a moment in case Miranda wanted to interject. The line was quiet all but for the faint sound of breathing on the other end.

"Miranda, you are in a place where the powers of hell are fighting for your soul. They aren't going to stand by idly and let you walk away from your old life. You weren't a threat to them before when you stayed drunk 12 hours of the day and mildly sober the other 12. Your home, your car, your friends, your job, and your finances seemed to be going well because your walk was in accord with what they wanted for your life: death, unrealized loss, and destruction. The alcohol was slowly killing you. Whether you knew it or not you would eventually lose everything, and your very soul would have been destroyed along with any testimony that could help another lost soul."

"Well... I can't be held responsible for someone else. I can barely handle myself," Miranda quipped, her voice very much like that of a child throwing a tantrum.

"Oh, but you are. The moment you confessed that Jesus Christ was your Lord and Savior, you were given the responsibility to live by example of what it means to be a living testament, a living sacrifice; one whose life is not their own. You are a prisoner for the Lord; a walking and breathing monument of His love and a representative and ambassador of Christ. Your salvation was bought with a price and rendered unto you as a gift. You chose to take that gift and be born again into a new kingdom. II Corinthians 5:17 tells us, 'Therefore if any man be in Christ, he is a new creature: old things are passed away; behold, all things are become new.' Galatians 2:20 says, 'I have been crucified with Christ; it is no longer I who live, but Christ lives in me, and the life which I now live in the flesh I live by faith in the Son of God, who loved me and gave Himself for me.' In Romans 12:1, Paul wrote: 'I beseech you therefore, brethren, by the mercies of God, that you present your bodies a living sacrifice, holy, acceptable to God, which is your reasonable service.'

So yes, you are responsible. As soon as you accepted Christ, you became responsible for how your children saw Christ. You are responsible now for how they see Him because you represent Him. I know you didn't think everything was going to be roses because we talked about that in the beginning. Just like I know now that you aren't going to turn back – at least not today."

"How do you know that?" Miranda raised her voice in a slightly threatening manner.

"Because you called me while you were sober. You didn't call me slobbering and incoherently drunk. You made a choice at that moment to reach out instead of giving in. You aren't ready to give up, but I will not attend the pity party you are trying to invite me to so that you can have an excuse to waiver. You made the choice to seek an answer that will help you, and I chose to give you one. Miranda, I would be lying if I told you that this would be the last time you felt like this, but you can't rely only on what you feel. Whether you feel Him or not, God is with you. The reason you can hear the bottle louder than His voice of peace right now is because your relationship with the bottle is still stronger or more real to you than your relationship with God. I am not just speaking out of the side of my neck. I have been there with a different type of drug. When thoughts of drinking come to you, instead of turning your thoughts immediately towards your relationship with God, you indulge in the thought and how drinking made you forget. You don't immediately open your bible; you reminisce about the foggy sensation where the pain and anger have been numbed to such a degree, they are barely perceptible.

39

It is a choice. A moment-to-moment choice. Some temptations you see from far off and are able to avoid. Some you will walk right into, but how you combat them is what strengthens you. Use the Word. It is what we have it for. It is powerful, pure, and living and it has the ability to change you from the inside out if you apply it. What and who you think about most is who you will have a stronger relationship with.

I am going to take this a little deeper. You are made of three parts: the body, your temple, the mind, your will, thoughts, and emotions, and your spirit.

The enemy will attack your mind. He will remind you of anything from a bad argument to a bad bout with the bottle. It is up to you to combat it with the Word, or music with the Word, so that your spirit will grow stronger. If you let the thoughts go unchecked, your body will follow. Understand?"

"Yes. But how do I know He is there? It is not like it was in the beginning. I don't wake up with Him on my mind all the time. I don't want to pray like I used to. Things are so busy now, and it doesn't seem like He is trying to keep my attention like He did in the beginning. I don't feel as special." Miranda's voice took on a whiney tone.

"Well then, by all means, you have every right to stop reading your bible and praying. It sounds like the honeymoon is over for you and God. Maybe He already got what He wanted from you and has gone on to someone new."

The silence on the other side was deafening. Then finally, Miranda spoke. "You don't mean that, Elder Paige."

"Don't I? If you don't feel special to Him anymore and you feel like He isn't paying attention to you, who am I to say you are wrong? If you don't believe God feels the same way about you as He did in the beginning, I can't do it for you." Silence met her once again.

"But the Word says that I am the apple of His eye, that His thoughts of me out-number the grains of sand near the sea. You led me to that scripture."

Paige said, "Then you use the same words against the enemy or any doubts you have about the love God has for you. You are precious to God whether you feel it or not. God is consistent, and His love for you is unconditional. He is real, and the relationship you have with Him is real, so you need to treat it as such. You wouldn't do this with a husband. You wouldn't just spend time with him when things were good. You are committed to him. You go home to him and live with him, working on deepening your relationship with him day by day. This is the same way

40

you treat your relationship with God, but with the knowledge that His love for you is unconditional."

The weeping began again, quietly this time, and it touched on something deep within her. A faint whisper came through the receiver. "I don't have a relationship to go by. I don't know what to do… I don't know how to love."

Silent tears were blurring Paige's vision. She knew exactly how this woman felt. It was hard to imagine yourself being worthy of such love and adoration and attention when you were treated so differently in reality. There was very little to reference in the way of a positive relationship.

"Are you still there, Elder Paige?"

"Yes ma'am, I am here."

"What should I do?"

"Start by looking in the mirror and praying that He will show you what He sees when He looks at you. It is hard to have a loving relationship with someone when you don't have one with yourself. You can also do for Him as you wish someone would do for you in a relationship. Be attentive, spend time with Him, and patiently get to know Him in His word and in prayer. And lastly, stop giving in to the enemy's condemnation of you. Before you deny it," she said quickly when she heard Miranda take a breath, "the proof is in the pity party you were having when you called me. Romans 8:1-2, Miranda. 'There is therefore now no condemnation to them which are in Christ Jesus, who walk not after the flesh, but after the Spirit. For the law of the Spirit of life in Christ Jesus hath made me free from the law of sin and death.'"

She paused for a moment to let the words sink in. "You are no longer bound by the sins of your past. So don't walk around bound by guilt, shame or regret for something you have already been forgiven for. You are not a victim of your old life or the circumstances that you used to characterize yourself as; you are a victorious child of God who will live and not die, and you will live an abundant life because you were, and are worthy of, being saved. Repeat after me Miranda," Paige said in a tone that left no room for argument. "I am worth it."

"I am worth it," came a scarce duplication of the statement from Miranda.

Paige repeated. "I am worth it, and God does not make mistakes."

After a small hesitation, Miranda repeated with more volume, "I am worth it and God does not make mistakes."

"Are you sure Miranda?"

"I am sure."

"Good, now let's pray. We could both use a little time talking to the lover of our souls."

Miranda agreed and Paige started them out in prayer.

CHAPTER 10

Two words stayed in Mason's head from his latest visit with his daughter. He had finished his tests and was told his ankle was healing well, but the doctors were more worried about the stress factor. His worry over his daughter's state was causing stress to his heart. His blood pressure was up and if it didn't come under control in the next few days, he was going home with a new prescription. The news he received upon opening his daughter's door did not help his cause.

Vivian sat up in her bed with a hopeful smile on her face. "Gram is here. She visited me while you were seeing your doctor. She really came! I hope you aren't mad, Daddy. I called her and she actually came."

At first, Mason thought he heard wrong, but when the realization came to him that Victoria was in the same town, panic began to grip him. Why was she really here? Was she going to try to take Vivian away from him? Did Vivian want to go with her?

When his wife first passed, Victoria didn't seem to want to have anything to do with either one of them; but one day out of the blue she called and asked if Vivian could come out and spend some time with her. At first, he was so afraid he flat out refused, but with coaxing from his daughter, he reluctantly let her go. He had never known Victoria to be warm or affectionate let alone nostalgic, but when Vivian came back full of joy, glowing for the first time since his dear Rachael had passed, he didn't see any harm in allowing her to visit on occasion. Maybe he was overreacting. No matter how tense their relationship was Victoria was still Vivian's grandmother. Maybe he should have called her to let her know that Vivian was in the hospital. He was so used to doing things on his own, and the thought hadn't really crossed his mind.

Super... Just one more thing for Victoria to hate him for.

"Earth to Daddy..." Vivian's touch brought him back to the present. He smiled at her, raising her small hand to his cheek while he looked at her heart-shaped face. He observed her eyes, clearer than they had been all week. The dialysis was working.

His heart gave a tug. So close – he had been too close to losing her. He looked down trying to mask the pain behind lowered lids, but as usual, Vivian looked right through him. She and her mom were both gifted with that talent and not just with him. They had such sensitivity about them. They were able to read people with such accuracy he sometimes found it unsettling.

Knowing she'd seen the worry in his eyes, Mason was quick to take her mind off of the subject. "So kiddo, are you up for a little sight-seeing today? I could ask the nurse for a chair and we could take a trip to the cafeteria. I know you must be as bored with this food as I am. Maybe some apple juice in a glass bottle instead of a box, or I might be able to smuggle some chocolate pudding. What do you think?" Vivian smiled widely and nodded. She allowed him to help her get ready, call for the nurse, and help her get into the chair with all of her different tubes without uttering one word.

Mason maneuvered the chair through the hall, careful not to get any of her tubes caught on odd pieces of furniture or people they passed. He turned two corners and wheeled her to the elevator before he realized how quiet she was.

"Honey, are you alright? Do you want to turn back around?" He came around to the front of the chair to take a look at her. She didn't appear to be winded or tired, just somber. What had happened from the time he offered to take her out, to now? He crouched down so that he was face-to-face with her.

He was a little surprised when she took his face in her hands and peered at him with those stormy, gray eyes. "I am twelve-years-old and, might I add, an intelligent twelve-year-old." Her tone was quiet, like steel wool encased in velvet. If he hadn't been so startled he may have considered reprimanding her.

"I know when you are hiding something from me and when you want to change the subject. I know these things, so don't treat me like I don't know or that I am not old enough to understand. I do understand."

He saw and felt the anger rising in her and was a little stung by the fact that she could feel this way towards him. He thought to defend himself by looking away but her hold tightened. "Daddy, I love you. I will always love you no matter what but don't think I don't know what you feel. If you keep trying to hide your hurt for Mommy, I can't show you my hurt and if I can't show you my hurt, I can't feel better. Daddy, I don't want to feel bad anymore."

His breath caught in his throat, unable to get past the lump forming there.

Vivian continued, tears brimming. "I want us to be happy or at least feel better. Mommy didn't want us to feel bad always. I miss her too, but at least I remember the good parts. I don't think you remember the good parts, Daddy." She began pleading with him, the tears streaming down her cheeks, wetting her gown. "I need to talk about the good parts, Daddy. Please, Daddy? I want you to remember good parts. I don't want to be sad anymore, Daddy. I am sorry if you do, but I can't…" The rest trailed off in uncontrolled sobs.

The pain in his chest grew with each word she spoke. It was met with the lump in his throat but when she began pleading with him, the pain splintered into a thousand pieces, shattering the dam he'd worked so hard to maintain. The realization of what he had been doing to his daughter cut him to the soul. He had no strength left. He placed his head in her lap and began sobbing openly right there in the middle of the 5th-floor lobby, the elevator doors standing open.

CHAPTER 11

Victoria carefully picked each article of clothing from of her suitcase and laid it out on the bed. It was a routine that brought her comfort and helped her get acquainted with new surroundings.

Victoria didn't like to travel much. She was one who believed that she lived in one of the most beautiful places on earth and since the farm sat on four-hundred and eighty acres of lush Oklahoma land. There was always plenty to do in the way of directing, answering questions, event-planning, charity events, and working in the garden she dedicated for the use of the children in the nearby city that were less fortunate. It took her a whole day to write out a schedule of things that needed to be done by the hour.

Her husband, Richard, was the one who loved to travel. If he had his way, they would still be flying, sailing, riding, walking, or bicycling around the world. He had been able to coax her off the property twice a year for a couple weeks at a time, but the preparation took so much out of her she wasn't able to really enjoy herself until the second week of the trip. She didn't mind the hiking or the skiing and actually had fun the time they road on the Orient Express, but it was the sailing that she could easily do without. Those cramped, tight places; even the junior suite they reserved on one of their last trips together was slightly claustrophobic, not to mention all of that water. There was nowhere to go if there was an emergency except a smaller boat, which did not sit well with her at all.

There were a lot of things Richard loved to do that she didn't care much for. In fact, they didn't have an awful lot in common, but he was good to her. He was kind and patient. He made her laugh and made her feel secure. She could not remember seeing him angry but two times during their marriage and only one was directed towards her and well-warranted. She knew people talked and wondered how they had stayed married as long as they did. She wondered herself; she knew she wasn't easy to get along with. Her own parents didn't even try to hide their irritation with her, especially after she took over the farm her grandfather had left her and brought it back to life.

Richard was different. He saw beauty in her and had said so on many occasions. He taught her how to appreciate her quirks instead of trying to hide them in shame. He encouraged her to use her eye for detail and compulsive characteristics to help build a small city on those acres. With him, she learned how to love herself and find value in things others laughed at. He was the love of her life and she was happy with him.

She wished he could be here with her, but he was already on his trip to Uganda with his group of friends. Over the last two years he'd become a philanthropist. This trip was more along the lines of missionary work, but she wasn't terribly interested in his 'guy stuff'.

She knew if she'd asked he would be on the first plane back, but this was something she felt she needed to do. Not that she didn't think Richard would approve of her true intentions, but it would be better if she dealt with this business of Mason on her own.

A light breeze rustled the coral-colored bedroom curtains, breaking Victoria away from her thoughts. She walked over to the dresser, pulling out the top drawer she had lined earlier. Methodically, she placed each piece of clothing from the bed into the drawer until it was full, and then opened the next, until each drawer had four pieces of clothing laid side by side, three layers deep. After storing her suitcase and garment bag in the hall closet, she walked to the kitchen to put away the rest of the groceries she had the market deliver from around the corner.

She looked around the sparsely furnished apartment she was leasing for the month. It met her tastes. The dark, cherry wood chairs and tables were heavy but the curve was delicate enough to appeal to her. She ran her hand along the edge of the beige chaise lounge, also outlined in cherry wood, admiring the feeling of brushed cotton beneath her fingertips. She had taken a few minutes to go through the rooms, eyeing the furniture and pieces of art when she first arrived, only to make a mental note of anything amiss that she may be charged for on the back end. She really didn't intend to stay the whole time, but it was a better price by the month.

It was almost too quiet in the apartment. Walking through the living room and looking through the floor to ceiling window, she watched the hustle and bustle of Chicago's city life. This wasn't really a place for a child to grow up and be free to roam and use their imagination. It was stifling, polluted, and too close for her taste. If she had her way, her granddaughter wouldn't live in this place where people were too close to not be in your business, not to mention the poor display of the few trees nestled together in front of her building called a "park."

If it was the last thing she did, she would convince Mason that Vivian's best chance for a life of privilege would be with her. Surely Mason could see that she would have more influence on getting Vivian what she needed most? She wasn't going to stand by and let his poor judgment take another life. She had come to adore Vivian a great deal more than she thought was possible. Rachael had been a light in her life and, when she became ill, Victoria had begged Mason to bring her back to the ranch where the fresh air, food, and environment were sure to help the healing process. They argued constantly, but Mason wouldn't budge. He insisted that he had her under the best of care in a hospital in the city and that he had paid for the top specialists to take care of Rachael, and beyond them, there wasn't much more that could be done. Besides, each doctor he had spoken to said that there was nothing that could be done in the country that couldn't be done in the city. It was only during the last two months that they thought it might be best if Rachael came home to be with family. By then, Victoria had ceased to speak to Mason, and, due to the many arguments they'd had, Rachael thought it would be better for everyone if they had as little contact with one another as possible. For the last two months of her daughter's life, the only communication she had was through her husband, who still had an open line of communication with both of them.

Then, on an uncomfortably hot afternoon towards the end of May, she received a call from her daughter. The call started out somewhat superficial, both of them conversing as if they had been talking all along. They discussed the weather, the farm, and its few changes since Rachael had been there. They talked about Rachael's hair, and the irony of how it had begun to grow straight instead of her normal, curly locks since she'd stop taking the chemotherapy and radiation treatments. They talked about Vivian and her latest antics; her growth-spurt, inquisitive nature, growing love for Christ and children's bible study, and her new collection of favorite animals, frogs. In all of that, it wasn't until the end of the conversation that Rachael even brought up Mason's name.

Rachael asked if Victoria might consider forgiving herself and Mason for the lack of communication. Not wanting to compromise the delicate truce that had been formed by the conversation, she tried to make light of the situation and tell her daughter there was no need to even ask. But her daughter was adamant, and wouldn't let go until Victoria actually formed the words.

"Mom, please don't. I need to know if you forgive me for my behavior for the last few months."

"Oh, honey, you don't really need to ask. I don't blame. We have all been very emotional, but if you need to hear it then yes, honey, I forgive you."

"And Mason? Do you forgive him too?"

Victoria had never lied to her daughter. She didn't believe there was a need for it.

"I am sorry, honey, he will have to ask me himself. There is more to it."

Rachael interrupted. "There doesn't have to be. You can choose to forgive him right now. It would make things easier on all of us."

"Did that coward ask you to call?"

"No, Mom. He doesn't even know that I am making this call, but I need this for me. And he is not a coward. I love you, Mom. Most of all, I need you to know that. I know we haven't seen eye to eye on a lot, and I did truly hope that my life would have caused you to want to get to know God more, but I let anger get the best of me and I am sorry for that. I feel like I failed you when you needed me most."

"Honey..." Victoria tried to break in, but Rachael kept going as if she had not heard her.

"I never expected it to go on this long between the two of you. I thought for sure Mason would give in first, what with Vivian and I working on him. Who knew he was even more stubborn than you?" There was a sigh like Rachael had finally gotten something heavy off of her chest.

"You know, most women marry men that remind them of their fathers. I messed around and married one just like my mom."

Victoria knew the comment was meant to lighten the air. Rachael did that often to help discharge the tension in the atmosphere, but it stung nonetheless.

"Rachael, I love you. I am proud of the strong, resourceful, and loving woman you have become. I am sorry too because I have missed you, but let's not talk about Mason. We have so much more we can speak on."

Rachael conceded, not wanting to continue distressing her mother, but she did have one last thing to say. "I need you to hear me out, no matter how hard it is for you. Regardless of how you feel about Mason, please don't take it out on Vivian. She loves you and she needs her grandmother in her life. When I go, she is going to need you even more. I need an affirmative answer from you. On this, I will not waiver."

"Baby please, don't talk like this. I don't like it one bit." In fact, it was scaring the hell out of her.

"Mom, I want an answer," Rachael went on as if she hadn't heard anything her mom said.

Victoria couldn't catch her breath; it felt like she had been punched in the stomach. She worked hard to regain her composure. In what seemed like a haze she heard her daughter call her name, this time insistently.

"Victoria, Mom, I need an answer."

"Yes. Honey, yes. I will always be there for her."

"Wonderful. Thank you, Mom. Thank you. So, Dad's coming back out tomorrow. Will you come with him?"

"Oh yes, honey. Are you sure you want me to come?"

"Yes."

They spoke for a little longer, and when Victoria heard Rachael yawn for the eighth time she told her she would see her the next day and talked her into hanging up the phone.

With a knot in her stomach, she packed quickly, rescheduled some meetings that were set for the next day, wrote out specific instructions three times, and on the fourth attempt gave up and decided to just call an emergency meeting with the immediate staff.

By six the next morning, she was ready and waiting at the private airport with Richard, watching as a sudden and violent rainstorm delayed her flight. It rained consistently for four hours, not letting up until just before the afternoon. Seeing her agitation grow, her husband whispered in her ear just as they were leaving the small terminal, beginning to board the aircraft.

"Well, at least you won't have to water the roses when you get back."

She turned to him with a quick retort ready on her lips but was defused by the smile on his.

"Oh, you almost got it that time. Thank you for trying though." She touched her hand to the side of his cheek, a form of endearment.

Once they arrived at the hospital, all thoughts of her hopeful reunion faded when they exited the elevator and came face to face with a sobbing Vivian. Richard bent down and tried fruitlessly to console the child. Victoria raced passed them to her daughter's room where the doctor was talking to Mason over her daughter's body, now covered by a sheet. She was too late. Her legs threatened to give away beneath her so she sat down in the chair just inside of the door. The sound of the chair scraping the floor caught Mason's attention. He came towards her, arms reaching for her with the purpose to comfort.

The slap resounded through the room. Victoria watched as Mason's head snapped to the side. When he straightened she came at him again, catching him across the other side of the face and throwing him off balance. Reaching out to stable himself, he caught hold of the bed Rachael's body was laying on, pulling the sheet as he stumbled back.

Victoria would have hit Mason again, but the sight of Rachael's body momentarily paralyzed her. She watched as Mason righted himself again, and all she could think of was causing him as much harm as he had caused her daughter. Her daughter was dead. Her daughter was dead, and he killed her. He killed her with his inability to listen to anyone due to his selfish pride. "Rachael is dead" kept ringing in her ears until the volume drowned out every other thought or sound.

She stood there, staring at the arm that had been uncovered. It was unfair. It was so damn unfair. The anger built up in her, quickly turning to rage.

She charged at Mason with a sound coming from her, foreign to her ears. All she wanted to do was cause him bodily harm. She hit him with all of her force once, then twice. Why wasn't he defending himself or hunching to protect himself like the coward he was? He wasn't fit to even be in the same room as her daughter's body.

She couldn't control it anymore. She hit him a third and fourth time before he went to one knee, and the doctor that had been standing in shock on the other side of the of the bed grabbed her from behind, holding her arms to her sides. She cried out in frustration, using whatever part of her that was free to reach Mason.

She kicked at him, catching him in the shoulder once and the chest on the next try, but neither one of those blows was satisfying. They felt superficial like she was slightly off target. She struggled to kick him in the face but was pulled out of reach by the interfering doctor. She screamed and cried out again, the anger and frustration causing tears to spill from her eyes.

"No!" she screamed. "He killed her. That bastard killed my daughter! Don't let him get away. He has to pay. He has to!"

Two nurses came in to assist the doctor in holding her away from Mason. Then Richard was in front of her, holding her face in his hands so that he was the only thing in her line of sight.

"Victoria!" He shouted, shaking her almost violently.

He came into focus. His hair tossed, eyes red and wet. The energy drained from her body. She didn't think she could hold herself up any longer.

"Richard," she whispered as if she were afraid to hear what she was about to say. "Our baby's gone." She felt his hands tighten on her face, but it wasn't enough to keep him in focus. She sought the peace of the dark she was slipping into.

Victoria's reflection in the window came into view, startling her from her morose line of thoughts. Yes. It was time to take Vivian away from this crowded town, or it would kill her too.

Whether Mason chose to come or not would be up to him.

CHAPTER 12

"I don't understand. Why would you do this?"

Paige's head was swimming. The thoughts didn't seem to be coming together to form a logical conclusion. She was beginning to feel betrayed, and she knew that if she indulged in that feeling, this would cease to be a productive meeting.

"Did I do something to lead you to think I would welcome this? Did I say anything to make you believe I would…" she trailed off, trying to gain her composure. It would not do any good to get angry with her pastor. He was her mentor, her spiritual father. He was the one she went to when she had a problem. Ironically, she was in her pastor's office because she needed to speak to him about her last two weeks and the emotional turmoil she had been trying to keep a lid on until it was physically and psychologically impossible to avoid dealing with – and he has the gall to tell her that he's setting her up with a friend.

"Please forgive me, Paige, I didn't mean to offend you," he said, beginning to look extremely uncomfortable. He got up from around his desk, walked past her and to the door, which he propped open slightly.

Paige knew that move. She knew it was standing protocol that her pastor never hold a meeting with a woman behind a closed door, but it was one that they began disregarding due to her relationship with his wife, Menagerie, Pam, and himself. She was more like a daughter to him than a member of the clergy.

"Menagerie told me this was a bad idea. I should have listened…" he said quietly while expelling a sigh as he sat down. "I am sorry Paige, I thought…I don't know what I thought…I just…" The fragmented sentence ended in a shrug.

Paige sat there looking down at her hands, trying to decide whether she still trusted him enough to tell him what had happened. She reigned in her emotions and figured that he did what he did in love, and he was human.

"I wasn't offended, just very surprised. I made this appointment hoping you could help me sort through some of the things I have been through over the past two weeks. Most of it is clear, but I am having issues with my reactions to it." She didn't have the courage to look up yet, so she just plowed ahead.

"When we first started meeting, I told you about some of my past and you said when I was ready I could tell you the rest, so here it is." She took a breath. "Two weeks ago I eulogized my cousin's funeral. This was the cousin who molested me and who I had twins by, at 14."

She paused, allowing him to absorb the last part of the sentence.

"The eulogy went well. He gave his life to Jesus Christ before he died, and many at the funeral also gave their lives over to Christ and rededicated themselves. The book and speaking tour also went well." She lifted her shoulders and looked up in a nonchalant manner.

The look of pain and hurt on the pastor's face surprised her, and she began to ramble on just so she could finish what she had come to discuss.

"When I gave birth there were complications; only one of the twins survived. She lives with my older sister, Melanie, in Atlanta. Her name is Gladys, and we told her that I am her aunt. Her mom, my sister, wants me to tell Gladys the truth. I know it is the right thing to do but I need to be able to tell her without a shadow of a doubt that she is beautiful, and that looking at her does not cause me pain."

Pastor Lawrence interrupted her ramblings. "Paige, look at me." She obeyed him.

"I am not going to ask why you didn't share the latter of this information with me sooner. I guess I am just a little hurt that you didn't feel comfortable enough to tell me before." Paige didn't move or look away. She kept her face blank, but she was feeling like a child being chastised.

"Aaah, I know that look. I have seen it on my daughter's face when she thinks I am being too strict or passing too harsh a sentence," he read with accuracy, "Paige, I am not punishing you nor do I mean to chastise you. I am definitely not judging you. I don't know your reasons for not giving me full details on your situation earlier, but I am open and ready to listen."

"I…um…" *Blast these tears.* Paige blinked quickly, breaking his gaze on her. "I didn't tell you sooner because I wasn't ready to acknowledge it myself. I was desperately hoping that Melanie would keep Gladys at least for a few more years or at least until she got into college. Although I have been through counseling, Christian and Psychological alike, and I have dealt with a lot of the issues of my childhood, I didn't actually close the door with Stone until two weeks ago."

Feeling her composure strengthen, she returned her eyes to her pastor. She recalled the conversation she'd had with Stone, and his request to have her officiate his home-going. She shared details of their relationship: the estrangement from her mom, aunts, uncles, and cousins, her mother's search for someone that would perform an abortion, the twin's birth, and finally her pact with her sister.

When she was done, he asked her a few questions. "Has anyone from your family reached out to you, besides your sister, since then?"

"Yes. A few years ago one of my cousins came into town for a few days and we talked. I seem to be one of the family's black secrets, but she took the chance because we had been close as children. She worked for a pharmaceutical company that kept her traveling, so she got in touch with my sister to get my information. It was a comforting and healing reunion. I know I am not crazy or deranged, but it is nice sometimes to know that just a few others who know me well also think so." She gave a short, throaty laugh paired with a smile that didn't reach her eyes.

"How is your relationship with your sister?"

"I would say it is stronger now than when she first started taking care of Gladys. She was the one that named her and took care of her from birth. I was a wreck. I couldn't even look at her without crying. I was so angry."

Leaning forward, Pastor Lawrence asked, "Did you talk of your relationship with Stone while you were ministering?"

Paige shook her head. "Not in detail, but they knew we were kin and had recently resolved some of our issues.

I think I was also encouraged by the number of people that attended Stone's funeral, despite the noted absence of his immediate or extended family. He is going to be missed by quite a few people, and surprisingly, some knew his past before I eulogized him. It gave me the courage to put hope in the general, human ability to accept those named 'outcasts' by others."

"You said your concern with telling your daughter that you are her mother is how you are going to relay it to her, without making her feel like looking at her causes you pain. Does looking at your daughter cause you pain?"

"Yes."

"Why?"

"Because of the way she was conceived and the fact that I felt so much anger, guilt, and hatred for her in the womb and while I was in labor. If my sister hadn't taken her, I would have given her up for adoption. I didn't feel as I believe a mother should when they have a child. I wanted nothing to do with her. I thought she was a grave mistake, and it took my relationship with God to realize that she was a gift, and not a curse, that was going to follow me through life."

"So why do you still feel pain when you look at her?" He eyed her quizzically.

"Because I am not only going to have to tell her how I feel about her now, which is fortunate and wonderfully blessed to have her in my life, even as small as it may be, but I am going to have to tell her why I gave her up – and that is going to be painful."

"It doesn't have to be." He reached over, taking a tissue out of the box. She didn't even know she was crying until he handed it to her.

"Oh, sorry," she began, trying to find an excuse for the tears. He waved his hand to interrupt her apology.

"When you speak to women and young adults during the breakout sessions in those conferences, you don't get any that have had some of the same experiences that you did?"

"Some, but…" she trailed off.

"But?"

"I don't mean to be difficult, but I don't know of many people who openly admitted to trying to abort their children."

"Probably not, but you do know of women who were successful, even if the circumstances of their conceptions were different." She nodded in agreement to his statement.

He went on, "Yes, and have you not help lead services of repentance for those who have had abortions?"

"Yes."

"So why have you kept the shame of the truth, even though you have accepted God's forgiveness for the attempt?" She was quiet and actually surprised that it had never occurred to her. "Think on that for a moment because what I would like to know is how you feel about the child that died."

"I feel a loss but that she is much better off. In the beginning, I thought it was my anger and hatred that killed her, but I had to let go of that guilt just as I eventually let go of the guilt of hating the one that survived."

"Well, I have to say that you have come a long way with this. No doubt your relationship with God led you through some of your darker moments, but the shame is not yours to bear and it isn't fair for you to put it on her either. You need to find true resolution with this before you talk to your daughter; otherwise, it is going to be hard to communicate your feelings in love for her."

She nodded again, hesitant to tell him the rest. "I am supposed to go and see her on Friday."

She watched as her pastor placed his hands together in front of him, the index fingers touching, meeting each other in a point in front of his mouth.

"Mmm, well it looks like you have some praying and soul searching to do but I think you are on the right path. How old is your daughter now?"

"Twelve."

A slow whistle came from his lips. "That is a delicate age. Tread lightly, Paige. Wait…" He stopped as if a light bulb went off. "You are in your late 20's right?"

"Just. I am 26."

"Quite a bit to go through at such an age. Your ability to forgive and allow God to heal you is a true testament of what God can do if you let Him. What is it that caused you to submit yourself to God, initially? I mean, if you can remember. What first got your attention?"

Paige thought about it for a moment, tracing back to her first thoughts of God. "I have always thought of God, or at least sensed Him. My parents went to church and believed in Him, but left my Christian education up to my youth pastor. As a child, I learned mostly about the stories of the Bible and the people in those stories, but I didn't know that it was possible to have a relationship with God like they did. God was a man that lived in the clouds that looked down and helped you every now and then when I was in what I thought was big trouble.

When I was 17, a friend invited me to a bible study. She saved my life. The study caught my interest because I had never heard the Bible broken down and explained that way. I continued to attend class and eventually came down to the altar to receive the gift of the Holy Spirit.

I *so* wanted to be special to someone, not just used because of my talents, beauty, or trusting nature. I wanted to feel safe in that love, but I didn't know how to get it. I read the Bible and prayed. I wrote down my feelings like I had been taught by my therapist and I went over them later and prayed for help with them. It wasn't a fast process, but once I understood that you could have a personal relationship with God, it made things easier. Life wasn't as hard, and the past couldn't torture me as it had been. I continuously received new perspectives on people, their actions and situations that would have defeated me if I hadn't been open to seeing things differently. I had to be willing to let go of everything I had learned so that I could continue to embrace what He was teaching and showing me.

Most of all, I received peace; peace from the dreams that haunted me and peace from the memories that I let steal the true understanding of my value. It has been my oldest and most faithful friend. It was always there when I needed it, and now I no longer run from my dreams. I face them, look them right in the eye and rebuke them with the name of Jesus with the authority of the Holy Spirit and the surety that I am an heir to the Kingdom and a child of the Most High.

It took all-night prayer, consecrating myself, and reading books that were recommended by my pastor. I kept to myself quite a bit, but when God gave me the opportunity to visit the sick with some of the evangelists, I took it and found I loved it just as much as I loved praying. I went back to school during the day because I had taken a graveyard shift as an orderly at a convalescent home. I double-majored and received my B.A. in Theology and Counseling, but you already know that. I went for my certification of chaplaincy at Daniel Freeman Hospital right after I received my Evangelist License.

It felt like I was in school forever, but my thirst for knowledge was insatiable. I was curious but didn't agree with some of the things some of my professors said about certain books of the Bible. We butted heads sometimes, not because I was sure I knew the right answer, but because some of their thought-paths confused me. I didn't know how they got to that conclusion nor how that conclusion could lead to a deeper understanding or relationship with God. I learned that there were some people who wanted to have a relationship with God and some who just wanted to study Him. I learned quite a bit from both. I just tended to gravitate towards the ones with like-minds.

Originally, I thought God enabled me to go to school so I could serve on the Visitation Committee. I had such a passion for those that were home or bed-bound. The presence of God would fill the room while we had Bible Study or prayed. Sometimes we would sing, other times we would just pray, but there was never a time I didn't feel God there; to know that He was inclining His ear was always very humbling. I felt like those times were always the perfect opportunity for a miracle, whether it was the healing of their body, soul, mind, or all three."

Realizing that she had gone far beyond the answer to his question, she smiled sheepishly. The pastor smiled back, knowing all too well the need to express one's love for God and the beauty of being used.

"And what of men? Were there any that you were interested in?"

"Yes. There have been a couple who were intriguing, but I didn't let it go further than that. We had study dinners, but once they saw that I truly treated God like my father, they either thought I was 'too spiritual' or slightly intimidating." Paige giggled. "But I guess I can understand. Can you imagine having to go to God to ask if you can date His daughter?" Pastor Lawrence laughed with her for a moment but sobered quickly.

"So where does that leave you?" He leaned forward, not allowing her to break his gaze again.

She stared back, unwavering. "It leaves me waiting for the man that is willing to ask Him."

"Is this what you really believe or are you using that as an excuse to keep men at arm's length? If you never come across a man that will meet you where you are, then you have a good excuse to stay single."

Paige reflected on his conclusion for a moment and then spoke. "Forgive me for being direct, but wouldn't you want your daughter to wait for the man of God that would seek Him, for her?"

Pastor Lawrence nodded. "Of course, but then my daughter has not been through what you have been through." He went on, "I know men and women alike who give their life to Christ and then spend almost every waking moment in church, in the Bible and in prayer, but it isn't to deepen their relationship with God. It is to find refuge and escape from the hurt and pain, not knowing that the only way to combat the hurt and darkness of their past is to face it with the knowledge that greater is He in them than he that is in the world. To face it with the knowledge and love of God, they realize that they are worthy of the sacrifice Jesus made for them and in turn love Him enough to be obedient. Not because He says it is law, but because they don't wish to grieve Him."

"Pastor, I know that it is easy to try to escape through church, but what you didn't hear was that through my relationship with God, there is no hiding. I am nervous and uncomfortable about the unknown. Knowing that I will have to share my past and present with yet another person doesn't sit well with me, especially now that I am going to have Gladys with me. I come with a child now – one that I barely know. Aren't you glad we had this meeting before you set me up with your friend?" She wiggled her eyebrows at him.

A look of horror flashed across his face and it made Paige very uneasy, no matter how quickly he regained his composure.

"Just one moment, Paige, I need to make a call."

He pressed the speaker button and dialed the extension to Pam's office.

"Pam, could you get a hold of Elder Brandon Tatum?"

"Not a problem. He arrived a couple of minutes ago and is waiting in the lounge," came the voice from the speaker.

The look on her pastor's face was priceless. He looked like a little boy whose hand was caught in the cookie jar and could hear his mom walking down the hall. Paige laughed out loud before she could stop herself.

Her pastor's eyes flashed, causing her to sober up.

"You must agree this is something you are going to laugh about later." His expression caused her to think again about telling him what else she thought. "Knowing what I know now, I wouldn't have been so bold as to set this up the way I did but I thought it might be nice for you to meet him before I invited you to dinner tonight at the house."

Paige fumed, trying to think of a truthful excuse for not being able to go but couldn't think of anything at the moment. "How long do I have to come up with a reason for not being able to go tonight?"

"Before you see him. He is new in town and I thought you and Menagerie could show him around a little before dinner. If you are completely against it, which I can understand given your circumstances and new mission, you will have to say it now so that I can give my apologies for promising you without knowing your schedule."

Paige considered a few scenarios but kept coming back to one question.

"Pastor, who knows the most about this set up: me or him?"

"What do you mean?" Pastor asked, starting to look uncomfortable.

"I mean, I didn't know about meeting Elder Tatum until right now, but Elder Tatum doesn't know about what we just spoke on. What did you tell Elder Tatum about me and about today?"

Paige eyed her pastor, observing the way he shifted in his chair so that he was leaning back, away from her.

"I told my friend, Elias, Elder Tatum's father, that I would take Brandon under my wing, and I knew someone with like-values that I wanted him to meet. Brandon agreed, and I suggested that my wife go along since you two are like mother and daughter."

Paige placed her hands in her lap. "I was last to know."

The last answer wasn't up to him but she wanted to know anyway.

"So what do you think now? Do you still favor this match?"

"I would be lying if I said, 'Not much has changed.' It has. You have a child that is part of this equation and she comes first. It would be unfair for me to ask you to begin two new relationships at the same time."

The moment of excitement was eclipsed by the reality of what she was going to have to prepare herself for on Friday. Feeling somewhat deflated even though she had not completely made up her mind to meet this man, she nodded her agreement.

"So we are agreed. I will make apologies for you," he stated, getting up from his chair.

Trying not to look as forlorn as she felt, she pasted a smile on her face, collected her purse and stood up, ready to follow him out of the office.

Her courage leaving her, Paige separated herself from the pastor before they reached the outer door to the lounge area. "You know what, I am going to the ladies' restroom. I will be out in a little bit unless you just want to take Elder Tatum into your office and meet with him there."

"So you aren't even going to meet him?"

Paige answered even as she was walking back away from him, and the door. "No. Not just yet. He may see me and decide that he doesn't want to let me out of his sight and that would be nothing but cruel what with me going out of town on Friday..." She tried to make light of the situation.

"Or he may decide you are just too confident, mistaking it for arrogance, and wonder what his father's friend thinks he might see in you," came an oddly gentle voice from behind her.

Paige's breath caught in her throat, threatening to strangle her. She dare not turn if she wanted keep her dignity.

"Then again," she continued to keep her eyes glued to her pastor's face, judging her scoffer's expressions by her pastor's responses, "she could have concluded that she didn't like being the last man out and was going to teach her pastor a lesson by letting him explain her absence."

"Oh, but what kind of character is that, that she would allow her pastor to go back on his own to explain her unwillingness to make a mere acquaintance?"

She watched as Pastor Lawrence's face broke out into a grin.

"Pastor is used to speaking for himself, especially when he rushes into things," came Menagerie's voice from the hall leading to Pam's office.

All three sets of eyes flew to the hall as Menagerie stepped forward.

With a sigh of relief, Paige moved towards Menagerie, and was enveloped in a tight hug. Not letting go, she heard Menagerie whisper, "Keep your chin up." Then, so that everyone else could hear, "I missed lunch. I think I will take Paige out to catch up and see how her latest trip went."

Menagerie turned Paige around, one arm still around her. "Elder Morganson, I would like you to meet Elder Tatum."

Paige's eyes confronted a chest. She looked up to meet piercing, brown eyes, softly-tilted at the sides. *Mmm, nice.* He was very nice. She could feel it, but he had a biting wit that she had experienced first-hand.

They exchanged a handshake, all the while she took in as many features as she could: his pointy chin, full, lower-beveled lip, wide nostrils, heavy eyebrows, and loose curly hair. For once, she was happy she was single. This man was good-looking...maybe a little tall for her taste, but definitely good-looking. *Funny*, she thought to herself as she stepped back, disengaging her hand and meeting his eyes again. She didn't know she had a type.

"I am going to apologize," Paige began, "not for trying to avoid meeting you, but for doing such a bad job at it, that I may have offended you in the process." She noticed his eyes darken as he responded.

"Well I meant what I said about your character, but I am willing to overlook it since you are being honest."

His smile was disarming. "Thank you for being so gracious," she retorted. His smile widened, and she panicked.

Turning away, she addressed Menagerie, "Thank you for the introduction, First Lady. You said something about lunch?" Menagerie nodded, a small smirk playing at her lips.

Nodding at Elder Tatum once again, Paige turned towards the outer door, walked to her pastor and gave him a hug then walked to the door, holding it open for Menagerie.

"Wow, as first impressions go, you definitely won't be forgotten soon," said Menagerie as they walked down the staircase.

Paige looked back to make sure the door had closed. "I didn't mean to be rude."

When they got to the last step Menagerie turned to Paige. "Didn't you? You apologized, saying you didn't mean to offend him, but it looked to me like you were working at it really hard, or is that how you greet all prospects?"

Paige shrugged. "As you said, it keeps me unforgettable."

Menagerie leaned forward until their noses almost touched. "Yes, and alone." Then she turned and continued out of the door, leaving Paige no other choice but to follow.

CHAPTER 13

They sat there looking at each other for a good 30 seconds before Brandon decided to break the silence. "Wow. She has a great deal of fire in her. I am glad she is on God's side."

Pastor Lawrence shifted in his chair, leaning forward.

"I know I said I would make the introductions, but now that you have met her, I don't think it would be wise for us to talk about Elder Paige without her being present."

Brandon smiled widely, oddly touched by the protective tone. "I wasn't talking about Elder Morganson. I was talking about your wife."

Pastor Lawrence laughed out loud. It was a deep guffaw that filled the room; Brandon could tell that he didn't give into it often. When he gained some composure, Pastor Lawrence leaned back in his chair, a light in his eyes. "Yes, First Lady Lawrence is not someone to be reckoned with. She is a fierce lover of God and a powerful prayer warrior. That is probably why she basically adopted Elder Morganson. Don't have those two pray unless you are ready for the answer the Lord has for you."

Brandon's brow lifted at that. "Mmmm," he began, but heeding Pastor's request not to speak on Elder Morganson, he kept the rest to himself and instead began another sentence. "So, I brought my papers with me along with my reference letters." He reached into his attaché case, pulling out a thick binder and handed it to Pastor Lawrence.

He could see that Pastor Lawrence was impressed by the number of references he carried with him, along with his Bachelors in Communication, Masters in Business Administration and Certificates of completion in numerous theological courses. His train of thought was broken when Pastor Lawrence closed the binder, laying it on the desk between them and point-blank asked him the question he thought it was going to take at least a half an hour to get to.

"I am sure your father has told you that we have a ministerial position available, but before I give you details about it, I want to know how you would handle the following situation:

You get a call at what you would consider an inconvenient time, but on the other end of the line is a brother who has been struggling with pornography for a few years. He didn't think there was anything wrong with it at first but after a while, he began sneaking it on the job, and his work suffered. He is a member of the church and has been attending the men's prayer meetings off and on because he sometimes feels convicted. He wants to stop because he knows it is wrong, but late at night is when the urge gets the hardest to ignore. This particular night he decides to go down to the restaurant on the corner which doubles as a bar so that he can get out of the house. He calls you up and asks if you can come meet him. What do you do?"

Brandon sat there, giving the situation some consideration. He sat up straighter, placing the soles of his feet flat on the floor while he tried to decide which way to approach the subject. Head on was one that worked more often than not.

"I would ask if he would mind if I called another Elder to come with me –"

"Why?" Pastor interrupted, not wanting to assume anything.

"I believe in the power of numbers, both to show support of the one hurting and in bondage, and for deliverance. The addiction to pornography is not just a disease. I believe there is a spirit attached to it. Whether it be rebellion, perversion or something deeper, deliverance needs to take place and it is best if there were witnesses."

"What if the person just wants to talk?"

"I can't want them to be free more than they want to be so, yes, I would talk to them, but I would let them know they have an option and it is up to them if they want to keep suffering or if they want to be free."

"Now as I said earlier, this is a man who has been dealing with this for a couple of years. How do you know others haven't already tried?"

Brandon shrugged. "They may have, but if he is calling me in the middle of the night for help then I should come prepared to help him as much as possible, right?"

Pastor Lawrence nodded his agreement. "Okay, say he hasn't been exposed to the deliverance ministry, is hesitant, and is feeling uncomfortable. What would you say?"

"I guess I would ask him if he is filled with the Holy Spirit. If not, then I would pray with him until he was filled with the Holy Spirit."

Pastor Lawrence, studying him, interrupted again, "Right there in the bar?"

Brandon hesitated and then answered confidently. "It is just a bar, and God is everywhere."

With that, Pastor Lawrence got up and started putting on his jacket.

Startled, Brandon got up too, reaching for his case, believing the interview was over.

"Leave the case unless you have a bible in it."

Brandon's face became rosy. He had forgotten his bible.

"I have an old acquaintance to meet and I would like for you to come along. Do you have any objections?" Brandon shook his head.

"I don't mind at all, but I..." Before the sentence was completely out of his mouth, Pastor Lawrence reached over, picking out a bible from his bookshelf and handed it to Brandon.

Pastor Lawrence dialed the intercom and Pam's voice came on the line. "Yes, Pastor?"

"Pam, Elder Tatum and I are going to see Marvin. We will be back shortly."

"Very well, Pastor. What shall I say to First Lady if she comes back before you?"

Brandon watched Pastor hesitate for a moment. "Do I have any other appointments for today?"

"No," came the voice from the other end of the line.

"Very nice, then I will call it a day. Please let my wife know that I went home early, but will not be available by cell until after 4:30 pm."

"I will do. Have a wonderful rest of your day."

"You too, Pam." He picked up the items he had laid on the desk and ushered Elder Tatum out the door.

As they walked down the stairs Pastor Lawrence asked, "Do you mind if we take your car?"

Brandon, feeling honored, answered quickly. "Absolutely." But the next question made him regret his haste to answer.

"Do you have full coverage?" Pastor Lawrence asked as they passed through the front door and into the light of the afternoon.

"Yes..." was Brandon's drawn out answer that signaled a want for more information.

All he received was a curt "Good."

"May I ask why the question regarding the insurance?" He quickened his steps so that he could lead Pastor Lawrence to his car.

"Because we are going to a bar in the inner city and if something happens, I wanted to make sure you were taken care of. I am having you drive because my car is well known, and I would like to do this with some privacy."

Brandon's hand froze on the car door. He was astounded at the boldness of this man. *A bar in the middle of the day?* But he did say he wanted to visit someone. Brandon took a deep breath. He knew this man to be a good friend of his father's but still needed clarity. He straightened away from the door.

Pastor Lawrence eyes were expressionless.

Brandon cleared his throat. "I am going to have to ask you why we are going to the bar. If it is to meet with someone, I will be more than happy to escort you; honored, really. But if it is to get a drink in the middle of the day, I am going to have to decline." He watched for any signs of impatience, frustration or worse yet, anger from Pastor Lawrence as he spoke, but all he saw was a squint that came from the sun passing through the cloud.

Pastor Lawrence shielded his eyes with his hands and stepped a little closer so that his next words would be uttered in confidence.

"Elder Tatum, I have not touched liquor in a little over 20 years, but I appreciate your concern. I want to introduce you to an acquaintance as I mentioned in the office and I do not wish to be approached by someone that may see my car while we are there."

Brandon, feeling a few pounds lighter, reached back down, pulled open the door, allowed for Pastor Lawrence to fold his six-foot frame into the passenger seat and closed the door.

As they drove through the streets of Glendale on the way to Boyle Heights, Brandon took directions and stole glances of places the pastor pointed out as he gave him a small tour of the cities they were driving through. He was surprised to see that some areas looked just like his hometown of Garden City, Kansas.

A small case of homesickness pricked his heart. He couldn't believe he was feeling that way. He had worked so hard to get out when he was younger. He remembered his dad's encouraging words each time he brought home anything lower than a score equaling an A+, but his goal wasn't just to be the best in the school. His goal was to make sure that he had a full ride to any college he chose so that there would be nothing to hinder him, financially, from getting out of town.

He had a few friends that had also left the area and had never looked back, but he had a lot more that stayed. Some were happy and some were not.

As far back as Brandon could remember, he knew what he wanted; he wanted to get out from under his father's shadow. It was a lofty goal because his father's name seemed to carry a lot of weight in many states. As the dean of a small college, pastor, and member of at least 4 community organizations in the city, it was hard walking anywhere in the city without being called out. Even though he was number six of seven children, he favored his father the most physically and people thought that, naturally, he would follow in his father's footsteps.

After learning what was expected of him as a child, he felt hard-pressed to stay under the radar. If he did exactly what was expected of him, he was least likely to receive any unwanted attention. He did so well at blending into any new class, subject, or home situation that he often found he received no attention. It didn't bother him too much, as long as he reached his goal: getting out of town and getting a chance to be known as Brandon and not just one of the Tatums.

"Your turn is coming up on the left." Brandon was taken away from his thoughts and led to a corner plaza with storefronts squeezed together. He was instructed to park closest to the small, hole-in-the-wall restaurant on the far end of the strip mall.

As they exited the car, people sitting outside the bar with brown bags in their hands got up and came towards Pastor Lawrence. Some looked dirty and unshaven, others looked like they had just come from work, but they each had something in their hand. As they came forward, shook hands and hugged Pastor Lawrence, Brandon watched the pastor's face for any expression of disgust or caution in trying to keep his suit clean. He hugged each man the same and seemed to be even more at home here than he was in his own office.

Then he motioned over to Brandon and introduced each man by name to him. Brandon, in turn, shook each hand and quickly fell into step with the last man as the pastor went towards the small, bar-like establishment.

Pastor Lawrence called out to one of the men, "Is Marvin here today?"

The man named Jim answered. "Yep, he's inside. You're good. He just got here." Some of the other men looked back at Brandon, but no one said a word.

As the door opened, all Brandon could see were brick-red seats and wood paneling on the walls. The carpet looked blood red in the dimly lit room. As he walked in, he could see that each booth had its own candle to encourage intimate conversations and the ceiling fans and heavy iron sconces on the walls couldn't have held more than 10-watt bulbs in them. Brandon blinked slowly to adjust his eyes to the shadow-filled room. It reminded him of the front room of some of the haunted houses he visited on Halloween when he was in college. Whatever brought Pastor Lawrence here in the first place?

The actual bar that ran from one end of the room to the other was deep mahogany and looked out of place in the clean but old-looking establishment.

Everyone in the bar turned as Pastor Lawrence entered with the men and Brandon.

Brandon watched as the pastor shook more hands and gave hugs to some of the men in the booths as well as at the bar.

Still confused as to the real reason for the visit, Brandon hung back by the door waiting to see what was going to happen next.

Once Pastor Lawrence made his way to the end of the bar, he back-tracked. Brandon saw him scanning the faces as if he was looking for someone, but Brandon couldn't imagine who. The place was so small you could look to the end and see everything.

Once their eyes met, Brandon began to get an uneasy feeling. He watched Pastor Lawrence draw the attention of the bartender over to him and wished the place was even dimmer so that he could get lost in the shadows. He had just been set up.

"For those of you who haven't met him, I want you all to meet Elder Brandon," Pastor said while signaling with his hand for Brandon to come away from the door. "He is new in town. He only arrived a few weeks ago from Fort Lauderdale, but he is originally from Garden City, Kansas." Brandon would have groaned if he wasn't afraid everyone would hear him. He obediently came forward as the feelings of trepidation grew.

He finally came to stand next to Pastor Lawrence, turning so that his back wasn't to anyone.

Brandon felt Pastor Lawrence's hand on his shoulder. "Elder Tatum, why don't you share a little about yourself and your background with these men? Let them get to know you."

Brandon looked at the pastor, trying to gauge the situation and silently communicate all the questions that popped into his head in that instant.

What do you want me to tell them? What is too much? Who are these men to you? Do you trust them? Will you stop me when I begin to go too far? What are we doing here?

Brandon looked back at the men, scanning their faces, coming to rest on one particular man, sitting in a booth, writing something in a small book.

He concentrated on what the man was doing for a second to organize his thoughts.

"Good evening," he began with a slight bow.

The small crowd responded in kind, some of the men smiling at the gesture.

"My name is Brandon Tatum. As Pastor Lawrence said, I am here from Fort Lauderdale, Florida, but I was born and raised in Garden City, Kansas. I am the sixth of seven children and the son of a very prominent man in that state as well as surrounding states, Elias Tatum, who happens to be a good friend of the pastor's.

I am an ordained elder under the Church of God in Christ. I studied at NYU and Columbia and later moved to Richmond where I got a job with a pharmaceutical company that allowed me to travel all over the United States. I recently transferred to their headquarters in Torrance, taking a promotion and a desk 25% more of the time." He ended the last sentence with a shrug.

The men in the room all looked at the pastor, who then looked at Brandon, again. "Wow. You said all of that and no man in this room knows you any better than when you first started. You don't trust people much do you?"

Brandon backed away a second, feeling trapped with the bar to his back. "I am not sure of what you wanted. I don't know how well you know these men though you seem very friendly with them."

"Brandon, no one is asking you to give them your social security or credit card numbers. I am just asking you to tell them who you are. I know you are feeling put on the spot but I am asking you for a reason."

Brandon looked at the pastor wishing he could discover what he was looking for. Retrieving nothing from the blank eyes but a sincere smile, Brandon turned back to the group and tried again.

He took a deep breath, blowing it out slowly.

"Alright. You know my name, how many siblings I have, where I went to school, and my vocation. I consider myself to be a man of God. I enjoy reading the bible. It fascinates me in how it comes alive in my hands, and the words feed my soul. I love a good bible study where the teacher expounds on the Word to the point where you might only get through three or four verses because the discussion gets so deep, due to the different ways people perceived those words. I come away feeling like I have been gifted with centuries of knowledge.

I accepted Jesus Christ as my Lord and Savior when I was nine. As long as I can remember, He has been in my life, showing Himself in different ways. My dad is the dean of a college in a neighboring city, and he is a pastor of a small church. He is very intellectual and can exegete a passage in such a thorough way you'd think he was there when it happened.

It was my mom that I first saw Jesus through, though. She was always there when you needed help. Whether it was fixing a hole in one of our sweaters or a hole in the small fence surrounding her garden, she was there. She could do it all. From helping the girls with their hair to running a pass to help Theodore train for tryouts in football, she did it all. But the thing that sticks with me the most are the prayers she said over us every night. She used to come to each of our beds late at night and pray over us. I would try to stay awake, feigning sleep to hear her, but most times I would fall asleep waiting. I only knew in the morning when I had oil on my forehead that she had been there.

Her walk with God seemed so sure. I know now that she may have wavered in some things, but we never saw it. To us, she is a strong pillar in our family, but soft enough to make us want to go back and sit next to her and have her tell us what she finds so endearing about each gift God gave to her. As much as my dad piqued my interest in the Word, my mom showed me that God was a lover of individuals."

Brandon continued, feeling more at ease. "Let's see. I am 33. I am not married, though I came close once. I do not have any children, but I do have seven nieces and nephews that seem to have birthdays every day of the year. I enjoy living by myself because I am somewhat of a bookworm, but sometimes I miss the noise of having a lot of people around. I don't believe I have a temper, but I do talk before I think sometimes, which gets me just what I deserve.

I don't preach like my dad but in the few times that I have been before men and women expounding upon the Word, it has been said that I covered all the bases and have brought subjects to light that provoked thought. I am more hands-on with my form of ministering. I like helping people walk through some of the process of getting to know God better or getting to know Him in the sense of a close friend."

Feeling a squeeze on his arm he stopped, looking over at Pastor Lawrence.

"So men, it is time for our bible study. What do you say to Elder Tatum taking the lead tonight?"

Brandon, hoping the surprise didn't register on his face, looked around at the nodding heads and smiles. There was now a lump forming in his throat the size of a watermelon. This was proving to be a day full of emotional highs and lows.

"Gentlemen, what was it you were wanting to discuss tonight?"

"The dangers of porn," a man in the back called out.

Brandon bowed his head, a wry smile playing across his lips. He shook his head slightly and raised it again to look at the pastor, who watched it all with feigned surprise.

"Well, what do you know?" Pastor whispered, rubbing his chin. It was all Brandon could do to keep from laughing.

If this day was any indication of what this year was going to be like, he was going to die a happy man.

CHAPTER 14

Mason was oblivious to the stares and whispers coming from the nurse's station as he rolled by, his mind focused on getting to his daughter. He woke up this morning feeling better than he had in the years since Rachael's death. He had made a promise to himself this morning as he waited for the doctor to come and examine his ankle and check his blood pressure.

Letting go of some of the pain he had buried deep in his heart since he broke down in Vivian's lap on Monday had allowed him to think more clearly. He was going back to work. It had been a long time since he even wanted to indulge in the thought of taking up architecture again, but being busy and not giving in to the depressive state of mind would do him and Vivian a great deal of good.

His savings and investments were still in good shape, along with the trust for Vivian, but he knew that occupying his mind while Vivian was in school would be the big challenge. Later today, he would contact David at MarsdenTech, Inc. and see where his old position stood.

No more negative thinking. He still had his life and his beautiful daughter. He'd wasted enough time on feeling sorry for himself and cheating his daughter out of a childhood. He was going to work harder to give Vivian the life he felt she deserved, even if that meant her spending a couple more weeks with Victoria and Richard each year.

He slowed as he reached her door, knocked, and peered around the door as he opened it. "Is it all clear?" he asked.

Vivian, sitting up in bed, turned to him with a smile. "All clear," she responded, referring to her grandmother. "She said she may be late coming in today. She had to go shopping." Vivian made a face that made Mason smile. He knew he should have reprimanded her, but he was growing more concerned about the dark circles under her eye.

"How did you sleep, honey?" he said as he rolled closer.

Vivian's smiled faltered. "I slept well. The nurses barely woke me when they took my blood, but I am still tired. I think I am going to take a nap soon if you don't mind."

"Honey, not at all. I will stay right here until you wake up again, but first I have some good news to tell you."

He could see her eyes light up.

"After I get out of the hospital and make sure my ankle is better, I am going back to work."

"Really Daddy? You are going back to work? That is fantastic, stupendous, outstanding..." she stopped mid-sentence, trying to think. "What is another word for 'great'?"

"There is monumental, prodigious, phenomenal, spectacular..."

Vivian interrupted him. "I know, marvelous."

"Very good, that is a perfect word." He lifted himself up out of the chair and leaned over her on the bed to give her cheek a kiss.

"Honey, you just go to sleep and I will stay here until you wake up."

"Promise?"

"Promise, baby."

He sat back down, taking her hand, and watched as she began to fight to keep her lids up. "Shhh, I will be here," he said, coaxing her to give in to the drowsiness. He sat back, keeping her hand in his, and watched as her eyes closed.

He stayed there, suspended in that position for many minutes, watching a small smile play upon her face. The arm crossing her body reaching out to him, was gently rising and falling with her stomach. He loved watching her sleep since she was a little girl. He could practically feel the peace that enveloped her. Sometimes he thought that if he watched long enough, he could share in some of that. All the earth was right side up in moments like this.

He remained like that for another half an hour. Even when his fingers began to fall asleep because of the awkward position, he didn't move. The sound of the door caught his attention, and he looked up to see Vivian's doctor walking in. Mason placed his finger to his lips signaling the need for quiet.

The doctor nodded as he walked over to check her vitals on the monitor. He went back over to the computer in the corner of the room, used to keep a record of her progress. After pressing a few buttons he sighed and motioned for Mason to follow him out of the door.

Mason, checking Vivian to make sure she was still in a deep sleep, disengaged his hand from hers and turned his wheelchair so that he could follow the doctor.

"I have been monitoring Vivian's levels closely for the last 24 hours, and I am afraid she has stopped responding to some of the medications that help her kidneys function properly. I mentioned that due to the extensive blood loss and the cut-off of blood flow to the kidneys, in addition to the rupture of the left kidney at the time of the accident, she went into perineal renal failure. I was hoping it was temporary and that her age would be an advantage, but some of her other injuries seem to be what the body is paying more attention to in healing.

Though one kidney is stronger than the other, it isn't functioning at a percentage that is allowing the body to rid itself of enough waste and toxins. If she continues to be unresponsive, I am going to have to schedule her for more frequent dialysis sessions. During that time, I would like you to talk to your friends and relatives about being a potential donor for her."

"Are we at that stage already?" Mason asked rubbing his brow.

"No, there is still time, but a living donor is the best option and if someone in your family or circle of friends steps forward, the evaluation and testing process to see if they are healthy enough to donate takes 2 to 4 months. I want you to be prepared but I haven't ruled out all hope that they won't start functioning on their own. It is a major decision. One just doesn't just give up an organ. There are physical and psychological repercussions."

"Her grandmother just came into town. I will ask her." He said hesitantly.

"I could have a nurse talk to her." the doctor began, but Mason cut him off.

"No. I will take care of it. She can be…a challenge." He said the last on a breath.

"If you think of anyone else you believe may be a potential donor, please let the nurse know." The doctor said after a slight nod of understanding.

"It may turn out that we don't need them, but I would rather be prepared and move forward. It isn't always a quick process. Some people wait days; others have waited years."

"I would like to be signed up," said Mason.

The doctor looked down the hall at something and took a deep breath. "That may be possible at a later time, but with your elevated blood pressure, you are not considered a good candidate. If I were you, I would wait until you were fully recovered and worked on bringing your blood pressure to a normal level. Until then, you won't even pass the physical and it would take even longer for them to test you again."

Mason nodded in agreement, feeling helpless. He spoke in length with the doctor, looking now and then to make sure Vivian wasn't waking up.

His little girl…he could feel the heaviness start to fall over him. Was it his imagination or was the day getting darker?

After he finished with the doctor and the nurses came in to check her vitals, Mason came back to sit with his daughter as he had promised. He watched her face as she slept; so much like his wife's, it was still hard to believe that she didn't come from Rachael's womb.

He remembered the day he and Rachael went to the hospital to see her for the first time. They were actually surprised to get the call because they were told not only a week before that the wait would be longer due to complications with the latest case.

He had been so nervous, he could barely get the car seat in; people would have thought Rachael was in labor. When he finally finished she placed a hand on his shoulder, kissed him on the cheek in thanks for a good job and then informed him that she would be driving.

"What am I going to do with you when I am pregnant and in labor? I won't be able to drive myself. Maybe I should have mom and dad come down for that last week."

He looked over at her. "Do you really want your mom to be in the delivery room with you? You know if she comes, she is going to try and take over."

Rachael returned her attention to the road. "Yeah, you have a point there. I will just walk." She looked over at him, grinning mischievously.

The infant laid there bundled in a light pink blanket, asleep between two screamers. The caseworker gave very little information about the birth mother. They knew she was in good health until the labor, which seemed to have had surmountable complications. The mother died soon after giving birth, which caused a delay in the adoption; due to no next of kin coming forward to claim the child, they were free to go on with the paperwork and take the child home. They named her Vivian Leigh Jenson. Vivian, after Rachael's aunt and Leigh after his mother, who at that time was in a convalescent home. The "Leigh" was Rachael's middle name also. This child had a hefty legacy just in her name.

That night, he sat there watching her yawn and move around in his arms. She couldn't have weighed much more than one of his shoes. He brought her up to his face so that he could smell the scent of baby powder on her and felt her cuddle to the side of his neck. He was in love.

He continued to sit there. He couldn't recall how long it had been because he was reminiscing in and out of the years when the three of them were together, but when the door opened, he wasn't surprised to see

Victoria standing in the doorway. He knew this was going to happen sooner or later. He was just hoping that it would be later.

He nodded his head in acknowledgment and gestured to a seat near the door. He placed a finger on his lips to indicate that they should be quiet.

Victoria took the seat near the door and sat silently for a few minutes. Every now and then he would take his gaze off of Vivian so that she wouldn't think he was avoiding her. The second time, he saw her open her mouth as if to say something, but he returned his gaze to Vivian and dared not look back for another minute. The longer she sat there, the dryer his mouth got. His stomach began to turn itself into one, big knot before he began talking to himself to try and ease his tension.

Get a hold of yourself. There is nothing that she can do to you, especially while Vivian is in the room. I just won't go anywhere with her. Listen to yourself. You sound like a kid that is trying to avoid being punished. Who are you? A little boy or a man? You're not afraid of this woman, are you?

Mason shrugged his shoulders. Feeling the movement brought him back to the moment. He looked to see if Victoria saw the movement. She was just staring at him with a scowl embedded in her forehead.

He took a deep breath and motioned for her to come over. She got up and walked over. He could see the anger burning in her eyes. He was used to that.

"I can't talk to you right now. I told Vivian that I would be here until she woke up, and I don't want to wake her."

Victoria bent down until they were eye level. "Are you that afraid of me that you would use your daughter as an excuse not to speak to me?"

Incredulously, Mason leaned back to bring her whole face into view. "I'm sorry, Victoria. How are you? It was very generous of you to come all this way to visit my daughter in the hospital. Was the ride alright? No motion sickness I hope." He placed what he believed to be the most innocent look on his face that he could muster. He watched as Victoria's eyes flashed. She answered him between gritted teeth.

"Thank you for inquiring but you know that is not what I am talking about."

Before she could say anything else he whispered in a frank, nononsense voice. Even as he said the words, he was wondering where they were coming from.

"Victoria, I am sitting here in front of my child, your grandchild, whom I was told only an hour ago may be in need of a kidney. I am not prepared nor do I intend to speak to you about anything heavier than the weather in Chicago." His eyes never wavered.

"Do you mean to tell me that you won't speak to me about anything more pertinent than the wind in your fair city?" She said it as if she were cussing at him, an ugly sneer riding the side of her lip.

Mason sighed, working his fingers back and forth across his forehead.

"Fine, fine. I won't be unfair. We can talk about the weather in your city too."

CHAPTER 15

Paige closed the door after slipping into the passenger seat next to her First Lady. She quietly watched as Menagerie turned on the air conditioner in the car and hit the memory button which automatically set her seat and mirrors in the optimum position for driving. Then she turned to Paige and gave her one of her looks that said, "I am about to ask you a question that you may want to avoid but I will see right through you so you better just come out with it."

"So why was my husband allowing you to fend for yourself with Elder Tatum? Usually, he is as fiercely protective of you as he is with our daughter."

Paige looked away and then down at her hands, which she was now ringing together. She took a deep breath. She might as well get it out now.

"He was hurt because I kept something from him and then I got caught trying to sneak out on a meeting he had made between me and Elder Tatum. His hands weren't completely tied but, I made it awkward and downright hard for him to protect me."

Menagerie's right eyebrow went into a high arch, but she said nothing.

Paige, feeling the lump in her throat return, tried to clear it unsuccessfully.

"I...um...I." Blast it. She began to feel a burning behind her eyes and began to blink quickly before the tears formed. Better just to blurt it out.

"About two weeks ago, I eulogized my cousin. This was the cousin that I had been molested by. We talked on the phone a few times during his last days, and I am happy to say that he accepted Jesus as his Lord and Savior before he passed. Next Friday I am to go see my daughter and let her know that my sister who has been raising her is not her mother, but her aunt."

She finally looked over at her First Lady, whose expression except for a low whistle, was unchanged.

"I needed some counseling in regards to the door I just closed with my cousin and how best to tell my daughter why I waited so long to tell her I was her mother."

"Why did you?"

"I was running. At first, my sister and I discussed her taking care of Gladys until I was on my feet financially, physically, and emotionally. Once I got to a place where I had healed from a great deal of the pain my cousin had caused me and that I had inflicted upon myself, I was touring. I thought that my sister would just keep Gladys then because her environment was more stable."

"But she isn't her mom. You are," Menagerie broke in fiercely, surprising Paige with her degree of passion.

"Yes, I know," said Paige raising her hands in a gesture of surrender. "I know she is not her daughter, but before you pass judgment on my character or my actions, I need to you to know that you can't do any worse to me than I have done to myself."

Menagerie leaned back away from Paige, giving her the space and time she needed to explain. "The last time I saw my cousin, Stone, I was 14. I was over my aunt's house tending to her garden. I loved gardening. It made me feel like I was creating something.

I was outside when I heard the front door open. My aunt wasn't due back for at least an hour, but due to her new diagnosis of type II diabetes, I thought she may have forgotten her insulin. I walked in from the back and there was Stone who had just gotten home from boot camp. I told him his mom was due home any moment, and that I had just finished in the garden and would be leaving. I turned to walk out and he caught my arm." Paige hesitated for a moment, breathing through the moment of terror she felt when she saw the look in his eyes after he grabbed her. She squeezed her eyes shut trying to block out the image, even as she talked about it.

"I pulled away and ran down the hall. I'd just made it to the back screen door when my legs were pulled out from under me. All I could think was if I could just get to the other side of the door, I would be safe. I would be free. I don't think I turned around once. I kept my eyes on the screen door stretching, yelling, and pushing to get to the other side. I heard him say. 'Why are you struggling so hard? You always came willingly before. Don't I deserve a homecoming gift? You should be nicer to me. I can do things for you no one can. It has always been that way. The other times were just foreplay. This time, you are going to get what you have been asking for."

"I felt him go for my pants and I struggled and kicked at him, but I was still on my stomach trying to get past the threshold. I begged him not to do it. I pleaded. I tried to remind him that we were cousins. We were related and family didn't do this to family. That is when he hit me on my side, just under my ribcage. It knocked the wind out of me and I couldn't say anything else, but I continued to struggle."

Paige stopped, revelation dawning. "I don't think I was the first one. He seemed to know exactly what to do to shut me up. I didn't think about that until right now." She looked back down at her hands. They were shaking, but she wasn't surprised by the reaction. It was one she had felt many times while in therapy. The story hadn't gotten easier to tell, just less painful and the hatred wasn't there anymore.

She began again, noting the wetness on her hands.

"I fought harder. If I'd known my struggles made the pain worse I would have stopped, but my goal was getting outside, and I almost made it. I was halfway over the threshold when he took me. The pain was so searing it took whatever breath I had left in me, away. I braced myself for the push that would send me over, but he read my mind and dragged me back inside. I remember seeing the screen door slamming back on its hinge, and I knew then that there was no hope of me escaping. I gave up and I laid there, watching the door, wondering how many more times he was going to slam into me and if I broke in the process, what he would tell my aunt when she got home."

Paige saw a tissue come into view and looked up at her First Lady, whose face was now covered in tears. This was the first time she had told someone about the incident that cried when she did. She was moved by the love she saw in the woman's eyes. She wanted to apologize but knew before she formed the words that it would be in vain. Instead, she silently thanked her for the tissue and continued.

"After he was done, he left. Not just the hallway; he left the house. I laid there for a while, afraid that if I moved I would splinter into a million pieces. Then finally, the panic of being found in that position rose to such a height that I slowly lifted myself off of the floor, trying to calm down enough to think clearly. I got to my hands and knees, looking around me for any evidence of what had just happened. There was blood on my panties, pants, and the hardwood floor. I actually sighed in relief that none had gotten on the rug, just a few inches away. I crawled over to the wall and worked my way to a standing position. Every part of my body was in pain. I listened intently, making sure he was truly out of the house, pulled my clothes back on my body the best I could then made my way to the kitchen to get some towels to clean up the mess.

When I was done I put away the tools I had used in the garden and walked home. I was so ashamed and I didn't think anyone would believe it wasn't my fault, so I tried to hide it until I found out I was pregnant two months later.

When my mom found out six months after that, she went ballistic and I finally broke down and told her what happened; she accused me of lying and took me to get an abortion. But instead of the abortion, I went into labor. There were complications; one was that I was pregnant with twins. The doctors knew about one of them; the other fetus, they found during the ultrasound they gave me – 12 hours before I delivered them.

The pain was horrendous, but because of all of the confusion, I was too far along for an epidural. By the time the first one crowned, I was delirious with pain and tiredness. When the second one came, I was so out of it, I can barely remember pushing. They told me later she was still-born.

I was so filled with hatred for Stone, my mom, and the child that did survive, I wouldn't even look at her.

I ended up on suicide watch for a few days after that, due to a conversation my mom had with the doctor, my lack of response or diversion to my daughter, and my threat to harm myself if I had to go home with her and the child. It was just too much.

My sister told me a few days later that the baby and I could come and stay with her for a little bit and we could decide where to go from there.

My relationship with my mom was pretty much over. We just went through the motions of civility, but each time I saw her, I hated her more.

My sister and I agreed that since she was better off and married that she would take care of Gladys until I was able to.

I moved to Los Angeles to live with my dad and his new wife, using the story that my mom and I had irreconcilable differences and I needed a new environment to get over my suicidal tendencies. They were understanding, caring, and went a long way to help me try to pick up any pieces of my life that were salvageable.

I sometimes wonder what would have happened if I'd had a closer relationship with my father then. I considered all of the things I could have avoided if I'd gone to live with him immediately after their divorce, but I am way past the 'what ifs'.

Now that I think about it, I am glad I never shared with him the true reason why I came to live with them. I could see him behind bars doing 20 years for murder in the first degree, or he may have succumbed to his heart attack sooner. It's good enough that we patched up our relationship when we did. We had a few years before he passed away. We were able to spend a lot of time together, getting to know one another. He became the man I could set as a standard against other men. I can't say it helped me with my own insecurities, but I did know what to look for when I stopped running from relationships with men.

When I finally got my head right, I began to take his advice and I threw myself into my school work, graduating with a high enough G.P.A. to get into Pember University. The rest you know."

She looked over at First Lady again but was surprised when the woman opened the door. She got out and walked around to Paige's side of the car, opened that door, pulled her out and hugged her right there in the middle of the sidewalk. She just hugged her. Even when Paige thought she was ready to let go, Menagerie continued to hug her. Then she spoke softly in her ear, and Paige crumbled into tears.

Paige had been through years of therapy with social workers, psychiatrists and Christian psychologists, but Menagerie spoke the words that broke her free from the last of the binds that seemed to have a steel hold on her.

"Baby, I am your mother and I believe you. I pray for that man's soul and thank God for His mercy because I would have moved heaven and hell to bring you back to a place you felt safe, even if that meant doing him bodily harm. I am sorry I couldn't protect you then, but I am here now and you can come to me with anything, and I will trust and believe you."

When the tears began to subside, Menagerie released her hold on Paige, pulled back to look at her and gave her a teary smile then hugged her again. It seemed like another half an hour went by before they were back in the car and even then, Menagerie sat there with Paige's hand in hers, silently giving strength.

The buzz of Paige's cell phone dragged her back to the present. The time on the phone read 10 minutes to 4 o'clock.

"Oh, wow...maybe we should have lunch some other time. It's getting late. Aren't you having dinner with Pastor and Elder Tatum?"

"If I know my husband," Menagerie tilted her head slightly forward, "and I do know my husband, they are going to be a little late for dinner. We have plenty of time. Now tell me about Gladys. How old is she? What is she like?"

Paige took a deep breath, feeling exhausted but strangely light. "Gladys is 12 years old, full of life, and since my sister is also God-fearing, my niece...I mean daughter is as well. Her smile is contagious, and she loves being outside. My sister says she will do garden work faster than she will do housework."

Paige spent the better half of an hour telling Menagerie about her daughter's beautiful personality and some of her antics with her sister.

When Menagerie asked if Gladys looked like her, Paige paused, trying to recollect her daughter's features.

"Actually, she is quite pretty. We share the same shaped eyes, wide and set apart, but their color she gets from Stone. Boy, those eyes really made it hard to look at her in the beginning. She is tall for her age and a little gangly, but she does like sports so I don't see that being a problem. She has an olive complexion, but her hair is what I find the most beautiful about her: thick, loose, black unruly curls. They have fought my sister many-a-morning, but I think they are adorable."

Menagerie nodded and smiled, "You are already sounding like a mother. When do you see her?"

Paige turned her lips into an expression of feigned horror. "Next Friday."

"Wow. Do you know what you are going to say?"

"I think so, but could we discuss it over lunch? All of a sudden I am ravenous."

Menagerie laughed. "Sure thing," she said as she put on her seatbelt, looked in her side view mirror and finally put the car in drive.

CHAPTER 16

Brandon closed and locked the door. He placed his keys on the small coffee table near the door and loosened his tie as he walked down the hall to his bedroom. He closed the blinds to the window leading to the small balcony, hung the coat up he'd been carrying and walked over to his favorite lounging chair to lay back and reflect on the day.

He watched as the shadows played across the ceiling and the walls, waxing and waning by way of the blinds slowly moving with the breeze coming through the sliding glass door. This was one of his favorite parts of the day; he didn't get to sit in his chair much, and he relished the moments when he got them.

Thank you God for this time to sit and just take in the beauty of this day You have given me. It was full of many surprises – pleasant and perplexing. You move with such mystery and I often wonder what direction You will take next, but I am always grateful for being a part of your master plan. Thank you again for Your love and mercy. For every lesson You have taught me, easy and challenging, each test you have led me through: the ones I was able to ace on the first try, and the ones that I was taken through a few times. Thank you for the chastisement and the hindsight that showed me without a doubt that You were there all along. Thank you for this test and the gift of knowledge and wisdom that have allowed me to look to You and desire peace on the journey you have me on. I look forward to seeing Your face and am awaiting that fateful day…

The sound of the cell phone took him out of his meditation. He looked over, frowning in the dark, watching the light blink on and off. He touched the sides of the phone, muting the sound, just a little perturbed with himself for not shutting it off when he walked in the door. He turned his head back and set himself to commune with God, but a pair of wide-set golden-brown eyes raced across his mind. As the face owning those eyes came into view, he groaned and shifted his position in the chair. He shook his head as if to clear his mind of the small-statured woman with the biting tongue. Why would she even enter his thoughts? She was pretty and her eyes were hypnotizing, he had to be fair. But it seemed just a way to disarm people so that they would be ripe prey for the poisonous sting of her tongue.

He'd met women like her with the snapping wit. He had even dated one his second year in college, mistaking her snapping tongue for intellect, but once he really came to know her, he found that what came out of her mouth was only the fruit of what was in her heart.

What he couldn't understand was how Pastor Lawrence would tolerate having someone like her on his staff. He didn't seem the type to take any flack from his ministers or elders, but Brandon was new and therefore had to give him the benefit of the doubt. He would keep his eye on her for Pastor Lawrence. He corrected himself – he would keep his discerning eye on her so as not to be deceived by her beauty.

He forced his thoughts from her face and trained his mind on reflecting on the rest of the day's events. An unbidden smile came to his lips as he thought of how he came to stand in front of at least forty men in a bar in the middle of the afternoon, talking about the dangers of pornography and what was considered adultery in the eyes of the Lord.

He started with defining adultery from the judicial law which stated that adultery was a form of extramarital sex. It was having sex with someone other than one's spouse. This left a great deal of gray area for those single and married who played with their perception of the pros and cons of porn. He then gave the definition of adultery from Jesus' words: "You have heard that it was said to those of old, 'You shall not commit adultery.' But I say to you that whoever looks at a woman to lust after her has committed adultery already with her in his heart."

There came a small uproar from the men who groaned, mumbling in disbelief and whispered expletives that didn't even belong in a bar. He raised his hands to quiet them down, remembering the first time he had heard the scripture. He had an idea of what they were thinking. *What! I can't even look at a woman? What happened to look but don't touch? Where is the sin in that? It isn't as if I would go after her. She is eye candy; something to look at. What about the magazines like Cosmopolitan, Vogue, and Jet who have all of the beautiful women wrapped up in different fashions. Is it a sin to look at them?*

He told them just so, and they began to quiet down. One man threw out the question they were all thinking: "So what are we supposed to do? God gave us eyes and He knows that men are visual. Are we to ignore women and treat them like they aren't there?"

Brandon remembered struggling with that same feeling and questioned where the person was that should of have walked him through this and taught him the difference.

"What Jesus is saying is that to look upon a woman with adulterous thoughts is as if you were committing adultery. There is no problem looking at women, but when you begin to undress them with your eyes, fantasizing about seeing them in anything other than what they are wearing, or placing them in positions that evoke excitement and situations with you that you would have no business being in if you weren't married, then you are sinning.

When you look at a woman, whether she is walking towards you or in a magazine, you have to guard your thoughts, because those thoughts, if not set aside, will grow. When you continuously indulge in them, they will eventually evolve into acts – acts of masturbation or fornication, neither of which are pure acts of love. They are merely indulgences to satisfy the flesh and are a perversion of what God planned for us.

God created the sexual act as part of a healthy relationship between a husband and his wife. It is for recreation, to form a deeper intimacy with one another and for reproduction. Outside of these, the gift of sex is being abused.

Guard your heart and feed it with things that fortify your soul. How do you feed it? You meditate upon God, you read His Word, you listen to music that exalts Him and praises Him and His creations. Which leads me to Luke 11:33-36, 'No man, when he hath lighted a candle, putteth it in a secret place, neither under a bushel, but on a candlestick, that they which come in may see the light. The light of the body is the eye: therefore when thine eye is single, thy whole body also is full of light; but when thine eye is evil, thy body also is full of darkness. Take heed therefore that the light which is in thee be not darkness. If thy whole body, therefore, be full of light, having no part dark, the whole shall be full of light, as when the bright shining of a candle doth give thee light.'

This scripture speaks of what some of us call the 'eye gates'. Through these gates our soul is influenced. If what you watch and see through these gates is full of perversion, then you will be filled with it, meaning that this is what you will think on often and indulge in when your mind is idle. You will look for answers through those things you spend most of your time doing and the only true place to find answers is in God.

A danger of porn is that it breeds unrealistic expectations; it is not real. Your wife is not going to be home waiting for you every day in bed with a slinky negligee on. When would you eat? What would you eat?"

The last questions were met with a roar of laughter and nodding heads from the men. He raised his hands again to silence the men.

"I am kidding," he said chuckling, "but seriously, there is more to a marriage than just sex, and if you don't work on developing a friendship and a deeper relationship than that before you are married, then you are in for a rude awakening. And if you are already married, you have no business delving into that world. The marriage bed between a man and wife is undefiled unless you bring someone else into it, and even though those people are only on the TV they are in there with you too. Pornography is a weapon the enemy uses to blur the lines of God's pure gift. Don't think that you can go back and forth with it and remain unaffected in your soul and spirit. It is addictive, and once you open the door to it, you need to pray that the enemy does not get a foothold.

Sex is to enjoy one another, not the people on the television. If you have let it go so far that you can't get excited without stimulants from another source, then it is past the time for you to seek counseling because it only gets more immoral from there. You have opened yourself up for many different thoughts and spiritual influences, and you might also find that you are thinking or doing things that you would not have given a second thought to before.

The indulgent thoughts of sin only beget sin and the wages of sin, what you get paid for sinning, is death."

He looked around at the thoughtful faces, wondering if he was too "textbook." Maybe he needed to give then an illustration. One man raised his hand, taking his attention away from his thoughts. "Sure," he said, pointing at a man in the middle of the crowd. "What's your name?"

"Michael." The man cleared his throat, "I have a question."

"Go ahead, Michael."

"So you said porn, adultery, and fornication are perversions of God's gift of sex and I can understand that, but why is masturbation considered wrong? It is only something you do by yourself. What's the harm? I was even told that doing so would help prevent prostate cancer?"

"Let me try to be as clear about this as possible so that the answer is clear. From the beginning, it has been God's purpose and desire to redeem man unto a place of unity with Him. On the other side, it has been placed in man to desire and hunger after God to fill that void that only He can fill in their soul and have a relationship with Him. This is achieved by submitting oneself to the Lord, applying His word to their life, meditating, fasting and praying, and bringing the flesh under submission.

There are no direct scriptures against masturbation, but instead with no gray area, how it is used. Like the Bible stated before in Matthew 5:28,

'But I tell you that anyone who looks at a woman lustfully has already committed adultery with her in his heart.'

If what accompanies, or initiates the masturbation are illicit fantasies about people, then they are impure thoughts and you are sinning. The body is your temple. You are to honor that temple and to edify yourself with thoughts that will continue to keep your spirit man in a position to communicate with the Holy Spirit clearly. There is no scripture though that states that it is a sin when masturbation is done as a rote act in keeping the body in submission.

I can't say that I myself condone this. As with drinking wine, there are countries that drink wine as we in America drink juice with our dinner. The wine-drinking is not the sin, but drinking in excess and the reason for drinking beyond to quench the thirst, it can be considered a sin.

Masturbation, though there is no scripture stating that it is a sin, can become a slippery slope that you don't wish to slide down. Keep in mind the motivation and intent, and I will leave you with 1Thessalonians 4:2-8 that states, 'For you know what instructions we gave you by the authority of the Lord Jesus. It is God's will that you should be sanctified: that you should avoid sexual immorality; that each of you should learn to control his own body in a way that is holy and honorable, not in passionate lust like the heathen, who do not know God... For God did not call us to be impure but to live a holy life. Therefore, he who rejects this instruction does not reject man but God, who gives you his Holy Spirit.'

Any questions?" He saw the men nodding their head in understanding.

Then Pastor Lawrence spoke up. "What about the scripture in the Bible that talks about God punishing a man for spilling his seed on the ground?"

Brandon could feel the eyes that were on Pastor during his question, all come back to him with great interest. He looked at Pastor Lawrence, not completely sure if he was feigning ignorance and wanting to set the old myth straight, or if he needed help. Either way, he was there to give the truth. "Thank you for asking, but Genesis 38:8-10 which refers to Onan and Tamar, who was Onan's deceased brother's wife, had nothing to do with masturbation. Onan would bed his brother's widow, which was the law, especially if the husband died before there were any children, to keep the family line going. Onan would not spill his seed inside of Tamar when he bed her because he knew that the offspring would not be considered his. He was struck down due to rebellion, not because of the act itself of spilling his seed on the ground."

He looked back at Pastor Lawrence when he was done explaining, and received a nod.

On the ride back to his car, Pastor Lawrence was quiet until they were a few blocks from the church.

"You did a good job of explaining the dangers of porn. You backed it with the Bible very well. You know your Word."

Brandon knew the words were to encourage him, but he detected an underlying question. He took his eyes off the road for a second to make sure he heard correctly.

"But?" he asked when he saw the look on Pastor Lawrence's face.

"No 'but', just another question."

"Okay," Brandon said, dragging out the 'a'.

"When there is no one around, what is your relationship like with God? What is it that He does for you specifically that causes you to continue to serve and love Him, besides the obvious gratefulness for His gift of salvation and love? How does His love affect you? You were so matter-of-fact in your teaching that I was wondering if there was any room in your sermons or ministering for redemption."

Brandon was a little taken aback by the questions. He worked his jaw back and forth, going over the questions, trying not to take offense but knew even before he opened his mouth that he was.

"I am not sure what you are asking?" He asked, stalling to keep his emotions out of his answer.

"Yes, you are. Let me go back to the first question. What is it that you are most grateful for God doing in your life? How do you show your love and gratitude for Him?"

Brandon thought on the question as he maneuvered around a truck to make a right turn.

He waited until he was clear before he began.

"When I was young I considered God to be my dad's God. I knew that I was covered because of my dad's and mother's prayer life.

When I was 12, I was in a youth service led by a traveling elder, when I heard a particular sermon that resounded so deeply within me that it left a mark – one particular statement really. He said God didn't have grandchildren, son-in-laws nor daughter-in-laws. He has children, and He loves them individually, uniquely, and fully. It seemed in that moment I was given the permission I needed to pursue a personal relationship with God. It was amazing that He could see me and want to be so close as to think of me so often that He would sculpt me in such detail.

I don't think that I have shared this with too many people, but His way of dealing with me and talking to me is the reason why I love Him to the degree that I work not to grieve Him. I need to know that I am doing everything in the best of my ability to show Him how grateful I am for the individual attention He gives me."

Pastor Lawrence asked quietly, "Do you feel the need to work for the individual attention He gives you?"

Brandon shook his head. "No. It is quite opposite. I do it because He does. I know that He doesn't have to do it, but I don't have the comfort of being lax in my appreciation for Him. I have to be ready to do anything He wants me to do at any time. Time on earth is so short. He says in a 'twinkling of an eye…' "

"Brandon, I know what the scripture says and it isn't that I'm not interested in going over it with you, but I am more interested in what you say. I want to know what you say to those who have turned away and are trying to find their way back. What do you say to those who have been holding on 'just long enough' to their faith to get one, pure word from Him, and it is up to you to deliver it? I want to know what you say to those who have been closer to God than even we have known, but due to life and a moment of distraction that became many, have found themselves further from Him than when they were first saved? What do you say to those who hope upon the Lord to continue to deliver them from different wrongs in life? Those who, instead of becoming a 'victim' choose to trust in God and let Him be their strength. What do you say to people that would not relate to your story of keeping yourself?"

Brandon pulled into the parking space they had come from in the garage. He shut off the engine and handed Pastor Lawrence the keys.

"I would say, God's love is unconditional and His mercy and grace are used to cover a multitude of sins, but it isn't an excuse not to live holy. It is a cover we are given when we miss the mark, no matter what that mark is. My answers may seem textbook to some or short of compassion, but I will not teach complacency or lackadaisicalness. I won't give people tomorrow to do something they can get done today. They may not have tomorrow."

Brandon was beginning to lose patience. He was not used to defending his relationship with God. He was never questioned in the path he was on with God before. What was the man getting at?

"I am not recommending that you begin teaching anything less than God's love and holiness, but when you teach it there has to be a hint of God's love on you. God is love, and that is what draws people that your word will minister to. His word and His love are life-changing. The Holy Spirit aids and guides man into all truths which keeps him pressing past himself and into a place of full submission to the Lord. God may relate to you in a no-nonsense manner which works for you, but He will deal with me differently because I have a different experience with Him, and He will get the exact results He is looking for from me. It is like a different language that He speaks to me than He speaks to you, but the universal translator is His love. Everyone recognizes His love and the life you live in holiness is the speaker in which you deliver that language."

Pastor Lawrence looked at Brandon silently waiting for him to gain his composure and return the look.

Once Brandon turned towards him, Pastor began again. "It may help that when we have discussions that you remain open until I have clearly delivered my point. I am not so high-minded that I think I can tell you the right and wrongs in your personal relationship with God, but I do know a little bit about the people in my congregation and my community, and if I am going to let you talk to them I need to be able to trust that you will serve them in a way they can receive. They are precious and valuable to me, just as you are as my good friend's son. I will not sacrifice either one of you.

I have watched and kept up with you through communication with your mother. I asked you the initial questions to see how well you know yourself, not that I know you better, but I wanted to see how honest you are with yourself and how your relationship with God had developed; not to judge you but as an inquiry. Do we understand one another again?"

Brandon, pretty much rendered speechless, could only nod his agreement.

"Good. Come on, it is getting late and I don't want to keep First Lady waiting. I will have you follow me to the house so that you will have your car when the night is over."

The sound of the cell phone pulled Brandon back into the present. He checked the phone to get the time and see who was calling. He answered. "Hello?"

"Are you alright? Did you make it home?"

"Yes. Sorry I didn't call. I got wrapped in… I got distracted. I made it home without incident. All is well. Thank you again for a wonderful dinner and conversation. Please give your wife my thanks for an enjoyable evening and meal."

"I will do so. Brandon?"

"Yes, Pastor?"

"Welcome to Skylight Temple's clergy staff."

"Really? You are sure?"

"Absolutely. I believe you will be a great addition to the ministerial staff. You will keep them on their toes. I will have Pam draw up the paperwork tomorrow. Give her a call to see when you can come and sign it."

"I will do just that. Thank you very much for trusting in me enough to allow me to serve on staff."

"I just want to see if you feel the same way in six months. Have a blessed and restful evening, Brandon. Goodnight."

Even before Brandon could respond, the phone disconnected.

CHAPTER 17

That insufferable, insolent, obnoxious, bullheaded miscreant. Victoria saw red as she walked from the hospital room. She couldn't believe that he could be so stubborn. It wasn't as if she wanted to have an argument right there in front of her granddaughter, but he wouldn't even hold a conversation with her.

She was so deep in thought, she walked smack into Vivian's doctor.

"Mrs. Branchett, it is nice to see you. How are you doing today?"

Victoria pasted a smile on her face and lied. "I am doing very well. I just visited my granddaughter. She doesn't look very good today. Her color is off and she has been sleeping a lot. What is going on doctor?"

The doctor looked perplexed for a second then his face went expressionless.

"We have had a slight complication but Mr. Jenson is going to have to tell you what is really going on. If you ask him I am sure he will let you know."

With a slightly noticeable struggle for control, Victoria replied between her teeth.

"He hasn't shared anything with me. He won't speak to me. Ever since my daughter died, we have not exactly been on speaking terms. Will you please just tell me what is going on, or am I going to have to bring someone in here that will?"

"You can bring anyone you like in here, but it still won't change the fact that you are not immediate family and right now we have not gotten legal permission to share any news with you. Now whatever squabble you and Mr. Jenson have, don't you think it is best that you squash it for Vivian's sake? She needs all of the support she can get right now – from ALL of her family."

"If I was looking for a lecture from you, doctor, it would hardly be on family. Are you surprised?" she added stepping closer to him, taking note of the flared nostrils. "I have done a background check on all of my granddaughter's doctors and nurses. There is no one that has even looked at her that I have not gotten the skinny on, so don't you wield your self-righteous stick at me. I know you were under investigation last year for sleeping with members of your staff. Your wife even filed for a separation.

How many were there? A charge like that doesn't just show up out of the blue.

You see, I am not one to be reckoned with or tossed aside and told to go get in line. I set my own standards and you are sorely lacking."

She stepped back and brought her voice up an octave, but not loud enough for anyone else to hear.

"Keep your BS in your mouth and that staff in your pants around me and my family, Doc, or I will have you counting pennies for tips in that diner across the street." She turned before he could respond to her threat, but she threw a statement over her shoulder a few steps away.

"No worries, Doc. I will ask one of the night nurses about my granddaughter. I am sure you have your hands full taking care of so many."

She continued her walk down the hall thinking to herself, *That incompetent fool. It's good for him that he is book smart.*

She had just reached the elevators when Mason caught up to her. The doors opened and he motioned that he would follow her in with his wheelchair.

"I hope you understand my refusal to speak to you in front of Vivian. I wasn't trying to be rude but Vivian is very perceptive, and I don't want to give her any more cause for concern regarding our relationship or lack thereof. Were you actually going to the cafeteria like you told us or are you going home? It will let me know what button to press."

Victoria huffed. "I am just going to the cafeteria as I said. I am not in the habit of lying to my granddaughter."

Mason pressed the button that would take them to the 4th floor.

"As I was saying, whatever you want to discuss with me in regards to Vivian I am open to listening to, but if it deals with your feelings towards me or if you can't veil your disdain for me while we converse in front of her, then I will have to limit our conversation to greetings and the weather."

Victoria turned towards him, her mouth tightening into a thin line. "There is nothing we need to discuss outside of Vivian. Let me make it even plainer. Outside of Vivian, you don't exist to me. Now, so as to keep you from jumping to any more conclusions, I will let you know that I only want what is best for my granddaughter and I believe it is back on the farm with me. I can provide her with all the luxuries money can afford."

She saw Mason's eyes flash and braced herself for a physical assault, but it never came. The elevator door opened and Mason wheeled out, turned around, and held the doors back so that she could exit.

His voice was almost as low as a whisper as he rolled beside her to the cafeteria, which kept her from being able to gauge his anger. "I appreciate your help, Victoria, and I am glad that you decided to recognize Vivian as your granddaughter again; she needs to know she has other family. However, I believe we will be just fine with the arrangement we have now. She will continue to go to school here, as I and my wife wished, and she will visit you for extended holidays and summer vacations."

Victoria stopped in her tracks and turned to him in the middle of the hallway. "You talk about family, but you didn't even give the release to allow me to consult with the doctors or nurses about her condition. You won't talk to me; how am I supposed to help you or her in this situation?" She gave a snort that sounded like a cut-off laugh. "You don't have what it takes to go one round with me, so don't even try to play me. I want to know what is going on with my granddaughter and if I can't get it with cooperation, I will force the issue of your ability to raise my granddaughter."

"What is your problem, woman?"

Mason was holding onto his last ounce of will power. It was taking extraordinary strength to keep from getting out of the chair, placing his hands around her neck and squeezing until that venomous tongue of hers turned blue.

"You must be delusional. Why would I purposefully keep you from getting information about my daughter when I need your help in saving her? Has your hatred for me blinded you so completely that you would think I would jeopardize my daughter's life just to spite you? You think too highly of yourself. Now, the reason the records weren't open for you to receive information from the doctor is because it was an accident that brought us in here; they are cautious about press talking to her as a minor. Since I was not aware of you coming, I did not have time to adjust the paperwork, being that I am still admitted to this hospital myself for care."

He moved back from her and resumed rolling down the hall towards the cafeteria. Assuming she would follow him, he added, "What would be appreciated is if you could take a blood test to see if you were in any way compatible to help Vivian. Right now, it is a precaution the doctor is taking to find a matching living donor if it becomes necessary."

Despite himself, he looked over at her in expectancy.

"I can't do anything right now. I am sorry. I still have 6 months before the vaccines I took when Richard and I went to South Africa cycle out of my body."

She watched as Mason shrugged off the answer. It looked like he accepted her answer. She was glad she was quick on her toes. She absolutely detested needles. If she needed to she would find someone else to help out her granddaughter. She could find someone on one of those living donor sites. Yes, that is exactly what she would do. Wasn't she on the board of one of those organ donor organizations? She would have to ask her assistant when she got back to the apartment.

Mason suddenly stopped short. "You know, I am not really hungry and the nurse is probably going to start looking for me soon. I am going to go back up. Enjoy your lunch. Vivian took such a long nap, she should still be up when you are done." With that, he turned around and rolled back down the length of the hall, back to the elevator.

Victoria could only conclude that he had said what he wanted and was done with the conversation.

She made her way back to the apartment after sitting with Vivian for a while. She was so proud of how Vivian was fairing. She was capable of intelligent conversations, even though they were often sprinkled with scripture. She was indeed her mother's daughter.

She let herself in, placing her sun hat and purse on the kitchen counter. She walked to the bedroom and picked up her cell phone off of the nightstand.

She pressed the two buttons that would connect her with her attorney.

"Hello Mr. Danio, this is Victoria Branchett. I have a big job for you then I have a bigger job for you."

"Okay," came the voice from the other side of the line.

"I want you to get one of your private investigators to run a search for me for a living kidney donor. I will send you the files for the requirements needed for a perfect match or as close as you can come. I give you permission to offer the person up to $50,000. You are not to bribe them to donate. If they are on the list, then they have already given it considerable thought. The money is only to tip the scales and make it easier for them to take some time off work or take care of family while they are going through the different procedures.

Make sure he is thorough; I need to make sure they will pass all of the tests. While he is at it, let him check into Vivian's biological family and see if any of them have signed up."

"I didn't know Vivian's mother survived the labor?" Mr. Danio interrupted.

"I am asking for family information. Anyone who is still living in the family may be eligible to donate. You may also see if the father is alive. Clear?"

"All clear."

"Next I am going to need you to begin proceedings for a family restructure. I am going to sue Mason for custody of Vivian."

The quietness on the other side of the line actually tickled her. It wasn't easy rendering him speechless.

"Did you hear me? I am going to…"

"I heard you, and I have to say that I think you are making an incredibly big mistake. But I will do what you want; that is what you pay me for. Is this to scare him, or are you really trying to go after full custody of Vivian without any proof that Mason is an unfit father or has neglected her in any way, shape, or form?"

"Are you afraid you are outside of your pay grade? I want full custody of Vivian, and I want you to make it happen. Capiche?"

"Capiche. I will talk to you later on in the week and give you an update on the P.I.'s progress. My other line is ringing."

Victoria closed the phone, disconnecting the call. Mark was her favorite lawyer. He was willing to do anything short of killing someone for her. Well…she had never actually asked him to kill anyone for her yet.

CHAPTER 18

"Well, Mr. Jenson, it looks like you have been healing well. I think if you continue at this pace, you will be looking at the inside of your home in two weeks or less," said his doctor, turning away from the computer in the corner of the hospital room.

"Your tests have come back much improved and since you will begin physical therapy tomorrow, I would say it could be as soon as next Wednesday or as late as a week from Wednesday."

Instead of getting up, he scooted the chair along the floor until he was in comfortable, conversation range with Mason.

"I know you may be hesitant to leave your daughter, but I will not be able to put off the inevitable. She will have the best care this facility can give her and I will personally look after her safety."

Mason was appreciative of the doctor's sensitivity but was puzzled by the generosity. "Why are you being so attentive towards me and my daughter? It is not to say that I don't expect the best of care or truly appreciate you giving my daughter special attention, but why?"

"I ran into your mother-in-law yesterday. In my years serving as a doctor, I have not run into too many with her air of entitlement and none with her obvious pernicious intent. I don't know what you did to her or her daughter and it really isn't my business, but she has it in for you. All I can do is try to keep her from taking it out on your daughter while she is here."

Mason looked away, trying to get his emotions under control until he could shield his expressions from the doctor. "I thank you for everything you can do for my daughter. If you have a moment I would like to give you a little history behind Vivian's mother and myself. It by no means excuses Victoria's, my mother-in-law's, behavior, but it may give you some insight and ability to see things coming from her in the future that you may think would be beyond reproach, even for her."

The doctor looked at his watch, exchanged his stool for a more comfortable chair and relaxed against its back, crossing his long legs in front of him. He gestured for Mason to begin, smiling briefly to let him know he was sincere.

It took a moment as Mason tried to figure out where to begin, and just how much he was going to be able to share about his late wife.

He would go at it from the beginning and let the doctor tell him when to stop.

"I met Rachael, Vivian's mother, in college. It almost didn't happen, and that is how I knew it was meant to be. I was awarded a full ride to Rysden University near Witchita Falls. I majored in Architecture and Literary History. I was running late for a study group, so I decided to cut through this grassy field. I never took that route because I was afraid of soiling my shoes, and I could only afford one pair a semester." That would be as far as he revealed about his life with his mom.

"Rachael was resting against this huge oak tree, and I would have completely missed her had it not been for a ray of sun catching some of the highlights in her hair, and nearly blinding me with them. I stopped because I couldn't see where I was going anymore and looked over. She was more than beautiful; she was radiant and seemed to draw me to her, and she hadn't even looked up."

Mason paused. He hadn't talked about Rachael like this to anyone since she died. He realized it was comforting, kind of like telling an old bedtime story to Vivian.

"I walked over, all the while reveling in the way her red hair contended with the sunset. I placed my books down and asked if I could use the same tree to study. She looked a little weary at first and why shouldn't she be. There were dozens of places all around that would have been perfect for studying, reading or relaxing. She shrugged her shoulders and went back to reading. I couldn't take my eyes off of her, which she soon felt. I didn't want to scare her off so I opened one of my books and pretended to read until I couldn't stand it anymore. I introduced myself and apologized for intruding. She slowly closed her book, placed it in her bag, gave me a polite smile, you know like those you give people as you pass them on the street?" The doctor nodded.

"That was why it surprised me when she got up, introduced herself by giving me her first name then walked away."

"You didn't follow her?" The doctor asked, curious.

Mason looked at him, a smile playing at the sides of his mouth. "I made a move to get up and follow her, but she turned around and shook her head, giving me one of those looks your mom gives you when you are in a place she can't speak to you, but wants to relay that you are doing something wrong. I was so dumbfounded, I sat back down and watched her walk away." Mason chuckled to himself.

"She was so unassuming, but she was straightforward with everyone and in everything she did. She didn't lie. She never felt she had to. You never had to wonder with her.

Eventually, I tracked her down. I couldn't believe how many Rachaels there were at that school. It was like all the mothers of that generation got together and decided to name all their girls Rachael."

Mason shrugged, knowing even as he spoke he was giving away a great deal of himself, but it was therapeutic.

"Anyway, once I found out what her major was, I worked hard to be in the places I thought she would be. I spent so much time in the history building that my G.P.A. dropped two points that semester. I wish I could say my plan was clever enough to allow me to get close to her, but she saw me coming from a mile away.

I waited for her after class one day thinking that I had finally gotten up the nerve to ask her out. I walked alongside her and for the umpteenth time, I greeted her. She greeted me back, and I took that as an opening. I asked her if she would have lunch with me sometime and she stopped and took a long, hard look at me. She said she would because she was afraid that if she said 'no' I might flunk out of school. I didn't know how she guessed, but I was not going to look a gift horse in the mouth. I know she thought I could have been some crazy stalker but to tell you the truth, I was more afraid of her and the way she made me feel than she could have ever been of me. If I could have, I would have turned tail and run."

A picture of Rachael sitting across from him at lunch on that day came into clear view, and he had to swallow the lump forming in his throat before he could go on. He rested his head back on the pillow allowing the tension in his neck to ease a few seconds.

"You know the whole time I knew her, we only disagreed on two things. One was her decision to end all communication with her mother in hopes that a serene environment would extend her life, even though the leukemia was voraciously eating her alive. I thought she should spend as much time with her whole family as possible, but we only argued about it once because she threatened to leave and take Vivian with her and I would not sacrifice whatever time I could have with her.

Victoria, on the other hand, believes it was my idea to keep Rachael away from her and her insistence in introducing Rachael to new medical studies that 'could possibly be cures'. When I asked Rachael why she didn't even want to consider any of them, she said that she was not going to spend her last days with us as a guinea pig.

She was extremely protective of Vivian, and wanted to give her as much of a 'normal' childhood as possible. Those last six months were heaven and hell. One thing I am thankful of is that she didn't have a great deal of pain. She just didn't have as much energy and she became winded more easily. It could have been so much worse, but instead she left us with good memories. Well, at least Vivian, Richard, my father-in-law, and myself."

"Mmm, that explains quite a bit of the resentment I saw coming from Victoria when she thought you had signed paperwork keeping her from receiving information on Vivian. She is not well, and she means trouble for you," said the doctor, unfolding his legs.

Mason could only nod. He had tried so hard to like that woman, and now he just felt sorry for her. He wasn't dumb though. He had gotten a peek of her ruthless side when Rachael passed, and she fought for every piece of control of the funeral arrangements even though Rachael had stated it clearly in her will what she wanted. He had been in no state to argue with her.

"You mentioned there were two instances where you and your wife did not see eye to eye. What was the other, if you don't mind me asking?"

"God. God was where we were split. She believed He is as real as you and me, and that He loves us and has only the best plans for us. I, on the other hand, don't."

"And your daughter? What does she believe?"

"She has insisted on siding with her mother on the subject, and on this she will not be moved. I just don't understand. She has had it rough, and it is only going to get harder, yet still she loves and adores Him and credits Him for every good thing in her life, including me. It is frustrating, to say the least."

"Why are you convinced He doesn't care?"

"Because the beauty and peace I have found in life have very little to do with Him."

The doctor was quiet for a moment, and Mason could see that he was pondering something.

"What is it, Doc? I can see you want to say something."

The doctor hesitated a little while longer then placed his fingers under his lips as he looked at Mason.

"If your wife devoted her life to God and your daughter has followed in her path, and you know both of them to be grounded, why are you so averse to believing in Him?"

"You have me wrong. I believe there is a God. I just don't believe He is to be trusted nor that He cares enough about me to try to prove my opinion wrong."

The doctor stared at him so intently that he began to feel uncomfortable.

"What? What are you thinking?"

"I believe I am in danger of crossing a line here, but I am hoping for a little grace." He took a deep breath.

"All I have to say is I hope for your sake and the sake of your daughter that you give God a chance to prove you wrong. I think you are going to need Him to get through situations that you have no control over."

"Such as?" Mason asked, beginning to grow irritated. He had heard conversations begin this way before. He almost knew word-for-word what this doctor was going to suggest as far as his salvation was concerned.

"Such as healing your daughter."

The wind went out of Mason's sails. That was not what he expected, nor what he wanted to hear.

"So, it's that bad?"

"It is slightly worse than yesterday, but it could be better tomorrow. I am just saying, you need support and it is very obvious that you are not going to get it from your mother-in-law. You need help. As a doctor, it is not part of my traditional practice to endorse a religion. I stand behind the science and practice of medicine that I have studied, and continue to study. But as a person that has come to know you as a friend, I suggest that you get in the corner of someone I know to have the answers when I have none. Whether you think He is for you or not, trust that the God your daughter and late wife loves will be there for her."

After expelling a deep breath, Mason couldn't seem to get all the air back in his lungs. He was deflated. How could he even think about trusting the same God that his father, a lying, cheating, bigamist, professed was the way to all right roads, and true peace and happiness? He had made his own peace and happiness and now that it too was being threatened, he couldn't conceive of trusting the same being to step in when He didn't so long ago.

The doctor stood up and patted Mason on the shoulder.

"I am going to attend to my rounds and I will come back by before my shift is over. You get some rest and I will let you know if there is any change with Vivian."

Mason lay back against the pillows, now deep in thought. His daughter was lying in a hospital bed two floors down with failing kidneys, and he was about to be discharged. His mother-in-law was out plotting some fiendish plan – he was sure of it – and his doctor just told him that the last being he believed would care could possibly be the only one that could save her.

Once again he was 15 years-old, listening to his mother cry in the night, cursing God.

He wondered as he looked out the window what could happen next.

CHAPTER 19

Paige walked into what she counted as store number seven of the day, her hands still half-filled with small packages. She couldn't believe that it took three days for her to realize that she would have to go shopping for bedroom accessories, such as sheets and blankets, small knick-knacks for the dresser, and hangers for the closet in the second bedroom. If all went well in Atlanta, Gladys may be coming home with her.

She got yet another cart and proceeded to go through the aisles looking for decorating books and magazines that would give her ideas for a different type of decor. She was flipping through a book on bathrooms, enthralled with the colors, when her phone rang. She fished through her purse, vowing for the umpteenth time to clean out all of the receipts and spare pieces of makeup. Finally successful in her search, she pressed the answer button quickly so as not to miss the call she assumed was from Carmen.

"Ms. Paige Morganson?" came a male voice.

"Yes." She was tempted to hang up like she usually did when solicitors called, but as usual, she didn't want to be rude.

"Ms. Morganson, I am calling on behalf of the Donating Life organization."

"Oh, yes. I have already signed up as a donor with another organization and I am not interested in signing up again." One particular magazine on living rooms caught her eye and attention. She reached down and picked it up.

"Yes, Ms. Morganson, we network together. I would like to know if you are still interested in being a kidney donor."

Paige paused, forgetting the opened magazine in her hand. "I am confused. Do you have a different protocol than the other organization? They said they would contact me by mail first and if I responded, I would then receive a call."

"Yes we do work differently, but I can assure you that your privacy is as important to us as it is to you. We know that if you are still interested, it would be a great asset. We are not allowed to share how well of a match you are to our client because we don't wish to pressure you, but we are calling you because you are a match."

Paige's head reeled. Distracted, she placed the magazine in the cart, picked up her purse and previously purchased items, and walked out of the store. She listened intently during her walk back to her car. Once inside she interrupted the caller.

"I'm sorry. I am going to need to test the validity of this call. Could you give me a number where I can get back to you?

"Sure. We can be reached between the hours of 9 am to 6 pm CST.," he said just before he recited the number.

"Thank you. I will call you back."

Paige sat there for a moment. Wow, what bad timing. She couldn't afford to be laid up for two to four weeks. She had a daughter to reunite with, a book to finish, and a tour…but then she guessed the person who was in need of the kidney was also having a field day.

Paige drove home in a daze. She wished she had programmed the donor organization's information in her phone, but then it was more than six years ago since she filled out the paperwork. She was anxious to see if the call was legitimate. A few years ago, she wouldn't have given it a second thought but Carmen taught her, signing by signing and tour by tour, that she needed to be careful of people looking for information on her. All the way down to digging up information about her and Gladys. She told Carmen that she was willing to put everything out in the open in the beginning so that no one could accuse her of hiding anything. Carmen suggested that they not offer information, but not deny it if it came out. She reluctantly agreed.

Once in the house, Paige put the packages in the spare bedroom, giving them a cursory glance as she walked back out and to her office. She opened her strong box which held insurance information and other personal, important documents. She found the contract in regards to being placed on the donor's list and looked through the paperwork for a number. She picked up the phone, dialed the number and waited for a receptionist to answer. On the second ring she was sent through a thorough voice prompted directory, and it took almost three minutes to reach a live person.

"Hello, I have a couple of questions about your procedures. I am a registered donor and instead of my name I would like to give you my number."

No sooner had she completed her 10-digit donor number than she was asked to hold, and then was transferred to another department.

"Ms. Morganson, this is Leslie Stans. Could I get you to confirm some information for me?"

"Sure." Now this was what she was familiar with and liked – security. She gave Leslie all of the information she asked for, and was finally rewarded with, "Thank you, Ms. Morganson. I appreciate you calling back so soon. I know the call you received earlier seemed to stray from our regular procedures, but at no time was your information in danger of getting out. In fact, the call came from this office and was patched through."

"Wow, so much trouble just to inform me that I am a match. What is going on?"

"I can only tell you that the client's family is insistent and slightly anxious, but we have done our background check and have found the need to be legitimate."

"Okay. If I say 'yes', what is the next move? Do I have to go in right away to see if I'm still eligible?"

"Not just yet. I would like to catch up with you and see if this is something that you can still do."

"Yeah, that might be a little harder. As it would be, my calendar just got very busy. So busy, I don't know if I would have enough time to go through the whole procedure now. I have a very important person I am going to visit in Atlanta, Georgia, and depending on how it goes after my tour, they may be coming to stay with me. Is the client looking for a donor right now, or would there still be an opportunity in four weeks?"

"Well, the sooner the better. Is there any point in these next few weeks that we could get any of the process taken care of?" asked Leslie.

"I guess it depends on how invasive the procedures are for checking my eligibility and complete match. Will I be able to meet the person I am donating to?"

"Some of those questions I can't answer just yet. From what I know about the patient, there is a little time but the people that represent the patient seem to have a lot of pull and money. If you are available over the next few days, we can get some of the preliminary work done. You can get some blood and tissue work done and meet some of the family, along with a case worker."

Paige thought about it. She could do it over the next few days and still be able to take the flight out to Atlanta at the end of next week.

"That may be possible. Is there a facility close to where I live now? The last one I went to was in Atlanta, Georgia, but I can't do that while I am in town there this time."

"Well, the family would actually like to meet with you before you begin to go through the preliminaries. Like I said before, they are a bit anxious."

"Where is the family?"

"Chicago."

"Chicago?"

"Chicago."

"How long would it take for me to meet with these people?"

"Three days tops. If they like you, then you would start getting some tests done."

"Could you give me a day to think about this? It is sudden, and I will need to see if I can work it into my schedule." Paige prided herself on her ability to keep focused at that moment. She was going to have to write everything down.

"Absolutely! I was only looking to see if there was a possibility or if you were still interested in donating at all. I will await your call. Could we say 3 pm tomorrow?"

*   *   *

Paige sat in service Sunday, trying hard to concentrate on the announcements, presentations of appreciation and dedications. In fact, she couldn't remember when a service was so full of special events. Usually service was filled with praise and worship and a more than satisfying Word. If there was time left in the two-hour block usually scheduled for morning service, the special events would come forward.

Paige let her mind wander as the announcements rolled on the screens in the front of the sanctuary. She looked around, taking a mental note of the unfamiliar faces so that she could introduce herself later. As a member of the clergy, all of the ministers and elders took it upon themselves to get to know visitors and members they didn't know, new and otherwise. As she scanned the room her eyes came upon Elder Tatum, who she had to admit looked very much like the new minister.

He looked a little uncomfortable standing at the edge of the pulpit. That was where all the new clergy had to sit or stand during their first four Sundays. This allowed them to recognize the congregation, get comfortable looking on from the pulpit, and it gave the congregation a chance to become familiar with them.

She remembered her four weeks; it was nerve-racking. Actually, she felt more like she was on display, which for all intents and purposes, she was. She felt a slight ping of pity for Elder Tatum, but if his quick wit this past week was any hint at his strength, he would get through it with flying colors.

She had to admit though, he was well put together. His three-piece beige suit was immaculate; the tie he'd chosen: an olive green with hints of gold. Paige admired men who could match their suits, shirts and ties perfectly. It was the only piece of clothing men wore that she envied. She scanned down to see if his shoes matched, already knowing that they would. A small smirk lifted the side of her mouth. Why was she looking for a flaw in this man? She looked up and caught him watching her. She was sure the surprise could be seen on her face. She knew if she looked away quickly it would look like she'd gotten caught doing something she wasn't supposed to be doing, so she lifted up the other side of her mouth in a smile of greeting, and received a reply in the form of a slight incline of his head.

She looked away, continuing her scan of the room, gazing at the screens every now and then. She looked down at her bible, turning the pages to a familiar scripture. Before she reached the chapter, she came across a picture of Gladys at 5 years-old. She gazed at it, praying once again that the Lord would word her mouth with what He wanted her to tell Gladys when she saw her on Friday.

Friday… it seemed so far away, and there was so much to do even before she could head that way.

After much prayer and a night of sleeplessness, she had called Leslie back and agreed to go forward with meeting the family of the kidney patient in Chicago. If that went well, she would go through an assortment of tests, consultations, meetings with the caseworker, and schedule pre-op.

After the call, the rest of the week went by in a blur with buying and changing tickets, cleaning the apartment (she'd decided it would give her time to think), going over her schedule with a fine-toothed comb and moving back appointments that she had scheduled for the following week. She barely had any time to write, and she was getting precariously close to getting off her timeline, something she had never allowed herself to do with any of her books.

She'd called Mel to let her know when she would be arriving, but she didn't tell her about what she had decided to do. It was still too early. Why send Mel through the whole gambit of emotions when there may not be anything to worry about in the first place?

She forced herself to come back to the service, and participate in congratulating the people that were now being given a certificate of appreciation for their volunteer work in the church. For the next hour, she concentrated on keeping her mind in the present.

After service, she was making her way through the crowd to shake hands, hug and greet those she wasn't familiar with. She offered her services as an elder of the church and gave her card to them, just in case they were in need of special prayer or resources.

As she was heading toward the back of the church, she heard her name. She turned to see Lady Menagerie signaling for her to come back to the front.

"Elder Morganson, it has been a few months since we have been able to fellowship after service. Would you be able to come to lunch with me and a few of the elders? It is nothing formal at all, just an opportunity for us to catch up with one another."

The use of her title made Paige aware of the fact that Lady Menagerie was not asking as a close friend but as the First Lady of the church.

"Sure. Are we going right away or will it be a moment? I still need to give Pamela my schedule for the next couple of weeks, since I will be traveling."

"We will be leaving in a half hour for Ming's. If you would like, you can caravan with the rest of the group."

"Okay, I will be out back in a half hour."

Paige walked over to the offices and found Pamela packing up. "Good morning, Pam, I was hoping I would catch you. I won't be long. I just wanted to give you my schedule for the next few weeks. Things have changed a little and I will have to leave earlier than I planned."

"How much earlier?"

"I will be leaving Tuesday instead of Thursday. Just two days off from my original schedule. I am going to Chicago for a couple of days for business."

"Chicago? You don't like Chicago. I remember last year when you got back from speaking in St. Louis you had to go through Chicago and you got stuck there and vowed never to go to or through Chicago. It must be awfully important," Pam said, scribbling something on the Elder's Calendar.

"Very," said Paige, now regretting the spectacle she made in front of Pam last February when she finally made it home after getting snowed in at O'Hare for two days, catching a very bad cold and missing First Lady's birthday celebration. She had rushed in for a meeting straight from the airport and looked a sight. When Pastor Lawrence asked her why she was late, she went through the whole ordeal between Detroit, Michigan, Chicago, Illinois, and Los Angeles. When she was done, he just patted her on the shoulder and said, "Praying for you will not be difficult tonight. I know exactly what to pray for."

"It wouldn't be a husband and children so that she would stay home, would it?" quipped Pam.

Pastor Lawrence turned to her, pointing his finger and said, "No it isn't and you stay out of grown folks' business."

This elicited a giggle from Pam and she went back to her work.

"So...you have that?" Paige said, while reorganizing her belongings in her arms. "I am going to head out and meet with some of the elders for lunch. I will talk to you when I get back. Okay?"

"I pray that you have traveling mercies and the weather is mild."

"Thank you, Pam."

Paige walked back out into the sunlight of the early afternoon, heading towards her car. She was sincerely hoping that her car wasn't too hot. It seemed the older her baby got, the longer it took for the air conditioning to work.

She had just taken her keys out of her purse when she heard an unfamiliar voice to her right, causing her to jump. It was much closer than she thought it should be, given that she didn't see anyone on the way to her car.

"I didn't mean to startle you."

Paige saw the beige suit first, but as she looked up the sun shown in her eyes and she couldn't make out the expression on Elder Tatum's face. "No problem. I just didn't see you when I walked out to the parking lot. How are you doing? If I remember right, you are new to town. How is our fair city treating you?"

"It is beautiful. I have never experienced so many clear and sunny days in a row, especially this time of year. I hope I never get used to it. It's hurricane season where I just came from."

"I don't think people really do get used to it. Where are you coming from?" she asked, trying to juggle her keys so that the one to the car would slip between her forefinger and thumb, her bible, shawl, notebook, and purse were tilting precariously to the side.

"May I?" Elder Tatum asked even as he took the keys out of her hand and selected what looked to be a car key. He held it up. "This one?"

Surprised, she only nodded. Their last conversation didn't give her much to go on but she didn't expect attentiveness. Most men would have watched her juggle all of the things in her hand just to see if she could do it.

He unlocked and opened the door, took the items out of her hand one by one until she held only her purse and placed them in the car on the passenger side. "Are you okay now?"

She found her voice, gratefully. "Yeah, thank you very much. I saw that going all wrong in my head. I appreciate it."

"Well, where I come from, when we see someone in need of another hand, we offer it."

"Mmmm. Where I come from, if most people see you in need of a hand, they run the other way, afraid you will ask them for one." She smiled sheepishly. "You don't know it is out of the ordinary until someone steps forward and does something we all secretly wish they would."

She looked up again since he had moved out of the line of the sun, and was surprised to see that he looked uncomfortable under her small rain of praise.

"Are you coming to lunch with Pastor and First Lady? Is that why you are waiting out here?" She glanced at her watch, noticing that she had another 10 minutes before they would be ready to go.

"Yes, but I was afraid I was late when I came down and didn't see anyone. I was just going to go back up when I saw you come out."

"Oh, where are you parked?"

Elder Tatum turned to her right, pointing at the dark car which was now in the shadows of the parking structure.

Paige sighed inwardly in relief. That was why she didn't see him coming.

"Give me one moment," Paige said, lifting one finger so that he would excuse her interruption of the conversation while she got in her car, rolled the windows down, and turned the car on so that she could get the AC started.

She got back out, closed the door and leaned against her car. "We have a few minutes before everyone comes down. So what brings you to California, Elder Tatum?"

He shifted his weight to a more comfortable stance. "I came out for a new position in my company. It is more of a desk job, whereas before I was traveling 75% of the time."

"What about your family? Do you see them often?"

Paige surprised herself by the questions. She was not usually so inquisitive.

He looked almost as surprised as she was. "I don't get to see my mom and dad as often as I would like but with work and ministry, I expected it would be so. What about you? Do you have family out here?"

Yep. She thought to herself. This was the reason why she didn't ask people questions like that. It was usually reciprocated.

CHAPTER 20

Brandon watched as Paige's eyes went dark. He thought the question was safe enough. She'd asked him and he thought it only polite to repeat the question to her. That, and he was so distracted by her change in demeanor and how her mint green suit brought out the colors in her eyes he couldn't think of much else to say.

"No, no family here right now. My sister lives in Atlanta and we are very close. I don't get a lot of chances to see her, but I will be going that way on Friday."

"Really? I know a few people in Atlanta. It was my second choice. I really like the culture."

Paige wanted off of this subject before it became more personal. She feigned disinterest in it, shrugging her shoulders. "As I said, I don't get a lot of chances to go to the ATL. I think it is rich with a diversity of cultures and African-American pride, but I can't seem to get over the weather patterns there. Humidity and I don't get along too well and "Hotlanta" has more than its fair share.

Elder Brandon nodded his agreement. "True, but eventually you get used to it. I thought I would feel the same way when I moved to Fort Lauderdale, Florida, but to my surprise it was easy to adjust. I think I was just too busy to notice after a while." He was hoping Paige would have something to ask or say because his mind had once again gone blank.

Reduced to talking about the weather. He chuckled to himself as his hands found change in his pockets to rub against each other.

There had to be other topics that weren't too personal that they could discuss that would allow him to get to know her better. Since their brief introduction on the previous Tuesday she had invaded his thoughts mercilessly. There was no rhyme or reason for it. They were only in each other's presence for a few seconds and from what he could surmise, she was a disobedient and arrogant woman – not someone he wanted to get to know better anytime soon. But when he went to sleep he would be haunted by a pair of huge, golden eyes and mischievous grin.

She was unknowingly the motivation behind many minutes of prayer that week.

Even when he went in to fill out some paperwork in the office the next day, the scene of their introduction replayed in his mind. He'd even asked Pam for a list of auxiliaries and ministries, their leaders, and their scheduled meetings. The reason he gave Pam was that he wanted to get antiquated with the church and its working, active ministries. His true motive was to find out what ministries Elder Morganson was a part of and to make sure he was somewhere else.

It seemed the more he fought thinking about her during the day while he was getting settled at work, working on unpacking, preparing his dinner, and sitting in Midweek Service, the more she entered his thoughts unheeded. The only time he seemed to get a reprieve was when he was praying or studying in his Word. It was unreal.

For half of a week, he dreamed about her. The dreams would always begin the same: just as they had met in the pastor's offices, with her back to him. He knew she was talking and what she was saying, but he couldn't hear her. Then she would turn around and he would feel as though she captured him. He couldn't move or speak. It was as if she hypnotized him with her smile and he was incapable of breaking out of her spell.

Each night the dream would go a little further: meeting, her turning, him momentarily paralyzed, her walking towards him; finally last night, he had enough courage to let it play out.

The former nights he'd forced himself to awaken, feeling that the only reason for the dreams was because he subconsciously lacked some self-control. The fact that she was beautiful didn't help the matter any.

She turned around this time and he was waiting expectantly for the paralysis to set in. He didn't fight it when she stepped to him and curtsied low, all the while keeping her eyes on him. As she came up she held something in her hand. Breaking her gaze with his, she looked down at the object in her hand. He followed her gaze, confused to see an arrested heart cupped in her palm. She looked back up, placing one hand at the side of his face, her eyes almost apologetic. He felt warmth and security and well-being, and something indescribable all at once then she raised the heart. As he watched, he noticed that she stopped just at the left of his chest, which to his surprise, had a hole in it the same size as the object. The moment she placed it there, the scene brightened and he knew what the feeling was.

Peace…overwhelming, joy-creating, embracing peace. The heart started and with each beat, he felt warmth rush through his feet and legs, then hips, waist, and chest. He opened his mouth to thank her for the wonderful gift, but she was turning into stone with each of his beats.

114

All he heard before he woke was, "It fits."

He lay in bed, heart beating quickly, trying to hold onto as many details as possible. He didn't understand all of the parts, and he had asked God seriously the night before to reveal to him why he was continuously having these dreams.

He turned his head to his left to check the clock, and noticed the warm liquid spilling to his hairline.

He touched his hand to his eye, already knowing that he had been crying.

At that moment he decided to go about exorcising her in a different way. He would prove to himself that Paige in person was not as good as the woman in his dreams. Nothing like the reality to kill a dream you'd made of someone.

"Do you like your job? You work with a pharmaceutical company, if my memory serves me right," he heard Paige ask.

Brandon blinked a couple of times to reorient himself with the present. He was thankful for the reprieve from the onslaught of thoughts coursing through his mind.

"Yes, very much. I like meeting new people and this job gives me the opportunity to meet all kinds. I find the industry fascinating. I actually went into pre-med but I cared too much. I was having a hard time detaching myself from patients. I figured if I was having issues at that early stage in my career, it would only get worse. I believe my sensitivity to people's hurts and needs is a gift rather than a curse. I found one of the next best things: working in the pharmaceutical industry and helping to judge the effects of certain drugs."

"How does that work with your belief in God and His ability to heal?"

Brandon smiled to himself. He had gotten this question from a few people that served as clergy. Some of them open to his answer, some of them not so open.

"I believe pharmaceuticals, just like doctors, can be used by God. They are used by God as an extension of his ability to heal. When Jesus healed the blind man with His spit and some clay, I believe that was a type of salve. The knowledge and wisdom we are obtaining more of every day in regards to our bodies are taken for granted. How we take care of them, how to prevent sickness, and how to use home remedies with prayerful direction, are all things I consider to be God-given and therefore tools to help in the advancement of the human race. I love medicine and I find the human body an awesomely-built machine. I don't think I could ever get tired of researching it. Though I strongly believe in the laying on of hands, anointing people with oil and praying, I also believe there is a place for Western medicine."

He was about to state more of his opinion when he looked down and caught a smile tugging at the side of her lip. He was arrested by it and smiled sheepishly. "Sorry. I tend to get a little defensive and passionate about the subject. You wouldn't believe the flack I get for being in this field. Some people think I am just a legalized drug dealer."

"Wow. They have actually said that to your face?" Paige seemed astonished but he didn't think she would have been terribly surprised to find that many church people thought that way.

"One or two. I wasn't too fazed. I mean, it only comes from ignorance. I don't mind helping to educate people though, if you couldn't tell," he said, trying to make light of his speech. Some people were turned off by this more passionate side of him. He noticed that she seemed content to listen to him on his soapbox; the small smile appearing and disappearing with certain points he made, as if she truly knew and understood what he was speaking on.

"May I ask you what you do for a living, or do you minister full time?"

He watched the way her eyes sparkled at the question and found himself transfixed while she explained that she was a writer and motivational speaker. Her hands started moving in an animated fashion, helping to draw him deeper into her form of communicating. He leaned his side against her car as she talked about her love for writing and the creative drive behind it. Naturally, how grateful she was to be used to bring people into a deeper understanding and more intimate relationship with the Lord by doing what she considered to be such a gift-giving and endearing thing.

He watched as her facial expression softened and her whole persona glowed. He was struck by a cord deep within as he related with her regard and love for people and almost desperately wanting them to feel what she felt for her Maker.

Then he saw it: the wry sense of humor that she used to cover up her slight embarrassment. This time, it was at openly portraying her unrestrained adoration for God her Father. He was shaken by his disappointment to see her come back to herself in their conversation. The rapture that had shown upon her face when she spoke of the lover of her soul was...he was almost ashamed to admit, attractive.

He wondered if she could look at him even something close to that way.

This wasn't working out quite as he had planned. So far he was finding more likenesses than contradictions in her.

He righted himself from her car, feeling now that the position was too familiar. The now-discarded thought seemed to come from far off.

He consciously shook himself, willing himself to reign in his emotions. *Get a hold of yourself Brandon before she thinks you are a lunatic. You don't know her from Eve. What you see could still be a mirage.*

He took one more step back, reinforcing himself against her dazzling eyes as she looked up at him with shy questioning. He wondered if he had missed an actual question while he was berating himself, but guessed that she just wanted to know if he understood how she felt.

"I know how you feel. To think that He who is perfect in everything, the Creator of everything, the Knower of all of my faults and transgressions – now and to come – would want to use me to spread His Word. It amazes me, and I find myself continuously humbled by it. He could use anyone to do the things that He has me do. The tasks are not rocket science and there are certainly more qualified people to do it, but He picked me and I am happy about it."

Her nodding let him know that he had guessed right. It was nice, the next moment of silence. Instead of trying to force her into more conversation, he was fine with just allowing the moment to solidify the shared passion they had for the One that had extraordinarily changed their lives.

This was a nice beginning. Not too personal, but slightly intimate. He liked what he was shown about her. She was definitely different from what he could surmise from their first introduction. He still wasn't sure about what the issues were concerning her reluctance to meet him, but if God gave him just a little more time, they would be good friends; no more. It would be selfish of him to want more from her. It would only end in hurt for her, and he was starting to feel oddly protective of this pint-sized woman who loved God with such a fierceness that it made him want to follow her around to see if she felt that way about all the things she loved.

"So, have you been to Ming's before? Do you know what type of cuisine they serve?"

"It is Korean and Mongolian. It sounds weird, but their ribs are fantastic and their wontons melt in your mouth. There is a walnut shrimp dish with a peanut sauce that I also love. I am a creature of habit so those are the ones I usually get, but I am willing to try what other people get. That is what we all usually do when we go. Each person gets a different dish and then we share. The restaurant has a family style menu, which makes the dishes huge. Otherwise, I would still only know that they have great ribs." She giggled, forcing a smile from his own lips.

"You seem to have fun here," he said, wanting to elicit yet another smile from her so he could see her eyes dance.

She nodded. "Pastor Lawrence and First Lady Menagerie are great. They pretty much adopted me when I joined several years ago. I kind of get the royal treatment, but I don't think they spoil me...not too much anyway."

And there it was, the hint of a smile – this time a little more apologetic, but still very disarming.

"Everyone should get the chance to know what spoiling feels like. Sometimes what you might think is spoiling is pure, unadulterated love in action," he replied, defending her voiced thought.

This time he was rewarded with a full smile, twinkling eyes and all, and he was so distracted by his different reactions to her various smiles that he didn't notice the couple watching them from the side door leading to the parking lot; one with a self-congratulatory smirk and the other with a concerned frown.

Paige saw them and the smile quickly left. She stepped away from the car, lengthening the distance between them, and smoothed the imaginary creases from her skirt. He caught the direction of one of her glances and followed it to the Pastor and First Lady, now coming out of the side door.

He fought the urge to take a step back so as not to look like he was doing something he wasn't supposed to. After all it was only conversation. Why should he feel guilty? He looked back at Paige, and her expression seemed to mirror his thoughts. He wondered then for the first time if she had been thinking of him as well in the past week. If so, then they would have a problem on their hands and he would have to forfeit his research to find out why this woman haunted his dreams, and abandon any thoughts in developing a friendship with her. Simple precaution only if things were to get out of hand, not that he could even fathom that they would. She seemed to be a very grounded woman and from what he had gleaned from their conversation today, not easily prone to fancy.

He searched himself again, judging the feelings conjured up by the dreams, and the ones he was experiencing due to their brief interlude. They were much the same, and as much as he disliked admitting it or using the word for that matter, he was bewitched.

This was so outside of his plans, ideals for himself and the heavy, protective shroud he had held onto to keep his sense of sanity in check since his diagnosis. It wasn't fair to himself or anyone else for him to indulge in these types of thoughts when they had no future.

"Well, are we ready to go?" Menagerie asked as she came forward, hugging Paige and then taking the couple steps to hug Brandon, "It looks like the others will meet us there. They headed there right away. Do you want to take one car and we'll drop you off back here after dinner?" Brandon thought on this for a couple of seconds and decided that being in that close of proximity with Paige wouldn't be a good idea with his warring feelings. Before he could say anything though, Paige spoke up.

"That's alright. I have some packing to do and it would be best if I took my car so that I could go straight home and get started." She was already moving to get in her car so she missed the brief disappointment flash across the First Lady's face, but Brandon caught it and placed himself on guard.

Later that evening as Brandon found himself unpacking the last of his boxes, he came upon a photo album he had kept on one of his shelves in his old living room. He sat back on the chair and began flipping through it, taking note of the backgrounds in the pictures more than the subjects at first. He glanced at a picture of the high school where he and his siblings had attended; the park where each of them had a birthday party. The party in this particular picture was his sister, Marjorie's. He had given the piñata that year the deafening blow, even though he'd been the smallest. He remembered being afraid that Marjorie was going to be mad that his hit was the one that broke the hat. *Was it a hat?* The memory was fading. But instead, she hugged him and jumped to the ground amongst the other children, scooping up handfuls of candy. She was always so gracious. She didn't see things as others did. He had actually been looking forward to a sound, verbal lashing from his father that night, but he got nothing. He found out later that she had gone to his dad earlier that evening and thanked him for the party, and praised Brandon for getting to the candy so quickly.

She had always looked out for him that way. He was closest to Marjorie. Actually all of the children were closest to Marjorie, which seemed odd because she wasn't the oldest but rather the middle child. It meant a lot to Brandon though because he felt he was misunderstood by most people. They thought him the "golden child" for his accomplishments in academics and athletics, but no one ever asked him what motivated him. They just assumed that because he was the son of a preacher, he was simply following his father's footsteps.

He snuck a few calls to her that first semester, begging her to come back home. After the third time, she made him a deal saying that she would call him once a week right before his bedtime, and she had kept her word. In his 8th grade year, he had made friends with a boy named Dominy who had recently moved into town. They found that they liked the same movies, subjects like Science and Math and were halfway decent in P.E.

Dominy was great to talk to. He was very quiet, but not so much shy as observant. He seemed a little intense at first because his eyes, the color of night, would watch every hand movement and expression almost as if he were memorizing the person and how they spoke each word. But because he watched, he was also able to pick up on what Brandon was really saying when he talked about his family and things he really liked. Dominy also asked the questions no one else seemed to, like, "Does your father talk to you like he speaks to people in church? Which sibling was his favorite?", and if he would actually follow in his dad's footsteps and become a preacher. When Brandon answered 'yes' to the last question, Dominy asked him why.

"I am not completely sure why but people keep telling me that I am the one in the family that is most like him, though I don't really see it. They say they see 'The call of God on my life'." Brandon had just shrugged after that.

"Have you ever thought of what you would do if you didn't become a preacher?" Dominy asked.

"Not really, it just seems inevitable."

"That's too bad. But it isn't too late. You could find something that you really like to do now and work on that." Brandon shrugged at that too. At that time, the thought seemed like some sort of blasphemy against his family and father, but as he lay in bed that night he thought back on some of the things he had found an interest in over the years and judged them in varying degrees.

He and Dominy had remained close friends, becoming inseparable even during their second year of high school when Dominy started dating Robin, whom he married during Brandon's second year in college. One thing he'd envied about Dominy was his confidence. Once Dominy made up his mind on something he wanted to do, he didn't look back or waver. It always looked so easy. Brandon asked him how he could be so sure things would work out and not want to change his mind.

Dominy, in a matter-of-fact manner just stated that he wasn't as sure as he seemed about things, but he only allowed himself to go back and forth until he made up his mind. Once he had decided on something, he moved forward. He said it was the same way with Robin.

"But how do you decide? Did you know when you first started going out that you were going to marry her?"

Dominy laughed. "There is no science behind it and I am not going to let you analyze like you do everything else. In some ways, she is the hardest decision I've made because I have to make different ones about her with every new move we make, but from the moment we started talking I did know that she would be a very special part of my life."

Even after Brandon graduated, he and Dominy kept in touch: calling each other, emailing, or texting twice a week. It was Dominy he called in regards to his introduction to Paige and all of the dreams he was having about her, and as usual Dominy asked the hard questions.

"Why do you think she made such an impact on you?" He had not been willing to ask himself that question about her. He didn't really want to know if she had but obviously she had made some type of impression because it was her face that stared up at him each night, the eyes laughing and playful.

"Is she beautiful?" Dominy asked.

"It isn't like that. I am trying to understand what this means now?" Brandon asked becoming a little agitated.

"So she is beautiful, but you are not willing to admit it because you are trying to figure out how she got past your defenses?"

"No, I don't believe her beauty has any bearing on the reason why she has shown up in my dreams. My first impression of her was that she was spoiled and rebellious."

"I know about your impressions, Brandon, and most of them are more like prejudgments. What I want to know is what your second impression of her was?"

Brandon could hear Dominy's smile through the phone. He hesitated to answer the question. He was holding out the few seconds he could before he heard Dominy's knowing laugh.

"There has been no second impression." Brandon stated, through his teeth. He expelled his breath waiting for Dominy's reply. He was met with quiet.

"Dominy, you there?"

"So, you are introduced to this woman, who, from what you said, seemed as reluctant to meet you as you were to meet her. Spoke to her all of 30 seconds, and now you are having dreams about her. Do I have that right so far?"

Brandon nodded into the phone; he was beginning to panic.

"Bran?"

"Yes. So far."

"Well, you say you keep making yourself wake up from the dream. Stop doing that. Let the dream run its course, and then you may be able to get it out of your system. If that doesn't work you can always just interact with her. Find out if she is as bad as you say she is. You never know, it could be your subconscious doing something for you this time that you never do for yourself."

"What is that?"

"Take a chance. Live some. I've always been a little worried about your 'all on my own' attitude. I don't think it is healthy."

"What are you talking about? We have been friends for years. I am calling you even now when I know you aren't going to let me live this down."

"Brandon, when was the last time you even considered following your heart more than your head? I don't recall the last time you talked to me about a woman you've met."

"Not everyone finds the love of their life in high school, but if your memory was better you might remember that there was Rowan in college."

"That wasn't love, and if my memory serves me right – and you know it will – she was more real in your mind than she was in life. I know she sent you for a loop and it set you on edge regarding women, but you trust God in everything else. Why not your relationships?"

"I can't believe what I am hearing. You know why. There isn't going to be a relationship. There is no time, besides it would be absolutely cruel for me to start any kind of relationship with anyone right now. It can only end in heartbreak for them."

The other end of the line was quiet for a few moments. "No change in the diagnosis? What number of opinion is this?"

"This is five," Brandon responded quietly.

"How much time did he try to give you?"

"He was a little more hopeful. He thought that since it was still in the early stages there were a few things that I might want to think about in regards to surgery, chemo, etc., but he said that he had only known that to extend life, not guarantee it. At least he said a little over two years."

"Wow," came the response, accompanied by a gust of wind.

"He did give me a referral to one of his friends who also studies a little, less traditional medicine. I am supposed to give him a call on

Monday," he finished, allowing for a lull to envelop the last part of the sentence.

"This is a different type of situation, I know, but I still think that instead of running or hiding from this, you should embrace it and let it run its course. I am sure there is something you can learn from this. Just be open. I know you will continue to seek God on this and you should, but stop waiting for your life to end and live what you have."

"And you don't think that isn't just a little bit selfish? I don't know what she may have been thinking or what Pastor Lawrence may have said to her before he introduced us. I think it would be foolish to lead her on knowing that this will not go anywhere."

"Wooo, don't get ahead of yourself – or of me for that matter. I am not talking about you trying your rudimentary seductive skills on her. I am just telling you to be open. Be polite, be decent, be open."

"You already said be open," Brandon reminded him.

"It was worth repeating," mimicking Brandon's tone.

"It took all of two weeks for me to know that Robin was the one for me. The rest of the time was me trying to talk myself out of it because of what society, friends and family said. I can't tell you how much easier it would have been if I had someone like me to talk to, then. Brandon, I am trying to be that one for you now. The future is uncertain, no matter what the doctors say about you. You have more insight than most of us in regards to Who really has the last say. Maybe you need a reason to fight harder. I can't think of anything better than love."

"See, you are getting ahead of me. I was simply asking how to exorcise her out of my dreams. Love is way out of the question. Besides, my idea of love is all encompassing, all consuming. It embraces everything and sets it on fire. There is nothing left afterward. To do that to someone knowing that there is not a lifetime to allow us to grow in it is cruel."

"Wow! Is that what you have been waiting for? Is that what you have been holding out for? My goodness. No wonder you have been by yourself for so long, but I wonder if that isn't also a form of defense you are using to keep from feeling for anyone. You have always been pretty extreme with your opinions, but I didn't know it went that deep. I have to say, I am a little concerned Brandon. You never struck me as the obsessive-compulsive type. I have always thought of love as a warm blanket that one may embrace, but it goes with you and it grows, yes…but consuming everything in its path? No. I think it is just the opposite. I think it brings things to life: thoughts, perceptions, dreams, hopes, cares, and wants or desires that we may otherwise go through life without. It changes things, yes, but gradually and permanently because you make decisions that you may otherwise not have made. It isn't something that destroys in its wake but revives and sears itself into your very soul. To know it can only make you stronger, even when it doesn't last."

"Well, look who's deep today? If I didn't know better, I would have thought you were in your Bible today. Do you even have a bible, Dominy?"

"You can try to make light of this to make yourself feel better, but still just remember what I said. Just keep yourself open."

"Yes sir. Well, I am going to finish this box and I will talk to you later, and let you know how it's going."

"Very well, before you spend too much more time thinking about all this, you might consider the possibility that she really may not want anything to do with you. I'm sure that would make you much more relieved, right?"

"Goodbye, Dominy." Brandon said through his teeth, pronouncing each syllable and then stabbed the end call button.

Brandon blinked his living room back into focus. He placed the photo album on the shelf, freeing his hands so that he could place them against his temples, his elbows resting on his knees.

What is this Lord? Why are you not giving me help against this? I don't understand what you want me to gain from this? If we are to be friends, that is fine, but can you take this attraction I have for her away? This pull that I feel towards her that I have never felt for anyone else. I am pleading with you God to take this away. I am content with my life. I have accepted what is and I am well with it. I have come to a place where I am expectant, hopeful, and in wonder; I am ready to embrace it. Please don't give me a reason to want to stay. I am afraid I will not be ready or worse yet, I will not want to leave this place, which up until now, has held no chains to me. You are who I live for and what I have lived this life to be a glory to. Please don't make that harder for me.

Brandon sat back in his chair reviewing the day, looking again for signs that he was imagining the character of Elder Paige Morganson. He had watched her from across the table, making sure he sat just far enough away that his continued glances would not catch anyone's attention.

She seemed just as animated with everyone else as she was with him when she spoke of her love for God and her vocation. Her eyes lit up as she talked about her tour, looking his way every now and then to bring him into the conversation since he was new to the group.

She seemed to react to everyone the same way, with a loving openness as if she was surrounded by family instead of colleagues. When the food came she made sure they passed the dishes to him, explaining that he was new to the experience and he needed to taste everything. He even watched to see if she interacted differently to the male elders that didn't have rings on their fingers, and all he could detect were slightly less intimate gestures. She didn't whisper in ears or touch them but there was definitely familiarity, respect and even admiration. She listened, asked questions that reminded him of Dominy with their profoundness, and joked. But what caused him to pause and look over time and time again was her laugh. It was unadulterated joy and he could see that he wasn't the only one affected by it. He looked around the table and saw that almost everyone interrupted their side conversations or found themselves smiling in mid-bite at the sound. It was unabashed and it seemed to blanket everyone.

He searched in his mind for what was in it that caused this reaction, when he heard a child's laugh from one of the neighboring tables. That was it. She laughed like a child: unguarded with abandon. No stifled shrill or insignificant giggle. It was joy, and he was finding it hard to fight against its appeal.

As they were leaving the restaurant, he angled his way around everyone so that he could walk her to her car.

"Thank you for the food suggestions. You were right. The ribs are great but I think I like their sweet and sour chicken more."

"Awwww, a sweet and sour man," she said, wiggling her eyebrows. He heard the laugh before he knew it was coming from him.

"So you are going out of town on Tuesday?" he asked, slowing his pace to lengthen the amount of time they had for conversation.

"Yes," she sighed, but didn't offer any more.

"Who takes your place in your ministry when you are out of town?"

"Have you met Sister Marsha Sands? She is over the sick and shut-in committee that I serve on. I am not over it; it would be selfish for me to be over it and travel the way I do, but she sends me the phone numbers of the people while I'm away and I make it my business to call and talk to them when I can't come and see them. If they need a resource or special visitation, then I pass them back to Sister Sands. Not rocket science either," she said, shrugging and recalling his words from earlier that afternoon.

"Do you mind if I talk to Sister Sands? I was a part of my visiting committee at my former church. I know I have been brought on staff to head up the men's ministry, but that one also has a special place in my heart."

He watched the different emotions cross her features over the next couple of seconds before she gave her answer. "I don't believe there would be a problem with that. We overlap in ministries all of the time, but I would pass that by Pastor Lawrence before I approached Sister Sands. Just to make sure you follow protocol. You wouldn't want to step on anyone's toes."

He watched as she played with her keys in her hands, every now and then giving him sideways glances, picking up her pace to the car. He didn't have any choice but to match it.

"Thank you for the advice, Elder Morganson. I appreciate it. Have a nice flight and I pray you have a very successful trip."

He waited for her to get to her car and get in, wondering if he'd spooked her.

CHAPTER 21

"Vicki, I thought you were smarter than this. You do know that if you lose, the chances of us seeing our granddaughter again are slim to none."

"What judge would possibly pick him over me? His lifestyle, questionable health, and his ability to care for her adequately since he has gone back to work will prove to be in my favor."

"Maybe, but her love and loyalty to him will be your undoing. No judge would separate a decent father from his daughter because the grandmother has more time, more money and more land. That does not always afford a child more in life. That day is over. You are playing with fire and I for one am not going to support you in this selfish scheme fueled by the anger you never let go of because you thought you were cheated out of time with your daughter. To tell you the truth, you cheated yourself with your stubborn need for control; you can't control everything. It is an illusion you have built around you. I am tired of holding a cold, angry woman in my arms where there used to be a soft, warm, loving one."

"Life has a way of doing that to a person."

"Life didn't do this to you. You did. I went through the same thing you did. I lost a daughter too, but I didn't go around trying to find someone to blame. Instead I looked for someone with the answers. I might as well let you know now that I haven't been just traveling with friends. I have been going to conferences and doing some missionary work.

A few weeks after Rachael died, I found myself with half a bottle of scotch and a lot of questions. I was desperate to find out why, with all of the money, influence, knowledge and success that we have, why there was no way to save our little girl. You were lost in your own world. You wouldn't talk to me, let alone let me comfort you. I needed to mourn with you. I needed to make sense of some part of what was going on.

One of the last conversations I had with Rachael was regarding a bible study she had gone to during her last visit. She said that she had received the answer she had been looking for in all of it and it gave her such a peace about what she was going through. She didn't tell me what it was specifically, but told me she was alright and God's grace was more than sufficient.

I thought about our talk through a cloud of single malt, and found myself walking to the same church she had told me about. I am ashamed to admit that I burst in on the group in the middle of the bible study and demanded they tell me what was so great about their God that He could take someone as wonderful as Rachael away from me and expect me to continue to see anything worth living for.

Now that I think about it, I am surprised that they didn't throw me out. Rather, the pastor slowly got up with two other men and walked towards me.

They asked me my name like I had just walked in, welcomed me, sat me down and out of nowhere a cup of coffee appeared.

The pastor sat down in front of me and asked me to repeat my question. I could barely remember why I was there. I began to mumble my apology, but he interrupted me saying that I was there for a very important purpose, and, if he could, he would try to help me find the answer to my question.

All those times Rachael would come back from bible study with her friend, she would be singing and whispering like she was communicating with someone special. I didn't get it. But the love I felt from those strangers on that night couldn't be a mistake. We must have been there for hours. Me, angrily accusing God of taking my precious daughter away one minute, then crying, begging them to pray that He bring her back the next. I was a mess. That night, I didn't get my answer to my question but I did get to know a small facet of God through these people, and it was enough to lessen some of the pain because I saw that God didn't have it out for me. He wasn't punishing me or Rachael, or even you. He didn't take Rachael because He wanted her more with Him than with us. He was a God with purpose and He had a special purpose for me. I was part of His perfect plan, and for me, that was a great load off. It didn't mean I wasn't still angry about not having my little girl nor that I wasn't hurt or wretchedly lonely without her. It just meant that it wasn't all in my hands and that it wasn't up to me to come up with the reason. Life was still going to go on even if I didn't get the full answer. It gave me an open door to healing.

That night I gave my life to Jesus Christ. I asked Him to come into my heart and I told Him I believed Him to be my Lord and Savior."

"How could you not have shared that with me all of this time? How could you have kept such a thing from me?"

"No love, my question to you is how could you not have noticed?" His voice took on an icy quality. You know how, because you are so consumed with your hatred and anger for a man who did nothing but love our daughter with every fiber of his being. You are consumed by it so much that you couldn't even accept the love and comfort I was trying to give you. I can't even imagine what it must be like for him, but he has pushed forward for that child and I will not stand by and let you take her away from him.

"Richard, you have betrayed me." Victoria was happy her voice didn't give away her full body tremble. "You have been lying to me and keeping things from me. You are not the man I married." She began pacing, hoping the use of energy would help dissipate some of the anger. After a full minute she stopped and took a deep breath. "I don't know if I can forgive you. You were the one stable thing in my life, and now I find that you have been stealing away to play savior to people you don't even know. How irrational is that?"

"Victoria, the anger and hatred you gave into has taken control and turned you into someone I don't know." The disappointment she heard in his voice hurt, increasing her anger to rage. She could barely hold her tongue as he continued "It isn't as though I was cheating on you. I am a better person because of God. I can love you better because I love myself. But what I can't do is make you happy. You are going to have to do that on your own."

"Don't you preach to me! I want you out of the house when I get there, you lying hypocrite!" She didn't even try controlling her voice anymore.

"Listen to who is being irrational, but I will give you your space. If you look at the caller I.D., you will find that I am not at the house. I am in a small village in Uganda. I was thinking about coming back early, but I will remain here for the next two months until this project is done. That should either give you enough time to come to your senses or build up enough loathing for me that we will divorce. This may truly be the one thing you have control over honey: whether or not I remain in your life." The line went dead.

She sat there looking at the phone in her hand until the off-the-hook signal began its annoying peal. She quietly placed the receiver back on the hook and waited for the phone to ring with Richard apologizing on the other end.

She sat there until the first rays of dawn began to climb past the skyscrapers. Then she cried herself to sleep.

CHAPTER 22

Mason was passing by the nurse's station on Vivian's floor when Phyllis caught his attention.

"Mr. Jenson, this was delivered for you today." She handed him a thick envelope, smiling warmly.

Mason mumbled his thanks, accepting the package. Things had gotten a little strange lately with the nurses. He didn't want to look a gift horse in the mouth, but it had been a more attentive group of nurses he had never seen before. Even during his wife's last days, he only knew the nurses to be thoughtfully quiet and almost invisible in their monitoring of his wife. He could probably thank his daughter for this. Everyone who met her seemed to fall in love with her. He would tolerate the extra attention for her.

Though Vivian's prognosis wasn't getting better, she was in better spirits. The doctor's latest attempt to get her kidneys to respond had brought back some color to her cheeks. It was getting close to the afternoon when he told her to take a nap. He would come back later to check on her.

He wheeled himself to the elevator, pressing the button that would take him to his room on the 11th floor. He looked at the package lying flat on his lap. He did not get an easy feeling from it. What could be so urgent that it would be delivered at a hospital? He refused to open it while he was with Vivian. If it was bad news, he didn't want to have to share it with her. She was able to see right through him.

He positioned his wheelchair by the bed so that he would only have to put his weight on his good leg for a moment while he transferred himself from his chair to his bed.

He was perspiring by the time he'd settled into the bed, but he was happy with accomplishing the deed on his own.

He took one deep, cleansing breath before he picked up the envelope and slowly loosened the back. He recognized the structure of the paperwork right away. It was a court document. He stared at the huge type in the middle of the page. The perspiration turned into beads of sweat on his forehead and above his lip. Icy fingers ran up his spine, causing the hairs on the back of his neck to stand up.

NOTICE OF CUSTODY HEARING: BRANCHETT VS. JENSON
(On grounds of party's inability to properly care for the child in question)

That snake! That conniving, evil bitch! She can't do this. There is no way she can win…how dare she?! That's it, she has gone too far. He leaned over to retrieve his cell phone from the bedside table and pressed the speed dial number 5 for Richard Branchett. It rang twice before he picked up.

"Hey, Mason. What's up?"

Mason shook so hard he found himself momentarily unable to speak.

"Mason…how is Vivian? Is she worse?"

Mason hesitated. Maybe he had been hasty. Richard didn't sound different or wary in any way. Maybe he didn't know what Victoria was up to. It wouldn't be the first time. He would try to remember this when he told him.

"Hi Richard. Sorry about that. She's fine. How's your trip?" He waited for Richard to respond.

"Alright. It is actually going better than I planned. We are not getting a great deal of resistance from the government here and that should allow us to finish this job on schedule. How is Vivian?"

"Her spirits are up but she still isn't responding to the medications. The doctor is still pressing for a transplant." Mason tried to keep the strain out of his voice.

"Mason, how are you doing? How are the headaches? I hope you aren't trying to walk on that ankle yet…and what about your heart?" Richard's voice sounded concerned, but the connection was so bad he seemed to be trying to get the information out of Mason as quickly as possible.

"I'm okay. I should be out of here in a few days. I want to talk to you about something. Have you talked to Victoria lately?"

"Not really. We have been going at it night and day here. I love the way the people work for one another here," he said, more to himself than to Mason. "I think the last time I spoke to her was early last week. Why?"

Mason hesitated.

"Why, Mason? Did she do something?"

"Richard, she has filed for custody of Vivian. I just got papers for an informal hearing." He still needed to ask, "Did you know anything about this?"

There was a long pause on the other side of the phone before he responded.

"What do you mean? She is going after custody of Vivian?" Richard's voice sounded like grating steel against steel.

"Yes. At least, that is what the paperwork says. I need you to answer. Did you know anything about this whatsoever?"

Mason heard a sigh from the other side of the receiver.

"No, Mason. I didn't know this was what she was up to. I do keep certain tabs on her, but since Rachael's death, she has been keeping less than favorable company from time to time. This came about without the knowledge of my lawyers, I can assure you. They would have informed me of it right away."

"I thank you for not getting angry with me for asking you that question. I know at times it has been very strained, but I do appreciate your friendship. I appreciate everything you have done for myself and Vivian since Rachael became ill. I just want to let you know that it has not escaped me that you have been suffering as much as we have and, in some ways, more since our continued relationship has placed you in a precarious situation with Victoria. I am sorry about that, really I am. I so wish that things could have been different."

The voice on the other line was very tired all of a sudden.

"She actually had you served in the hospital?" His voice was incredulous. "Mason, I am sorry. I knew she was working on something, but I didn't think she would take it this far. I have been trying to shield Vivian in any way I can from her animosity towards you. I thought that we were finally making progress during Vivian's last visit. It was still budding, but there was definitely a connection there. What she is thinking now, trying to separate Vivian from the only home she knows, is a tragedy for all of us." Richard's voice broke, but he cleared it before he continued.

"I will try to do whatever I can, but I cannot promise you anything. I don't know how long she has been working on this and what she may have up her sleeve, but do know this: if there is anything I can do, I will endeavor to keep your daughter with you."

Not completely convinced of the outcome, but definitely assuaged by the fact that Richard wasn't cosigning Victoria's latest scheme, Mason let the subject go for a moment.

"Have you heard anything from the donor foundation?"

"Ah, yes. We have a candidate. I was completely distracted by this mess with Victoria. There is a woman coming in to meet with your caseworker, Amanda, on Tuesday."

"This Tuesday? Wow, that was fast. Has she agreed to donate? How far along in the process is she? Can I meet with her myself?"

There were so many questions vying for first place in his mind, he was having a hard time concentrating.

"It's still in the early stages. She agreed to fly out here, so she must be pretty serious about it. She is meeting with the caseworker and going through a myriad of tests, just to be certain she is still eligible. I don't see there being any reason why you can't meet her. I am sure Amanda can set that up with the three of you, but I am asking you not to jump the gun on this. Things may still turn around for Vivian and she may not need the transplant at all."

Mason's heart was beating a mile a minute. The news was like a ray of sunshine, breaking through menacing storm clouds that had been threatening to burst open, showering him at any moment.

"Thank you, Richard. I really appreciate all of your help on this. I can't express my gratitude enough."

"Nothing to it. She is my granddaughter as well." There was a pause. "Mason, I was wondering if you thought about the offer I gave you last year? I could still use your help."

Mason recalled the conversation close to nine months ago where Richard shared his plans for building some small homes for villagers in a small town in Uganda. He was assured that he wouldn't have to travel; most of his expertise would be used in regards to drawing plans of the actual homes. The zoning, geographical-mining and soil samples would be done onsite by another company. Richard had assured him that this would allow him to spend more time with Vivian, and work at home. It sounded great, except in the last two years he'd begun to miss the workplace and he doubted his ability to be a self-starter now. He felt so disconnected from everyone. He just wanted to be moved for a while, instead of having to generate the energy to move on his own.

"I considered it and it is a great offer. I don't know too many people that would even consider passing up such an offer, but for me right now, it would be too hard. I need to be pushed for a while. If you could give me maybe another year to get back into the swing of things, self-motivation may not be so hard. Do you understand what I am saying?"

"I believe I do understand and though I may not be able to hold off until then, I will welcome you whenever you are ready."

"Thank you Richard. Thank you for everything."

"Mason, when you thank me like that it makes me feel uncomfortable. We are family. That didn't end when Rachael passed...okay? Families are supposed to look out for one another. Sup...pos...ed to." He drew out the last two words as though he was trying to get them to stick.

Mason could hear the wry humor in his voice.

They finished their conversation with Richard referring Mason to Amanda, and giving him her office number.

"I'm going to see what's up with that custody notice. I will call you back later. If it gets too late, I will call you in the morning."

"Alright, I'll talk to you soon."

Mason laid back on his bed, hoping that Richard could talk Victoria into dropping whatever crazy scheme she had up her sleeve. He was really getting tired of her. He had worked so hard to try to keep Victoria in Vivian's life. He didn't relish the thought of keeping his daughter from her extended family, but if he had to protect her by taking her out of their lives, then he would do so. How he wished Rachael was here now. She would be able to stand up to Victoria and give her a sweet and truthful what-for.

He decided to go down and see Vivian a little sooner than he had first planned, but he called first.

"Hi hon. How are you feeling?"

"Hi Daddy! I am feeling better. I even ate all of my lunch today, but dinner was nasty. The only thing good was the applesauce. How was your lunch?"

"It was fair."

"Small town fair or too much fare?" she giggled, repeating the question either one of them responded with when the other used the word 'fair'.

"Small town fair. Just as good as a Ferris Wheel."

"That good?"

"Almost that good."

"Are you going to come back to my room today?"

"Sure, honey. Um...did your grandmother come visit you today?" He tried to keep his voice light.

"She said she had some things to do today and that she would come tomorrow. You can come. You don't have to be afraid."

"Who said I was afraid?" He was finding it even harder to keep the edge out of his voice. "I am not afraid of your grandmother, sweetie. I just know that she likes to spend time alone with you so I try to respect her space."

"Really?"

"Yes. You don't believe me?"

"Umm. Yeah." Her answer was hesitant.

"But," he said, hearing the hint of something in her voice.

"It's just that everyone else is afraid of her. Why aren't you?"

"Because she has no control over me. There is only one person in my life that can hurt me, honey, and that is you. If you ever decided that I wasn't your main man, I would be heartbroken and I don't know if I would heal." He let his smile be heard over the phone and was rewarded with a giggle from her on the other side of the receiver.

It didn't matter that the smile didn't reach his eyes or that the words were too close to home. She didn't need to know that she was the one that had the true power to break him in two. That losing her was now his only fear.

"I will be down in a minute."

*   *   *

Mason's phone rang early the next morning. Reaching for it groggily, he was instantly alert when he heard Richard's raspy voice.

"Are you alright, Richard? You don't sound too good."

"I actually don't feel that good, if you must know. I had a talk with Victoria last night and it got a bit out of hand. I don't think you have anything to worry about. I will supply you with my lawyers so expect a call in a couple of days–"

"But what is her reason for this?" Mason asked interrupting Richard.

"She believes she can give Vivian more than you, more opportunities and more gifts, but she will never be able to give Vivian the one thing she needs most because she can't give what she doesn't possess: love." The resentment dripping from the last word sent chills down Mason's spine.

"Richard, is there anything you want to share with me?" Mason wasn't even sure he wanted to know. He didn't know he was cringing as he waited until he felt his muscles begin to scream in protest.

"No son. It will all be fine. Just don't worry. You need to get better for Vivian. I will be talking to you in a couple of days, okay?

Mason didn't want to press the issue. "Okay, Richard. Take care of yourself. Vivian told me last night that you promised you would come and see her after your trip to Uganda. She is already asking me to take pictures of what is in the gift shop with my phone so she can pick out something for you."

"She is absolutely precious. Mason. You have one beautiful jewel there. Never doubt that you have more than many."

Were there tears in his voice?

"Richard?"

"I will call you in a couple of days, Mason."

The line went dead.

CHAPTER 23

*Toiletries, hair oil, body oil, flat iron, curling iron, shower cap...*Paige continued to go down the list of items on her paper, comparing them to what was present in her suitcases.

She shut the last bag, looking around her to make sure one more time that she had not left anything out. She knew that she was procrastinating, looking for any reason to stretch out this chore, but she was finally finished.

She walked into the kitchen and looked in the refrigerator. Her lunch was already made. "Humph!" She walked out to the living room, heading towards her window. She still had three hours before she needed to be at the airport and everything was packed well. There was no reason to leave this early; rush hour was over and there were very few cars on the side streets she would be taking to LAX.

This restlessness was driving her to distraction. What was she so pent up for? She was only going to answer a few questions, take a few tests...but even as she thought it, she knew that wasn't the reason for her agitation.

Of all things, of all times, and at all places...

Even as her thoughts started to dart back and forth from the present to last night, she couldn't help but give in to the memory of the conversation she had with First Lady.

Menagerie had called her in the early part of the evening with the excuse of needing the phone number of one of the members of her auxiliary. At first she had thought nothing of it, but then came the hinting questions.

"Did you enjoy yourself Sunday?"

"Sure I always enjoy service. There seemed to be a lot going on, but I credit that to Pastor's recent trip."

"And how did you enjoy fellowshipping at lunch?"

"Oh, that was nice too. Thank you for inviting me."

"Paige?"

"Yes?"

"Did I interrupt something? Did I catch you at a bad time?"

"No, just putting the finishing touches on my packing list."

"Put it down for a second. I want to talk to you."

Paige laid her paperwork down obediently, "Okay. You have my undivided attention."

"I was talking to Pam this morning and she let me know that Elder Tatum has asked to join the Visitation Ministry."

Paige, not knowing where this was going, had no comment, though she had the feeling she should.

"I was just wondering if this is something you may be aware of."

Paige frowned to herself. Why was she asking her?

"Uh…Sunday Elder Tatum did mention that he had served in the same ministry at his former church, and wondered if he could be allowed to visit the sick along with his other duties. I told him he would have to ask Pastor first. Why? Was I wrong? Did he take offense to that?"

"No, because first thing this morning he asked Pastor just that. I was wondering if there was an ulterior motive."

"Ulterior motive? I'm not following you, Lady Menagerie."

"Wow! Are you really that obtuse?"

Stung by the question, Paige was silent.

"Paige, I watched the two of you from the side door on Sunday and also at the table during fellowship. The man couldn't take his eyes off of you. Are you telling me you really didn't notice?"

Paige was taken aback. She was at a loss for words. *Elder Tatum?* But he didn't know anything about her or her, him, except what they shared in the parking lot and though it was a more pleasant exchange than their first meeting, she couldn't pull anything from it that would have made her think he was treating her with any partiality.

Menagerie took her silence as an answer.

"Oh, then maybe I am jumping to conclusions. It wouldn't be the worst thing in the world, though. What do you think about Elder Tatum? You got to talk to him for a little bit."

Paige was starting to feel trapped. What could she say? What was Menagerie looking for?

"He is very nice. He is polite and courteous. He seems to truly love the Lord and he comes across as genuine. While I am gone, I don't think it would hurt to have him fill in. We can always use the help."

"So there is no attraction there? I was almost sure I saw something on Sunday between the two of you."

"Really, Lady Menagerie? You know my situation. I don't think I have the right to have those types of feelings right now, what with the responsibility I am about to accept. I can barely see myself through to reconciling one relationship, let alone starting another one."

"True and wise you are, but I also want to make sure that it doesn't take you off guard. Is that your honest opinion of Elder Tatum?"

"That is the one I have room for," Paige said stubbornly.

"That is not what I asked you, Paige."

"Ugh. Elder Tatum is very nice looking." She paused for a moment. Yeah, that was all Menagerie was going to get on that end. "He did surprise me on Sunday. He is softer than my first impression gave him over to be, but that was probably due to my refusal to meet him. He is forgiving, I will give him that; very interesting too, but for the next few weeks to two months, I have a twelve-year-old that will need my attention and I am already shortening her time because I committed to being a living kidney donor. I just don't have time to consider it right now."

"Understood Paige. Would you be too against a game of bowling when you get back... nothing too small, about eight of us?"

Paige knew Menagerie meant well, but on this occasion she sided with Pastor Lawrence. No one really knew how Gladys was going to impact her life.

"Thank you for the invite, but I can't promise you more than that I will think about it."

"That is all I ask."

And think about it Paige had; from the moment they got off the phone until she pushed him out of her head so that she could finish her packing. Now with nothing left to do but wait, *he* was wiggling his way back into her mind. She bet Pastor Lawrence didn't know what Menagerie was up to.

She thought back to Elder Brandon Tatum inclining his head to her in church, Elder Brandon Tatum taking her keys from her and placing her things neatly in her car, Elder Tatum's long form leaning against her car, his spoken heart for God, his passion for his job, the way his shoulders blocked out the sun. She couldn't think of anything that would make Menagerie think he was interested in her, but now he was on her mind and she was having a hard time thinking of anything else. Hopefully, her time in Chicago and Atlanta would remedy this.

She continued to watch the cars pass, taking no real notice of their make or model which she sometimes did when she was working through her thoughts on her books.

She wondered if this was common for him. It didn't seem like him – not that she was even looking for something. She didn't discern any misgivings. He didn't even seem interested beyond curiosity in her job and family, both perfectly safe conversations for getting an understanding of those you would be working with.

She worked again at recalling any signs that he had hidden motives towards her. He only seemed to watch her intently when she was talking, his eyes rarely leaving her face. His answers and reactions were thoughtful, but could never be misconstrued as working with an ulterior motive. He didn't monopolize the conversation. In fact, it was as if he were waiting for her to introduce the next subject. If this was a new way of drawing in one's prey, she was unaware.

There was only one time she thought she saw uneasiness in his eyes, but that could have easily been her projecting her feelings on to him when the pastor and first lady came out of the side door. Ever since she'd had the talk with Pastor Lawrence, she felt guilty about the hurt she saw in his eyes at her failure to be more open with him about her past.

She shrugged, slightly impatient with herself at her lack of intuitiveness in these areas. She called up an image of Brandon in her mind, checking her reactions as she thought of his sloping forehead, nicely groomed black eyebrows that contrasted against his smooth cocoa colored skin; dark eyes, slightly tilted at the corners that would have been intimidating if the lashes weren't so long. The high cheekbones, more rounded than angular, and the full, lower-beveled lip made her wonder who he received most of his features from. Now that she thought about it, if it weren't for the nicely-lined mustache and goatee and the small cleft in his chin, his facial features would border more on pretty than handsome.

The rest of him was unmistakably masculine. The distance he'd kept during most of their conversation, which she was now surprised she appreciated, allowed her to watch his full body language. His broad shoulders didn't look like they came with too much effort and there was something very relaxed in the way he held himself, like he was lounging standing up. She thought about the way he stood in front of the church and it was much the same way except for the wry expression that crossed his features every now and then.

It was nice to see someone so comfortable in their own body. She had often felt cramped in hers; always reaching for something, just out of arm's length.

With this assessment of him, she found herself curious and very appreciative of his looks, but the thing that caught her interest was the passion that warmed his eyes when he talked about his work and how he was so open about his adoration for God.

Sadly, quite a few of the men she knew only spoke like that when it was their turn to do the exhortation during Sunday service.

She could tell that God was real to him, and that, she found flat out attractive. She wondered if that would be considered odd if she were ever asked what she liked most when she first met him. It sounded right to her. Why shouldn't the most beautiful thing about a man be his expression of love for God?

She'd caught his eye a few times at the table during lunch but she had also invited it, trying to make sure that he was included in at least some of the conversations.

She tried to compare it to other instances. It had been a while since she was approached, but she'd seen the last one coming – and so had her pastor. The slow assessment the man gave her when she was introduced to him had suddenly made her want to cover herself with her hands. *Ugh.* She shook her head to dislodge the mental picture.

No, she was sure Menagerie was just imagining things. If Brandon Tatum had any interest, it seemed purely platonic to her. Her final analysis made her feel the most comfortable about the entire situation than she had in the last ten hours.

She walked away from the window, taking one last, cursory glance around the living room and walked to her office to make sure there were no last minute emails she missed.

CHAPTER 24

Brandon looked at the clock on his computer for the fifth time in so many minutes. This morning was dragging out. He was just filling in reports today, a job he sometimes found tedious because he was only really doing some end of the month data entry. But today, it left too much room in his mind to wander.

Was she on the plane yet? Was she still going? When did she say she would be back? Was it closer to or further from the date of the bowling party First Lady was throwing?

He'd followed Elder Morganson's (Paige's – he rolled the name around in his head) advice and called the office the day before to ask Pastor Lawrence about the possibility of helping out on the Visitation Committee. Pastor Lawrence was in a meeting, so he was about to leave a message with Pam when she paused in mid-sentence and asked him to hold the line. He obliged her, but when the phone was reconnected it was First Lady Menagerie's voice that came across the line.

"Hello Elder Tatum. How are you doing this afternoon?"

"Quite well. How are you doing?"

"Wonderful. Is there anything I can help you with?"

"I just had a question or two about the Visitation Ministry that I wanted to run by Pastor Lawrence."

"Well I would be willing to answer any questions you have if I can."

Brandon figured if anyone besides the Pastor would know, it would be First Lady.

"I was wondering what the procedure was for helping in ministries you are not assigned to. I was talking to Elder Morganson on Sunday and she informed me that she would be going out of town. She said that they had people to cover her on the Visitation Committee but since I was on one similar to it at my former church, I was wondering if I could participate from time to time?"

"I don't see any reason why you couldn't. I will let Pastor Lawrence know and have Pam contact Sister Sanders. She will inform you of their meeting times. Was there another question?"

Brandon smiled into the phone.

"Just what time the meetings were, but I can wait. Thank you for your help and thank you for the invite to lunch on Sunday."

"You are welcome. I'm glad you could make it. Did you enjoy yourself?"

"Yes I did. Your eldership is very close, like family. I felt very welcome. Do you fellowship like that often?"

"Not as often as I'd like, but I am trying to do more with each group to maintain the close, working relationship. In fact, I already have another outing in the works. Do you bowl, Elder Tatum?"

"It has been a couple of years, but I wasn't too bad the last time I played. I think my average was something like 160-180."

"Nice. Would you be willing to come out and show some of us how it is done? It would be Friday, September 5th."

Brandon looked through his calendar on his phone.

"Yes. That sounds like it would be fun. Would it be all the same people that came on Sunday?" He was hoping she didn't see through his question.

"I am pretty sure, plus maybe two more. So what did you think of the food? Ming's is one of my favorite restaurants. Whenever I can find an excuse to go, I am there."

"I liked it. Elder Morganson suggested the ribs and they were very good, but the sweet and sour chicken was some of the best I've tasted."

"Aahhh. A sweet and sour man."

Brandon paused, his curiosity piqued.

"That's exactly what Paige, I mean Elder Morganson, said." *I am going to have to watch that...*he said to himself. "That's funny, is there a story behind that?"

Menagerie laughed a little sheepishly. "Oh, just an old joke, nothing of any significance really."

"I am really curious now. Could you tell me?"

He heard a pause on the other end of the line.

"No...I don't think it would be...appropriate at this time. I think you should wait and ask Elder Morganson."

Disappointed, Elder Tatum conceded. "Understood."

"Elder Tatum?"

"Yes?"

"I am the type of person that says what they feel – no veils, no masks, no pretense." There was another pause. Brandon felt a little apprehensive, but he kept silent.

"My husband and your father are good friends, but where he may not be able to distinguish between you two, I don't hold the same prejudice. From your recommendations and paperwork, you seem to be a man of good, moral character. That is the easy part. I would like to know what your plan is, if I may?"

Puzzled, Brandon responded. "Plan?"

"Yes. I am asking you what your plans are regarding your ministry? Is your time here a stepping stone for something else? Is it your intention to stay?"

"Hmmm…" His mind raced. *What brought this on?* He took a breath to help compose himself. "Honestly, I am open to where this path leads." He cleared his throat, organizing his thoughts.

"I just made a few, big transitions in my life. I changed my job, I moved to another state and with that, not choosing to go back home. I live in a city where, until a month ago, I knew three people; your husband, you, and your daughter. I left my church family to be transplanted here. I just finished with a plan. Right at this very moment, I am just extremely grateful to know beyond a shadow of a doubt that this is where I am supposed to be." He took a breath, confident and pleased that he was able to express himself so clearly.

"Meaning no disrespect whatsoever, if that isn't what you were looking for, I don't know what else to tell you. I am just looking forward to learning here. Not just in this ministry or this location, but in this part of my life." He shrugged with the last of the sentence, even though he knew she wouldn't be able to see it.

As the silence thickened, he wondered if he had offended her with the last sentence. He was preparing to apologize when she spoke.

"Thank you, Elder Tatum. I appreciate your honesty. May I ask you another question?"

"Mmmm…Sure."

"Was it very hard, making that transition?"

"No. Not once I knew which way to go." He stopped, wondering if she was more intuitive than he could discern. Well, there was only one way to find out.

"I find that in my relationship with God, I don't have the luxury of moving and just hoping I got it right. I'm in a place where the hardest part is remaining quiet enough to hear him correctly and staying still long enough to get the whole story. Once I have it, most of the work is over."

"But your friends and family relationships, what do you do with them? Are they not also important?"

The question immediately put him on the defense and he had to work his mouth to relax his jaw. He dispelled a breath, reminding himself that this woman didn't know him well and couldn't know how many arguments started in his family with the same question.

He switched his phone to the other ear, consciously using the movement to cool himself, but subconsciously hoping to better hear the meaning behind her words.

"Well, technology is awfully funny that way," he replied, working at keeping his voice light and nonchalant. "It allows you to talk and see each other from distances these days."

He was met with silence…again. *So much for that.* He started again.

"My friends and family are extremely important to me. I love them very much and I discussed my decision with each one of them. They knew this move wasn't going to be easy for me. After their initial denial and questions, most of them realized it was something I couldn't deny."

"May I ask you a personal question?"

"Those weren't?" He tried to keep a teasing tone in his voice.

She ignored his reply, choosing to take it as a sign of compliance.

"Did you leave anyone significant in Florida?"

What! What kind of question was this? Did he look the type? What could he have done to prompt her to ask this kind of question?

A light went off in his head. *Ohhhh. This was a scouting mission.* He stood up, beginning to pace up and down the length of his small hall.

"First Lady Menagerie." He hoped the use of her title would help his answer to register with all the seriousness he felt. "I consider all of my family and friends significant to my well-being, to my life, but if what you are asking me is if I left a woman or girlfriend in Florida, the answer is no." There was no longer any hint of humor in his voice.

"Elder Tatum, I appreciate your patience with my line of questioning. I wanted to get to know you better. I know sometimes etiquette suggests more subtle means, but I have never been known to be subtle when I want a question answered. Now that you have been so gracious and honest. *I* want to welcome you to *my* Skylight Temple family. I really think you are going to like it here…oh it looks like I have another call. Was there any other questions you had?"

"Ummm, no. Thank you."

"You are very welcome. I will see you later on this week at service, alright? Have a good evening."

"Uh, you too."

Brandon shook his head, still trying to catch up with her last few sentences. They had taken on the characteristics of a spinning top. Not wanting to dwell on the conversation, he walked to his bedroom, picked up his jacket, and went to have dinner in a very loud sports bar and grill. He knew the atmosphere would keep him distracted long enough to allow some of the feeling of anxiousness and excitement to ebb.

Now as he thought back on that odd ending, he was beginning to form some questions of his own.

He sighed, shifting another piece of paper from the 'in' to the 'out' pile, glancing at the clock again. It was only five minutes later.

The phone at his desk rang and he picked it up on the first ring, welcoming any work that would distract him from the hazel-eyed beauty.

"Why didn't you call?" Dominy's voice came on the line as soon as he answered.

"Ugh. Is this a conspiracy? What do you want, Dominy?"

A low whistle came from the receiver. "Wow…who's been grating on your nerves? I almost feel unwelcome."

"What do you want, Dominy?"

"That's it. I am going out right now and buy myself another friend. I wonder where your receipt is, because I think you are broken."

"Warranty expired. Why do you think I haven't replaced you?"

"What's going on?"

"Nothing. Just feeling tired. I didn't sleep too well last night." *Ah, why did I mention sleep?* He could already hear it…

"Are you still having the dreams? Did you get to talk to her on Sunday? Is she a fantasy or real?"

Brandon groaned to himself. This was going to be one, very long day.

CHAPTER 25

"That is not the answer I'm looking for, Marvin." Victoria tapped impatiently on the small kitchen counter.

"I don't see why you are having such a hard time fulfilling this one little request."

"There are some new developments. Mr. Jenson has representation – good representation. It isn't going to be a quick win."

"What do you mean 'good representation'? How could he…" She stopped in mid-sentence, a feeling of dread washing over her. It was quickly replaced by a heat burning in the back of her eyes. Her voice was barely a rough whisper when she spoke again.

"Who is his representation, Marvin?"

There was a long pause.

"Who Marvin? Don't make me ask again."

"Felix and Houghan."

The name was like a flare being thrown on gasoline. The blaze behind her eyes lit everything in the room, turning it into a red haze. She bit her lip hard, trying to keep some composure.

The feeling of betrayal caused bile to rise in her throat so thick, she walked over to the sink and hovered there momentarily, waiting to see if it would continue its journey out of her mouth.

He was lending his lawyers to that scum against her. This was what it felt like to have everyone turn on you.

Richard had crossed the line. She had spent all day yesterday going over their conversation from the night before, and though she didn't think she was wrong for wanting to give Vivian every opportunity her money could provide, she was willing to listen. But now…what was left? Had he decided not to wait for her answer? How was she supposed to forgive him for this?

"You still there?"

"Yes. Let's move on." He didn't need to know any more than what he'd found out for her.

"Were you successful? Were you able to get any leads on a donor?"

"Um, yes…and no."

"Don't play with me, Marvin. I am not in the mood and I have never felt less obliging. What are you saying?"

"We found three on the list that would have matched. One passed away last spring, and the other declined. She is pregnant." He stopped there.

Oh, he was really going to push her. Did he not understand the state his last information had put her in?

"Marvin...so help me...if you don't quit being a punk and give me the rest of the story, I am going to find out whatever miserable excuse for an office you work out of and I will have it burnt to the ground..."

She paused to make her point stronger. "...with you in it. Now, you are an informant. Give me. The information I asked for."

"The third was Paige Morganson."

The room started to spin with a sickening tilt. She hadn't heard that name in – what had it been – six or seven years.

Well, the little girl had signed up to be a donor. She was probably trying to redeem herself and find a way to relieve herself of the guilt; pathetic thing. She had no idea what Victoria was capable of.

"And?"

"And...I had one of my men speak to her and lead her on a wild goose chase."

"Alright. So where is she headed to?"

There was a long pause.

"Marvin. I believe I am at the end of my rope here. I don't think I will be needing-"

"It looks like your husband was also looking for a match and he came upon her name as well," he said it with the rush of one breath. "The reason why I was blowing up your phone yesterday was because I found out that she is coming into town today to meet with a caseworker at the hospital."

"What!? Please tell me you are kidding. No, never mind, don't say anything. I want you to get in touch with that case worker and cancel the appointment. I will take care of the Morganson woman."

There was a brief pause.

"Marvin?"

"Yes?"

"After you talk to the caseworker, lose my number. I am no longer in need of your services. Oh, and Marvin, you will do what I ask or the severance package you are in need of, you know the charges with the minor you need dropped, will hang you. I will see to it. Goodbye, Marvin."

She hung up the phone and walked into the bedroom so that she could get dressed.

If the Morganson woman couldn't meet with the caseworker, she might try to contact Mason and her granddaughter and Victoria had to make sure that didn't happen.

She thought of how she could intercept this woman so as to discourage her without actually coming face to face with her. This would take a little planning, but she was very low on time. Maybe she could warn the women at the nurse's station to send the Morganson woman away if she made it up to the 5th floor.

She could feel the dread that had come over her earlier begin to absorb under her skin. She shook it off, not ready to give into the uneasiness. She had worked too hard for it to come to not.

CHAPTER 26

Paige stepped out of the elevator. Her stomach, already a breeding ground for butterflies, didn't fare any better with the sterile smell of the hospital floor. She walked forward to the nurse's station, taking deep breaths to calm herself. She stood at the counter, quietly waiting to be recognized. To her left, a woman's moans caught her attention and she watched through a doorway as the woman was being moved from her bed onto a gurney. She began silently praying for comfort and healing for the woman.

She turned back to see the nurse patiently smiling at her. "May I help you?"

Paige tried to mimic the smile through her nervousness. She cleared her throat noisily. "I am here to see Mason Jenson and Amanda Carter. I was directed up here. I believe he is visiting his daughter, Vivian, in room 538B. May I go ahead in?"

"And you are?" the nurse asked quizzically.

"I...um." Her nerve was failing her. She held onto the counter to keep from bolting back through the elevator. "I'm here to..." She cleared her throat again. "I am Paige Morganson, the donor."

The nurse's face broke into a grin. "You are the woman who responded to little Vivian's need for a kidney? It is wonderful for you to come. I know she would like to meet you but because she is a minor, I am afraid you will have to meet with the father first."

"Okay. I have a meeting with the caseworker today."

"Oh yeah. No problem. Mr. Jenson just went down to the cafeteria. He should be back soon. You can wait in the waiting room over there," she said, while pointing off towards a small room to the left.

Paige smiled her "thank you" and went to sit and wait.

This was torture. She wanted to turn tail and run. She had so many opportunities to back down and oh how she wanted to, but this was a promise she made, even if it was over a decade ago, and she wasn't going to break it now.

As she sat there, the thoughts of the last time she was in a hospital waiting room came back to her sharp and clear. She had been asked by her pastor to visit the sick on occasion and after the initial fear of what it might be like to enter a hospital again, she was pleasantly surprised to learn that when she was praying and concentrating on others, the memories were not overpowering.

She sucked her teeth at her lack of thought. She began to gather up her belongings. Surely the nurse would not object to her going around to the different rooms, minus Vivian's of course, to pray with the patients until Mr. Jenson came back. Still deep in thought, she stood, glancing around her to check that she didn't forget something. She turned forward taking a step into someone before she could halt her movement. As she bounced off of them, she began juggling and shifting her things to keep them from slipping from her hands. Hands came out to help right her and her small pile. She looked up to thank the person for their help, but the words along with the beginning of a smile were frozen on her lips as she stared into the face of the most ruggedly-beautiful man she had ever seen.

*　　　　*　　　　*

When Mason came off of the elevator the nurse at the front desk directed him to the waiting room, giving him the message that the donor had arrived. His nervousness heightened. He chastised himself. *Don't get your hopes up too high. Just see it for what it is: a chance.*

He covered the distance quickly then forced himself to slow down and take a few, deep breaths. As he reached the doorway he scanned the room, stopping at the sight of the back of a woman. He watched her, trying to assess her and find out anything he could before she had a chance to put on airs. She seemed to be gathering her things. Did she change her mind? Was she leaving? *No, she couldn't leave!* The panic that rose up in his chest cut off his air supply.

As she stood he noticed her small stature, wondering fleetingly if she would even be strong enough to donate a kidney. He took a step forward, misjudging the distance between them and her agility. Her shoulder bounced off of his rib cage causing what remaining air there was, to leave him. He reached out to keep her from falling and dropping her load, but was not prepared for his reaction to her face.

He took in the glassy, black eyebrows, shaping wide-set and deep, hazel-brown eyes which stirred something deep within him in that instant. Her olive complexion caused her lashes to stand out, framing her eyes delicately, but there was something vaguely familiar about her face on a whole. It was beautiful, but it caught him off guard.

151

His body went fever hot, then ice cold as a chill raced down his back. He shivered but still said nothing. He watched her eyes widen and her lips part slightly, and the thought that crossed his mind made him feel ashamed. This sobered him up immediately. Afraid she could read his thoughts from his expression, he tried for his most pleasant tone in order to distract her.

"Sorry. Are you alright?" Mistaking her lack of response for fear, he apologized again.

"I didn't mean to startle you."

It could have been five seconds or five minutes that she stood there awe-struck. Then just as everything had stopped, it all started again. All of her senses came into play at the same time, threatening to overwhelm her. She took in the big, deep-set eyes, high cheekbones and angular jawline. He smelled of vanilla and mint, and the hand that was helping her keep her things off the ground had found hers under her jacket. She watched his mouth move, but it still took a moment for the words to register once she could hear them over the loud beating of her heart in her ears.

"Sorry. Are you alright? I didn't mean to startle you."

Get it together Paige. Snap out of it…and say something before he mistakes you for a runaway patient!

"Oh, umm, fine. I'm fine. Thank you," she said, taking a step back and tearing her gaze away from his.

She tried to concentrate on her things, but was still very aware of the hand still on hers. She stepped back again, this time out of his reach. Taking a few deep breaths to gain her composure, she feigned complete preoccupation with her belongings until she felt she could trust herself to look at him again. She squared her shoulders, steadying herself and this time when she looked up, she was the perfect picture of cool reserve.

"Are you Paige Morganson?"

She nodded. "Yes," remembering her voice.

"I'm Mason Jenson, Vivian's dad." He held out his hand.

So that she wouldn't have to touch him again, she shifted her things making it look too awkward to reach out to him.

It would have worked, but he reached out to help her right her items again, brushing her arms, sending electricity through her in the process. She dropped everything, but stood still as he mumbled apologies yet again, and stooped to pick up her purse, coat, hat, umbrella, and satchel full of references; something she had packed just in case he asked for more information.

"You come prepared, don't you?" he said, straightening while trying to avoid putting too much pressure on his bad ankle.

"I try, but you can never be too sure with this weather. Chicago is so unpredictable. I have gotten stuck at O'Hare quite a few times, so I tend to overdo it when I come here."

"Where are you staying, or are you staying?" He placed her umbrella and hat in her satchel then handed it to her along with the coat and purse. Then put his too warm-hands in his pockets. She smiled wryly, berating herself for being so clumsy.

"Yes. I am staying at the hotel on Mannheim Road." The name escaped her. "I am not good with names and I have not visited here enough to be familiar with the regular hotels."

He frowned slightly. "You just said you have gotten stuck in Chicago quite a few times."

"I've gotten stuck at *O'Hare Airport* quite a few times, usually when I had a layover though. I have only stayed in Chicago a couple of times. It isn't usually on my circuit."

"Circuit...you said you were a writer. You speak too?"

She nodded, allowing the interrogation. If it was her daughter, she would want to know everything she could about the person she was getting an organ from too.

"Does it keep you traveling a lot?"

"Not if I can help it. I would say about three months out of the year."

He made a low whistle. "Is it spread out throughout the year or is there a certain season?"

She shrugged. "It is a little of both. There are some annual engagements, but the rest depends on my manager and how much I fight her." The side of her mouth raised in a quirky smile, which he thought was endearing. It distracted him and there was a small lull in the conversation.

"Do you want to continue these questions with Vivian?"

He shook his head quickly. "No. Not just yet. I would rather wait. There are offices downstairs. I am sure they will let us use one for just this purpose. I spoke to Amanda, the caseworker, and she told me where to go. Do you mind?"

"Will Amanda be joining us?" She sounded too hopeful.

"Um...actually I was surprised you came. I thought she told me that you had called in to reschedule or cancel your appointment with her, but maybe it was the opposite."

"I missed my transfer and it caused me to fall behind a few hours. I would have checked my messages, but I went straight to the hotel and went to sleep. When I woke up I found out that my cell battery was dead so I never got the message. Should I call her and make another appointment with the both of you?"

"No, I have some time and some questions. If it wouldn't be too much of an inconvenience, we can go down to the areas designated for interviewing and get started with the process. Tomorrow or later today, if she is available, you can meet with Amanda."

Paige inclined her head in agreement. "I already set aside the time for this today and tomorrow. I am available and willing to answer your questions the best I can."

He watched her chin come up, noting her earnest annunciation of the last sentence.

She seems pretty honest. Mason thought to himself as they walked towards the elevator. Yet, there was one thing that kept bothering him.

"Mrs. Morganson, when I arrived at the waiting room you looked like you were packing up to go. Had you changed your mind? I need to know before we go any further." He turned towards her as the elevator doors opened and he motioned for her to step in.

As the doors closed, Paige couldn't help feeling a little trapped. How much was she supposed to tell him about her life, personal and otherwise?

Was he always so intimidating and … big? She felt on the verge of panicking. *Girl, get a hold of yourself and calm down. One breath at a time. One breath at a time. One…*

"Mrs. Morganson. Are you okay? You are starting to look a little pale."

"Ms. Morganson." She corrected him. "I am not married, but it is safer to let people think so especially when I am traveling alone." As the elevator began its descent, she concentrated on the movement to help calm her. "I wasn't leaving. I'm just not all that comfortable in hospital waiting rooms. I thought if I visited some of the patients and prayed with them, it would get my mind off of…of…my nervousness until you came back."

"Do you do that often?" He turned back to stare at the elevator doors, keeping his voice even.

"Do what?"

"Go around praying for sick people."

"Mmmm. Not as often as I wish. I used to do it more before I started traveling. I am part of a visitation committee at my church and we would go and visit different hospitals in our community."

"Did you know any of the patients?"

"Sometimes, but mostly they were people who reminded me of my mom, my dad, my sister, maybe my niece or a good friend. I always figured that, since I would want someone to come and pray for them if they were in that situation, and I couldn't get to them, that I would do the same."

"Interesting."

"'Interesting'?" She turned to look at him.

"What do you pray for a person you don't even know? Shouldn't that be reserved for their family or friends? Someone who has an idea of what they are going through?"

Paige looked up, searching his eyes for an answer even as she asked the question. "Mr. Jenson, are you saved? I mean, are you a Christian? Do you believe in God?"

The elevator door opened, but she didn't move. She waited, watching a host of expressions cross his features. Surprise, confusion, sadness and a ghost of something she couldn't quite place. *Was it disgust?* Why would such a question provoke such intense emotions?

Now it was Mason that felt uncomfortable and a little intimidated. He was transported right back to one of the many discussions he'd had with his wife and it made him defensive. He raised his chin slightly, reigning in his feelings.

"Why?"

"I need to know how to answer your question so that you can understand."

"Why don't you give me both versions?"

A doctor came into the elevator, drawing their attention away from the conversation. Once again, Mason motioned for Paige to go first, but this time she caught a smirk playing at the side of his mouth.

She walked out and stepped aside so that he could lead the way to one of the examining offices set aside for patients and families working with donors.

She was relieved to find that it was more of a cubical in a bigger office than a closed-in room. Separating the chairs as far as the small space would allow, Mason sat down facing Paige, his long legs eating up the space between them.

"Okay. Enlighten me." Mason invited with a crossing of both arms and legs.

Paige took her time placing her things on the desk next to her, gathering her thoughts, praying for the right words.

"Mr. Jenson. I believe we are all connected. Whether it be through blood, social status, religion, or culture. If we talk to one another, we will find something in common. From the love a mother has for her child and the way she nurtures that child, to how we face and comfort each other in crisis; that is why I have the confidence to pray to God for the peace, comfort, healing, saving grace, and the gift of salvation for people I may have never shared a word with. It is the compassion of Jesus Christ that even allows me to stand, let alone want to pray for others. It is the unselfish love of God that would compel me to want to be like Christ in every way so that no matter how scared or nervous, I would still say 'yes' to a call, fly into one of the coldest places I know and offer a part of me to a child I don't know, just so that their family doesn't have to experience the heartbreak of living without them."

Speechless, Mason watched as this woman's face lit up with an expression of joy mixed with the closest thing he'd seen to love, outside of his wife and daughter. She actually believed what she said.

Amazing.

For his daughter's sake, he wanted to believe that she wasn't a fanatic. It also would have been a shame for such a pretty woman to be so far above reality.

"So…Mr. Jenson. I answered your question. Will you answer mine?"

"And what is that?"

"Do you believe in God?"

"Does it matter?

Paige shrugged. "God's existence doesn't rely on whether or not you believe in Him, but yours does. For your sake, I would say it does matter, but first things first. Whether you don't believe in God or don't believe it matters," she slowed her speech, trying to calm herself, "I was wondering who has been praying for your little girl, because I go where God calls me."

Mason stared at her. He was slightly taken aback. He wasn't used to such…arrogance. It was unnerving.

His wife became very matter-of-fact with her relationship with God, especially towards the end of her life. After days and months of asking and pleading for him to join her in a bible study class or church service, she became thoughtfully quiet about his relationship with God, but resolved in hers. It didn't cause him to completely change his mind about God, but he didn't mind His "presence" so much since it made his wife so happy.

"What are you? A soldier for God? A messenger, a prophet?" he sneered, his defenses going up.

Paige looked down, masking the hurt in her eyes. "No, Mr. Jenson. I am just a child of God who loves people." She looked up to stare back at him and shrugged again. "And that includes everyone."

Now that reminded him of Rachael.

Against his better judgment, he was intrigued.

CHAPTER 27

They continued with the interview; him asking her questions about her family history that she could recall, followed by her touring schedule. She answered more questions about her ministry, her books, her family relationships, and then the question she was expecting and fearing.

"Do you have any children?"

She thought it ironic and slightly funny that two weeks ago, she would have easily answered "no," but in two days, she was going to see her daughter and if she wanted a future with her. It was time to start being truthful with herself.

"Yes. I have a daughter, but she currently lives with my sister."

Even as she finished the sentence she saw the curiosity in his eyes, and knew she may have to tell the whole story. Was she ready to tell a stranger about the best and worst part of her life? *What would he do with it?* Then she thought, *What could he do with it?*

She waited, not offering any more information, just watching the wheels turn. She was surprised it was taking him this long to ask the next question. He seemed hesitant.

Mason received a great deal more from her expressions than he did from her answers. He was still not sure she was being honest, but her eyes were so open, they told him what she couldn't seem to in words.

He wasn't used to this process and, if he was going to be truthful, it actually wasn't his job. But he was impatient; if she wasn't going to be a candidate, the sooner he knew the better.

Meanwhile, he found her fascinating. He was having trouble asking the questions that he had been going over and over again throughout the afternoon. Her answers were so direct; he found it refreshing. *Finally, someone without an ulterior motive, plotting, or scheming…at least that is how she looked.*

He could tell his last question wasn't a surprise, but she was not too generous with information. He saw the pain flash ever so briefly in her eyes and wondered if she was dealing with some type of custody battle. It caused him to hesitate in asking why, but he was growing more curious about this woman and that made him uneasy. He didn't want to care, but he told himself that for his daughter's sake, he needed to get the whole story.

"May I ask why your daughter is with your sister?" He seemed uncomfortable, like he didn't want to ask the question or didn't want to hear the answer.

All of a sudden, she wanted to calm whatever assumption he had jumped to. She wanted to comfort him more than she cared about what the answer would do to her mentally.

"My daughter, Gladys, lives with my sister because when she was born, I wasn't able to care for her. My sister promised to raise her as her own until I was able to do so. In fact, I am going to see her in a couple of days. This meeting with you was a detour on my way to Atlanta to visit with her for a few days while my sister takes a vacation with her husband."

She looked away from him, finding the next words hard to speak out loud let alone in front of someone else.

"If things go well, she will come home with me after a little while."

She took a deep breath trying to slow her racing heart. She rubbed her palms against her pant legs to dry them and raised her eyes once again to meet his now intense gaze.

"If you decide that you may still want me as a donor, I will have to rearrange some things of course, but I am willing. If it is at all possible, could you let me know before I go to Atlanta on Friday so that I can proceed accordingly?"

"You seem to have a lot going on. Would you be able to go through with the pre-op, surgery, give yourself the necessary time to heal, and deal with your family issues?" He placed his elbows on his thighs, rubbing his hands along his face. "I am not going to kid you. I am desperate." He raised himself up, his face looking haggard all of a sudden; vulnerable and tired, but his eyes kept the same intensity.

"But I will end this right now if I have any reservations about you seeing this through. I am not going to give my child hope only to have it dashed and I will not waste time with you when I can be looking for someone else."

Paige stared at him, noting that she had unconsciously begun leaning back in her chair as his voice gained emotion. She was almost rearing back on two legs by the time he was finished. She forced herself to sit straight. She hoped when she spoke, her voice would ring with the conviction she felt in her heart.

She wanted to help; to be able to help this man who obviously loved his daughter very much. Who intimidated her with his size, mesmerized her with the intensity of his gaze, and scared her with the feelings he evoked in her just by being in close proximity of her. This man who, if it wasn't for that love, would have her cowering in the corner of the cubicle.

"I know that my answer has caused you to doubt my conviction, as you put it, but I wouldn't have come knowing what I do if I didn't think I could fulfill my promise. I knew before I got here that this wasn't going to be easy. Even if I didn't have a new chapter unfolding in my life it would be a challenge, but I am up for it."

She took a deep breath waiting for his reply, watching resolve wash over his face. His eyes now clear and his jaw set, he seemed to be looking for something from her, but she didn't know what it was. She was about to ask when he responded.

"Why did you decide to become a donor?"

Here it was. The question that would make or break this interview. It was inevitable, and she would answer it honestly. If she was to be this child's kidney donor it would be decided right now, and she would have peace with the outcome.

"There are two reasons, and I am going to ask you to save your judgment until after I give you both."

He nodded.

"I originally registered as a living kidney donor to bring closure to a situation in my life. It was one of the ways I forgave myself for some of the behaviors and unresolved issues I had at that time." She took a breath hoping that he would let it go at that.

"Now, I am here because I have a twelve-year-old daughter, who I would try to move heaven and earth to keep happy and healthy. If the tables were turned, I would hope that the person I was sitting across from would not only keep their word, but understand how much of my life would end if she died."

She resisted the urge to break eye contact. She wanted him to know that she was resolute in what she was saying and that he was also gaining a confidant.

She waited as he studied her, feeling more like a specimen than a person. Then he blinked and she was released. She didn't know she was holding her breath until he looked away, and she clutched the sides of the chair to steady herself as she took a deep breath to clear the foggy sensation.

"So…Can you meet me here tomorrow, at the same time? I will introduce you to Vivian. I accept your offer to be my daughter's donor."

He stood up to shake her hand and she clenched her teeth as she placed her hand in his. She worked on, ignoring the way his palm swallowed hers up, the warm and slightly rough edges of the side of his hand, and the unmistakable heat that was crawling up her arm. She pulled her hand from his grasp as quickly as she could without bringing attention to how his touch unnerved her.

She began collecting her belongings in order to keep her hands and her mind busy. *Really! What is wrong with you?*

Heat began to creep up her neck to her ears. She could feel him watching her while he waited for her to get everything in hand. The cubicle seemed to be getting smaller with each breath she took. She needed to get out of there.

Mason watched her as she turned to pick up her purse. He could hear her breathing in the quiet room, and it was starting to come and go quickly. She seemed agitated, but for the life of him he couldn't understand why.

He stepped closer to see if she needed help.

"Do you want me to help you with anything?"

"No. I've got it." She responded quickly trying, not to jump at the close proximity of his body to hers.

She closed her eyes, swallowing at the lump in her throat. She changed the position of her satchel, letting it ride on her hip so that she would have to be given a wider girth of room to get by him.

Mason stepped back noticing that she had stopped moving. He walked slowly around the cubicle, maintaining a short distance in case she needed help.

He held the door for her. "When you get to your hotel could you give me a call?" He took out his wallet, withdrawing a card and handing it to her. "I want to make sure you get back safely and once you talk to Amanda, we can discuss what time to meet tomorrow."

It was much cooler in the hallway and the peaked feeling was retreating, allowing her to regain composure. She looked up, craning her neck slightly. His expression was anxious.

Paige forced a reassuring smile to her lips and took a deep breath.

"Thank you very much for your time, Mr. Jenson. I will call you to let you know I got back to my hotel safely, and I will see you and your daughter tomorrow."

"No, Ms. Morganson. Thank you. I will be waiting for your call."

As he watched her turn to walk away, he clenched his teeth so that he wouldn't say anything to interrupt or delay her departure, even though that was the very thing he wanted her to do.

Why had she acted so oddly those last few moments? What was such a beautiful woman doing traveling alone, offering up an organ? And why was she so distracting?

Her demeanor, her honesty, her expressive eyes – beautiful, expressive eyes – were magnetic and if he hadn't forced himself to continuously think of his daughter and her well-being, he would have made up a few dozen more questions to ask this woman just so he could spend more time with her at that close desk.

Paige could feel him watching her as she walked away. She resisted the urge to turn around or hasten her steps. She was going to coolly and calmly walk down the hall, around the corner and out of the lobby. She would then hail a cab, try and remember the name of her hotel, and not think of this man until she reached the safe haven of her room.

She repeated every step until she was sitting on the bed of her hotel room. She took Mr. Jenson's card out of her pocket and dialed the number. He picked up on the third ring.

"Hello, Mr. Jenson? Yes, I just wanted to give you a call and let you know that I made it to my hotel safely."

"That didn't take long. You must be very close. Very well. How would you like to handle tomorrow?"

"Well, I was thinking that I would call Amanda and make an appointment with her. She can call you to give you the time and I will see all of you tomorrow."

There was a pause.

"Um…well if that is the way you want to do it..."

"I think it would be more efficient and less personal that way. I don't want to keep bothering you with all of the calls. I will just see you tomorrow. Okay?"

Another pause.

"Alright, Ms. Morganson. I will see you tomorrow."

"Goodnight, Mr. Jenson," Paige said in her most professional voice as possible then pressed the end button.

CHAPTER 28

Brandon sat in Dr. Connor's oncology office only half-listening to the directions he was being given for the anti-nausea medicine, pain reliever, and four other drugs he was being prescribed to help him cope with the side-effects of the chemo and radiation he would be taking.

"Are you listening, Mr. Tatum?" The doctor watched him as he came back to the present then looked over at Dominy sitting in the chair beside him.

Dominy turned to Brandon, seeing the glazed look in his eyes, he turned back to the doctor. "It's alright, I will make sure everything you say is written down and heeded. That is why I am here."

"Are you in the same household?" The doctor asked, sounding slightly uncomfortable.

Dominy, still looking at Brandon, wiggled his eyebrows, bringing a small smile to Brandon's lips.

"For now." Then he turned back to the doctor. "I have just as long as my wife says I have. Not a day longer, so I am hoping that your prescription list won't be too much longer otherwise I will spend the whole time writing."

The doctor looked back at Brandon, who shrugged, a tolerant look plastered on his face.

"Moral support. Don't worry; he is taking this far worse than I am and much more seriously. Shall we continue?"

The doctor glanced back and forth between them, warily, then looked back down at his paperwork.

"If the chemo and radiation are not successful, surgery at this point is still an option, but I urge you to consider it sooner rather than later."

Brandon's face went stony. Surgery was not something he was willing to consider again. He wanted to wait as long as possible before he took any type of sick leave or told his family that he was out of remission.

"I understand." Brandon couldn't seem to dredge up any feeling. *What was wrong with him?* "Where is the treatment center?"

"Both of your treatments can be taken here at this facility. Here is the schedule for the fractionated-dose chemotherapy." He lifted the paper up from the folder to show it to Brandon. He leaned forward to hand it to him, but Brandon couldn't seem to make himself move forward to cover the space between them.

"Thank you." Dominy leaned forward, taking the paper from the doctor, studying it for a moment and then handing it back.

He took the paperwork for the external beam radiation as well, giving it a scan and returning it.

"Mr…Elder Tatum, are you alright?" the doctor asked, showing real concern.

Brandon cleared his throat, forcing himself to respond.

"Um…yes. Just a feeling of déjà vu I was trying to avoid. Are we almost done then?"

"Yes, unless you have any questions."

Brandon shook his head and looked at Dominy.

"Do you have any?"

"Sorry. Not a one."

Brandon looked back at the doctor and shrugged.

Dominy drove them back to the apartment after stopping off at the pharmacy, grocery store, and video rental store.

"So what was that back at the center? Are you alright?"

He glanced over at Brandon, who had partially reclined his seat and was looking out of the window.

Brandon shrugged, feeling more tired than he had in a very long time.

"Oh no you don't, man. I know that look and I am not going to spend the next few weeks serving you at some pity party. Get it over and done with and then we can have some fun poisoning you again."

Brandon didn't move. He knew Dominy was pulling out all of the stops. He just needed a few hours to reconnect with himself. Just enough time to prepare himself for the fight of his life, again.

"Alright. One glass of Ensure for you and one glass of Moscato for me." Dominy emerged from the kitchen with two glasses in hand, gave one to Brandon who was sitting on the couch and then walked over to sit on the edge of the recliner.

He made a really loud sound like a buzzer, and Brandon looked up at him quizzically.

"Time's up. I let you mope through the shopping, the ride home, dinner, and the first movie. It is over. I am not even going to threaten to leave you if you don't stop because I know it won't work, but I won't stand for it either. Besides, I think it is time for my payment."

Brandon became skeptical.

"Awww. Well at least that is better than 'lost in space' man. Now, I have been sensitive – to a degree, helpful – very helpful." He stood up and started pacing.

"I have been patient, painfully so, and I have been quiet, for me. I believe that entitles me to a question or two, or three, or..."

Brandon interrupted him. "What do you want, Dom?"

"I want to know how it went with Paige."

"You don't call her Paige. You call her Elder Morganson," Brandon said with warning edging his voice.

He saw Dominy's lifted brow, took a deep breath, and gave up. He was just going to bother him until he got what he wanted, anyway. Dominy was incorrigible that way.

"Fine, what do you want to know?" He shifted himself on the couch so that he was lying across the full length of it.

"I want to know if you took my advice on Sunday and spoke to her?"

"Man, you are worse than my sisters."

"You told your sisters about her?" Dominy asked incredulous, his voice going up an octave.

"No. I was talking about your love for gossip."

"It's not gossip if you ask the person directly. Now stop stalling and answer the question."

"Yes I did speak to her on Sunday. Matter of fact, we ended up talking in the parking lot after service."

He saw her face before him, her eyes squinted with laughter, her hands telling a story as she spoke, her suit lighting up her complexion...

A slow whistle interrupted his train of thought.

"Wow. That good, huh?"

Brandon looked over to see Dominy shaking his head.

"Are you still dreaming about her?"

Brandon placed the back of his hand on his forehead and turned his gaze to the ceiling.

"I will take that as a 'Yes'. Is it the same dream?"

Brandon shook his head. "No. I let the other one play out." He shrugged, trying to act nonchalant so that Dominy wouldn't be able to tell how much it still affected him.

"Now it is just pictures scrolling, like a slide show, but each one is of her laughing, smiling, or smirking. Just her, in varying degrees of mirth. I'm thinking it is just one way my subconscious is telling me that she can't be taken too seriously."

An odd cough, sounding more like a stifled guffaw came from Dominy. "You do, do you? You are a piece of work. Okay. Go ahead. Tell me what you talked about."

"Not a great deal. We talked about our ministries, our jobs, Florida compared to California." He tried to make it sound light and superficial.

There was silence in the room; deafening silence. He snuck a glance at Dominy and right then, he knew he had failed.

"Quit playing around, Brandon. You know you can't hide your expressions from me so you might as well lay it all straight. If you don't tell me the truth, I will have to find it out for myself. Save us both some trouble and embarrassment, and tell me what I want to know."

"Psh. What would you do?" As soon as the question was out of his mouth, he was sorry.

"You wouldn't dare," he said reading the expression on Dominy's face.

"Does your church make visitors stand up and tell where they are from?"

"Don't play Dom..."

"I wonder if anyone knows her by her first name." Dominy sat back down on the recliner, laying back. "I wonder-"

"Fine...fine...fine." Brandon sat up, turning to Dominy. "I will tell you about Sunday, but you have to keep your mouth shut and you can't jump to any conclusions. None, Dominy." Brandon warned, waiting for a response.

Dominy gave him a look that made it clear that he was growing impatient but he was willing to agree.

Brandon thought about it for a moment. He was sure he was going to regret this, but honestly he did want Dominy's opinion.

One hour, eight questions, and three warnings later, Brandon had relayed his entire conversation with Paige in the parking lot before the elder's lunch, after it, and the full dream.

Brandon sat on the edge of the couch, his hands together, elbows resting on his thighs, waiting for a response from Dominy.

After a few moments, Dominy pressed his lips together then sucked his teeth.

"So what do you think of her? Honestly this time, Brandon."

"I find her fascinating to watch. She is definitely interesting, beautiful, and her obvious love for people and what she does makes her...attractive." He'd said more than enough.

"Well...that's a good start I guess," Dominy said flippantly.

Brandon frowned.

"Okay. I will try not to be hard on you, but honestly I have good news and bad news for you concerning this woman."

Brandon took a deep breath, expelling it slowly.

"Man, this is not the inquisition. Calm down. Now, bad news first. Well, actually it isn't really that bad, it-"

"Dom!" Brandon yelled, completely on edge.

"You have had two conversations with her and you remembered everything: what she wore, her expressions, her smiles – which you are counting by the way – some of her hand movements when she talked, what she talked about and you have offered to help out in the ministry she is a part of when she is out of town." He paused to look at Brandon squarely. "Are you kidding me? You don't know how you feel about her yet?"

"Huh?"

"Sorry. I keep forgetting that you are emotionally inept." Brandon opened his mouth to make a comment, but Dominy interrupted him.

"Back to the good and bad news. The bad news is…you are well on your way to actually liking this woman."

Brandon picked up one of the pillows from his couch and threw it at Dominy.

"Seriously, Brandon. It is already too late. Unless you find out that she's a serial killer or…I don't know… a man, it is done. You are already smitten, but that can also be part of the good news."

Brandon could feel his stomach tightening up.

Not noticing the slow panic creeping on Brandon's face, Dominy went on.

"The good news is…you can use this as a reason to fight. You could fight to live for her."

Brandon stared at Dominy from across the room. The panic he'd felt moments before was replaced with a deep sadness. Not for himself, but for all the people he was going to leave behind who loved him. He wasn't going to add to that number.

No more daydreams, no more advice, and, prayerfully, no more dreams. He would leave Paige Morganson alone from now on.

He cleared his features, pasting on a smile, and nodded. Dominy looked back at him skeptically, shaking his head.

"Sure…go ahead…make it harder on yourself. Don't say I didn't warn you, but just so that it will make it easier for you, let me know when you come to your senses; I will promise not to tell you 'I told you so'."

CHAPTER 29

Victoria was pacing in Vivian's room when Mason walked in.

"We need to talk."

She heard him groan, but clenched her teeth against her retort. She walked passed him and back out the door to wait. He joined her after a few minutes, wearing a bored expression.

"Victoria," he said flatly.

"Let's walk down to your room. What I have to say to you is confidential." She started walking down the hall.

He stood where he was. "Victoria, if this is about the custody hearing …"

Victoria turned around quickly, walking back to him, addressing him with an icy whisper. "No, Mason, it isn't, but if you don't listen to what I have to say, *that* will be the least of your worries." She turned back around and continued forward again.

Mason rolled his eyes at the dramatic performance she was giving and followed after her.

Once they were back in his room, Mason sat on his bed, making himself comfortable.

Victoria pushed a chair by the door forward. The sound grated against his nerves, but he remained still.

Victoria sat down, smoothing her skirt as she prepared her speech.

"We don't normally see eye to eye, but one thing I do know is that we both want what is best for Vivian."

She could see from the sardonic expression that raced across his features before smoothing back into a look of boredom that he was listening,

"So, I took it upon myself to do some research for a kidney donor. I have many contacts and I knew my network could be put to good use." She paused, surprised he didn't interrupt her. She jumped ahead.

"There were three that I happened upon right away, but unfortunately none of them can be candidates. One passed away recently, so recently in fact that she had not been taken off of the list yet. The other is pregnant, so that is out of the question and the third, well, that is an entirely different situation altogether."

Still no comment. She was happy to see he was finally giving her the respect she deserved.

"The reason I'm sharing this information with you is because I found out that Richard has been doing some digging of his own on your behalf." The name tasted like rust on her tongue. She couldn't get it out fast enough. "I thought that we could join efforts so that we weren't duplicating ourselves."

He continued to stare at her, but she saw the wheels turning. He was trying to see if he could trust her, but she knew he was too desperate not to.

"What happened with the third, potential donor?" he asked.

She waited, making it clear that she wanted an answer from him first.

"It looks like we are at an impasse," he said, bluffing "Victoria, I don't have time to play cat and mouse with you. It has been a long day and I need to make some arrangements."

Victoria's patience was wearing thin. "Arrangements for what?"

The ugly smile marred his features. He didn't elaborate.

He was so damn infuriating.

She huffed. "The third one isn't a likely candidate due to her past. The background check isn't coming up complete. It is like she dropped off of the face of the earth for a while. I don't think we can trust that. For all we know, she could have been in rehab or in another country selling herself."

"Did anyone ask her?"

"Do you think I am a fool? I am not letting anyone with shady character around my granddaughter."

She was met with silence, but she could have sworn she saw a brief look of irony in his eyes.

"I am thorough. I like to make sure I have a good view of all sides before I move."

"What if, despite her questionable past, she is the only eligible and viable donor? Then what of your need for a spotless character?"

"If her past is questionable, then so is her character, her moral standards and thus, her habits. What if there are things that she has done that won't show any signs on her kidneys until later?"

"Alright." Mason said with his hands held up in surrender. "There is no reason to beat this into the ground. I spoke to a potential donor today and she will begin the process with Amanda tomorrow. I am just waiting for a call from Amanda's office."

Victoria's mouth went dry. *No!* Her mind screamed. *How did he...Victoria calm down. Maybe he is talking about someone else.*

"What is the potential donor's name?"

She watched as Mason stared at her warily, obviously trying to decide whether or not to share the information with her.

"Her name is Paige Morganson." He watched her intently.

The roar of blood in her ears was deafening. She swallowed, hoping she could maintain her dignity. It would not do to throw up now. She took a deep breath and swallowed again.

"That is the same woman I am speaking of. You cannot let her near Vivian. I believe you would be putting your daughter in jeopardy."

She tried to gain control over her emotions.

"I don't know what you're up to, Victoria." Mason's control was slipping. "I talked with this woman for over an hour and I saw nothing in her character that would warrant your reaction." He watched Victoria, catching every nervous flutter and frown.

"I also consider myself to be an excellent judge of character. Like you, for instance: a devious, maniacal, spiteful, malicious, loathsome excuse for a woman who won't even do what it takes to save her granddaughter's life because of her need for control."

Victoria's smile was pure, unadulterated hate. A lesser man would have shivered.

"You dimwitted, trifling piece of a man. You don't know what you are up against. If I didn't love my granddaughter, I would let you continue on your quest to destroy the only good thing you have going for you. But today, I feel like being merciful, so I am going to ignore that pitiful tirade."

"Whatever, Victoria! I think we are done here..." he was turning to lie on his bed.

"We are not! You need to listen to me or..."

Mason got up off of the bed, working hard not to limp as he walked over to her.

"I am done with the threats, Victoria. I will not be manipulated or moved on this decision. Now get the hell out of my room!"

"Fine! Go ahead and meet with her tomorrow, let her go through all the procedures, but you cannot allow her to meet Vivian."

"Victoria, stop with the games. I don't see why Vivian shouldn't be able to meet the person she is getting a kidney from. She is going to want to at least thank her. You know that. Go back to your farm and order your servants around if you want to feel useful; go shopping and abuse the store clerks. Just get out of my..."

"She is Vivian's mother," Victoria said, her voice barely audible.

"What." He was sure he heard her wrong.

"The Morganson woman is Vivian's biological mother."

Mason went still. His eyes glazed over, losing focusing, then clearing.

"No. Vivian's mother died in childbirth," he spat in denial.

Victoria just shook her head.

"What are you saying, Victoria?" He was having trouble getting a full breath. The floor started tipping. He staggered back to the bed, hoping it would break his fall.

He caught the edge and brought his head down between his knees, trying desperately to fill his lungs.

"What...you are saying... is impossible. How could it happen?" He took a labored breath. "How would they let a child go home with a complete stranger when the mom was still alive?" He raised his head, eyes blazing. "If you are lying, Victoria, so help me, I will make your life a living hell."

Victoria sat there unmoved by him and his threat.

She had been through it all herself six years ago. She'd been doing some medical history-searching of Vivian's birth mother, just in case there was an emergency. She stumbled upon the truth almost immediately, denying it even as more and more proof came forward. The deceased woman had been producing an antigen from a blood transfusion which during pregnancy, crossed through the placenta that was foreign to the fetus. The result was a severe form of hemolytic disease in the fetus. The medical records were found in a small clinic a state away, showing the early signs of distress in the fetus.

Though Vivian was small for a full-term pregnancy, she had no symptoms of the disease from what Victoria could remember, not even jaundice.

She searched further, having her men pull the records of all the women who gave birth that night and then they found Paige Morganson, a 14-year old child, who came in with the initial thought - or so the unfinished paperwork said - for a third-trimester abortion procedure, but instead gave birth to twins. The records further indicated that one was healthy while the other was stillborn due to a severe form of Twin-to-Twin Transfusion Syndrome.

It didn't take much to get contact information. Then there it was: an envelope full of pictures, delivered by messenger.

The child looked exactly like Vivian. Vivian had an identical twin sister, states away, thank God, but nonetheless she was out there and so was her mother.

Little did she know that her search would send up red flags not only allowing for Paige's mother to find her, but approach her on behalf of her daughter, making her an offer she could barely refuse.

"Victoria. I am talking to you. How long have you known?"

She shrugged. "A while."

"A while... a while...." He began to repeat to himself. It sounded like he was on the verge of hysterics.

"Get a hold of yourself. No one needs to find out," Victoria said, her voice raspy. She cleared her throat, collecting herself.

"The Morganson woman doesn't need to find out about her."

Mason placed his face in his hands. What was he going to do? He couldn't lose Vivian. She was all he had left. Even as he tried to think of ways around this whole situation, his heart revolted against the deception. He felt like he was being torn in two.

"Oh my God, Victoria. Do you know what you have done?"

"What? What have I done, besides making sure my daughter and her husband stayed blissfully ignorant? If it wasn't for your father-in-law, you never would have known. Now I am left trying to clean up after him."

Mason didn't say a word. He was horrified by his thoughts, terrified by the possibility of losing his daughter.

"It doesn't have to be a hard decision," Victoria continued on, "It's not like Vivian was the only child. The Morganson woman had twins. She has hers...well, at least her sister does. She didn't even want her child enough to raise it on her own. You see, it is for the best that we were given Vivian. She will have so much more with us than she ever will with that woman."

"Stop calling her that. She has a name. She is not a separate species from us. She is Vivian's mother for goodness sake!"

"Her biological mother. That woman has no more a mark or influence on Vivian than the DNA she passed on to her."

Mason shook his head, but he didn't say anything. They were more alike than she knew.

He needed to think. He needed to get some clarity, and he couldn't do that with this little demon chanting in his ear.

"I need you to go, Victoria."

"Go? But we haven't discussed what we are going to say to the caseworker."

"I will be the one to make the decision, not you. You…you have done enough." He reached over and pressed the button for the nurse.

"I need to think. I need to be alone." His eyes were bleak.

Victoria began to panic.

"Mason. Be reasonable. Don't throw this away. Vivian loves you. She loves her life. I will not go after custody. We can come to some understanding in it all. It can all be worked out." She was grasping at anything she thought he would want to hear.

He said nothing more. He just stared at her with empty eyes.

"Mason! Don't be stupid. Vivian is the last piece of Rachael that we have left."

The hospital door opened and in walked Mason's RN. "Are you alright? Do you need pain medication?" She asked, seeing the distress on his face.

Mason smiled ruefully. If only there was a medicine that could cure this. He was dying on the inside, and he didn't suspect he was going to get any help from that "silent god" in this situation either.

Hardly able to raise his voice loud enough to be heard, he whispered hoarsely, "I need to rest."

Victoria sat up, her back straight as a steel beam. She stood up, still watching Mason, pleading with him with her eyes.

He stared in her direction for a long moment then turned away, lying on the bed.

Resigned to leave the room with as much dignity and pride as she could, Victoria turned towards the nurse who was waiting quietly and mumbled something akin to, "Goodnight."

Before she walked out the door, she turned back.

"Think of Rachael."

CHAPTER 30

Mason didn't know how long he'd lain there, staring unseeingly through the blinds, but the sun was setting when the phone began to ring. He looked at it for a moment, then decided he'd better pick it up.

"Hello." His voice was still rough with emotion. He cleared his throat.

"Hello, Mr. Jenson?"

"Yes."

"This is Amanda Watson, your caseworker for Vivian."

"Yes."

"Are you feeling alright? Is this a bad time?"

"No. I'm fine." He sat up in bed.

"I heard from Paige Morganson. We had an interesting talk. She said she met with you today?"

"Yes. I found her in the waiting room this morning."

"You do know that this is not protocol."

"Yes, but since she was here I didn't see the harm in it," he said quickly.

"Well, I am going ahead, but I would advise against you having Ms. Morganson meet Vivian just now. There are still a lot of tests that need to be run. She will be with me for the better part of tomorrow and we will begin with some of the process. If that works out, well then we will move forward. How does that sound?"

To him it was a relief, especially Paige not meeting Vivian right away. It meant he had more time to try and figure all of this out.

"Fine." The storm clouds were beginning to part.

"Ms. Morganson also mentioned that you might be joining us tomorrow. I don't particularly think it is necessary, but if there is a question or concern, I would be more than willing to pass it on."

Mason paused. Had he really been that out of line in regards to his dealings with Paige Morganson, or was there more? He wouldn't put it past Victoria to have intervened.

"Have you spoken to my mother-in-law recently, like in the last few hours? Her name is Victoria Branchett."

"Mmmmm, no. Should I have?"

"No. It was an idle thought…never mind. Is it Ms. Morganson's wish that I not be personally involved at this stage?"

"She just suggested that we keep this as professional as possible and follow protocol strictly so that if she can help, nothing would jeopardize that."

Mason took a deep breath, letting it out evenly.

"That is what I want as well. I will not interfere anymore. I know you will keep me up to date on the progress. Ms. Watson, I have a question for you."

"Sure."

"If the donor or receiver of the kidney want to meet, when would it be most beneficial?"

"Usually a few days to a week before the procedure. It helps with bonding, resolution, and sometimes with some of the pain. Sometimes there isn't time for it, but if Ms. Morganson is the one, then you will have a little more time due to the stage of renal failure Vivian is in. There is a possibility that things could turn around."

"Thank you, Ms. Watson. You have given me something to think about. One more thing."

"Yes?"

"If Victoria Branchett should call you and have you deviate in any way from the procedure, please let me know."

"Is she going to be a problem?"

"Let's just say I wouldn't put it past her. Just don't take her word for anything. If you do your research and confirm everything with myself and Ms. Morganson, this should go smoothly."

"Okay Mr. Jenson. I will give you a call later on tomorrow."

"Thank you Ms. Watson. Have a good evening."

"Good evening Mr. Jenson." The phone line went dead.

Mason got up from his bed. All of a sudden he was desperate to see Vivian. The last few hours were like a nightmare and he needed to reassure himself that they had no ill effect on his daughter.

Feeling a little unsteady, he picked up the crutches in the corner. His ankle was throbbing but he had felt worse.

He made his way downstairs to her room and found her lying in bed, asleep. He quietly made his way to her bedside, sitting in the nearby chair and waited until she woke.

As she lay there, he studied her features looking for similarities between mother and daughter.

The eyes were very close in shape, though the colors were as different as silver and gold. Vivian's nose was thinner and more angular, whereas her mother's was fuller and more rounded. He surveyed the cheekbones and mouth and found vague similarities, but as he examined the jawline and chin, it became unmistakable. The small jut of the chin and square jaw were undoubtedly hereditary.

It was funny how perspectives changed from person to person. Though his daughter was still developing, he saw her chin and jaw as a part of her very strong character and confidence.

On Paige, it was more stubborn and hinted at a certain sensuality he didn't think she was aware of.

The similarities were there but they were muted by the eyes and nose, which caused him to wonder what the biological father looked like and then if he was still in Paige's life.

Ms. Morganson's demeanor and maturity would have caused him to assume that she was somewhere in her early 30s, but her face put holes in that theory. She didn't look a day over 24, but that would have been too young to have twelve-year-old children, wouldn't it?

He wondered how much information Victoria had been able to glean from searching through this woman's records. He briefly considered asking, but his very being revolted against the thought. He didn't want to have any kind of contact with that woman in the near future.

What if she was in her twenties? That meant that she had Vivian and her sister when she was in her teens. He shuddered mildly, wondering if she was the victim of incest or rape, but how could someone so sweet and precious come from something so dark and violent? He negated the thought and berated himself for being so morbid.

He thought about Googling to find out more about her, her career, and books; that wasn't illegal or intruding. It was merely searching for more information about his daughter's mother.

It was weird to even think that since Rachael had been the only one ever to hold that title in his mind.

"Hi Daddy."

He looked up. He had been so lost in thought he didn't realize she had awaken.

"Hi baby. How do you feel?"

"Better now. I was so tired before. I am a little thirsty. Could I have some water?"

"Sure sweetie." Mason reached for the pitcher on the bedside table and poured her a cup. He helped her sit up while she drank. She looked so pale and fragile. He just wanted his bright beauty back.

"You were smiling in your sleep. What were you dreaming of?'

"Mommy." She smiled over the cup.

He waited until she was done, then leaned her back against the pillows.

"Mommy?" He asked. "Do you dream of her a lot?"

He put the cup back on the table and sat back in the chair.

"I didn't before, but since I have been sick, it's almost every day."

"What do you dream about?"

"It changes. Sometimes we are in places that we have been together, sometimes we are talking in my bedroom at home." She lifted up her shoulders as if she wasn't quite sure she wanted to share the information.

"What do you talk about?"

"Lots of stuff. Gram's farm and the animals, school, you." She looked up fleetingly.

Mason was surprised. "Me? You talk about me? What about?"

"How sad you are since I've been ill."

"Awww, baby, I am not sad all the time. I am concerned about you. That's all."

"Daddy, I told you. I am going to be fine. Mommy even said so."

"Really, Mommy told you that?"

Vivian nodded.

"She also said that you worry too much about what isn't going to happen."

"She said that, huh." He gave her a wry smile.

Vivian smiled. "Yeah."

"I am so lucky to have two wonderful women looking out for me, but don't waste your dreams on me. I am right here and I am not going anywhere."

"I know that, Daddy. Mommy keeps saying that too; you and I will be together for a long time."

"Your mom was always the smart one."

"Daddy, do you ever dream about mommy?"

"Every now and then, but not too often. Why?"

"I just think if you dreamed about her more, then you wouldn't miss her so much."

"No, honey, if I dreamed about your mom all the time, I would stay in bed every day and then you wouldn't have anyone to take you to school, ice skating, the movies, to make you dinner…"

She giggled. "You burn dinner."

"Yes, but I try. That should count for something."

"Yes. A whole lot." Vivian looked down at the sheets, all of a sudden very preoccupied with the lines in the fabric.

"I just want you to be happy, Daddy."

"Ah, baby, I am. When I am with you, when you smile and talk to me about your day, everything is right side up."

She frowned as though she was going to argue, but then her face relaxed and she yawned.

"Are you still sleepy? I know you just woke up, but maybe your body is asking for rest. Are you hungry? I can call the nurse."

Vivian shook her head. "I had dinner before I fell asleep."

"Anything good?"

"Just the pudding."

"Sorry hun."Come on, snuggle in and relax so your body can rest."

He got up to bring the covers up around her neck. She brought one hand out from underneath and touched the side of his face. "I pray you have dreams about mommy too, that way you won't miss her so much, and she will tell you that I am going to be fine and there is nothing to worry about."

Emotion stuck in his throat. He leaned forward, kissing her on the forehead.

"Go to sleep my princess and dream good dreams. I love you."

"Daddy, don't go."

"I won't leave. I will stay until you go to sleep, okay?"

He sat back down in the chair, holding her hand and watched until her eyelids began to droop. She yawned again and closed her eyes.

He felt like he'd just had one of the longest days of his life. He never would have thought that the woman he would meet today would bring about so many emotions. True, most of them were distressful, but the others were strong too. Like the way she looked at him when they first met and his reaction to her. He'd never felt such a strong, physical attraction for anyone like that instantaneously.

Her face came into view. Those beautiful eyes going wide, her lips parting, her agitation and nervousness, which he first thought was due to the interviewing process, never abated. It waxed and waned, but it never really went away. Right before they parted and he was waiting to help her with her things, he could have sworn her breathing became labored.

Was she afraid of him? Was that why she'd told the caseworker she didn't want to meet with him again? It was a bittersweet thought; he did want to see her again, maybe in a less formal setting. She was strange enough for him to find curious and beautiful enough to find alluring. Maybe it was good that she wanted to keep everything strictly professional. He wouldn't know where she would fit in his life right now, the mess that it was.

But even as he shifted in the chair, hoping the change in position would help direct his mind to something else, he pictured her again, wondering how someone so petite could hold such passion in them for the world that it would cause them to give up such a vital part of themselves. The more he thought about her, the more beautiful she became.

He wanted to call her up and ask her more questions. *To see if she would allow me...*

What was he thinking? He was still in the hospital himself. He needed to come back to reality. Donor or no donor, Paige Morganson was off limits. But one decision had been made while he watched his daughter sleep.

He was going to tell Paige about Vivian. Not right now, but soon. It was the right thing to do. Once he had decided on it, he felt relieved. He couldn't explain it; he just felt better.

It was right. Vivian should know that she had history – living history. History she may actually be proud of. No wonder Vivian was such a lover of people; both of her mothers were.

CHAPTER 31

Paige took one last, long look out of her cabin window. She couldn't count how many times she thought of calling Mel and telling her she couldn't come, but that would have been worse to live with.

She'd been so preoccupied with the interviews, paperwork, the battery of tests which left her just a little sore and her reaction to Mr. Jenson which left her shaken, she hadn't given a great deal of thought to what she was going to say to Gladys.

Oh God, I need your help.

She sat there through the landing, the switching off of the seatbelt sign, and most of the disembarking of the other passengers. Finally, without an answer, she turned away from the window, took a deep breath, and began gathering her things.

One week. One week. One week, she repeated to herself, through the gate, on the underground terminal shuttle, at baggage claim, passed the MARTA station and into the waiting arms of her sister Mel at the small coffee shop close to the entrance.

"Hi beautiful," she said, returning the hug.

"Hi Paige, you look tired. What have you been doing the last few days?"

"Mel, you don't want to know, but I will tell you about it later anyway."

They walked the long distance to the car in silence. Mel helped her pack her luggage in the car and then they were off.

"The weather is much nicer than I thought it would be for this time of year," Paige said, adjusting her seat. "I was actually wondering how far I would get out of the door before the humidity would have me on the ground."

"I know. I am glad it is nice for you too. It might mean you will come and visit me more often." Mel smiled wistfully at her as she started the engine.

Paige just shrugged.

"I came to pick you up alone so that we could plan how we are going to tell Gladys."

"I figured. I haven't been able to really think of a way to begin, but I have been thinking about what you said for the last two weeks. It occurred to me that I was trying to deal with things that were no longer an issue. Why put all of the hurt and shame that I no longer feel on her? She is beautiful and I want her to feel as loved as I can."

Mel nodded. "What are we going to do about visitations and custody?"

Paige shivered. "Custody is such a formal and restrictive word. I am not going to fight for any more than you are willing to give. I think we can do this out of court."

Mel nodded again. "So what do you think?"

"I am not trying to continue to put her off on you, but if you could give me some months to get my calendar in order, then I can arrange it so that she is with me at least for the summers so that we can start to create a bond. I don't want to take her away from her school friends. In a few years, we should be able to revisit this and see if she wants to relocate to Los Angeles for high school. What do you think?"

"I thought you hadn't given a lot of thought to this?" Mel asked, a small smile playing at her lips.

"I have been extremely selfish. You know it and I know it, so don't argue with me. I also understand the love you have for Gladys and I don't want to replace or come in the way of it. I just want to have a chance to get to know her. It is about time, isn't it?"

"It is. What really happened over the last two weeks?"

Paige took a deep breath. "I was called last week by the Living Donor Foundation." She looked over at Mel to see how she would process that information.

"As it turns out, I may be a match for a young girl who recently had an accident and is in need of a kidney transplant."

"Isn't that painful for both of you?" Mel glanced over, concern etched on her face.

"What is a little pain compared to a life?" Paige shrugged. "This child is Gladys' age. Can you imagine? It really got me thinking about how fragile life is. I just assumed since she was healthy and in your care that I would always have an opportunity to get to spend time with her.

I met the father and he seemed to really love his daughter, but, in an instant, she was almost taken away from him. I have the opportunity to get to know a beautiful girl. I am going to take it."

"Be patient with me. I am just trying to absorb this 180 that you have done. So you are saying that you want to tell her tonight before we go? I was thinking that you might want to spend some time with her first and then tell her."

"I am thinking that it may be easier if we told her now and then she could have time to get to know me as something more than 'aunt'. She would be able to ask me questions and at a more comfortable pace, come to understand my decisions. Is that alright?"

"That is fine. I will just let Marcus know. We will eat in tonight. Meanwhile, you will be set up in your usual guest room down the hall from Gladys. I will run through all of the emergency numbers as normal with you and Gladys, as routine. Marc and I leave out tomorrow morning, so I'll let him know this might be a late night for us." Mel paused. "You say you may be a potential donor. When will you know?"

"I will get a call in the next few days. The operation could be as soon as the end of September."

"That soon? Will it conflict with your tour schedule?"

"A little; I am already working around that. Carmen is fit to be tied, but we are a ways out from the holiday season, when the real push begins for me. I should be more than fine by then. I could be back on my feet and ready to travel between two weeks to a month."

Paige had barely exited the car when Gladys embraced her, knocking her back onto the door.

"Auntie Paige!"

"Oh my goodness, you have grown! What are you now 5'4', 5'5"? Let me see you."

Paige pushed Gladys away from her slightly so that she could get a full look at her. She gave her a thorough look up and down.

"You are beautiful," she said breathlessly, "When did you get to be so beautiful?"

It had been rhetorical, but Gladys looked like she was actually trying to think of a date. Paige smiled, placing her hand on Gladys' cheek. Gladys smiled back shyly but brilliantly. Then they both laughed and hugged again.

"How long has it been?" Paige asked Gladys as she began opening her suitcases they'd placed on her bed.

"Over a year," Gladys answered, a playful pout on her face.

Paige froze, a pair of socks in her hand. "Has it really been that long?"

Gladys nodded, walking over to the chair at the desk in the corner. She turned it around, sitting down with her arms resting on the back.

"Wow." Paige said, trying to go back in her head. Was Gladys right? Had it been that long? She wasn't even that great of an aunt. How would Gladys forgive her for being such a horrible mother?

"So....'Glad to Know Ya'." That was the nickname she had come up with when her niece was eight. She said it whenever she wanted to lighten the mood. "What are we going to do this week? Did you make any plans for us?"

Gladys started nodding. "I hope you took your vitamins, 'Page Turner'."

Paige laughed at the regular retort for her name-calling.

"There are a few concerts in the park and we are also going to Lennox Square so I can do some school shopping. I saved that for you. Mom's tastes are so ancient." She rolled her eyes.

"I am sure your mom's taste is not that bad."

"You think? Hold on right there." Gladys raced out of the room and was back inside of 30 seconds with a sweater and pleated skirt that looked like it had been matched by Osh Kosh B'Gosh.

Paige grimaced. "Well at least they match." She shrugged. "You don't pick out your own clothes?"

"This is what happens when she goes without me. It happens a lot. See, if you go with me then I can pick out some, and you can help. You know kinda like...um....what's that word...referee?"

"You mean mediator?"

"What does mediator mean?"

"I would be the middle man."

"Exactly!"

"It would be great then; we would both get what we want."

Paige smiled to herself. She hoped that one day would be a sleep-day, otherwise she would be no good when she got back to Los Angeles.

They used the rest of the afternoon to catch up while Paige unpacked and Gladys moved from one piece of furniture to the next.

When Melanie came to the door announcing it was dinner time, Paige's stomach knotted up, her mouth going dry. Gladys got up quickly. "Come on, Auntie Paige."

"You go ahead and save me a seat. I am going to use the bathroom and change my clothes really quickly."

Gladys sucked her teeth. "Aaaight. Hurry though. I am hungry and mom won't let us eat until you get to the table."

"Okay, brat. I will hurry."

Gladys laughed and left the room.

Paige was relieved. She needed a moment to gather herself.

Lord please, word my mouth. Give me what to say and how to say it. You know how precious a gift she is. You gave her to me. Please prepare her heart for what we are about to tell her. Let her see that we did it in love, even though it may not have been the right thing to do. Let us listen to her, truly listen to her, so that we can help mend what we have broken. I love you, Lord. Thank you so much for this second chance. I didn't and still don't deserve it, but I will take it.

She quickly changed her clothes and went downstairs.

They ate dinner in relative silence, everyone except for Gladys having a lot on their mind. She talked a mile a minute – eating up the quiet – regaling the table with her summer activities which, in her opinion, were sad and uneventful.

Melanie began after dinner was finished.

"Gladys, we have something very important to discuss with you. Since Paige was coming into town, we thought it would be a perfect time."

Gladys looked at all three of them. "Ugh. Is this about boys?"

Paige looked down, smiling to herself. She almost wished.

"No honey, it is a little more complicated than that. At any time during this conversation, you may ask any question you'd like. We only ask that you don't get up from the table until it is done. Okay?"

Gladys was quiet now. She just nodded.

Melanie looked at Paige, giving her the go-ahead to speak.

Paige took a breath, expelling it slowly. She looked Gladys squarely in the eye. "What I am about to say to you will change your view of me, but I do hope it doesn't change our relationship because I really do love you." She saw Gladys swallow and understood that this was scaring her more than the new information might. She launched ahead.

"Gladys, I am your biological mother. Melanie is your aunt."

Gladys stared at them glassy-eyed for a moment. "Huh? When? Why?" Then she shut her mouth.

Paige could see she was still trying to absorb the information and they all stayed quiet, patiently waiting for the real response.

Gladys looked back and forth between Melanie and Paige. Paige's heart was beating so hard it was almost painful in her chest.

"Why?" Gladys repeated after a few minutes.

"Why are we telling you or why did we do it?"

"Yes."

They waited a little bit longer.

"Why are you telling me now?"

"Because we thought you were old enough to understand, and mature enough to be able to handle it. If we are wrong, then we will help you in any way we can."

There was more silence.

"What does this mean?" She looked very concerned and more than just a little anxious.

"It means you know the truth. It doesn't have to mean more than that if that is not what you want."

"So you aren't going to fight for custody of me and split me between the two of you?" She looked at Paige.

"I didn't come here to disrupt, displace, or divide you between two families. We thought it was time you knew the truth. The repercussions, the consequences, or things that happen from it are what we are trying to openly discuss with you right now." Oh she was starting to make a mess of things. *Get it together, Paige.* Paige looked at Marc and Melanie, a pleading look in her eyes.

Melanie frowned, making Paige roll her eyes. *Dang.*

Mel was right; this part had to come from her. She tried again.

"Nothing will change if you don't want it to. Well…nothing in regards to your living arrangements. Mel and I are sisters who love each other and you even more. We are not interested in any custody battle and neither one of us is insecure about how you feel towards us. We just wanted you to know."

Paige took another breath. She opened her mouth, and then thought better of it; no need to introduce any options now. They would just confuse the issue.

"So nothing would change. I would get to stay here with Mom…I mean…Auntie Melanie?" She looked back and forth again between Paige and Melanie.

"Yes, and you can still call her mom. In all ways, besides giving birth to you, she is your 'mom'. She raised you and has cared for you these twelve years."

"So why would you even tell me now if nothing has to change? Why would you tell me at all?"

"Don't you want to know the truth?"

"I don't know? It is so confusing. I need to think." Gladys began shaking her head.

No one moved for a long while. Then, Gladys began to cry.

Melanie got up from her side of the table and came around to kneel in front of Gladys. Gladys leaned into her arms and the quiet sobs turned into open weeping. It didn't sound like it came from the grief of being betrayed but from fear.

"Sssh, honey, it's okay," Melanie crooned rocking Gladys side to side.

After the tears subsided a little, Melanie whispered something into Gladys' ear.

Gladys pulled back. "You mean it?"

Melanie nodded looking her straight in the eyes.

Paige was curious, but a great deal more relieved with what seemed to be Gladys' acceptance of the news.

Then Gladys turned to Paige. "Why did you give me up?"

Paige worked at keeping the answer as truthful as possible without giving too much information.

"I was too young to take care of you and Melanie was more prepared, financially and emotionally. We didn't want you to go to another family, but I wanted something better for you than what I could give you."

Gladys seemed to take that in quicker than the initial information.

"Do you know who my dad is?"

Paige nodded, her breath catching in her throat.

"Do you still talk to him? Will I get to meet him?"

Paige, very close to tears now herself, could only shake her head at first. She took a deep breath to gain some composure.

It was so unfair.

"He died."

"Oh," was all Gladys said.

"But I can tell you that you have his color eyes, though they are shaped like mine. You have his forehead, your grandmother's nose, and my jawline and it makes you one of the most beautiful young ladies I have ever seen."

"You are biased," Gladys accused, a small smile coming to her lips.

Paige shrugged. "Whatever."

This time, Gladys laughed.

They stayed at the table for the next few hours, answering as many questions as they could. Each took their turn hugging and holding Gladys trying to physically repair some of the damage and instill the reassurance of their love for her.

It was long after one a.m. before they got to sleep, so it was no wonder that Melanie and Marc were rushing around the next morning trying to tie up loose ends and catch their plane. By the time things settled down, Paige was tired again.

She forced herself to go downstairs and start making breakfast. Gladys came down a few minutes later.

"You want to help me make breakfast?"

"Mom doesn't usually have me in the kitchen when she cooks," Gladys said, leaning against the door frame.

"Well, I don't have an aversion to you being in the kitchen with me. If you would like to at least learn how to make eggs, I can show you that now. In fact, I can show you a different recipe a day and when your mom gets back, you can surprise her."

Gladys shrugged, but came closer to the counter.

"Why do you use so many big words?"

Paige looked at her as she handed over the bowl of pancake mix. Paige showed her how to stir it then went to the refrigerator for the bacon.

"I think of words as a pallet of colors. As a writer, the more words I have to my....the more words I know the easier it is; it is easier to paint pictures with them. Sometimes I forget who I am speaking to and I go for the word that comes first."

"Auntie Paige, you don't mind that I want to stay with Mom...Melanie...here, do you?"

"No, and like I said last night, Melanie is your mom, and you continue to feel free to call her that." Paige put the meat down on the counter and turned back to look at her.

"I am very sorry for hurting you the way I did. I don't want you to ever feel like you are unwanted because I was young and selfish. Okay?" Paige, not waiting for an answer, hugged Gladys.

Hearing a stifled, "Okay," she relaxed her hold, allowing Gladys to breathe.

"So your mom told me that you want to get your ears pierced?" Paige said, slyly.

"Are you going to take me? Did she say 'Yes'?" Gladys said, her voice full of excitement, the bowl of pancake mix forgotten in her hand.

Paige nodded, not looking away from the package of meat.

"Oh, Thank you! Thank you! Thank..." the sudden silence caught her attention.

Paige turned around to see Gladys covered in pancake mix.

It was obvious the excitement was too much to contain without jumping up and down. Paige pressed her lips together hard, trying not to laugh. She came undone when she glanced back and one large clump fell from Gladys' nose onto the floor.

She burst out laughing and was joined quickly by Gladys.

"Maybe we will just have cereal," she said, before getting a towel.

CHAPTER 32

"Don't be such a baby."

Brandon glared at Dominy. "I think it's time for you to go back home."

"We have been through this. I can't go back until I believe I have given Robin a chance to miss me. A week is hardly enough time. She is just beginning to enjoy her vacation away from me. It looks like you have me for a few more weeks, at least. Now drink this and I may consider leaving you alone for at least an hour."

Brandon took a deep breath, held his nose and began to swallow the heinous-smelling, nutritional drink with the chalky protein. He emptied the glass and set it back on the tray. He breathed too quickly and the taste made him gag. He picked up the glass of water and chased the taste away.

"You are enjoying this," Brandon accused, solemnly eyeing Dominy's slightly amused face.

"Not at all. I would rather be out golfing and if you weren't bent on feeling sorry for yourself, we could be on a course right now." He put the tray on the bedside table and sat down on the edge of the bed.

"Really Brandon, if you don't think you're going to heal from this, why are we wasting our time with the chemo and the radiation? Why aren't we just making funeral arrangements?"

Brandon laid back on the pillow. The movement made the liquid he just drank slosh around. He clenched his teeth taking deep breaths to calm his stomach. He slowly sat back up and his stomach stopped its rolling.

"I am not in the mood to play with you right now, Dom," he said through gritted teeth.

"I'm not kidding; I just want to know if I am wasting my time. I mean it will be much easier if we were on one accord, whichever way you pick, but this half-hearted attempt…frankly, is just pissing me off. I need you to decide today what you really want to do. I will stick by you whatever you decide but once you do, you'd better be ready to give it 100%"

"Or what?" Brandon asked, tired of the idle threats.

"Or I'll call your mom. I still have the number to the house. Don't think I won't use it. You decide, Brandon, but I warned you in the beginning that I wouldn't serve you at your pity party."

"So you have already resorted to threatening me. It has only been seven days. You are getting impatient in your old age."

"What I am getting impatient with is your pathetic need to sulk and feel sorry for yourself. You are a man of God. You encourage and pray for others to receive understanding on how to move forward in times such as these. I know this was a blow to your hope, but it doesn't mean it's over."

"You don't know anything. You are not in here." Brandon growled pointing at his head. "Or here." He poked at the center of his chest. "You are out there with dreams and desires; not just to survive, but to see your children grow, invent another great business that you can sell for millions, and to grow old."

"What is your problem? The desire to survive is in all of those things. It doesn't just take cancer to stop those things from happening. It could be an accident of any kind, being in the wrong place at the wrong time, or just being in God's will. If I were you, I would do the one thing you should have done first: ask God what His will is for you in this situation, and then get up and do it. Meanwhile, you're only wasting time—mine, yours, and most importantly, His."

Dominy picked up the tray and walked out of the room, leaving Brandon to stew.

Brandon was angry and he didn't want to be angry. He just wanted the numbness to come back. He didn't want to care; he was too tired to care right now. He laid back down, gingerly placing his arm behind his head, staring up at the ceiling.

The phone rang in the living room and he heard Dominy answer, "Hello? Oh, hello, Pastor Lawrence. Yes, still a bit under the weather, but I believe today may be at a turning point. I'm not too sure he is up for visitors just yet. Oh, well I guess that is different. Alright, we will see you in an hour."

Brandon's heart began beating a mile a minute.

Dominy came back in the room. "Well, it looks like your decision has been made for you. Pastor Lawrence won't be put off anymore. He is coming by and I suggest you tell him the truth. It may be the only thing that saves your position on staff and you and I both know that this is something God has assigned you." He went to the closet and pulled out a shirt and slacks. "I suggest you take a shower. I'm your friend, but you are starting to offend me."

"Shut up Dominy, I need to think."

"Don't you just love it when God answers prayers?"

"What are you talking about? I haven't heard anything."

"I'm talking about me. I asked the Lord for help just this afternoon. I am going to go put on some worship music because the cavalry will be arriving any minute." Then he walked back out of the room.

Brandon sat there for another 15 minutes, trying to decide what he would tell his pastor. Finally, he gave up and decided on the truth. He would lay his chips on the table. It would be his pastor's choice whether or not he could still use him. But first he would have to make him promise not to share this news with his family.

*   *   *

Brandon sat on the edge of the recliner, waiting for Pastor Lawrence's response to all he'd shared with him. They were alone in the living room; Dominy had made himself scarce after he'd reintroduced himself to Pastor Lawrence, then excused himself to go out to do some shopping.

"How long have you known?"

"A little less than a month."

"How many opinions did you seek?"

"Five." Brandon said studiously.

"This is the second time in how many years?"

"Eight. I have been in remission for six years."

"I wonder why Elias didn't share this with me," Pastor Lawrence said more to himself than to Brandon.

Brandon shrugged nonetheless and answered. He might as well be as forthcoming as possible.

"The first time I made him promise not to share the information with people outside of our family. You know, mouths and all. Plus, I'd already gotten my word."

Brandon took a breath.

"This time he hasn't said anything because he doesn't know yet and I would really appreciate it if you wouldn't say anything to him until after I tell him."

"When are you going to tell him?"

"Once I am through this cycle of chemo and radiation. I want to know how the cancer reacts to these sessions. From there, I will have a better idea of what I have in store. This all is, of course, unless I get another Word from God."

"Did He have a Word for you last time?"

"Yes. That the illness was not unto death."

"What has the Lord said concerning your health this time?"

"He just said to work. I have not heard Him address my health this time. Not clearly like the last time."

"Are you expecting Him to answer you the same way?"

"It would be nice. It is the same disease."

"But you are different."

Brandon just nodded.

"How is the treatment going?"

"I am taking shorter sessions more times a week. I have an abbreviated work schedule on the days I have my sessions and work longer on the days I don't. I am one of the fortunate ones; besides the really bad taste in my mouth and sleeping very hard, the side-effects I am experiencing are minimal. Still, it would be a lot harder without Dominy."

"You two have been friends for a very long time."

It wasn't a question, though Brandon could hear curiosity in his voice.

Brandon looked the pastor squarely in the eye, waiting to be asked.

"How long will he be staying?"

"Until my first round of sessions are done. This is usually the hardest time for me and I am almost ashamed to admit that I have not done so well this time."

"Mmmm. Why do you think that is?"

"This time it really seems to be out of my control. I am staring my mortality in the face every day and I am afraid. Truthfully, I don't know how to handle that emotion."

"You didn't experience this the first time?"

"No. I got my answer early on from the Lord. It seemed that the first time was a testing of my trust in His Word, whereas this is more of a trusting in what I know to be true."

"Which is?"

Brandon had wrung his hands together. When had this become a counseling session?

"That He will never leave nor forsake me and that He will comfort me, but honestly right now that is not doing it for me. I am trying to grasp and hold onto something that will motivate me to fight through this and remain positive and uplifted. It is a constant fight and not just day to day, either. Sometimes it is by the hour and others it is by the minute."

"Your friend believes you may need a distraction."

Brandon was instantly wary.

"What did he say?"

"He wanted to know if there were any special events he needed to be aware of so that he could make sure you were in attendance."

Brandon slowly let out the breath he'd been holding, then shrugged. "As I said, this is a challenging time and Dominy has been doing his best, but I know I am wearing on his patience. He was there the first time, but since we both didn't know what to expect, he was more open. This time, I think he was expecting less resignation from me and more fight. I believe it frightens him a little though he won't say anything; he will just hover like a mother hen."

"Yeah, he is very nurturing for a man," said Pastor Lawrence, frowning slightly.

"You should see him and his wife, Robin. He can drive her crazy. It was her suggestion that he come and stay with me this time, at least through my first session."

"Is there a problem there?" Pastor Lawrence said frowning.

"No. Robin is smart. She knows herself very well. To her, it is all a balancing act."

"So…it sounds like you need to keep busy," Pastor Lawrence said sitting back on the couch, crossing his legs.

Brandon sat back as well understanding that the interrogation was over. He nodded.

"Good. Your first assignment is dinner with First Lady and myself this evening. Dominy is also invited. He is a very interesting person. I have two more people to visit so let's say, 7:30 pm? Meanwhile let's pray."

He nodded at Brandon then closed his eyes and began.

"Dear Heavenly Father, we thank you for life and the life we can live in acknowledgment of You that allows us to live more abundantly. We thank you for the gift of the Holy Spirit and His leading and guiding. He is our Comforter and confidant; a wonderful friend in our time of sorrow, joy, need, and overflow. Thank you.

Lord I thank you for Your wisdom and understanding that You impart to us in regards to each situation and level in our lives. We appreciate with these things that You appreciate in our eyes because we are able to see You in each move. Thank you for revealing different facets of Yourself to us.

Lord I lift my son, Brandon, up to You. I ask that where there is confusion, You would bring clarity. Where there is lack, You would provide. Where there is weakness, You will undergird him with strength. Where there is sickness, you will heal. I thank you, God, for my son's insight and perspective that You have allowed him to see with. I thank you that in that very ability to see things Your way. You are confirming Your presence and gifts to him.

I ask that You meet the need within him and reveal to him the pathway to having that need met. I thank you for Your word in Jeremiah 29:11 that says, 'For I know the plans I have for you, thus saith the Lord. Plans to prosper you, not to harm you to give you hope and a future.' I thank you for the hope that comes out of the struggle and that he need not be afraid for he is on the journey to that hope even now.

Lord I ask that You give him peace and a renewed vigor for the work You have set his hands to, for in it is the very thing he is looking for in You. I thank you for providing him with friends that love him and hold him up to You. I thank you for their loyalty and servitude to this servant of yours, and I ask that You strengthen them on this road towards his healing. These things I pray in Jesus name, Amen."

"Amen." Brandon repeated.

"Also, I am going to want that outline soon on your plans for the men's ministry for next year. As I said before, we want to make sure there is an event that will bring the men together every month. This is above and beyond the weekly prayer, bible study, and Men to Men fellowship."

"I have half the year done. I am just waiting on a confirmation for an event I thought would be fun in June."

"Nice. I am looking forward to seeing that."

Pastor Lawrence pulled himself off of the couch.

"Well then. I will see you at 7:30 tonight. How is your appetite?"

"Just fine. My taste is off just a little, but I manage to represent." He laughed, getting up from his recliner.

When Dominy got back, he was thrilled to find out that they would be going out. A ping of guilt struck Brandon as he realized the burden he'd been placing on his friend. At this point, Dominy would have been happy if he told him they were going to an Italian Opera, and Brandon knew he could barely stomach one in English.

*   *   *

Brandon realized he had allowed more time to slip by in his morose state than he first counted when he and Dominy entered the living room of Pastor Lawrence's home, only to find Elder Paige Morganson talking with their daughter, Dana, and First Lady Menagerie on the couch.

He made a mental count of the days since Paige had left as he and Dominy stepped into the sunken living room.

Lady Menagerie came forward, hugging and welcoming both himself and Dominy, whom she had met the prior Sunday.

"Hello Mr. Hartemen, it's a pleasure to see you again. I didn't know you would be visiting for such a length of time." She went on before he could form an answer. "May I introduce you to my daughter, Dana, and Elder Paige Morganson."

Brandon noticed the slight change in his cadence when Dominy greeted Paige, but it was only because he was looking for a sign of recognition. He breathed a sigh of relief when the greeting ended only with Dom repeating her name.

Brandon then stepped forward, offering his hand to both women. He noticed right away that Paige looked tired. There were circles under her eyes slightly darker than her caramel-colored skin. She offered up a smile which didn't reach her eyes. It must have been some trip.

They sat in the living room for a good twenty minutes waiting for Pastor Lawrence to arrive. Brandon let Dominy do most of the talking. He was quite content to sit back and watch the interaction between his friend and the three women.

Dom had always been at such ease with women. It was as if they migrated towards him. It was a scene Brandon never got tired of, but when Paige laughed out loud he was unnerved by the fact that his friend was able to elicit such a reaction with little effort.

He worked to keep his features as light as the conversation.

"What do you think, Elder Tatum?" asked Lady Menagerie trying to pull him into the conversation. "Should Elder Morganson consider changing her next book to a pen name to protect herself?

Brandon shifted his gaze from Lady Menagerie to Paige, her eyes still shining with laughter.

"In the brief time I've known Elder Morganson, I have not known her to avoid confrontation nor to fear conversations that could be controversial. With her quick wit, I think she might welcome the opportunity rather than shy away from it by using a fake name."

Lady Menagerie clapped in delight. "Well said, Elder Tatum. I quite agree."

Paige was now a slightly darker shade due to the flush that had covered her face at his comment. She was most likely remembering their first encounter.

"How was your trip?" he asked in order to shift the conversation to what he thought was a safer subject.

"It was very..." she paused while thinking of a good word, "productive," she finished vaguely.

"Really, how so?" Dominy asked.

Bless him, Brandon thought.

Lady Menagerie answered. "Paige here was selected to be a living kidney donor to a child in Chicago."

"I thought you were going to Atlanta to see family?" Brandon spoke before he could stop himself.

They all looked back at him. Dominy had a curious expression on his face, but said nothing.

Brandon cleared his throat. "Sorry. I just remembered that part because I have friends in that area. Go ahead, I didn't mean to interrupt you, First Lady."

"That's alright. The world would be a better place if all men listened more attentively." Brandon watched Paige's reaction to Lady Menagerie's praise, and recount of what Paige had obviously told her earlier that evening about the early part of her previous week.

She looked harassed by the attention...and beautiful.

"Is it a painful procedure?" Dominy asked. Brandon unknowingly clenched his fists. He didn't want to think of her in pain.

"Um...yes," she said to Dominy, not offering any more information.

"How painful?" Dominy asked, pressing for more..

This woman was such a surprise. Brandon found the knowledge unsettling. He couldn't seem to place her. She seemed to be moving a mile a minute in many different directions.

"It will take two to four weeks for me to recover, but it is not as painful as it will be for the child I am donating it to. There is also a chance that her body rejects it, but I don't believe it will."

"Aren't you a little...petite for such a surgery? Were there no other candidates?"

Once again everyone turned to stare at Brandon, wondering at his outburst, but this time Dominy came to his rescue.

"What Brandon is trying to say, very poorly I might add, is 'Isn't it dangerous?'" He then looked at Brandon for confirmation. Brandon could only nod. He was dumbfounded at this violent reaction he was having at hearing about the procedure she would endure.

"I am fully aware of the risks, but I trust that God will keep me and heal me in this process."

He was going to be sick.

"May I use your restroom?" He directed his question towards Lady Menagerie. His body was already starting to betray him. A small sheen was breaking out on his upper lip.

"Sure, just around that corner." She pointed in the direction he was to take.

"Excuse me," he said as he took long strides out of the room.

"Is he alright?" he heard Paige ask. He was too engrossed in reaching the bathroom before really embarrassing himself, to hear the answer Dominy gave.

He closed the door and breathed as slowly as he could while running cold water over his hands, and wiping the back of his neck to cool himself down.

He leaned down, placing his face on the cool countertop, and sweet relief came over him. He had to divert his thoughts in order to keep the reaction from starting over again.

Yes, I hear you. I know you will take care of her. I trust you will take care of her. You did way before I met her. Please, Lord, I need peace in this.

Such a huge overreaction his body was having; he couldn't even blame the chemo.

You have my attention. I am admitting only that. You have my attention. Now can I get back to them before my time in here becomes embarrassing?

He took several deep breaths, sitting down with his head almost between his knees, and finally his body began to relax and return to normal. He washed his hands, checking his reflection to make sure the person looking back was the picture of cool reserve.

He joined the group back in the living room.

They were now on the subject of Dana's school. He would have to hold his questions until later. Dominy gave him a sidelong glance, but said nothing.

A few minutes later, Pastor Lawrence walked in offering his apologies for being late and the party of six moved to the dining room.

Dinner was pleasant. Brandon resigned himself to only speaking when asked a direct question. He concentrated on eating the food on his plate at slowly as possible. Not completely trusting his body, he only placed half the amount he might otherwise eat on his dish.

He only gave himself permission to watch Paige when she spoke, noticing her looking more tired as the evening went on. When she took longer than normal to bring her coffee to her lips during dessert, he began to get concerned. He didn't know how far away she lived, but she was in no condition to drive.

He offered to help Lady Menagerie by carrying some dishes into the kitchen for her and asked her if Elder Paige shouldn't stay overnight because she looked exhausted and he doubted she could make it home.

She turned from what she was doing and looked Brandon squarely in the eye. "You seem quite …concerned about Paige."

Brandon chuckled, covering his embarrassment, "Did you see her in there? She almost fell asleep in her coffee. I just thought since you two were close that you might not mind suggesting that she stay."

"I love Paige like a daughter, but I also know that she is stubborn, and less willing to do something for herself than she is for someone else." She took the dishes out of his hands, placing them in the dishwasher.

"You will want to remember that when you begin to feel overprotective. She will fight you unless you are clever with it. Follow me." She walked back through the kitchen towards the dining room, allowing him to hold the door for her.

She sat back at the table. Dominy had engaged Paige in a light debate regarding the Kansas City Chiefs and the Oakland Raiders and their game history. She showed a lot of knowledge in the Raiders and some in the Chiefs. *She knows football? When did she have time to watch football?* Brandon thought to himself.

"I am sorry to interrupt this most educational display of football history, but before you continue could I ask a huge favor of you Paige?"

"Sure," Paige took another sip of coffee.

"Could I get you to stay over tonight? Pastor has a really early appointment tomorrow and Dana will be using my car because hers needs new brakes and I will need to take it in the morning so that it will be one of the first."

Paige contemplated on the request briefly. "Of course. I still have my overnight bag here right?"

Lady Menagerie nodded.

It wasn't too much later that Brandon and Dominy excused themselves for the evening, wishing everyone a good night. Pastor Lawrence walked them out to the car.

"Brandon, will you be able to make it to the Elder's bowling night on Friday?"

"I believe so. I don't foresee any reason why I shouldn't."

"Could you meet with me an hour before, in my office? I want to go over some things with you then we can go there right after."

Brandon nodded. "I will be there."

"This is not a closed elders' event. Some are bringing their spouses, so if you'd like, you are more than welcome to come, Dominy." He turned to Dominy.

"We would love to have you."

"Sure. Looks like I will have more fun on this trip than I initially thought. Thank you for inviting us tonight. I really enjoyed myself. Please give your lovely wife my regards," Dominy said, shaking Pastor Lawrence's hand.

They were a full two miles away when Dominy, who had been staring out the window, turned to Brandon.

"That Elder Morganson is something else, isn't she? A living donor; I don't know if I would have the nerve to do something like that, especially knowing that I would have to stay in a hospital in a city I was not familiar with. She is quite bold and has a passion for life that rivals an old friend's I used to know."

Brandon kept his teeth firmly together. He knew if he made any comment, Dominy would take it and run. They had almost reached his apartment before Dominy spoke again.

"You might want to try a little harder to hide that protective streak she seems to bring out in you if you want to keep with your plan to leave her alone. At one point, I thought you were going to outright forbid her to go through with the surgery. I don't think she is the type to take orders either. It would be more of a challenge for her to prove you wrong. I also believe that tonight, it became apparent to Lady Menagerie and her daughter that you have feelings for her and you know how much women love to talk. I suspect your ears will be burning by the morning."

Brandon pulled into his parking space, turning off the car. "Was it really that bad?"

Dominy gave Brandon a sympathetic look, nodding his head. "You, sir are fighting a losing battle. Throw up your hands and concede to it before you make it worse. I don't believe Paige noticed though, which is good for you. She must be considerably obtuse to the attention men give her. If I didn't already have the perfect wife, you would have some competition on your hands."

Brandon gave Dominy a dark look.

Dominy just chuckled. "Yeah, see... that. You might want to start practicing your poker face and find things she is interested in. At work tomorrow, you might want to Google her."

"I am not going to Google her," Brandon said, a little disgusted with the thought of snooping on her like that.

"Mmmmm and that is why I would win. You better hope no one else has their eye on her."

Brandon turned to him sharply, staring at him. He hadn't thought of anyone else being in the picture, but then again she was a very private person. He wouldn't have known about the Living Donor procedure if they'd not been there this evening.

"Did you ask her when she would be having the procedure?" he asked Dominy after a few minutes.

"The end of September. She will be on tour in a week or so. I wonder when she has time to do it all." Dominy turned to Brandon. "I like her, Brandon. I think she is amazing. Come on, put away the fear before regret takes its place. Don't answer now. Just think about it."

"And if I decided to do something, what would you suggest?"

Dominy became thoughtful. "Well for one, don't come at her like a bear. I really suggest you do a little research so that you can ask her some poignant questions. Be her friend. It seems as though Lady Menagerie is on your side. You could definitely do worse than to have her pulling for you."

"Maybe not after this evening. I know Pastor Lawrence will share with Lady Menagerie what I told him. I may become persona non-grata."

Dominy shrugged, not at all affected by the news.

"Just be her friend. If it is going to happen, it will happen. You don't have to do more than be yourself and be her friend."

Brandon opened his car door. "That seems easy for you. Women seem to flock to you. Besides my sisters, I have never really been able to talk to women, let alone ones I was interested in."

Dominy got out of his side of the car and came around to walk with Brandon upstairs. "That's because you treat women outside of your sisters like another species. Just talk to her and ask her questions you might want her to ask you about, like the things you love to do. How many books has she written? What was her favorite? What does she want to do next in her career? What are some of her dreams and aspirations? Speak to her and, when you get that overwhelming urge to be her protector, shut your mouth."

Brandon shot him a disparaging look as they walked in the apartment.

"Awww, don't give me that look. I can tell you are mentally writing down everything I tell you, but it is nice to be useful as more than just your nanny."

"And you just lost your star pupil. Goodnight Dom, I am going to bed." Brandon started walking to his room.

"Yeah. Don't you want to talk shop? I could teach you a lot."

"Goodnight Dom," Brandon repeated, continuing on to his room without turning around.

He could hear Dominy mumbling as he sat on the couch, turning on the television to the sports channel.

CHAPTER 33

"Martha, I am not coming home just yet. Some complications have arisen. I will be at least another two weeks."

"No problem, Mrs. Branchett, I will make sure everything is ready for your return."

"Martha, have you heard from Mr. Branchett recently?"

"No, Fabian said he extended his trip and wouldn't be back home for another two months at least."

"Oh, alright Martha, thank you. That will be all."

Victoria sifted through the paperwork on the bed in front of her. She let her hand glide over the pictures of Ms. Morganson, known as Elder Morganson to quite a few people. There were pictures of her in front of her apartment, in her car, with her niece/daughter in Atlanta, with her sister, an older press shot from a book signing and one of her speaking at a Women's Convention from the year before.

Victoria had never known anyone to have such a focused life. Besides the children and the recent eulogizing of her cousin, there wasn't anything on this woman. She led a very…uncomplicated life. She made a modest living by touring on a circuit which kept her traveling about a third of the year, but besides that, she stayed at home most of the time. And when she did go out, it was to church or volunteer.

Through records and the private investigator she'd hired, she'd learned that Ms. Morganson had one sister in Atlanta, a mother who now resided in Washington, and a father who'd been deceased for three years. She seemed to be very healthy, and besides visiting the sick, she had not been admitted to any hospital since the delivery of her children.

From what Victoria had found on the internet, the Morganson woman had written five books; three had been on the Best Sellers' list, and she was reportedly coming out with a new novel in the early part of next year. The woman was definitely a go-getter, she had to give her that. But she had rarely met anyone as good as their biography, and unfortunately, it looked like this woman was the real deal.

Victoria sighed. It was always so hard finding something to blackmail people with when they didn't have anything to hide. She wondered if this woman had shared her past with her pastors. Maybe she would send a small note to test the waters.

She needed some insurance, just in case Mason grew a conscious and decided to tell the Morganson woman about Vivian. It was already going to be hard enough for her lawyers to come up against Richard's; she and Richard had picked them together. And of course, they were men of integrity and fought fair---it was their only drawback from what she could see. It would be nearly impossible to take Vivian away if her mother were in the picture as well.

Victoria put the files away, stuffing them in her attaché case, and stowing it away in a corner of the room. She eyed the clock; it was getting late. She would have to leave now if she wanted to visit Vivian.

She didn't have to worry about running into Mason; since their discussion over a week ago, he'd been avoiding her. She hadn't caught sight of him once. Vivian let her know that he still came to visit every day, even after he'd been released from the hospital.

In the taxi on the way to the hospital, she rearranged her packages and considered the ramifications of Vivian's kidney transplant.

Vivian, who began looking more and more fragile by the day, was now going through dialysis twice a week, so Victoria had her make a list of movies she wanted to see so she could watch during her sessions.

The thought of the Morganson woman coming back to the state was bittersweet. She wanted to see her granddaughter well, but she feared that woman being in close proximity to her. There were too many scenarios she couldn't account for.

She walked out of the elevator onto the 5th floor. She balanced the packages once again and made her way down the hall to Vivian's room.

Her hand was on the door when her name was called.

"Victoria."

She turned to see Mason coming from the waiting room down the hall.

"Mason," she responded drolly.

"I waited for you because I need to let you know that I will be out of town for a few days on business. It will be easier on Vivian if you come by more often next Wednesday, Thursday, and Friday."

Victoria watched the strain on his face. How difficult this must be for him to be civil towards her, let alone to ask her for anything. The love of a child could weaken anyone; she should know.

"I would be more than happy to spend more time with my granddaughter. That is why I am here." She pasted a smile on her face.

Mason stared at her for a moment, then continued. "Thank you." Then he turned around and hobbled back down the hall to the elevators.

She watched him retreat. A suspicious woman by nature, Victoria worked out a few possibilities as she walked into Vivian's room.

She eyed the child sitting up in bed, a pout on her lips. She took a deep breath, letting it out slowly.

"What is this? You know you shouldn't pout. It misshapes your lips, and you have such lovely lips my dear."

Vivian pulled her lip back in, but it was the only feature that changed on her face.

Victoria's patience was wearing thin. It had been 10 minutes and Vivian was still sulking.

"Oh, come on Vivian, he will only be gone for a few days. You spent 10 times more days away from him this summer. What is the big deal?" She came forward sitting on the edge of the bed.

Vivian looked like she was going to cry. "I wasn't sick. I could come home at any time. I can't go home now." She looked up at Victoria, eyes brimming with tears.

God this child. Victoria was at a loss. She usually wouldn't put up with anyone in the throes of irrational behavior. She sat there for a moment, knowing she would have to think fast.

"Well, he has asked that I come a little more often so that you are not alone so much for the few days that he is gone. How about I see if we can't get a little better food for you? You really must eat something more than pudding."

Vivian sniffed. She looked at Victoria, eyes a little brighter. She blinked at the tears in her eyes. "You will spend more time with me?"

Victoria was caught off guard by the small glimmer of hope in Vivian's eyes. She'd underestimated this child's love for her. She nodded her head. It took three swallows to clear the lump in her throat.

"You just tell me what time you want me to be here and I will do my best to be here, but be reasonable, Vivian, about your request. You know I am not my best before 9 am"

Vivian giggled. "I remember. How about 10 am? It still gives you time to spend with me before any of those boring sessions."

"I believe I can do that," Victoria smiled, seeing that Vivian's face lift. "You didn't say anything about the food. Do you have any requests?"

"Spaghetti. They don't make it right here. It smells funny," she said wrinkling her nose.

Victoria smiled. "Spaghetti it is. This will be our little secret though, okay?"

"Okay." Then Vivian held out her arms.

Victoria, surprised by the gesture, hesitated slightly then leaned in. She held still while Vivian wrapped her small arms around her, but after a moment, she brought up one hand to pat her back lightly.

When Vivian finally released her there were no traces of the tears left, but there was curiosity on her upturned face as she glanced back and forth between Victoria, and the packages on the floor.

Victoria laughed. She didn't notice that Vivian was staring at her dumbfounded.

"What child? Why are you looking at me like that?" she asked, the smile slowly fading.

Vivian looked away shyly. "I like your laugh."

Victoria stared at her for a moment judging if that was a true statement. She shrugged after a while, then bent down to retrieve one of the packages she'd brought for Vivian to use while in dialysis.

"Gram, can I ask you a question?"

"Yes, you may ask," Victoria replied, putting one of the packages on the bed.

"I was wondering if I could ask you a favor." Vivian hid her face inside the bag, her voice muffled.

"Go ahead."

"Could you be nicer to daddy?"

Victoria's mouth opened then closed. She didn't have a reply.

"I was hoping that you and he would be nicer to each other for me." Her eyes were downcast. Victoria didn't have a response that she thought this child could accept.

"I…I don't…"

"Pleeeeeeeease."

"Don't beg Vivian, it is beneath you."

Victoria watched Vivian's face as she looked away.

"Don't you want to see what I bought you? I had to go to three stores to find it."

Vivian shrugged, the pout coming back.

"Really, you are trying my patience." Victoria was growing concerned. This was not like Vivian. She was normally such a well-mannered child.

"Really, you are trying my patience." Vivian repeated in a voice as close to Victoria's as possible.

Victoria's eyes narrowed. This little chit of a girl was actually trying to challenge her. Good for her.

"Don't be insolent, child. When you don't see things going your way, you don't antagonize the person. You find out what they want and then compromise with them."

Vivian cocked her head to the side. "What does ant-gonize mean?"

"To annoy or irritate – exactly what you are trying to do to me. Do you want to tell me what is really wrong?"

Vivian hesitated.

"Vivian, I know you think I am hard on you sometimes, but it is for your own good. Right now, I just wish you would let me know what is causing you to behave like this."

"Gram, I'm scared."

"But there is nothing…" Victoria began.

Vivian interrupted her.

"I'm afraid they won't find me a kidney, and I will leave daddy all alone. He can't be alone." Vivian finished quietly.

Victoria found herself speechless for the second time inside of 5 minutes. This child was running on an emotional roller coaster. Maybe she would make a call, see if she could find a good child psychologist.

"If your father is alone, it is his choice," Victoria said, a stoic expression etched in her face.

"I want you to make up with Daddy," Vivian nearly shouted, her voice adamant and stubborn.

Victoria saw Rachael clear as day in Vivian's contentious expression: the way her brows came together, shoulders taut. It pricked her heart.

"It isn't so easy," Victoria said, her voice gentling.

"But it is. All you have to do is say it."

Victoria wouldn't tell Vivian that she would sooner cut out her tongue than say anything remotely close to Mason. That was even a line she wouldn't cross. Instead she just stared back, her face expressionless.

Vivian crossed her arms, tears forming in her eyes and brimming over. She huffed twice then began to cry… loudly.

"If you don't stop this instant I will walk out of that door."

Vivian continued, taking it up an octave.

"Vivian Leigh Jenson, if you don't pull yourself together and behave like the young lady I know you to be, I will leave here and I won't be back for the rest of the day."

Vivian stopped for only a second, drawing in a deep breath and let out a blood-curdling scream before she continued to cry, then she launched herself back against the pillows, rolling over onto her stomach, and began bawling in earnest.

A nurse came in to investigate. "What is going on in here?"

Victoria got up from the bed, moving the packages out of her path, placing her purse on her shoulder. She lifted her chin.

"Have you never seen a child throw a tantrum before?" she said, walking past the nurse.

"Vivian, I will come back tomorrow when you have remembered yourself."

"Don't come back!" Vivian sat back up, yelling. "If you're not my daddy's friend then you can't be my friend."

Victoria turned around, watching as the child started kicking her legs, as if the movement could take the place of any explicative she couldn't verbalize.

The nurse moved towards Vivian making cooing sounds, trying to soothe her.

Victoria turned back to the door in front of her and walked out.

The stubborn child definitely had Rachael's ways, no matter who her biological mother was. She was her granddaughter through and through.

She would have to think of another way to widen the gap between daughter and father and Mason had inadvertently given her the time she needed.

She could see that gifts were not going to be enough. She was going to have to feed on this child's emotional needs.

CHAPTER 34

Mason made the final arrangements for his trip to New York. Thursday morning, he would be on a flight and by that evening, if everything worked as planned, he would be sitting across from Paige Morganson, trusting her with the most important piece of his life: the knowledge that his daughter was also hers.

All week he'd gone over the different ways he could tell her. He was wondering if he should make it short and to the point or go through the story of him and Rachael, and their desire to adopt before having children biologically.

It was finally decided that this he needed to do in person. It wasn't because he wanted to see her again, he'd told himself. This was just too important not to be in front of her, to see her reaction and maybe even to comfort her if need be. Plus there was always the chance that she may make a call to the caseworker and that may delay the whole process.

He'd made reservations at the Belvedere Hotel, since it was close to the bookstore she was having her signing. He'd even scouted out some restaurants in the area on the internet, just in case she would allow him to take her to dinner. Though it would guarantee privacy, by her reaction to him, he knew his room was out of the question.

Mason had looked up Paige Morganson, hoping her site had a speaking engagement calendar. He was pleasantly surprised to find that it not only provided a calendar with addresses, times of engagements and book signings, but also contact information for media junkets and a press page. He read over her biography and list of books she'd written. He even looked back to see other places she'd spoken and found the list quite impressive. She was busier than he'd first realized. He would have wondered why he'd not heard of her before then, but their worlds were as far apart as if they were born in different centuries.

It wasn't until he reached the gallery page that he caught sight of a picture of her with some young women. Paige, looking only a couple of years older than them, was dressed in a peach-colored suit that complimented her complexion and brought out the flakes of gold in her eyes. He studied her face as he had his daughter's, once again going over the similarities and differences, wondering now how he'd missed the connection.

He knew how. He had been mesmerized by her and even if they looked more alike, he would not have noticed. She had a certain allure that couldn't be hidden in a suit, high neckline, or low skirt. It was as if the very essence of her called to him, even as her eyes stayed demurely masked after those first few moments.

Not since Rachael had he been in a woman's presence that affected him so thoroughly. After deciding how and when he was going to talk to her about Vivian, he'd not been able to fully get her out of his mind. He wondered what she was doing, where she was, if she was feeling trepidation or anxiety about the procedure, had she thought of him or their few moments together...

He organized the papers he'd printed on her and placed them back in his briefcase, along with his flight itinerary and hotel arrangements.

He checked his watch as he picked up his coffee thermos; he had just enough time to get to work. At least today he was leaving five minutes sooner. He didn't realize how long it had been since he'd been to work until he had to be someplace before he was ready to be there. Being manned by a clock or watch again was taking some getting used to and he was finding the adjustment cumbersome. This was the first time this week he had a good chance of getting to work on time; it was a good thing he had kept in touch with Bill Parker, the CEO.

Well, it was more like Bill had kept in touch with him, continuously asking him when he might consider coming back to work and letting him know that there would always be a job for him as long as he was in the position to give it to him.

When Mason had finally called Bill and told him he was ready, Bill sounded like Christmas had come early. He even allowed him to make his own, though structured, hours so that he could still visit Vivian in the middle of the day when she was going through dialysis.

He was actually thankful to have something else to think about besides the last two years of his life. It felt good to be part of something that made a difference in the lives of people he would never meet. He was happy to use this creative part of himself again. He'd had moments of anxiety the day before he was to come in. He nearly called Bill and told him he'd changed his mind.

The elevator ride up to the 23rd floor of MarsdenTech was the longest he'd ever taken, but once the doors opened, he forced himself not to look back.

He was more than surprised to see some familiar faces in the old office, and though he was now at another desk, the workers on this side of the huge office were very friendly and open.

During his first day back, a man by the name of Sam Parker came over and walked him through the new version of the Application Architecture they were using, giving him a crash course in the quick keys and going over changes in tools.

Mason spent the rest of the day playing with the different applications, making up mock projects and familiarizing himself with some of the latest designs the company had come up with.

By the end of the week, he'd joined a team in an ongoing project for a supermarket chain that was buying out old warehouses and using some of the materials to rebuild.

With his days filled with work and Vivian, he felt the storm clouds lift and begin to dissipate. But when he would come home after a full day, he would sit at the kitchen table with whatever frozen dinner his hands would touch first, turn on the television for background noise, and reminisce on how he'd once had it all.

Without Vivian to check on him, he didn't even bother going to the bedroom to sleep. After two years, no matter how many times he washed the sheets or cleaned the carpet, *she* was still there. It was as if she were in the walls and he knew it wasn't true, but Rachael had stamped herself so incisively on his person he couldn't seem to get away, and until recently he had no thought or reason why he should want to.

*   *   *

Mason got off the plane at LaGuardia Airport and hailed a cab to Midtown where his hotel was. He sat in his hotel room after unpacking and calling Vivian to see how she was doing. She sounded so down, he was considering coming back early.

She'd had a perpetual pout on her lips from the moment he'd told her he was going out of town for a few days. At first he thought it was because she wouldn't get to see him every day, but as the days passed and the same sour look greeted him, he pressed deeper to find what was really bothering her.

The closest he'd come was a few mumbled words of how she would miss him. He'd seen something more in her eyes and he'd alternated between asking, begging, and waiting for her to elaborate, but she would say no more. She just cried in his arms until she fell asleep.

He'd sat there shaken, hoping she would wake up before he had to leave. He didn't want this to be the memory he took with him on his trip, but he already knew that even if she had awakened before he left, her response would have been no different.

Mason left the hotel to make his way to the bookstore where Paige would sign later that evening. As he walked past the bookstore window towards the door, he saw the poster advertising Paige's latest book. He noticed that her picture was placed small and low on the poster, the book cover and teaser taking up most of the space with a few forwards in italics. He wondered why there were so few pictures of her on her website as well.

He walked through the aisles, perusing the different genres. It had been a long time since he'd been in a bookstore, let alone taken the time to walk through each aisle.

He eventually found himself in the children's psychology section. He fingered through the titles, picking up a book every now and then and reading its description.

An hour later he headed toward the checkout with three books. At the front of the aisle leading to the cashier in the middle, he spotted Paige's book. Without a second glance he picked it up off the shelf, adding it to his purchases.

Over lunch at a corner diner near the hotel, Mason scanned the three psychology books, picking out places in chapters he wanted to read more in depth.

He finished his lunch and walked back to his hotel room. He was going to wait until the signing was almost over before he got in line. He wanted to be one of the last ones she saw so that she could heed his urgent plea to meet her later.

Picking up Paige's book, Mason sat on the bed leaning against the headboard. He stared at the cover for a few minutes then turned the book over to read the brief summary.

It was a fictional novel. The story caught his attention immediately causing him to wonder how, if at all, the tragedies in the beginning could lead to any type of redeemable ending.

He turned each page wondering how people could go through such devastation and survive with their sanity. He was so engrossed he lost track of time and had to rush to make sure he got to her signing before it ended.

He walked in the door of the bookstore that for the lateness of the evening was still very busy. He made an immediate left to the edge of the store, taking a side aisle to where the direction for the signing pointed.

As he passed each row, he briefly glanced to make sure he hadn't walked by her; seven rows down, he saw the end of the line. There were still quite a few people waiting to speak to her. He crossed through an aisle suddenly feeling more like a stalker than an acquaintance. The thought that she may not remember him briefly occurred to him, but he dismissed it almost as quickly.

Book in hand, he stood at the back of the line. Every now and then, he would look behind him to see how many people had gotten in line. When the number was more than five, he would step out of line and get back in behind them. He did it twice.

Finally, when he'd stayed the last person for a while, he began to get nervous, trying to keep focused on his spiel. As he inched closer his heartbeat escalated, and by the time he was a few feet out, he was warm enough to feel a trickle of perspiration roll down the back of his neck.

The few glimpses he'd caught of Paige did no good for his stomach, which was already tossing and turning. He worked to stay out of her line of sight, but couldn't help staring.

The look of her had no less of an effect on him than the first time he saw her. She was beautiful. Her hair was put up in a French roll; small wisps of hair fell around her ears, framing her face. The hairstyle was still not as soft as when she wore it clipped loosely at her crown the day he met her. It was more severe, as though she dared someone to start something with her. How he wanted to take the pins out and see the dark curls fall around her shoulders. Up this close, he could see small smudges under her eyes. She looked tired and he felt a tinge of guilt for causing her further unrest, but he couldn't go back without fulfilling his purpose.

Her skirt suit was black with white piping along the edges; tailored to fit, but still too angular for his taste.

His heartbeat going a mile a minute, he placed his copy of her book on the table and waited for her to look up from something her manager was showing her.

He stood there staring at her as she looked up and waited as recognition crossed her features.

"Mr. Jenson!" The surprise on her face was expected, but the next few expressions that crossed over her features turned the warmth of his nervousness to heat, then she blinked and her eyes cooled.

"Hello, Ms. Morganson, congratulations on the success of your new novel," he said, pushing his copy of her book toward her.

She frowned. "I didn't know you read." She blinked again. "I mean I didn't know you read Christian novels."

He shrugged, but didn't say anything.

"Why are you here? I mean here in New York?"

"A bit of double-duty. I have some business here, but I also came to share some important information with you."

"How is Vivian doing?" She opened the book, still looking up at him.

"She is a trooper and is fighting hard."

Paige nodded. "Who would you like me to sign this to?"

He shifted from side to side. "To uh, Vivian. V-I-V-I-A-N."

She looked down at the book and began to write.

Mason knew if he was going to say what he needed to, this was the moment.

"Ms. Morganson, I need to talk to you. It is very important. It is about Vivian."

She looked up, more concerned with how he said Vivian's name than the thought of talking to him away from the hospital.

"Is there something wrong?" Her pen was now hovering over the page.

"She isn't really doing all that well, but there have been some new developments that I believe you need to be made aware of. Would it be possible for us to discuss it after your signing here?"

She just stared up at him for a long moment. He felt like a child called to the principal's office.

"What are you talking about? What is going on with Vivian? Has she gotten worse?"

"She was declining slowly, but the dialysis has been helping. She should definitely be strong enough for the transplant though."

"Then what Mr. Jenson? What is so urgent?"

"It isn't something we should discuss here. There is a restaurant down the street. It is public enough where you shouldn't feel uncomfortable, but the atmosphere should allow for some privacy."

"Uh, um, uh." She opened and closed her mouth. Then she looked up at her manager who had yet to be introduced.

"I'm sorry. I am Paige's manager, Carmen Menascal, and you are?" Eyes lit with curiosity as she looked back and forth between Mason and Paige.

He reached forward to shake hands with the woman standing next to her.

"Mason Jenson," he said.

Carmen leaned down and spoke close to Paige's ear. He watched Paige's face become stern as she shook her head, and the woman spoke again waiting for Paige's answer. This time she nodded then looked up at Mason.

"Yes, I will come since it seems to be urgent. I will have to bring Carmen with me of course."

Mason nodded. Knowing that this may be the only way to come out with him, but she may regret it later.

"I don't mind at all if that is what makes you feel comfortable. I do realize that you hardly know me, but I must warn you that it is a very sensitive matter." He looked back and forth between the two women. He would have said more, but thought better of it with both women present.

"I will wait until you are done then I will escort you to the restaurant. I will let you finish here and meet you near the door."

Paige's mind was reeling. Was he really here? She had managed to finally exorcise Mr. Jenson from her mind over the last few days, going over her conference materials more meticulously than usual. Her long days and nights left little time for her to think about anything else.

She thought she had seen him when she'd glanced up to see how much longer the line was, but thought that her mind was playing tricks on her. She was tired and she was ready to go home for a couple of days of recuperation before she went back to Chicago. Normally, her energy level was high and contagious, but the signings had dragged on and what Paige would have usually reveled in, she found to be draining. She was contemplating that again as she first looked up and saw that the line stretched to the door. Carmen had definitely done her homework this time and the marketing strategy had paid off.

She even noted that Carmen was more attentive than normal, periodically asking if she wanted some more coffee or water, or needed to take a break. She shook her head, wanting to get done as quickly as possible so that she could return to the privacy of her room. It was bitterly cold in New York this autumn, and that did very little to lift her mood.

She kept a smile plastered on her face and continued to listen with undivided attention to each person's show of appreciation, small story, or their perception of the characters in her book, until Carmen politely gained their attention to let them know there were many people waiting behind them.

She'd looked down to read a note Carmen handed to her in regards to a small women's group that wanted to see if she would be willing to add to her schedule late morning of the next day. They were willing to pay, but it was their affiliation with her pastor that helped guide her decision. She told Carmen she would accept and reached for the book that had been placed in front of her to sign.

She looked up at first thinking she was seeing things yet again, but after blinking a couple of times, he was still there in front of her, calmly waiting for her to show signs of recognition.

He was dressed warmly in a black wool coat that enhanced his square shoulders, and charcoal-gray slacks. His eyes were wary, as if he didn't know how she would respond to him being there, but it didn't take away from the reaction that he evoked. He was better looking than she remembered, not like she was trying to remember. Not just his face, but her reaction to it caused a decent amount of inner turmoil.

Once again her face became flushed and she tried to hide her reaction to him behind a professionalism she no longer felt. What was he doing here?

Carmen bent down to whisper in Paige's ear after Mason departed.

"Oh my...that's the father of the little girl you are donating your kidney too?" Paige could hear the excitement in Carmen's voice.

She just nodded, trying to regain some composure, taking the next reader's book so that she could concentrate on something other than her agreement to meet with Mr. Mason Jenson.

Soon with the last signing of books and the store's closing, Paige gathered up her belongings, very much aware of Carmen's curiosity. She decided to get it over with. She straightened up and looked Carmen squarely in the eye.

"Alright, better now than in his presence. What do you want to know?"

Carmen's eyes were dancing. "Really? Okay. I want to know what you thought when you first met him. You gave me the polite and general overview, but I can see that you left some things out like just how tasty of an eye-candy her father is."

"Carmen, behave yourself. This is a purely professional relationship."

Carmen waved her hands. "I never thought anything less. That wasn't my question anyway. I want to know what you thought when you first saw him?"

"Why is that important?" Paige said looking down, busying herself with rearranging her things.

"I want to know if you are alive under there."

Paige looked up to see Carmen wearing a mischievous grin and she couldn't help smile herself. The woman was a hopeless romantic for all her practicality in business affairs. She had tried more than once to match-make, until Paige told her in no uncertain terms that she was not interested and would embarrass Carmen the next time she tried.

"The first time I saw him I thought he was very handsome" Paige said, hoping that would satisfy her. The look Carmen gave said otherwise.

"What do you want to hear? That the first time I saw him he took my breath away. That I have never met a man I thought was more physically beautiful than him. That I can barely think when he is around?"

"Yes. Is it true?" Carmen asked expectantly.

Paige nearly laughed. "No, not completely, but I will let you pretend for a little while."

"You could have not said anything." Carmen said with a sardonic smile, "Was there any part of it that was true?"

"Yes, but I am not going to tell you which part," Paige said, laughing.

Carmen just made a sound deep in her throat, then sighed. "Do you want me to stay with you through the whole meeting, or if things start to get really personal do you want me to make myself scarce?"

Paige thought about it for a moment. She had no real idea what he wanted to discuss, but didn't think she would feel comfortable enough to be alone with him at any time. She felt pretty confident that anything he said, Carmen could be privy to, and told her just as much.

At the door, Mason helped the two women with their coats and escorted them to a quaint late-night café, close to Broadway.

Once seated in a booth in the back, Mason took a deep breath. He wiped his forehead with the back of his glove, trying to calm his heart. He straightened his place setting, working out the speech he'd recited over and over in his head. Finally, he cleared his throat and looked up at the two women.

His agitation was beginning to make Paige nervous and she began to feel the hairs on the back of her neck raise up.

"Ms. Morganson, do you remember mentioning your daughter Gladys to me in the hospital?" He looked uncomfortably from Paige to Carmen.

Paige nodded, aware of the shift in Carmen's attitude. Bless her heart, she could also be very protective.

"Not to bring up what may have been a very tumultuous time in your life, but could you tell me what you remember from the day you gave birth to her?" His eyes were pleading, but for what?

"Mr. Jenson, I don't see what this has to do with my being your daughter's donor…"

"Please humor me. I am getting to that. This has more to do with it than you know."

Paige eyed him for a moment trying to gauge his sincerity while working her mind to make the connection.

She wasn't sure just how much to share with him, but gave him what he asked. She explained that she had gone to the doctor earlier that day for a physical, leaving out that she was intending to get an abortion, and was told that she was pregnant with twins. She was far enough along that they kept her. She went through the ordeal of the labor, feeling Carmen take her hand underneath the table for support while she relived the scene in the delivery room when the nurse came back to tell her that one of her twins didn't make it.

She didn't feel the need to share her relief at the time that at least one life was spared in the tragedy, which she had begun to consider was her destiny. One of her children was able to escape and go straight to God. She knew that if she were to die with her she may not be so fortunate, but had still prayed for it.

When she had finished, the silence that surrounded them was thick. Carmen squeezed her hand a few more times, then slacked off.

"Did you ever see the other child?" Mason asked through a choked voice, overwhelmed with emotion for the child that had to endure the delivery of twins.

Paige shook her head, not wanting to give away the fact that she's had no intention nor interest in seeing the deceased product of hate.

She took a deep breath. "Now Mr. Jenson. It is your turn to explain yourself and these questions. I think I have been more than obliging. Overly so."

"May I ask one more question?" Mason looked at both women, hoping Paige would meet this one last request.

Exasperated, Carmen sighed and was about to say no but Paige squeezed her hand in return. "Go ahead, Mr. Jenson. One more."

"Could I see a picture of Gladys?" His eyes were beseeching.

Paige's stomach twisted into a tight knot. She didn't like where this was heading. "I don't understand what she has to do with any of this. I only told you about her as part of my interrogation that day."

Mason didn't say anything. He lifted his wallet from his back pocket and took out a photo from the wallet. He looked at it briefly before looking at Paige.

"I want you to take a look at a picture of my daughter, Vivian, taken earlier this summer but before I do I need you to promise that you will remain here and allow me to explain."

Paige knew a huge question mark was stamped dead in the middle of her face but as if she were moving in slow motion, she reached out for the picture. When she turned it, she saw a child that looked exactly like Gladys but the background was no place familiar.

She continued to stare at the picture trying to place it in her mind but couldn't seem to make the pieces fit.

"I don't understand…" Paige began, but her thoughts were muddled. She couldn't seem to get a clear one through.

"My mother-in-law is a very influential woman. She has a lot of money and a great many connections, and she uses them to her advantage." Mason paused as the waitress came back with their drinks and asked if they were ready to order. Carmen ordered a strawberry cheesecake and Paige ordered a blueberry muffin, thinking that she was going to have to work hard to get any of it down.

"Victoria is not the most giving person I know, but she is thorough. My wife and I knew we wanted children early on but instead of having one of our own first, we wanted to adopt. Rachael was special that way. Well, we did adopt a beautiful baby girl twelve years ago. It was a simple process and everything looked well in accordance to any other adoption someone might have, plus we had my mother-in-law's lawyers double-check everything. Like I said, she is thorough. I shared with Victoria that I'd met with you, and she became greatly agitated to the point that she didn't want to use you as a donor even though you were the likeliest candidate. I know Victoria to be neurotic, bitter, and angry, but I know she loves her granddaughter. So I pressed, and she finally told me the story of how she had looked into Vivian's biological mother's medical records, just in case if anything happened to Vivian, she would be prepared. Things didn't quite add up and she hired a private investigator to do some digging." He took a deep breath, his intense gaze never leaving Paige's face.

Paige felt like she was in the clutches of a dream that slowly turned into a nightmare. She could see and hear Mason and feel Carmen now rubbing her hand under the table but it all seemed like it was far away, like she had been detached from her body and the scene was playing out on some weird type of movie screen.

"Victoria found out that the woman who delivered the child that night died and that is what we were told as well about her, but what we weren't told was that her child supposedly died soon after her."

There was a loud rushing in her ears, she could barely hear him over it, but she knew what he was saying almost before he said it. She reached out to hold on to the table, needing to feel something bolted down to keep her on the ground.

"Ms. Morganson, what I am saying is, Vivian is your daughter. Your other daughter."

"Paige? Paige, honey, are you alright?" Carmen's concerned voice broke through the haze, but Paige couldn't seem to get herself to move.

Her other daughter was alive. Both of her twins lived. She didn't die? She wasn't in heaven? *Sweet peace, please, please have me, have me. Sweet darkness, take me please.*

"Paige please, you're scaring me. I think you need to drink something. Paige? Come on honey, this is good news."

She could hear the fear in Carmen's voice. She didn't handle extremely emotional situations well.

You will have to pull yourself together.

She gritted her teeth, making the feeling pull her back to herself. She blinked and stared across the table.

Mason leaned across the table, placing the back of his hand on her forehead and then cupping her cheek with his hand. The look in his eyes was one of tenderness and concern.

"I'm sorry to give you such news in this way. I didn't know any other way than being direct. Are you alright? Maybe you should drink something? Do you want something stronger than water?"

He finally removed his hand after the last question, sitting back in the seat, seeming to have remembered himself.

Paige, caught in a surge of emotion, didn't trust herself to do anything but lift up the glass of water to her lips. Her hand shook violently and Carmen helped her steady it.

The cool liquid helped her get back in touch with more of her body as she concentrated on the feel of the liquid sliding down her throat and esophagus. She blinked again and took a deep breath, and with it came a rush from Carmen.

"You scared me for a moment there. Your face became as white as a sheet. Are you alright?" Carmen exclaimed, her voice agitated.

Paige nodded, looking at her then back at Mason who was looking just as concerned. His brows were drawn together but he was biting his lip.

"Give me just a moment," Paige said, leaning her back against the booth and looked down at the forgotten picture on the table. She picked it back up, staring at the child again, looking for differences now instead of similarities between her memory of Gladys and Vivian. From what she could see there were very few except for the clothing and the smile. She bet Vivian had her mother's smile.

She swallowed, closing her eyes. She was her mother, too.

God what are you doing? I don't know how much more of this I can take. I am so tired. I need help on this one. I need an answer, Lord. I am desperate for one. What should I do?

"I...uh....I will be here for one more day. Will you still be in town?" She looked at Mason. He nodded.

"Will you phone me late in the morning? Carmen will give you my contact information if you need it. I need to go be alone and lay down right now." She moved out of the booth, but found that her legs weren't as steady as she wished. Mason moved quickly around the table, placing his hands on her shoulders to help keep her upright.

"Are you sure you don't want to wait for a moment longer and see if you are stronger?" He said, peering down into her face, watching her eyes.

She looked up and found that his closeness mixed with his aftershave was doing nothing for her stomach or the haze that still clung to the outside of her peripheral vision.

"My hotel is just around the corner. I should be able to make it."

"The least I can do is accompany you to your hotel, just to make sure you get there. Please let me do that. It will go a long way in easing some of the guilt I feel in how I told you."

She nodded, stepping from under his hands to lean on Carmen. Even after they'd walked a few feet, her shoulders were still warm.

CHAPTER 35

Paige sat on the edge of her bed for what seemed like an hour, staring off into space before she picked up her cell phone and pressed one of the speed dial numbers.

Lady Menagerie picked up on the third ring.

"Good evening, Paige."

Paige's mouth lifted slightly. Lady Menagerie truly believed in Caller I.D.

"Good evening, First Lady. I am sorry to call you this late, but I really needed to talk to you. Do you have a moment?"

"Sure. I was just doing some reading."

"Are you sure I am not interrupting you? I could call back later."

"No need to back-pedal, Paige. I am fine. Actually, I am surprised to hear from you tonight. You are still in New York? Isn't it rather late?"

"Yes I am and yes it is, but so many thoughts are going on in my head right now I won't be able to get to sleep until I talk some of it out."

"Alright. I am listening."

Paige suddenly didn't know where to begin. So many different emotions were trying to rule at once. The life she saw coming together before tonight and the one she saw continuing to unfold in front of her, to a degree, left her helpless. Another whole different scenario came to mind from her participation in the Elder's Fellowship, but in all, the news of that evening was now second place.

"Paige, are you still there?"

"Yes. Sorry. I was just trying to put things into perspective or at least in some semblance of order."

"Okay. Take a deep breath and start with the facts."

"My other twin daughter didn't die at birth. She is alive."

"What?! How do you know?" Menagerie's voice was one of sheer shock.

"She is the one I am donating my kidney to. Her father came to my book-signing tonight and…" Paige's hand started shaking so much she could barely keep the phone to her ear.

"Paige do you have some water near you? Get some water, honey. I'll wait."

Paige retrieved a bottle from her nightstand, taking in the cool liquid, trying to calm herself.

"I am back."

"Alright. So you found out that the child that you are a living donor for is actually your biological daughter. How did you find this out?"

Paige tried to recall everything that happened that evening starting with the book-signing. She had already shared her encounter with Mason and the kaleidoscope of feelings he evoked in her when she'd spent the night at First Lady and Pastor's house.

It was one of the reasons she had given into her hesitancy towards Elder Tatum.

"Did he tell you how long he'd known about her being your daughter?"

"I honestly don't remember…I was too shocked to think of anything but the fact that both my twins lived and I don't know either one of them."

"But you have that opportunity now. I am sure he wouldn't have told you if he didn't have any intention of letting you get to know her."

Paige nodded then remembered she was on the phone. "Yes, but I am not sure I deserve another opportunity. I hated my babies. I didn't want to have anything to do with them. What mother hates the children she carries and bares?"

"A child who goes through the trauma you did with little support, cannot be faulted for the emotional turmoil such circumstances bring about. You were 14, pregnant with twins, and were being pushed into killing them by your mother who believed your rapist over you. I can't imagine what you went through emotionally and physically during and after labor at that age. It's a wonder you kept your sanity."

"Just barely. I think I was too angry to lose my mind, though sometimes I wished I could have just disappeared. If someone had shown me how, I would have," Paige said stoically.

"But you are here now, relatively on the other side of things. How do you feel about her now?"

"I feel truly blessed to be given another chance. It is one I never expected or thought I would want. I thought she had been spared from all the darkness of my life then by dying. I always imagined her in heaven and I found comfort in that. Now I want to see her. I want to know that she is happy, that she has a childhood and that she is safe."

"Do you doubt any of those things? You told me about her father, Mason, was it?"

"Um, yes, Mr. Mason Jenson. It is obvious that he adores her and puts her happiness first but with her mother passing away, I wonder if he doesn't have ulterior motives for telling me," Paige rubbed her palm back and forth across her forehead.

"Or, knowing that you will be his daughter's donor he thought you should know. Which takes me back to my first question of how long he has known."

"I am supposed to meet with him tomorrow morning to talk with him about this more in depth. I am afraid I was working too hard just to take it all in and keep breathing."

"I understand. So are you meeting with him alone?"

"I don't know. I was thinking of keeping Carmen around. She didn't seem uncomfortable with the cause for my reaction, just the reaction itself tonight. She isn't the most nurturing of people but she did handle herself well."

"I know he provoked some pretty strong emotions in you when you first met. What about now?"

"His looks still take my breath away, but there are so many different dynamics to all of this than how I react to him physically and emotionally that are now starting to take a backseat to it all."

"Are you sure?" Lady Menagerie seemed to be leaning towards something.

"I believe so…why?"

"I just want to make sure that you are not taken by surprise. You yourself said that it has been quite a few years since you responded to someone that way…if ever."

Paige thought about her statement. Mason did seem to throw her off guard easily. His uncanny looks and the intensity of his gazes left her feeling vulnerable and feeling naked.

It was unnerving and strangely exciting, and though his love for his daughter was endearing and made Paige thank God for the affectionate environment she was raised in, Paige was still wary of him.

The last thing she wanted was to lose her head around him. She understood enough by their conversations to know that they were unequally yoked. She moved and lived by God's direction. Her relationship with Him was the most important aspect of her life and therefore she could only trust a man whose relationship with God was as important to him.

She wanted to submit to and be loved by a man who she knew submitted to God. But Mason, though he stirred up many things in her body and mind, she sensed was angry and felt God needed to prove something to him. It was not a good combination for a trusting relationship… just more hurt.

"Paige, are you still there?" She heard Menagerie as she pulled her out of her thoughts.

"Yes, um, yes, thank you, that is true. It is just so weird that all this time I have not been remotely attracted to anyone, and then out of the blue it is like my eyes are open to it."

"Mmmm, while your eyes are open…*who* have you been seeing while your 'eyes have been open'?" Lady Menagerie hinted.

Paige was quiet. She wondered how it would sound if she admitted her attraction to Elder Tatum as well.

"Is it wrong to be attracted to more than one man at a time?" she asked quietly, her voice barely audible.

"It isn't necessarily wrong but it may complicate things if you aren't clear on why. Do you want to talk about it?"

"I do but I am not sure where to begin. Everything is so fuzzy and all mixed up."

"Mixed up how?" Lady Menagerie pressed.

"Elder Brandon Tatum. He is confusing."

"So you are attracted to Elder Tatum?"

Paige winced hearing it out loud. She was tempted to deny it but that wouldn't help her get the answers she needed.

"Ah, um, yes," she finally finished with a sigh.

"When did you realize you were attracted to Elder Tatum?"

"Well, I noticed how nice he looked when I first met him." Paige answered recalling her first reaction to him. "I even enjoyed interacting with him the first Sunday I was back and we sat out in the parking lot talking before and after lunch." She took a deep breath. "But I would have to say that it wasn't until the elder's bowling night that I began to see him as more than just a very compassionate and caring elder." Nervously, she began to ramble.

"I didn't mean to. I know it will make things a bit uncomfortable for everyone but I will work on ignoring it even if I need to avoid him, so if you… " Menagerie cut in.

"Wait, why would you avoid Elder Tatum?"

Paige flushed. She was hoping to get through her spiel without interruption or having to explain.

"Well...um…you know the day I met with you and Pastor and I went to lunch?"

"Yes."

"Pastor let me know he had planned to introduce me to Elder Tatum with the intent that I show him around and we get to know each another. After I told him about Gladys and the trip I was to take regarding my relationship with her, he reconsidered it. I know Elder Tatum is his best friend's son and since I now come with even more baggage than we both originally knew, I figured he would want to pick someone else to show him around."

The line was quiet for a moment. Paige, embarrassed and reluctant to hear Lady Menagerie's agreement on the subject didn't want to be the one to break the silence.

"Mmmm. I find this interesting," Lady Menagerie finally said.

Paige didn't respond.

"Paige I was under the impression that your unpleasant surprise at Pastor intruding into your personal life was the reason for his reconsideration in Elder Tatum. When I spoke to him about it I didn't recall him having any intentions on 'shopping' Elder Tatum around. He was merely going to patiently wait for things to take their own course, which I told him he should have done in the first place."

"Take their course? What do you mean?" Paige was both relieved and confused. She found the mix of emotions to be puzzling.

"What was it that 'opened your eyes' to Elder Tatum?"

Paige thought back to the evening of the bowling party. She couldn't think of any one thing that happened. It seemed like the whole night brought him slowly into focus.

"If I have to try to think of one particular moment... I would have to say when they were picking teams. Pastor Lawrence made Elder Tatum and Elder Michaels the team captains, and I have to admit that being picked for a team has always been a sore spot for me because though I was never the last one picked for any individual sports team, I was close many times. It was downright nerve-racking.

Elder Tatum, not knowing how well or poorly I played, picked me first. Well kind of... his friend, Dominy, was there so he was automatically on his team – but that didn't count. He didn't even get huffy with the gutter ball I threw but encouraged me louder than the rest, and he just waited until I sat back down and quietly gave me a couple of suggestions he said worked for his sister.

He also was more relaxed but I think that was more from Dominy's antics than anything else. They are very close friends, don't you think?"

"Yes, I do." Paige could hear the smile in her voice.

"Paige, do you think you would welcome it if you found that Elder Tatum was interested in you?"

The line was quiet for a few moments.

"No."

"No? Why 'no'?"

"I think I would have given it more thought if I didn't have so much baggage. I have twins now, not to mention my book tour and I am about to go through surgery. It isn't fair to consider things like that."

"It isn't fair to whom to consider living life?" Lady Menagerie counteracted.

Paige fumed for a moment. She bit her lip in consternation. "I am being practical and realistic. It is a lot to handle. I'm not even sure I am ready to deal with it all."

"Do you mind if I make a stab at breaking some things down here?"

"No, please go ahead. If it can bring me some clarity, I am all for it." Paige replied gratefully.

"Okay, so I am going to just separate what you have told me into two categories: what you are seeing and what you have in your grasp."

"Okay." Paige was barely following her.

"Let's go through the things you see first. You see yourself as an elder of Skylight Temple, an author that has a good amount of success that has been able to make a career out of writing and speaking. You volunteer as a chaplain and are a member of our Visitation Committee. How am I doing so far?"

"All of that is correct."

"Okay. You recently reunited with one of your twins and told her the truth about her biological ancestry, and today you found out that your other twin is alive and will be the recipient of a life-saving procedure that you will be taking part of at the end of the month."

After a moment's pause, Paige responded.

"Also true."

"Now for what is in your hand." She heard Lady Menagerie take a deep breath, which meant Paige may not want to hear everything that she was about to say, but it was going to be said nonetheless.

"Though you carried and delivered two children, you are actually a mother to neither. Your sister has given you the chance to get to know Gladys and develop a relationship with her in truth, but she still remains with her aunt. Your other child has a family that is more than capable of taking care of her without you, and you would not have even known she was alive if it hadn't been for these extenuating circumstances."

226

Paige opened her mouth to interrupt but Lady Menagerie heard the breath.

"No interruptions, Paige, just listen. All I am doing is showing you the real reality of things."

"You will be going through a rough procedure that will take a few weeks to heal from but it is not life-threatening nor is it terminal. You will recover and you will heal quickly, and be able to move on with your life. Your book tour is no more taxing now than it has been in the past. So you tell me: what is the real reason why you would say 'No' to a relationship right now."

The silence was deafening on the other end of the line while Paige fought through the different reasons and was forced to sort them out by the emotions that ruled them.

"It is easier to just not get into any type of relationship. I don't know how I will handle one."

"Are you afraid of getting hurt? That you will be betrayed?"

"No," she said, but didn't continue.

"Paige. I am trying to help not coerce you into anything."

"I know. It is just embarrassing to admit. I am not afraid of getting hurt. I am afraid of hurting them or hurting myself by doing something wrong."

"You are definitely going to have to elaborate on that, Paige. This is not something that I will share with another living soul, but I can't help you if I don't know all the facts."

Paige sighed deeply. She had never shared what she was about to say with anyone.

"I have already shared with you what happened to me at 14, but what I didn't share with you was my promiscuity and 'devil-may-care' attitude I adopted for quite a while after."

"But that is in your past." Lady Menagerie interrupted.

"Yes, but it has effects on my life today. Not directly, but indirectly and until I come to terms with my fears and insecurities with myself regarding that, then I can't chance getting close to anyone."

"What are you talking about? Make it plain, Paige."

"I don't trust myself with men. I don't trust being alone with them. I spent so much time looking for a way to fill that void and those places in me that I hated that I lost control of." She took a shaky breath.

"I know that my relationship with God has been the only thing that has taught me how to love myself, get over what I did to my children and family, and even consider myself worthy of love from another individual.

I haven't thought of being intimate with a man in over five years, but what I am afraid of is whether those urges are just dormant or if I have actually gained enough knowledge and moral character to put things in their perspective order when it comes to dealing with a man."

"What do you think you are going to do? Invite them home and sleep with them?"

"No. Nothing that extreme, but maybe give hope where there shouldn't be or worse give no sign of interest because I am so worried about moving too quickly..."

The phone line was quiet for a moment.

"How about just getting to know them? Ask questions, stay in public places or around groups of people when you are with them, and depending on the degree of your attraction to either one of them then the more people you should keep around you.

"Cover yourself. If you feel weak in some areas, have a contingency plan so that you can't be tempted beyond a certain point."

She heard Lady Menagerie sigh.

"There is no instruction besides being holy and following God's direction and precepts for your life. You will have to deal with your desires and lack thereof, individually. What you must not do is allow fear to keep you from trying at all. We won't always be victorious but you have a relationship with God. Ask Him first and ask Him for individual help, not what you think someone else would do or should do. He knows you specifically, so ask him for what you need and get clarity before you make any type of move. If you keep your eyes open, He will show you the flags.

You are looking for the outcome so that you don't have to make any decisions or live through these moments yourself; that is part of the process, honey. God isn't questioning if He can trust you. He places you in these situations so that you can answer with all surety that you know you can be trusted with all that He gives you. It is part of living in Him."

Paige was thoughtful for a few moments. She saw that she had begun to blow things out of proportion, turning her circumstances into problems when they could be blessings. She took a deep breath, deciding to step out.

"So what do I do now?"

Lady Menagerie gave a short but distinctive chuckle. "Uh uh, not so easy. I will not tell you which way to turn or who to direct your attention to. Just live your life to the fullest. Take it in and open your eyes to what is around you. God has set a great deal in front of you. You have been presented with more opportunities in the last few weeks than most people get in a lifetime. Don't let it overwhelm you. Let Him guide you on what you should do first, just don't run away from it. Will you promise me that?"

Paige laid in bed staring up at the ceiling for a while after hanging up with First Lady. She contemplated what she had been told in light of what she had shared with her. Feeling a huge weight lifted off of her shoulder, she finally gave herself permission to think about the bowling party with Elder Tatum in detail, wondering if the glances and demeanor were new or just something she was finally noticing.

*   *   *

"Hello?"

"Finally, I have been calling your room for the last half-hour waiting for you to pick up. I will come to your room in 10 minutes and don't worry, I will have room service sent up to your room on my way."

The phone disconnected and Paige hung up, eyeing the clock on the nightstand next to it. It read 7:40 am. She shifted onto her back, staring up at the ceiling while memories of the night before began playing in her head.

Her daughter lived. Both twins were alive. It had felt so much like a dream, sitting there across from Mason and him revealing the news frankly and calmly and her struggling to remain lucid.

She pulled herself up, sitting on the edge of the bed and glancing at the window a few feet away. She felt the beginnings of anger creep up on her. She questioned the emotion. Why should she be angry? It wasn't as if she would have welcomed twins at 14, but as she thought it over she realized knowledge of this daughter had been kept from her whereas Gladys was always accessible and made a part of her life.

She had missed the firsts with Vivian. The first steps, first words, first smile, the first day of school. Even though she wasn't there personally for some of Gladys' events, her sister had always kept her abreast of them, and pictures filled up at least five photo boxes just of Gladys. Her sister didn't want her to regret missing anything, though it had taken time for her to look at them without just seeing Stone.

Another child, another family and from what Mason shared, it wasn't a close one.

God please, I need your help with this pain and anger. I want to hurt someone, Lord. I want to scream at the injustice of it. I want to cry and just sit on Your lap while You right this wrong. Turn back time God. Turn it back for me. Just this once…please.

But even as she pleaded, she knew that this was where it would begin for her and Vivian. She would be introduced to her daughter just a few days before she gave her life again by donating her kidney. Her daughter…that was lying in a hospital room because she was in the wrong place at the wrong time.

She laughed at the irony of it. One would think that she would have been better off away from the whole story of her conception, and saved from the knowledge her whole life which may guarantee fulfillment and happiness…but not her child. This beautiful second part of her was withering away in some hospital bed with life trying to cut its ties from her.

God. I am so sorry. Please forgive me for being so selfish. Please Lord, spare her life. I am so sorry for not acknowledging the gift sooner. I am so sorry, so desperately sorry.

The tears ran down her cheeks as sobs choked out of her, racking her body. She wrapped her arms around her middle, trying to hold herself together feeling as though she would splinter. She began taking deep breaths to calm herself, but had to try four times before she could begin to smother some of the trembling.

She sat there trying to come up with answers, but just kept creating new questions. How long had he known? How long had his mother-in-law known? Why wasn't she told sooner? Did Vivian know? Would she be allowed to get to know Vivian?

The knock on the door drew her out of her trance. She wiped her eyes and cheeks as she made her way to the door.

"Awwww, sweetie, you look a mess. Good thing I come bearing gifts." Carmen moved forward into the room, followed by a cart with a carafe of coffee and four, silver-covered dishes.

Carmen winked at her as the attendant pushed the cart in the room, and came back so that she could sign the bill.

"So, rough night huh?" Carmen commented as they sat down at the makeshift table, drinking their second cup of coffee.

Paige was surprised Carmen had waited for them to finish breakfast before she began. She must have been dying to ask.

Paige nodded, staring out the window, knowing before Carmen left she would have the whole story. It was odd how their relationship had developed over the years, but Paige, who had kept Carmen at arm's-length at the beginning of their relationship, had begun opening up to her, especially when she shifted her writings to novels.

Carmen, originally questioning her motivation for the new projects listened thoughtfully while she shared of her desires and of her history. By the time she was finished, Carmen was almost as excited as she. After reading the first finished product, Carmen encouraged and supported her 110%.

"How are you fairing?"

The question pulled Paige's attention back to Carmen. She glanced at her briefly before turning her gaze back to the window. "I am afraid I am not doing so well." It registered to her ears that her voice sounded strained.

"I have a twelve-year-old daughter that I barely know and another that I don't know at all. Now I am realizing that I got just what I asked for."

She turned to look at Carmen again, then turned away seeing the tenderness in her eyes. She didn't deserve tenderness or pity. She deserved exactly what she was getting.

"I was so consumed with anger and hatred for my cousin, my mom, those babies...I couldn't see straight. I could barely think straight; I actually thanked God that one of them didn't make it, and I hated what the other symbolized. I hated my mother for looking at me like I was something that should have been thrown out with the garbage, and so easily came up with the idea to kill what was inside of me. She was determined to see it through, too. It was a side of her I never should have seen but in the end it was my decision.

When the doctor told me that I was carrying twins, my mom had just walked out and when given the option to go ahead and have them right away, I thought that I had been spared the guilt and shame of killing my babies because they were a nuisance. But at the end of that dark tunnel of pain, I ended up thanking God for taking the one I thought had died and giving up the one I couldn't bear to look at because she had his eyes."

Carmen touched Paige's hand, drawing back her attention. "But see, now you have been given the chance to redeem yourself or at least rectify the situation. You will be giving your own daughter a life-saving organ. You will be saving her life like you thought you would be able to before, but this time you are ready to get to know her."

"Yes, but do I deserve this chance? Do I really deserve this second chance with her?"

"Maybe not, that is up to you to decide. But regardless of whether you deserve it, you are worth it and you owe it to yourself to take it because it has been given to you."

Carmen lifted her lips in a wicked smile and continued. "Besides you are not only getting your daughter back. From what I saw last night you might just have her father too."

Paige's eyes widened. Surprise registered on her face as she looked at Carmen.

"Oh come on. You can't tell me you didn't notice the way he watched you." Carmen sat back in her chair.

"He was just concerned about me. To tell you the truth, so was I for a minute there. It felt like I was having an out-of-body experience."

"I wasn't talking about at the diner. I'd noticed him staring at you while you were signing books. He isn't a hard one to notice either. He is very easy on the eyes."

Paige rolled her eyes.

"What is that for? You know I am a multi-tasker. Someone has to watch out for you and that is what I do. I constantly watch to make sure you are not accosted by some overzealous fan or stalker." Carmen refreshed their coffee cups.

"I am not kidding you, Paige. I think Mr. Jenson is attracted to you, and not just a little. It could be to your advantage, getting to know your 'baby-daddy' and all."

Carmen raised her eyebrows and pursed her lips, eliciting a chuckle from Paige.

"Carmen, I don't know what I am going to do with you."

"Invite me to your wedding," Carmen laughed.

"Seriously Carmen?" Paige branded her with a look that stifled any more similar comments.

"What is it, Paige? What's with the fortress?"

Paige smiled more to herself than Carmen.

"Very honestly, I don't think I have any more guards up than the next person. But in the case of Mr. Jenson, I have a few reservations that make seeing him as more than a grieving father challenging. Like the fact that though he acknowledges the God his wife served, he has a huge grudge against Him."

Carmen shook her head. "And you don't think you are being just the least bit prejudice or judgmental?"

"Prejudice?" she shrugged. "Judgmental, no. What I am saying is mere fact. I asked him if he believed in God and he basically asked me if it mattered…like God owed him an explanation or something."

"And?"

"What do you mean 'and'…" Paige looked at her quizzically.

"You were there once. You were angry and hurt and blamed God for your pain, and look where you are now?"

"Yes, but I was also in no way, shape or form ready for any type of meaningful relationship. I was looking to get even and use like I had been used. Even when I began to look for something more I had no clue how to find it and until I surrendered to God, I found myself in a cycle of self-hate taking me down like a whirlpool."

Carmen sighed seeing that Paige was resigned to her thinking.

"I am not blind, Carmen. I'll admit when I first saw him he took my breath away, and being in close proximity to him makes thinking clearly very hard. I thought about it, more than I wanted to. It was like he invaded my senses and wanted things I haven't wanted in a long time. It has been a moment since I noticed someone enough that my body reacted that way, but the anger and lack of reverence to God is a reminder of a place I don't want to revisit."

"Do you really think that is fair?"

Paige shrugged again. "What do you think?"

Carmen shook her head. "So… what then, you continue to live the life of a spinster-elder?"

"Who said I was living the life of a spinster?" Paige replied, nonchalantly.

"Are you seeing someone, Paige Rosen Morganson?"

"No, but there may be a little light at the end of the tunnel," she said.

"Are you kidding, and you haven't said a word to me. Why?"

"Because you make too much of too little, and I don't need to be clouded by your romantic sensibilities."

"You say that a lot, 'romantic sensibilities'. What does that mean?"

"It means your notions on romance. Your fanciful, romantic notions. The ones that are larger than life."

"I think I like romantic sensibilities better."

Paige laughed, but remained quiet.

"Aren't you going to tell me about him?"

"Not just yet. I want to see if there is something to tell. Meanwhile, Mr. Jenson will be here soon, and I need to make myself presentable. Will you stay while he is here, please?"

Carmen gave her a leveled gaze. "If that is what you want, not a problem, but don't think I am going to forget about 'Mr. Light at the End of the Tunnel'." She wiggled her eyebrows, making Paige laugh.

*   *   *

The doors of the elevator barely closed before Paige closed in on Carmen. "What were you thinking? I thought I'd made my feelings clear about Mr. Jenson earlier. Why would you not back me up?"

Carmen rolled her eyes. "Who am I, Paige? I mean, to you?" She turned to Paige, not backing down. "I have been privy to some of your history and granted I learned a lot more this weekend...but then so did you.

Last night, while you were trying to come up with new ways to construct walls to keep you hidden from life, I was having a background check conducted. I wouldn't throw you to a wolf, even if he was a devastatingly handsome wolf.

Even if you don't think so, I have your best interest at heart and if you apologize I might just tell you something I found that you might find intriguing." Carmen folded her arms across her chest, turning back towards the doors of the elevator, looking up to watch the numbers increase with the floors.

Paige took a deep breath. Maybe she was making too much of this. Mason had never conducted himself in less than a gentlemanly fashion. If she was to be completely honest, most of her problem with being in his presence was due to her reaction to him.

She didn't know what it meant – this strong, physical pull to him and as much as she had considered and asked God, she was no closer to receiving an answer than she was after the first day she had met him.

Lady Menagerie had given her a lot to think about in regards to her different reactions between Brandon and Mason. The feelings Mason evoked in her were almost frightening. It was almost as if her body was on autopilot and she had to fight hard to keep it under restraints. Her hands itched to touch the loose curls of his hair to see if they were as soft as they looked. To drown in the depth of his piercing eyes as his face came closer so she could taste –

"Paige?"

She was pulled out of her thoughts, suppressing the urge to groan in disgust at herself. She gave over her attention to Carmen, hoping she didn't see the flush creep up her neck.

234

"Don't you want to know what I found?"

"Yeah, sure I do."

They paused when the doors opened at their floor, and they walked to Paige's suite.

"Well, as I said, I had a background check done on Mr. Jenson that came in just before we met with him this morning. I was going to share it with you after our meeting, no matter how it concluded. He is a successful architect and makes a very good living for him and his…your daughter, though he just recently began working again full-time.

He was honest when he told you his mother-in-law had a lot of clout. It seems she owns a small city just outside of Oklahoma, and has quite a few investments in corporations in the area. Her husband has his own money and then some property he shares with her, but he is mostly a philanthropist as of late.

What I find interesting is that his wife left a sizable amount of money for him and Vivian, but he placed it in a trust for Vivian and has not touched it otherwise. A few weeks ago, he became involved in what may be a messy custody battle for Vivian."

Paige stared at Carmen as she allowed herself to flop on the couch that was nearest to her. "Do you think he will try and use me to keep her?"

Carmen shrugged her shoulders. "The thought had crossed my mind."

"And you encouraged me to see him again tomorrow?"

"Yep. If he brings it up during your lunch, then you know that he is coming at you straight and he isn't trying to hide anything. What the background check can't give is the emotional ties or lack thereof between him and his in-laws."

"If he loves Vivian enough to fight to keep her, what is wrong with you helping?"

"Because I have enough drama in my life already, plus I don't think he and I see eye to eye when it comes to who we ultimately go to for help. It may make things difficult because we may not be in agreement on how to get our answers. It may put us at odds."

"You are so stubborn, Paige. Regardless of who you go to for the answers and the help, you are in agreement for the results."

"And that is the difference between how we see things, Carmen. I am not being stubborn. I just know who I believe in and who I serve, and I know He brings about results."

"That is all well and frankly I wouldn't expect less from you, but how do you convince people who don't know or are struggling with the concept of Him, without being overbearing and offending them?"

"With love and leading by example…" Paige began before Carmen interrupted her.

"Yes, great answer, but what do you do in this situation, and before you answer I suggest you walk down that path for a while. You never know, you might even come away with another book."

Paige frowned. "You suggest I write about my life and sell it?"

"Haven't you already been doing that in different ways? The book you are writing right now, though it is labeled fiction, is about your cousin and his struggles and inability to accept what God had for Him until it was almost too late."

Paige's frowned deepened, but more in thought than at Carmen. She hated that she knew her so well. Would this chaos never clear? She just wanted to go back to the peaceful life she led up until a couple of months ago. She allowed the thought to be fleeting, knowing that she was no longer going to run from her responsibilities.

"I will go and have lunch with him tomorrow and if he doesn't bring it up in a decent amount of time, I will do so."

"Do you think that is wise? He will know we have been investigating him," Carmen said with concern in her voice.

"He had me investigated." Paige shrugged.

"It isn't the same. You are donating a kidney to his…your…Vivian. It is standard."

Paige just shrugged again. "No need to play games. The more he understands that I have nothing to hide, the easier it will be for us to work through this relationship."

"So matter-of-fact; so emotionless. Do you feel nothing?" Carmen asked softly, her eyes beseeching.

Paige returned her look squarely, revealing openly what she had been trying to hide before. "No, Carmen, actually there is too much emotion where Mason is concerned. I need to figure things out before I cause more bad than good."

Carmen only nodded.

"Alright, enough about my personal life. How are things looking for Denver in April?"

*   *   *

"So did you enjoy your time in New York?" Mason asked after the drink-waiter left them at a table boasting a beautiful high rise view of Manhattan.

A smile eased up one corner of Paige's lips. "I usually do, and this time was no exception. I love interacting with people. Whether there are two or 200, it is well worth the plane ride."

"You don't like flying?" he asked, watching the way her eyes gazed around the room behind him before answering. He was happy that she seemed less nervous around him. It annoyed him to think that she didn't trust him, but even more, that he cared so much that she did.

"I don't mind flying. I actually love the taking-off and the landing, but the cramped space and the filtered air make me uneasy. I usually try to bring enough work with me to keep my mind occupied."

"Are you working on something now?" Mason sipped his lemonade, surprised when she held his gaze for a moment then flushed, looking down at her coffee cup.

"Yes, I am. It is a fictional novel." She didn't continue.

He wondered if he should press. He decided to go at it from another angle. "Are you always writing something? I mean, how many projects or books do you average a year?"

He watched as she played with the cup in her hands, her well-manicured fingers tracing the rim. He looked up to see if she would look at him again. He had to admit that this conversation could have taken place over the phone but after the first night, seeing her had reminded him of some feelings he had locked away two years ago and evoked new ones. He was walking a fine line between mere interest and fascination, but he refused to hold anything else that could be taken away. He was already fighting for the one thing he cherished beyond his own life. He didn't have room for anything else.

Impatient with himself and his thoughts that kept directing themselves her way unheeded, he asked the question again just in case she'd lost focus.

"How many books do you average a year?"

She glanced up at his tone. A little sharper than he'd intended. Her eyes warily scanning his features.

"It depends on the type of book I am writing. The more research needed and the more analytical I get, the longer it takes; as far as the fiction goes, it is all about His timing and the prompting of the Holy Spirit. I really just have to make sure I listen and make myself available. In a lot of ways,

I consider myself more of a conduit. My job is to prepare myself and be open to what way He wants to use me and what He wants to say."

"Where are you in all of that?"

She smiled. *Good question.*

"I am in the style of the writing, the voice in which the story is told, and the experiences I bring with me. Just like a dancer that praises the Lord and allows herself to be used to interpret a song to minister to people. She may get her moves from the Holy Spirit, but her body, the skill she has acquired and her continued experience, will ultimately be a part of what is used to shape the dance."

"Are you always so sure about your work and what He wants from you?"

Paige frowned. "No. Absolutely not. It is a work in progress. Just because it is my job to listen and be available doesn't mean I am unerring at it. It takes practice in focusing on His voice so that you know that you hear it from here." She placed her hand on her upper abdomen. "Instead of here." Her hand then touched her ear.

He stared at her, unable to form an opinion to what she had just shared with him. He was more than relieved when the waitress came to take their order.

Paige was trying hard to keep her focus on Mason's word and not on his eyes or jaw, hands or heaven forbid, his lips. She was finding it difficult communicating with him without watching any of the features that gave her more insight into what his words meant.

This was ridiculous. How were they supposed to interact with one another on a professional level, when she was having problems just trying to control reactions to him being across a table from her?

Body, get yourself in alignment and submit yourself, and calm down.

Maybe if she started singing...*really*...How soon after eating could she excuse herself? She was already packed and ready to go but he didn't have to know that.

She was pulled away from her thoughts when Mason spoke. "I was wondering if you had any thoughts on how we could tell Vivian about you?"

Paige studied the view once again, watching the movement down below. "I think being direct is the best way, but it may do better with her knowing who I am before the procedure rather than after. I will not discuss anything with her that I have not already gotten permission to do so with you. We can play that part by ear."

She immediately regretted the last suggestion because it would keep them in communication. She would endeavor to have herself in order by then.

He was in agreement with her suggestions and made a few of his own where Vivian's curiosity was concerned. He knew his daughter was extremely inquisitive, and there were small things each of them could avoid in conversation that would keep her from moving forward quickly with questions neither of them would feel comfortable in answering.

Mason noticed Paige had become quieter as the meal went on, not that she was all that talkative to begin with. He had been playing with telling her about Victoria and the custody hearing all morning. So far, he had been as honest as he could be without bringing her into unnecessary drama with his in-law. This would be no different.

"I need to tell you something, but I need your trust that I am telling you this for information sake and not because I want something from you." His eyes were intense and unwavering as they held Paige's when she looked up from the plate.

"A few weeks ago my mother-in-law, Victoria, sent me some legal documents giving me notice that she is going for full custody of Vivian." He watched, but the look of surprise didn't come. He frowned. Did she already know and if so, how?

"You don't look surprised."

"It is not new to me if that is what you mean. You forget that I have a manager that is very efficient and even more protective. Last night she let me know about a few things she found."

"Were you not curious? Didn't you want to know why Victoria was taking me to court to gain custody?"

"You let me know a couple of nights ago that things weren't all that close between you and your mother-in-law, but from what you have shared with me I have no doubt that you love and adore your daughter. My concern was whether I could trust you." She shrugged. "It's nice to know that I can."

Amazing.

CHAPTER 36

Brandon had long since given up trying not to think about Paige. He figured since she would successfully breach the walls of his thoughts at random moments of the day, he would indulge until the scene or thought had played out and then go back to focusing on what he was doing.

Before the week was out he found himself wanting to hear her voice, but was hesitant. He knew she was just coming off her tour in New York because it was one of the few things they talked about while waiting for their turn to bowl.

Her laughter was entrancing. It made him search for stories in his past or recent incidences that would bring out the melodic sound from her throat. Dominy seemed to elicit the two, true guffaws from her with his comedic displays throughout the evening while Brandon sat back and witnessed the looks of surprise and incredulity on her face at his words and antics.

On more than one occasion her laughter would get the attention of the other players on their team and they would all be drawn in, strengthening the bond of camaraderie between the elders in their group.

In fact, it took them so long to finish the second game that they had to rush through, but promised to get together in a couple of weeks, even if it was just the six of them to share Sunday lunch.

Brandon came home to the quiet of his apartment for the second night. Dominy had left the previous morning to surprise Robin. She had recently finished her dissertation on Panamanian Women's Suffrage, and he said she sounded like she needed a little attention.

Dominy had a special knack for hearing his wife's needs in her voice, even though she wasn't shy about her thoughts. Dominy always seemed to go the extra mile to show his love and appreciation for the person Brandon heard him refer to as *mi aliento*, "my breath," in Spanish.

Brandon remembered coming upon them as he sought out Dominy for a road trip they were about to take in celebration of his fifth anniversary of remission.

He followed the whispered tones out into a large, ivy-covered courtyard between the house and the front entrance, until the couple came into view and he stopped. Momentarily entranced, he stared, feeling like a peeping tom watching two, intimately-shrouded lovers. He continued to watch as Dominy shifted his wife in his embrace, holding her face between his hands, communicating in words, tiny kisses and looks, his deep love for her.

"You are my words before I speak them. *Tu eres mi proximo aliento*, my next breath." He passed fluidly between Spanish and English, punctuating each word with a kiss to her eyelids, cheeks and the tip of her nose. The look in his eyes shared even deeper emotions that transcended all words. Brandon, finding his breath and remembering his manners, slowly backed his way out of the courtyard and went to wait for Dominy inside the house.

What must it feel like to love someone with such all-consuming passion that, just to see that person or be in close proximity to them made you feel whole? He had never envied anyone's emotional ability in his life until that moment. Even after 14 years, it was more than evident that Dominy loved his wife deeply.

That had been almost four years ago, and though he never asked Dominy about the details of his marriage with Robin, he listened more intently to what Dominy would say about her when they would greet each other.

As he laid down that evening, Brandon's mind went over his "to do" list for the next day, realizing that he was almost at the end of his cycle of chemo and radiation treatments. It was odd how the thought of this bout with cancer would sometimes be all-encompassing and others just be a distant thought, almost like an invisible garment that he wore day in and day out. It was more of an acceptance as a part of his life this time, whereas the first time his only thoughts were to eradicate it.

He wondered what Paige would think if he had the chance to share this with her. Would she think him less than a man? Would she be as fierce as Dominy about his recovery? Would she pity him? No, he knew she wouldn't pity him. She'd had too many experiences where she spiritually fought for the life of people she was assigned to intercede for. Pity didn't seem to be in her vocabulary, but he didn't want to be a case she was working on either. He wanted her to see him as a man first.

He had been thinking a lot about it since she'd left, and talked himself into quitting the fight between his headstrong determination to shut out everything but his battle with this illness and the uncompromising pull of Paige.

Friday night though, he didn't visibly respond to her obvious relief and gratefulness for being chosen early for his team to bowl. Her reaction made him feel like a man who'd rescued her and the experience was both humbling and empowering. So much so that he had looked for more opportunities to aid her during the game, but found that the conversation between them did more to ease everyone into a spirit of friendship, relieving them of the edge of competitiveness.

She had opened up even more and he found that she shied away from anything phony. She didn't put on airs or pretend to know when she didn't. She was more than open to suggestions and laughed at herself more out of fun than embarrassment.

It was a little unnerving to see how she reacted with Dominy. Their banter was light-hearted but her humor with him was just a tad dark and her quick wit, biting, as though they had known each other a great deal longer than the few times they'd shared company.

Brandon, even knowing the love Dominy shared with his wife, felt a possessiveness he'd not experienced for anyone else when Dominy elicited one of the unbridled laughs from her. He pasted a smile on his face and fought to suppress the feelings. Shaking his head to clear his thoughts, he turned his concentration to the scorecard, feeling only a little bit of ease at the fact that he was ahead.

At the end of the evening he'd asked if he could walk her to her car and she had accepted, eyes dancing in the light of the street lights leading to the parking lot. Dominy bid her goodnight at the door along with everyone else and continued on to the vehicle they were sharing. Paige's car was a few spaces across and back. Hands in his pockets, working hard to quell his nervous energy, he walked alongside Paige until they reached her car. Opening the back door, she placed her purse on the back seat then released it so that she could move forward to the driver's door.

"I had one of the best nights in a long time. I don't remember the last time I laughed so much," she said, turning to face him. "I appreciate the bowling tips. You really play very well."

Brandon shrugged. "I am a little out of practice, but I had fun. Greg is a riot. He is so competitive," he said, referring to the elder who captained the opposing bowling team.

Paige's giggle enveloped him like a caressing sigh. He shivered and took an involuntary step back.

"Thank you, Brandon," she said quietly, her eyes grew serious. She held his gaze for a moment, the light from the parking lot lamp bathing her in what seemed to be an iridescent glow. He was unable to make a sound passed the lump in his throat, so he furrowed his brows in confusion.

She glanced away towards a pair of headlights crossing their path as another car left the parking lot. He watched as she took a deep breath, deciding to hurry.

"Thank you for picking me early on for your team, even though you didn't know how bad a player I was. I really appreciated it. It was nice not being the last man out."

He thought the one statement spoke volumes.

"Have you been 'last man out' so-to-speak a lot?" he asked, retrieving the space.

She shrugged. "Let's just say that I wouldn't have won any medals in any one athletic competition. I prefer to take my time."

"If I may say, you look in excellent condition. Do you do any type of exercise?"

"Yes. I love to run, whether it be in place or outside, but I would rather do it alone. I find it peaceful and it aids in my thought process. It helps clear my mind."

He nodded, then leaned forward. "If you promise not to tell, I have a little secret to share with you."

A small smile tilted the ends of her mouth in the form of a conspiratory grin. She held up three fingers just before she flashed her teeth. "I promise."

"I would have picked you first if I didn't think Dominy would take it personally." He winked at her. Hearing her inhale, he decided to ask.

"Is that a problem?"

She stared up at him, going still. "Why?" she expelled airily.

Because I like you. "You were one of the first people I met here. I enjoy your company. So I wanted to make sure you were on my team." He shrugged matter-of-factly, but watched intently for her reaction.

She broke his gaze after a moment, looking down at her feet. She took a deep breath then looked back up into his eyes as if making the decision to accept his answer.

"Okay, but shouldn't winning have been factored in there? You didn't know how badly I played."

"I believe we did win."

He could see the question in her eyes.

"You just said you haven't laughed so hard in a while, and I know the others on our team had a great time tonight. Even though our score wasn't higher than the other's, we won something more important tonight."

She stared at him so long he wasn't sure she believed him.

"What did we win?" She finally asked breathlessly, not blinking, her golden eyes holding him hostage for a few, indescribable moments.

It would be so easy. So easy to lean just a little closer and share breath with her, see if her eyes would widen with surprise, acceptance, or rejection.

Knowing he wasn't ready to have that question answered if it were the latter, he moved back slowly, breaking the spell when he glanced down at the pavement.

"Friendship, camaraderie, a beginning of understanding of one another."

Her eyes narrowed as if she were trying to figure him out, maybe read his upcoming thoughts.

"That means a lot to you...friendship, huh?" she asked.

He nodded, glad she'd chosen to analyze that part of their conversation. She was intelligent. He knew it would only be a matter of time before she was able to access his true feelings but this was too soon.

"With my family so far away, it would be nice to have people that I share things in common with to talk to and fellowship with once in a while."

Her head tilted to the side.

"I bet you are a good friend."

Did she know what she was saying? How she was saying it? Did she know she had already woven a spell around him and each time she made a query or statement like that, he lost a little more footing on his ability to make a choice not based on what his heart was saying?

"There is only one way to find out," he said with challenge.

A light came into her eyes and her lips curled again.

"Ask Dominy?" she said then exhaled a gusty laugh that forced him to reply in kind.

He laughed because he couldn't help it. He laughed because she had met his challenge and beat him with it. He laughed because she gave him a glimpse at lighter times that finally seemed in reach.

*   *   *

He rolled on his side, staring out onto the balcony leading from his bedroom. He would call her tomorrow.

"Goodnight," he spoke out loud into the dark of the room not expecting a reply but feeling a peace surround him in acknowledging her.

*   *   *

Brandon glanced at the clock for what felt like the 20th time that day. Paige's number sat near his kitchen phone. Every time he went to it, his hand nearing the receiver, he found another reason to delay calling her. Finally, becoming impatient with himself, he sat down at one of the bar stools and forced himself to dial her number.

The phone rang four times before she answered.

"Good afternoon."

"Good afternoon," he replied.

There was a pause.

"Hi, this is Brandon."

"Yes," came the quiet response.

"Paige? It's Brandon." Brandon wondered if he had interrupted her.

"Yes? Oh, sorry. Just a second. I need to clear my other line."

"Sure," feeling a little guilty about disrupting her conversation without having a plan for discussion, but encouraged by her acceptance of his call, he waited.

He could hear her expelling a breath as she came back on the line. "Hello Brandon. How are you?"

"I am doing great." *Now that I can hear your voice.* "I am sorry for interrupting your call. If you are really busy I can call you back." *Please don't make me call you back.*

"Oh no, that won't be necessary. I was just finishing up some last minute travel plans with my publicist. It was the last bit of business I had to do today and a good thing because it is too beautiful outside to work today."

"I agree." There was a small pause while he swallowed furiously over and over again.

"I was calling to see how you were doing. I haven't spoken to you since before you left on your trip, and I was curious to see how it went."

"Really?"

"Sure. You sound surprised."

"I guess because I am. I am not used to the attention."

"I don't understand. Don't you get a lot of attention during your tours and speaking engagements?"

"Yes, but that isn't so much for me as it is for Paige the writer and speaker. I don't usually get too many inquiries about my experiences from my personal standpoint."

"Oh. Well, you can take your time answering. I don't have any place to be for a while. Meanwhile, I will ask you an easier question."

He could hear her smile through the phone. "Alright, I'm game."

"How was the food?"

"It was fantastic! If I wasn't so busy I am sure I would have eaten my way out of my clothes on this trip. I love New York's melding of cultures and the array of cuisines that are found on each street. It's like having small countries next to one another. Thai one night, Jamaican curry the next. I was in a small corner made from heaven."

"Wow. You are so expressive." He stated, moved by her passionate answer.

"Sorry. Sometimes I tend to ramble."

"No need to apologize. I meant what I said. I really enjoyed your answer. Which leads me to my next question."

"Mmmm?"

"How was your room? When I used to travel a lot, there was nothing like a nice bathroom with a great shower. The bed could be halfway decent and I could even deal with there not being complimentary breakfast but the bathroom was the deal breaker."

"For me, it should not surprise you: it's the room service. Not just the food, but I have to say that this particular hotel had a great bathroom, bed, and view. There is nothing like being home, but they went all out. Their staff offers to unpack your clothes, and I was only too willing to allow it. If I'd had a little more time to myself it would have felt more like a vacation than work. Even though sometimes I think of myself as a creature of habit, I like visiting different hotels when I visit a city more than once.

I like walking around the lobbies and any galleries they have. I even like looking in their gift and clothing shops."

"Do you eat in the hotel restaurants for a change of scenery from your room?"

"Funny enough, no. I'd rather pay for the comfort of room service than pay to eat a meal in the restaurant. If I am going to eat at a restaurant I want it to be as authentic to the city I am staying in as possible."

"Have you always been this inquisitive or do you do some of these things for material in your books?"

"Honestly, I love life. I hope I wouldn't start living it because I wanted to use it as research. I am much more into the motivation and achievement behind an experience. I am much more interested in why I want to experience a certain taste or sight, and the anticipation of reaching that particular goal."

He was silently taking in the undulation and the warmth in her voice.

"I have a question for you." she said, turning the tables.

"Shoot."

"When was the last time you went somewhere just because you wanted to go? Not because of work or because you were on assignment, but just because you were curious."

He thought about it for a couple of seconds, afraid he wasn't going to be able to come up with anything.

"There is a gym walking distance from my apartment and I finally took the time to go and check it out this week. Does that count?"

"Does it? Why do you go to the gym?" He could hear the laughter in her voice and wondered why almost every subject they talked about seemed lighter with her.

"I go to the gym to let off some steam, think, and relax. Are you one of those people that spend hours at the gym?"

"No," he said too quickly.

"Really?"

"I don't think so.."

"You aren't sounding too sure. What all do you do while you are at the gym?"

"I don't really follow a regimen." He carried the phone to the living room and sat on the couch. "I usually start with a half-hour to an hour of running on the treadmill or the elliptical..."

"You've already said too much," she said interrupting him, laughing, "If you start with a half an hour to an hour of anything and don't follow it with going home, you are one of those people."

He joined her in mirth. "Alright. Is there a problem with us people?"

"No. Absolutely not. I almost wish I were as dedicated to my body's fitness. Almost."

"Why almost?"

"Because I just am not. I prefer to do other things for that extra hour or two, and I like what I do. So… almost."

He could almost see her shrug.

"Are you always this matter-of-fact?"

"Just about what I want. I figure I spend enough time with myself, I should know what I want and what I don't want, but I am not going to apologize to myself for not wanting something whether it is good for me or not."

"What about vegetables? Do you like vegetables?" he said, barely able to keep the smile out of his voice.

"Most of them. I like all the green ones except for zucchini, unless it is fried."

"Well sure, 'cause there's nothing like frying a vegetable to make it taste better." He was laughing now.

"In some cases, but definitely not in others. I try not to categorize because I may find an exception to the rule at anytime…where food is concerned, anyway."

They continued to talk over the next half hour using light banter and sharing experiences regarding their travels, which brought Paige's mind back to the original question.

"I have an answer for you."

"Regarding?"

"Your first question about how my trip went."

"And?"

"It started out as it usually does with me trying to get over the initial nervousness of talking. It doesn't matter how often I get in front of a crowd. Be it 20 or 200, I get a momentary bout of nervousness and I have to remind myself that this isn't the first time I've gotten up to speak and the last time I made it through. I enjoyed this trip because there were a few organizations represented that I may be able to partner with to do some training and workshops under and that means helping more people. The book signings also went well, a little longer than I hoped. In all it was an even more successful and enlightening trip than I thought it would be."

"It doesn't sound like you had time to rest," he said, a little concerned.

"Will you be attending service this weekend?"

"Yes. It will be the last time I am able to come before I go into the hospital."

He was silent for a moment.

"So you are going to go ahead with the living donor procedure?" He held the phone away from his mouth, feeling pinpricks of anxiety traveling up his limbs.

"Yes. I go to Chicago towards the end of the week. I should only be away between two to three weeks, depending on my recovery rate."

"Do you think you will be allowed calls?" he asked, taking deep breaths in order to calm his runaway heartbeat.

"Yeah sure, after about a week. Why?"

"You know, just in case the hospital food is so bad you need someone to order some take out for you. There is nothing worse for recovery than bad food. Takes some of the taste out of life."

She groaned at his sad attempt at a pun. "I'm sure I would appreciate a call." She paused before continuing. "Just as long as you don't try any repeat performances of that last attempt at humor."

"Awww, you didn't like my joke?"

She laughed to soften the blow. "Not even a little bit."

Sunday service was followed by lunch with the elders that had been part of Brandon's bowling team. They picked a Thai restaurant in North Hollywood that boasted a great-tasting blue crab fried-rice and curry and mango sticky rice. Everyone continued with the tradition of ordering family-style by selecting dishes that could be shared with the rest of the table. Paige ordered the shrimp Pad Thai and Brandon ordered the B.B.Q. pork spare ribs.

Brandon elected to sit across from Paige, making it easier to watch her features. Michael Baler, the elder in staff over the Missions and Outreach Ministry, sat to his right. They'd met during the first elder's luncheon and found they shared interests in music and agreed on some of the same aspects of Biblical Hermeneutics.

The all-around atmosphere was light with conversations, ranging from family to the morning's sermon on man's ability to delay God's blessings through disobedience.

CHAPTER 37

Victoria closed the door of her apartment, eyeing her baggage lying next to the couch. Feeling an overwhelming sense of weariness, she walked past them, laying her purse down on the table in the hallway that led to her bedroom. She stood at the doorway of her room, knowing that if she got anywhere near the bed, she wouldn't be any good for the rest of the day.

Her heart ached so painfully she could feel a twinge with each beat. The goal was not to give the heaviness too much attention, otherwise she would be swept away in the loss. She wouldn't allow it to crush her from the inside out like a piece of aluminum coming in on itself under the impact of 20 gauge steel...

Making a quick decision, she swung around, rejecting the invitation to claim oblivion just yet and, placing one foot in front of the other, she hastily grabbed her purse and left her apartment.

He's gone.

The thought circled in her mind as if it had been picked up in the wind that now lifted her scarf off of the tailored travel coat she still wore from the flight she'd taken earlier that afternoon after her brief trip to take care of much-needed business in Oklahoma. She hugged her arms around her mid-section, as if to ward off any worse thoughts, but to no avail. The same taunting voice visited her again and again, speaking of the hopelessness of her future with the man she'd never considered being without.

She had tried using anger as a form of armor after not hearing from Richard over the weeks since their last call. She worked it into a heated fury by the day, only to have it fail on her as she walked into the bedroom of her home at the ranch to find most of his belongings gone and a sealed envelope laying on the nightstand.

She took a deep breath, allowing the chill in the air to soothe the lump forming in her throat. She was not going to give into another bout of tears. She'd wasted enough of those over the last month. It was not in her nature to cry. She knew the emotion behind such a show of weakness was no use to her. It didn't make things better. It didn't get her what she wanted. It just reaped havoc with ambition, drive, fortitude and moving the world in the position that benefited her.

She continued to walk down the broad street, passing an occasional pedestrian on the quiet block. She neither greeted nor acknowledged them as she made her way to the small park at the end of the street.

It was still too early for mothers to bring their children, so she had the park's benches to herself. She stared at a bench for a few minutes, wondering not if it would be sanitary enough to sit on, but if she would have the strength to get up from it if she sat down. After what seemed like several minutes, she sat down with lead legs.

She watched the trees sway, but the rustling of the leaves was oddly dimmed, as if the sound was being funneled through cotton. She continued to stare at the shrouds of foliage as they intermittently warned of the change in direction and intensity of the wind. What should have been soothing evidence of nature's ability to calm and quiet rioting emotions only liberated her morose thoughts of her immediate irreconcilable differences with life.

She hated Chicago, but was consoled in the fact that she was not in her home with these feelings, since the ranch was her only true solace.

She sat there for hours trying to dredge up any emotion that would motivate her to move, but as she randomly accessed thoughts flowing through her mind in disarray, trying to file them into permissible or unacceptable categories, she finally allowed herself to remember the previous weekend.

$$*\qquad\qquad *\qquad\qquad *$$

"Martha." Victoria acknowledged the housekeeper as she walked through the door.

The woman responded with a small inclination of her head. "Mrs. Branchett. It is good to have you back."

There was something in her tone that made Victoria raise her brow, but upon close scrutiny of Martha's features, she still couldn't guess at the edge in her voice.

"Have the papers arrived?" Victoria glanced around the foyer, seeing that everything was as she left it except for the bouquet of flowers, the centerpiece of the round marble-top table which was replaced from the garden every few days.

"Yes. They are on your desk," Martha responded as Victoria walked to the stairs, taking them at a leisurely pace. She turned, feeling Martha's eyes still on her.

"Yes?" She watched the tightness around Martha's lips slowly ease until her mouth took on what could only be described as a grimace.

"Nothing. I will have Ron bring up your things right away. Would you like me to bring up some tea?"

Victoria eyed Martha warily, but knowing the woman would say whatever was on her mind when she was ready, she let it go. "That would be good. Thank you Martha."

Martha found Victoria sitting on the edge of her lounge chair staring out of the window, lost in thought. She placed the tea service on the desk and then went about quietly unpacking Victoria's clothing.

"When did he come?" came Victoria's soft voice, stilted, but otherwise void of emotion.

"He sent a courier for his things on Monday." Martha turned back to the closet.

"Did you know?" Victoria didn't look away from the window.

"No, Ms. Victoria," Martha responded.

The answer drew Victoria's attention to the small woman who had now moved to the middle of the room. Martha, who had been in charge of the organization of work going on in the house, had also served as a child when the land had flourished under her grandparents. She kept it professional when anyone else was in hearing range, but she was closer to Victoria than her own parents were.

The use of her name as the old endearment let her know that Martha was well aware of the turmoil and pain she was going through and, if given an invitation, would share her compassion and maybe even some advice.

Victoria gazed at Martha for a while, trying to decide if she was ready to discuss what had happened. She wasn't. She turned back towards the window, staring unseeingly at the garden below.

"That will be all for now, Martha. I will take my dinner in here tonight."

"Yes ma'am," was the reply.

An hour later, Victoria finally gathered the nerve to open the letter and read it.

Victoria,

You have been the reason in my life for many, many years and I was more than fine with that. I accepted my ability to love and understand you when no one else could. I appreciated the task and goal of meeting needs in you that many have not been privileged to glimpse upon, let alone be assigned to. For a long time, you and your happiness were an obtainable and acceptable commission of mine.

Regardless of what was said a few weeks ago, I know that you love me in your own way but that is no longer enough.

Your propensity for hate has overshadowed my love's ability to reach you. It makes my love for you no less real, just impotent.

The space that I offered to you I am now taking as well. I see now that I took on a job that wasn't mine; I can't make you happy if you can't make yourself happy. I can no longer force upon you what you won't willingly seek out for yourself.

So now I need to reassess what our relationship is and what my true and pure purpose is within the confines of our marriage. I need to seek a healthier form of loving you.

I will be in and out of the country to visit Mason and Vivian. If you wish, I will try to avoid us running into each other.

I have collected some of my things and will be occupying my condo in Wichita Falls, TX until I decide on my next move.

Your husband,
Richard

What did it mean?

What was he saying?

"Healthier form of loving you"...was he calling his love for her unhealthy and if so, what was he going to do so that it would be considered "healthy"?

She began to shake with the realization that there was nothing she could do with the situation. There was no talking her way around a situation she knew nothing about. How did things get so turned around? What made him change his mind about waiting the two months he initially talked to her about on the phone?

She sat there pondering those questions and a few more, until Martha came in and found her sitting on the bed in the dark.

"Ms. Victoria?" Martha inquired quietly. She had come up to see if Victoria was ready for her dinner, but upon opening the door to find her sitting there looking bereft, her heart went out to her.

Martha closed the door behind her, then went over to a lamp in the far corner of the room, turning it on only to bring a minimal amount of light into the room. It cast shadows across Victoria's face and the letter in her hand.

She sat down next to Victoria and waited quietly. When Victoria did speak, though it was no louder than a whisper, Martha almost jumped.

"He's gone."

"No, Ms. Victoria. Richard loves you. He just needs time to heal. Like you need time."

Victoria's head snapped to the side as she pinned Martha with an intense stare. "Have you spoken to him? Did he tell you he was doing this?"

Martha shook her head sadly. "No, Ms. Victoria. I just noticed the signs."

"Signs, hints…does no one talk anymore? Richard said I was too consumed with my own life to see the pain he was in. Did he not see the pain I was in?"

"I believe he did, but was unable to reach you and make it better. I think that is what caused him to really seek outside help. A man not only wishes to provide for and protect his family; he wants to know that he can make them happy, feel secure and loved, and with you I think he felt that his hands were tied. It made him feel helpless."

"Did he tell you this?"

"Not all of it, but it only took watching him go through what he has been going through and you being absorbed in trying to cope as well to see his loneliness."

"But why now? Why after he, so-called "found God", is he leaving me? What is it about this God that causes my family to hate me so?"

Martha placed her hand on Victoria's. "You don't really mean that, do you?"

Victoria shrugged, feeling an emptiness so intense she was wondering how she was able to sit up.

"I am going to speak to you frankly, Victoria, and you may not like all that you hear but I want you to listen anyway."

Victoria could do nothing but nod. She didn't want to care anymore. She didn't want to love anymore. It hurt too much.

A cold chill shook Victoria out of the scene. She blinked a couple of times, feeling the moisture from her eyes reaching her cheeks. She felt restless and annoyed with herself. All of her ponderings, the talks, and the rationalizing only brought her to one realization. Richard had left her for reasons she was unable to embrace and the frustration grew with each attempt to bring his thoughts on paper into the realm of her logic.

As the frustration grew, so did her anger for this God who continued to take away everyone she loved.

*   *   *

Victoria walked back to her apartment to prepare herself for her meeting with Paige Morganson the next morning. Before Victoria went on her trip, Vivian had shared with her that Mason was allowing her to meet her donor. Victoria had tried getting a hold of Mason, but to no avail. She was going to give it one more try in the morning and, if she was unsuccessful, then she would make sure she was in the room when Vivian met her mother.

She would not lose her too. The past weekend only helped to strengthen her resolve in moving forward with her latest plan to become the most important person in Vivian's life.

Wednesday morning at ten a.m. exactly, Victoria stepped from the elevator onto Vivian's floor. She had not been to visit her granddaughter in almost a week and was a little anxious about her mental and physical health. Her last visit was spent trying to cajole the brooding child who went on and on in regards to missing her father and pouting about Victoria's and Mason's strained relationship.

Today, she would play nice and be the doting grandmother Vivian would want to spend more time with.

She knocked lightly before entering and found Vivian sitting up, her eyes bright with excitement were out of place, set in the almost yellow pallor of her skin.

Victoria pasted a smile on her lips as she walked towards her bed to give her a kiss on the forehead.

"Hello. I am back. Did you miss me?" Victoria asked as she brought a chair closer to the bed.

Vivian watched her. A surprised look raced across her face, but was replaced with steady adoration.

"Yes. I am really happy you are back." She lowered her head, her hands clasped in her lap.

When she raised her head, her eyes glistened. "I didn't know if you would come back." She paused, taking a deep breath. "I know I acted bad last week. I'm sorry I got mad at you. I don't want you to stop being my Gram." Tears silently rolled down her cheeks.

Victoria, momentarily at a loss for words, came forward and wrapped her arms around Vivian as gently as possible.

"I wouldn't stop being your Gram. You are the best granddaughter anyone could ask for." She pulled back slightly, rubbing the pad of her thumbs across Vivian's cheeks to wipe her tears.

"I have been thinking and I have decided to make you a deal." She watched as Vivian's eyes widened. She knew she had surprised her because Victoria was not one to make deals with anyone, but today she needed to feel special by someone who would love her unconditionally.

"If you promise to behave better and not pout, I will promise to be nicer to your daddy."

Vivian's eyes became as big as saucers. It was almost comical. Victoria may have smiled if she didn't know Vivian was sincerely incredulous.

"You will?" she asked, drawing out the second word, "Why?"

Victoria frowned slightly, confused by the question. "Don't you want me to be nicer to your father?"

"Yes, but that didn't change your mind last week. Why did it change it now?"

Leave it to children to ask the hard questions, Victoria thought to herself.

She shrugged. "I have been thinking a lot lately and what is most important is for you to be happy. I want to make you happy, so I will do things to make you happy." *So happy that I will remain the woman you love most, no matter who else enters your life.*

Vivian quietly thought about this last statement. Victoria watched as the expressions flitted across her face. She opened her mouth then closed it, took a breath then finally squared her shoulders with resolve and looked at Victoria with a shy smile. "Thank you."

Victoria's restraint weakened slightly and she had to swallow a few times in order to talk around the lump in her throat. "You are welcome." She patted Vivian's knee to lighten the mood.

"So what have you been doing since I last visited? Has the food gotten any better?"

Vivian giggled, shaking her head. She then laid back, breathing out a sigh, dispersing the last of the tension in the air. It was quiet for a moment as she glanced at the television mounted on the wall in front of her.

When she looked back at Victoria, she had a conspiratorial gleam in her eye.

She motioned for Victoria to come closer so that she could whisper. Victoria was going to reprimand her for the action, but thought better of it. She may not wish to share this information any other way.

"I am going to meet my donor today. Isn't that great? Daddy is bringing her here at 10:30. He says she is really nice. I was so excited I couldn't sleep. Do I look alright? Do you think she will like me? I hope so. I really would like her to give me one of her kidneys so that I would feel better and be able to leave here. I want to go back to school. I miss my friends and I don't know if they know I am here. No one but you and Daddy come to see me..." Vivian continued her diatribe as Victoria's mind began working. Her thoughts taking her away from Vivian for a moment, wondering just how much Mason had shared about her with the Morganson woman.

She knew he'd gone to see her in New York. It didn't take a detective, even though she had used one to check on him, to know that Mason wouldn't stay away from her.

Knowing this, Victoria was determined more than ever to become invaluable to her granddaughter – the person she wouldn't want to live without.

Coming out of her thoughts, she let her gaze roam over Vivian, placing a serious look on her face until the child became quiet. She allowed her eyes to rest on her hair, then come back to her eyes. Knowing that she now had Vivian's attention, she began.

"Why don't I help you with your hair? I have a wonderful idea for a style and when the woman comes she will see even more what a beautiful little lady you are."

"Really?"

"Really."

Twenty minutes later, the door opened and upon seeing Mason, Victoria's heart began beating quickly in anticipation of coming face to face with Paige Morganson.

"Vivian, hon -" The greeting died on his lips as he stalled for a moment, eyeing Victoria. His face became wary, but she saw him force himself to recover as a petite woman stepped through the door behind him, dressed in camel colored suit and a burnt orange sweater with a mock turtleneck that brought fire to her golden eyes. It looked like Vivian wasn't the only one that wanted to look their best for this meeting.

Victoria took in the smile that seemed genuine as well as the nervous energy that surrounded her. Did she know Vivian was her daughter?

"Victoria," Mason acknowledged dryly.

Victoria nodded, keeping her voice as soft and void of the resentment she felt. "Mason, it's good to see you again."

Surprise replaced the wariness for an instant, then was back in full bloom in his eyes. He watched her a second too long to be considered cordial.

"Vivian, honey, and Victoria. I would like you to meet Ms. Paige Morganson." He turned slightly, giving the woman space to pass him and come forward to greet both of them with a firm handshake.

"Ms. Morganson," he continued, "This is my lovely daughter, Vivian, and her grandmother, Victoria Branchett."

"It is an honor to meet both of you. I am very happy to make your acquaintance," she spoke with sincerity. Victoria watched close for signs of recognition or surprise and, finding none, had her answer. Paige Morgan knew who Vivian was and was discreetly keeping it to herself – for the moment, anyway.

An unusually shy Vivian almost whispered her greeting of, "Hello," but it was quickly followed by an unchecked response to her open admiration. "You are really pretty."

Paige's face registered first surprise then extreme pleasure as the corners of her mouth lifted, almost catching up to the flush rising to her cheeks.

"I was just about to say the same thing about you." Paige replied.

Vivian blushed, her wide smile mimicking her mother's.

This did not bode well, Victoria thought to herself as she forced her smile to remain. She felt Mason's eyes on her, trying to assess her reaction. She would give away nothing.

She stepped away from her chair by Vivian's bed. "Here Ms. Morganson," she said and motioned to her chair, "Take my chair. I am sure you and Vivian have a lot to talk about and would like to get to know each other better."

Paige hesitated briefly, her gaze moving from Victoria to Mason, then back. "You don't have to give up your seat. I can stand."

"Nonsense. I was just going to get a little treat for Vivian and myself anyway. Come sit down." She stepped over to Vivian, quickly pressing a kiss on her forehead.

"I will be back soon." Vivian nodded, enjoying the rare affection.

"It was nice meeting you, Ms. Morganson. We will have a chance to get better acquainted later, I hope." She turned to Mason as she walked to the door.

"You are looking very healthy, Mason. The trip to New York must have done you some good." She was pleased to see her comment take him off guard. He didn't respond.

She turned back one last time, waving at Vivian as she exited.

Once she closed the door she relaxed her face, working her jaw to remove the slight ache from the forced smile. Turning towards the elevators, she took her time walking down the corridor.

She marveled at the momentary victory of leaving Mason speechless and, she would guess, a bit leery. Let him squirm for a little while.

Now, what to do about Ms. Morganson? The woman was hard to place in the brief time they were in each other's presence. She could tell the meeting meant a great deal to her by her demeanor and inability to keep her eyes off of Vivian.

Though slightly perturbed by Vivian's uninhibited comment, Victoria couldn't blame her. Ms. Morganson was beautiful and did hold some promise to the beauty Vivian would be. Though the similarities weren't outright obvious, there were many small likenesses.

A shiver of apprehension crawled up Victoria's spine at the thought. If she'd noticed the woman's beauty, she wondered if Mason had. The ramifications of their union would definitely put a dent in her plan, but she wouldn't put any more obstacles in her way than were already there. She would cross that bridge if or when it came.

Meanwhile, she would just work to outshine the golden-eyed beauty and remain the foremost benefactor of her granddaughter's affection and loyalty.

She walked back out into the bright morning, just then remembering the earliness of the day. She shrugged to herself; Mason may frown a little at her choice of treat, but all adults knew that it was never too early for a child to want ice cream.

Maybe she would peruse the shops lining the streets closest to the hospital. If she took her time finding an extra special gift to go with the treat, she may be able to miss the rest of Mason and the Morganson woman's visit.

The thought appealed to her more and more as she looked into the different windows.

Passing in front of a hat shop she paused, her eyes alight with a new idea. Vivian wasn't a finicky child. Come to think of it, Victoria didn't recall a time before the past week's events when Vivian even pouted or complained.

Pleasing her wouldn't be hard once she put her mind to it. Vivian would get the doting and gift-giving grandmother Victoria believed she wanted and Victoria could also have what she wanted.

CHAPTER 38

Mason tried hard to concentrate on the scene in front of him, but his mind kept wandering as anxiety built in him over Victoria's suspicious greeting. What was she thinking? She'd made it known that she was aware of his trip to visit Paige, but he'd not received any calls from her since he'd gotten back into town, nor did she make any direct remarks regarding that fact. He knew she was plotting something. She was always plotting or scheming something, but this time he had a sinking feeling that his vulnerability was exposed in the form of his daughter.

"I like the color green too but I don't have a lot of clothes that color. My mom said that blue looked great on me because it made my eyes shine." His daughter's animated voice drifted over to him as she conversed with Paige.

"So I was thinking…you might be a little lonely with school starting already and not being able to see your friends…" Paige reached into her briefcase resting on the chair by her side. Mason had been so preoccupied by his thoughts on how Paige and Vivian would take to one another, he hadn't noticed the piece. Then once they entered the room and were met by Victoria; most thoughts had left him.

Even the thoughts that were returning now of how feminine Paige looked in her tailored, camel-colored skirt and jacket. He could see the dark, burnt-orange sweater flowing above the top of her jacket. Both brought a glow to her face and her quiet excitement made her eyes sparkle.

He couldn't blame his daughter for her outburst. Paige was more than pretty; she was stunning. He wondered, not for the first time, if she had someone special back in California. He'd been wondering a lot of things in regards to Paige since his last encounter with her, least of all what it would feel like if she looked at him with even half of the adoration she was displaying for Vivian right this moment.

He and Paige had discussed how they would approach the subject of her relation to his daughter. There was still another day before Paige had to start getting prepped for the procedure. He would allow Paige and Vivian to get acquainted and begin a rapport before they told her. She was a very smart and inquisitive child that had never been discouraged from asking questions. It was only a matter of time before she would begin asking questions that would place Paige in the uncomfortable position of trying not to reveal too much with her answers.

"I like your bracelet. It is very pretty. Did your boyfriend give it to you?" Mason's thoughts were held by the question. His ears were sharp, even as he glanced up at the television that showing a documentary on tigers in the wild on the Discovery Channel.

"No. It was a gift to myself a few years ago after one of my books landed on the New York Best Seller's List."

Vivian's eyes went wide. "Is that what you do? You write books?" He knew this would pique his daughter's interest. She was always writing poems or short stories. He accredited it to her maturity and sensitivity, but now he could see that it may have been passed down.

"Yes," Paige answered. Mason looked away from the television just in time to see her nodding.

"What do you write about?"

"At first I wrote self-help books for women – Christian and otherwise – on obtaining and maintaining a higher level of self-esteem." Paige cleared her throat at Vivian's slight frown. "I write books that help people show themselves how to feel better about themselves and show them how to love themselves."

At the dawning of realization in Vivian's eyes, Paige went on. "I wrote them for a few years, and then I would travel and speak to different groups and encourage them to be brave and go after what they wanted and now I write with the same thing in mind, but more in the form of a story."

"Are the stories true?" Vivian asked, enthralled.

"Maybe parts of them, but most of them are fiction."

"How does a story that is not true help people?"

Paige smiled in admiration for the brightness of this child who looked so much like Gladys, it was hard not calling out her name.

"Even though it may not have all happened around me or to me, there is definitely a possibility that it could happen. I know life isn't perfect, but there are things I believe we can do when things don't go our way that will help us remain happy and at peace. So instead of telling people what to do, I just kind of show them with words."

Vivian was in deep thought for a moment and Mason returned his attention to the television until she spoke again.

Paige took the opportunity to go back into her briefcase and pull out an oversized card. "As I was saying before, I thought you might be missing some of your friends, with school starting and all. Your dad and I thought hearing from some of them might cheer you up." Paige handed the card to Vivian, who took it with slow reverence.

"Wow," she replied breathlessly, extending the word, "This is a big card."

"Well, how else was everyone supposed to get to sign it? One of those small cards couldn't possibly fit all of your friends. You are a very blessed girl to have so many friends."

Mason watched as Vivian held the card in her hands. She didn't move to open it right away. She just stared at it.

Mason mistook her silence for sadness at not being in school with her friends. "Hon, you will be all better soon and you will be able to go back to school and see all of your friends."

Vivian looked up, unshed tears glistening in her eyes. "I know, Daddy. I am not sad, I am happy."

"Thank you." The words were just a mere whisper in the suddenly, overly-quiet room. Vivian was looking at Paige in such a way it brought moisture to both the adult's eyes.

Paige nodded in understanding. "My pleasure. I am happy to be able to do it. Now, open your card. I can't wait to see your face when you look at all the kids that signed it. "

Paige visited with Vivian for another hour, going over the card and answering questions about her writing while Vivian shared her love for writing as well. She even shared a poem she had written a few years ago about her mother before she passed away. They talked about hobbies, favorite foods, and places Vivian wanted to visit. Some Paige had traveled to and some she had not. They found they had a lot of things in common, especially their love for the Lord.

Paige checked her watch, noting the time. "Well young lady, I think it is about time that I give you a chance to rest. It was wonderful meeting you."

Vivian nodded, her somber expression relaying her reluctance to see Paige leave. "Will you come back and see me before...?"

Paige inclined her head. "That is why I came early. When would you like me to come back?"

"How about later this afternoon...if you aren't too busy?" Paige couldn't help notice the pleading in the child's eyes.

"If your father doesn't think it will tire you out, I will be back later this afternoon, right after you eat your dinner." Paige looked to Mason for his permission. He gave it in the form of a nod.

Vivian clapped her hands together a couple times, squealing in delight. "Thank you! You know you really are very pretty, inside and out." She turned to her father and in the same breath and asked, "Daddy, don't you think Ms. Morganson is pretty?"

Mason watched as a startled expression quickly fled across Paige's face, an impassive one replacing it. She kept her eyes averted, feigning interest in straightening Vivian's bedcovers. He stared at her, not realizing he had not replied until Vivian began to repeat her question.

"Daddy…?"

"Yes, honey, I agree," he said, never taking his eyes off Paige. "She is pretty inside and out." Those last words garnered another startled look from Paige, but brought with it a flush that he saw crawl up to the tips of her ears when she glanced at him to gauge his expression.

"Do you have a boyfriend, Ms. Morganson?"

Mason could see that Paige was beginning to feel uncomfortable. "Vivian. It isn't proper to ask such personal questions just after meeting people."

"Oh." Vivian frowned as if she were trying to work out a puzzle then looked at her father. "I just find it hard to imagine that she doesn't have a boyfriend."

"Why?" It was Paige that asked the question this time.

"Why wouldn't you? I'm sure boys…I mean men think you are also beautiful."

"I could say the same thing for you. How many boyfriends do you have?"

Vivian laughed out loud. "None. I am too young to have a boyfriend. Besides, most of the boys at my school are short and look funny."

Mason let out a long breath. Thank goodness for funny-looking boys.

Paige inclined her head. "Exactly. Men may think I look nice, but it's my decision. No matter how beautiful a gentleman thinks a woman is, it is still her decision whether she would like to have a relationship with them."

Noticing Paige had not answered the initial question as to whether or not she was single, Mason was about to ask a question of his own when the door opened and in walked Victoria. Her eyes instantly narrowed and, just as quickly, opened to reveal nothing.

"My…you are still here," she stated too brightly, carrying in a couple of bags on each arm, "I brought Vivian a treat. You are more than welcome to share…"

"That's alright. We were just leaving so that Vivian could get a little rest. It wouldn't be the best time to tire her out," Mason interrupted her, making it clear that she wasn't to keep Vivian up long.

Her lips thinned, but she nodded. "I just came back to give her what I promised and sit with her while she takes her nap."

Mason schooled his features so that Victoria couldn't read the confusion and anxiety her words caused. She was definitely up to something. She wasn't even this nice to her own child. He turned to Vivian who gaped at her grandmother until she realized that her mouth was open.

"Hon, I will see you later. Have a restful nap," he said walking over to her and gently yet firmly hugging her. "I love you."

"I love you too, Daddy."

"It was nice seeing you again, Mrs. Branchett," Paige said, shaking the older woman's hand, then turning to Vivian before Mason escorted her out the door. "I will see you later."

Vivian nodded right before she was obscured from their view by Victoria as she moved closer to the bed.

The walk to the elevators was done in silence as each was caught up in their own thoughts. As the door closed them in, Mason glanced at Paige wondering what she was thinking in light of his admission of her beauty. Would she ignore it or would she address it? And if she addressed it, would it be in acceptance or to reject the door he may have inadvertently opened?

After a few prolonged moments of silence, he guessed at the former. "Do you want to share a cab? I have to go by the office so I will have to pass right by your hotel." He tried to sound as nonchalant as possible.

Paige regarded him, a slightly wary expression roaming across her features, causing a small line to form between her brows. "Okay."

If he hadn't been watching her, the one-word sentence would have given nothing away. As it was, he was surprised and she stated as much.

"You didn't think I would accept your offer?"

"No."

"Why?"

"Because your features said something totally different. You looked guarded, like you had your defenses up and you frowned. They all read like a negative sign to me."

Paige nodded.

"Are you purposefully being evasive?"

"No. I was nodding in agreement with you." She watched him just as intently as he was watching her. He opened his mouth but closed it as the doors opened.

They walked through the lobby and out to the street. He hailed a cab, but didn't say any more until they had entered the car and had traveled to the end of the street.

"Are you afraid of me, Paige?" Mason watched Paige, waiting for her to look at him from across the seat. She had moved to the very opposite side upon entering.

"No. I just wonder what you might be expecting from me besides help in saving Vivian's life." She tore her gaze from the passing scenery outside her window to impale him with her dark golden gaze.

He worked through the lump in his throat, thinking it would best if he lightened things a little.

"You're very perceptive. I do want something else from you." His expression gave nothing away.

Her eyebrow went up, but she said nothing.

"I am so tired of hospital food, I am actually thinking about going home and cooking for myself." His voice was just a tad too drool for her to resist responding.

"What's wrong with that?"

He leaned over and voiced in a stage whisper. "I can't cook."

She looked at him with disbelief. "But you have a child…surely you are exaggerating. There must be something you can cook?"

Lowering his head, he shook it woefully then peeked up at her through his lashes. "I burn bread. It is either plain or burnt. Nothing in between. You've seen my child. She isn't thin only because she's been sick," he said with exaggeration, "It's because she won't eat my cooking. The only time I get a halfway decent home meal is when she cooks. It's rather pathetic."

He watched as she deliberated on this. She never took her eyes away from him, watching to see if he was indeed telling a story. Once she had surmised that what he said had a good deal of truth to it, she just shook her head.

"So now that I have shared this disgraceful secret, could you find it in your heart to show me a little mercy and allow me to accompany you to dinner this evening? It will be the last chance I have to dine with decent adult company for a while since you are going to be admitted for the procedure within the next day or so."

She laughed at his antics, an unabashed giggle that made his heart shudder. He watched as she bit her lip in consternation. Suddenly, it was very important that she accepted his invitation. He wanted – no, *needed* –

to hear her laugh again and he wanted another opportunity to elicit the emotion that could bring it about.

He held up his right hand as a symbol of the Boy Scout Promise. "I will be on my best behavior, the epitome of the perfect gentleman and at any time you feel the slightest bit uncomfortable, I will take you back to the hotel."

He waited for her answer, not knowing he was holding his breath until she spoke. "Alright. I will have mercy on you. If you want, we could go right after I visit Vivian again later this afternoon, that way we won't have to take too many cabs."

Mason would have preferred driving and picking her up, but he would settle with her plan. He was so happy she agreed to spend time with him he would abide by her rules.

"There is just one more thing I am going to need to know before we dine. It is more for my health and wellbeing than anything else."

"What's that?" She had gone back to looking out the window.

"Do you have a boyfriend? I am only asking because I wouldn't want him to get the wrong idea about me taking you to dinner, and come after me. I know I put on a good front, but I really can't stand pain."

Paige chuckled. "No. I do not have a boyfriend, but, even if I did, I'd hope he wouldn't be so insecure as to pounce on people I shared meals with."

Insecure or not, he knew he wouldn't have been too happy about any man dining with his wife and if he were to consider an involvement with Paige, it would be the same.

A few minutes later, he watched her exit the cab with the understanding that they would meet back at the hospital and go to dinner from there.

*   *   *

They sat across from each other in a restaurant known for its southern seafood cuisine. The homey atmosphere was fed by the single and family-style seating; gleaming oak tables for two or four sparkly placed around long tables able to accommodate parties of up to 14. The oak chairs were deceptively comfortable with swoop backs and arms that cradled a person while they ate. The high ceilings with huge exposed, wooden beams and homemade curtains gave the restaurant a rustic look; the wall of windows at the back that led to enclosed porch seating overlooking a mock dock,

Weeping Willows, and a real pond thoroughly affected the look of the Bayou.

Paige glanced around her, engrossed in the open seating arrangement that afforded just enough privacy for the more intimate dinners. She scanned the pictures on the walls. Family portraits began a long line of pictures ending with celebrity customers and a man who looked like the chef of the establishment.

Mason was enjoying her fascination. He had only been there a couple times himself, finding it during one of his many excursions through the city in the last couple of years as he took the time to study some of the older buildings.

When she finally turned back to him, he shared some of the history of the building. "This used to be an abandoned warehouse, that's why it has so much room towards the back. The owners told me it took about 8 months for the renovations but it is worth it. We are on the early side of dinner, but give it an hour and this place will be packed. Their blackened catfish is one of the best in the city, but if you like gumbo or Jambalaya, you are also in luck."

"I totally didn't expect to see anything like this in the middle of this city. How did you find it?" He could feel the excited energy flowing around her.

It reminded him of the atmosphere in the car on Saturday mornings when Vivian could barely contain her excitement because he always took her someplace new, educational, or entertaining. It was their time after a week full of scheduled practices, rehearsals, classes, and meetings.

"Before I went back to work, I used to drive around looking at different buildings while Vivian was in school. I was drawn to this particular place because of the outside structure. Unless you already know it is a restaurant, it is hard to fathom. I like peculiar uses of space." He watched as Paige nodded while scanning the area again and a drink server came to take their order.

When she finally shifted her eyes back to meet his, they were alive and dancing.

"I take it you like it?"

She nodded quickly. "It is so warm and inviting. They have made great use of the space. I wish it wasn't so cold outside; I would have loved to eat out on the porch. I bet it is perfect in the summer."

He felt drawn to the animation in her voice and the wonder flying across her features, lighting up her eyes, turning them to liquid gold.

"See, I may have you changing your mind about Chicago yet. My city does have many redeeming qualities. You just had to get away from the airport."

"You sound like a commercial for the Chicago Tourism Bureau, but I am willing to be open. What other hidden treasures do you know about?"

"Uh uh. I can't tell you about them. It's not allowed. I would have to show them to you and since there is no time before the procedure, you will have to promise to let me take you around for a few days once you are released from the hospital."

Barely concealed mirth seemed to be straining at her lips as they quivered at the force it took to keep them straight.

He watched her struggle for a couple of seconds, then finally and regrettably succumb to it. She shrugged her shoulders. "I will have to check my calendar and let you know."

"Fair enough." He nodded while opening his menu so she couldn't see the disappointment in his eyes. What was it about her that continuously drew him? One moment he wanted to protect her and the next he felt as if he was the very person she needed protection from.

She came off very stern and rigid, almost unyielding in the way she conducted herself in business and more personal issues. She was incredibly possessive about her privacy and was hard-pressed to reveal much about her life outside of her ministry and passion for people. And for all of this, she didn't come across pious or snobbish, but incredibly down to earth and very direct. So direct one wouldn't even think about asking her personal questions.

Just when he thought he had put most of the pieces together, she laughed that childish, uninhibited laugh that blew him away by giving him a peek into her soul. Most adults – at least all the ones he knew – didn't show such open emotion anymore. They had been taught, formed, stemmed, and cut short from expressing themselves so openly. He wondered how she had been able to keep that part of her innocence and remain comfortable in it. He opened his mouth to ask, but their server came to take their order.

Paige ordered the gumbo, stating it had been quite a while since she'd had really good gumbo and was hoping this would put an end to her drought.

Mason ordered a seafood platter with crawfish, shrimp, clams, crab, and lobster, all steamed and seasoned with a special rub that made Paige's mouth water when it was delivered.

Mason watched her look back and forth between their dishes. "Do you want to switch with me?"

"No, but if you would be nice enough to share a piece of your crab, I would be extremely grateful."

"Your wish is my command."

"In that case, I will take a piece of shrimp too," she said with a huge smile. He found himself arrested for a moment, but quickly composed himself and served her from his plate.

Their conversation was a little stilted at first with Mason doing most of the talking about his profession and Vivian, but as Paige began to relax she opened up more about her sister and Gladys.

"Are you still sure you want to tell Vivian about you tomorrow?"

"Yes." Paige said emphatically, nursing the last of her sweet tea.

"Do you know how you want to broach the subject?"

"No, but I am sure the opportunity will present itself."

"How do you know?"

"Because it is time."

"How do you know?" he repeated, becoming a little agitated.

"I know from here," she said as she placed her hand just below her solar plexus. "I am not sure how to explain it except that I know it is the right time. I believe she will be receptive and I will try to answer all of her questions as honestly and directly as possible."

Mason shook his head slowly. He needed more of an explanation than what she was giving him. He didn't want his child hurt any more than she had been.

"If you consider all of the things that look like a coincidence, then you would understand that everything has led to this. It could very well have been that I didn't sign up to be a living donor. There could have been someone else that was a better match for Vivian. I would not have been called and you still may not know about me." She directed her full gaze at him. "There were too many signs guiding me to this moment, and I am not going to ignore them because of fear. I have done that far too long."

You know I was recently reminded of a prayer request I gave the Lord almost a year ago," she continued, "There seemed to be so many pieces of my life in disarray, up in the air, floating around. I asked God to help me put my life back in order, to help put the pieces back together. I believe He has been helping me do that." She looked down at her fingers, studying the length of her thumbnails as she overlapped them.

"It took me actually wanting to face the pieces first, and that was a challenge in itself. I didn't know how good I had gotten at running away from my issues. Instead of confronting them with God's help, I used my work for God as a crutch to avoid them." She glanced back up at Mason, who was listening intently, even if he didn't quite understand the difference between the two, and he stated as much.

"I could be found in church at any time, on any day. I poured my heart and life into everything I was asked to do by my pastors, but it was my quiet time with God that showed me that I was pouring so much into the assignments they gave me, I was not putting forth any energy into discovering, learning, and healing myself from the pain in my past."

"But how did you know God just didn't have you busy? I have known of a few people that were very busy doing God's work, but were very happy in working for Him and never questioned themselves."

"I can't say for them, but for me it had to do with motive. I love my Lord. He truly is everything to me. I would die without him, literally and figuratively.

When it was still hard after five years for me to think about - let alone discuss - my past, I had to ask myself if I was really taking advantage of my whole relationship with God. I began to understand that there were parts of my life that I was more than happy to surrender over to Him and work through, but there were other parts that I kept strictly off limits from Him."

"Like what? If you don't mind me asking." He was hoping she wouldn't.

She looked at him so long at first that he didn't think she would answer. Finally, without averting her eyes she replied, "I didn't trust Him to help me resolve my issues with my cousin, men, or Him."

Mason was surprised by her honesty and even more so by her admission to him about her issues with God.

"Are you allowed to have issues with God? I mean, aren't you afraid of what He will do, knowing you have an issue with Him?"

He watched the small frown mar her forehead briefly before she answered. "Why? It isn't as if He didn't know I had an issue with Him even before I realized it. I think if He had a real problem with me admitting that I didn't trust Him, He would have taken me out before I came to realize it."

"But how can you love and believe in a God you don't trust?" Mason was more than intrigued.

"Was there ever anyone you loved that you didn't trust in some areas? Better yet, did you ever argue with your wife? I don't mean about what type of movie you decide to watch, but about decisions that had a profound effect on your lives together?" She had leaned forward, waiting for his answer.

Mason thought of a few occasions, especially their last argument about Rachael not interacting with her mother.

He nodded.

"Did you still love her?" Paige pressed forward.

"Absolutely."

Paige shrugged her shoulders. "It is the same with my relationship with God. Even though I may not agree with how He brought me to this stage or why my life is how it is, He is not afraid of my anger or admittance of feelings of distrust. It is up to me to be open to receiving His reasoning as to why He did and does things the way He does. I think that is one of the differences between treating God as a religious figure and having an intimate relationship with Him.

Just like your daughter wouldn't be afraid to be angry with you on occasion, because even though things may not go her way she knows you love her and want the best for her." She cocked her head to the side. "You don't seem like a tyrant or overly controlling, so she probably feels comfortable and safe voicing her opinion to you within the parameters of respect for who you are in her life, of course."

Mason was desperately trying to take it all in and see the parallel, but this was not the same God he knew. He was having a hard time reconciling the being that allowed his father to get away with destroying his mother and the loving and paternal figure she was portraying.

Paige must have read his scowl because her next question seemed to peg him straight on. "Why are you having such a hard time recognizing God as a loving being who wants nothing but the best for you? If your wife and now daughter have that type of relationship with Him, what keeps you from knowing Him in that way?"

Mason looked away, trying to decide whether he felt comfortable enough to share his anger with God. After a few moments and a sip of coffee, he decided to skim the surface.

"There were some things that went on in my childhood that I am finding it hard to see... 'God's hand' in, let alone His love. In fact, the situation made me even wonder if there was a God for many years and, when I opened up to believing that there may be some credence to what my wife and child go on about, all I can consider is that maybe He was preoccupied; His attention was needed somewhere else or that I just wasn't important enough for Him to keep the enemy out of my house."

Mason took a deep breath. He hadn't meant to reveal so much. He couldn't keep the bitterness or the pain out of his voice. Why was he wasting energy on such things? He was tired; just tired of it all. He set his cup down and glanced over to catch the server's attention for the check, before returning his gaze back to Paige. But when he did, he was startled by the tears brimming in her eyes.

Anger he had not felt for a while came up, threatening to spill over. Through tightly-clenched teeth he tried to hold it in check, but the edge was in his voice. "I don't want your pity."

Paige's chin came up proudly as she furiously blinked back the tears.

"I don't pity you, Mason. My pity wouldn't do you any good. I only feel your pain. "

"What do you know about my pain? You don't know me."

"No, in the full spectrum of things, I don't, but I have been where you are. I have my own story of when the 'enemy' came into my camp and took things from me that I will never get back, but it wouldn't do any good to share it with you right now because you wouldn't understand the things I gained and I don't feel like just swapping stories of woe with you."

Mason, feeling slightly chastised, was momentarily distracted. He still wasn't fully convinced she felt his pain. How could she and still be happy with her life, and laugh as carefree as a child? Her pain had not been as deep as his.

Even as he tried to convince himself, he wondered if maybe there was a way back to lighter times. If so, did she by chance know how to get there?

CHAPTER 39

"I promise I am fine, Mel. You really don't have to come. Things will be crazy around here, and you will wind up just sitting in the hospital room getting more and more anxious by the moment. I know you. You don't like hospitals and worse yet, you don't like seeing anyone you love in the hospital. Remember, we have been through this before."

"All I hear is static, Paige," her sister replied on the other end of the line. "We are both a lot stronger, but you are still the only sister I have. I have already made arrangements. I will be there right before you go in, and I will stay until we can have a decent conversation and I know you are out of the woods."

Paige laughed. "I am glad you elaborated. Your and my ideas of decent conversation may still be polar opposites."

"So you will put me on the list to visit you?"

Paige blew out a deep breath. "Yes. My sister, Mel, once again to the rescue."

"Is that what you think? That I am playing hero?"

"No, Mel, not playing." Before her sister got the wrong idea, she went on.

"I am already greatly indebted to you, and growing more and more each day. I want you to get on with your life and concentrate more on you and your relationship with Marc. I am okay now. I know there are some things I can't take back and that will forever…"

"Stop the madness," her sister interrupted.

"You are my baby sister. I love you and you love me. We take care of one another. Would you stop praying for me if I asked you to?"

"No, but…"

"Would you stop calling me, sending me and Gladys words of encouragement, sending gifts from your travels, putting money into Gladys educational fund and trust?"

"No, but…"

"You owe me nothing and I owe you nothing. This is what people do for each other that love one another. They care, they share, and they cover each other. You should be able to wake up to at least one, recognizable face, and I am going to be that one. I can be stubborn too you know."

"Yes, I know," Paige responded quietly.

"Mel?"

"Yep?"

"I love you. Thank you."

"Not a mention, not a word, already done," said Mel, repeating part of an old pledge they had begun to make to each other after Paige had come out of her depression.

"Done. I will see you in Chicago. Good night."

"Good night."

Paige laid in bed going over the past couple days and organized the emotions playing havoc with her thought process.

Before speaking to her sister she had made a call to First Lady Menagerie, who had practically grilled her about both Brandon and Mason and her recent interactions with them. She'd tried to be as honest as she could in regards to her feelings and thoughts for each man, but found both great points and winning flags where both men were concerned.

"When I get around Mason I can barely think straight. He's so good looking I get a physical reaction just being in close proximity to him. I find it disconcerting and I wonder if I am looking for things to dislike about him."

"Does he know this?"

"Are you kidding? I don't think it would be wise if he knew how I felt about him. I'm not sure I could trust him with that information."

"Do you think he would take advantage of you?"

"No, nothing like that. I just don't think he would understand that I won't be moved by my physical feelings towards him, and even my emotions are questionable. He makes me laugh once I relax enough around him, but I am so afraid of leading him on I think I might come off rigid sometimes."

"Well, from what you told me about your dinner with him, I would say that he isn't allowing that to deter him. Do you think he is looking for a mother for his daughter?"

"Actually, I think that is the last thing he is looking for. I just know that he has some serious trust issues with God, almost to the point where he's not 100% sure He exists. How can I trust a man that doesn't trust in God? How can I put my life in a man's hands knowing he will make decisions on his own knowledge of things?"

"How do you know men who know and love God won't find themselves doing the same thing? No man is perfect, Paige. We all lean on ourselves once in a while, when we think the answer has come easily.

Besides, I remember when you had some of the same issues, and look at you now."

"What are you saying? Should I work more to help him through this?"

"No, I am not telling you to become what my friend calls 'Captain, save and make a Saint'. That would and should never be your job. You are only to be open to what God is leading you to say or do and if He doesn't lead, then please don't do it on your own. I am saying again what I have been saying to you through all of this. Don't judge by what you see with your eyes, continue to ask God to reveal things to you and by all means please guard your heart with both men. Speaking of both men, we had dinner with Brandon and Dominy again last evening."

"How is he…they…How are they doing?"

"Good. Dominy was his usual, jovial self. Brandon was a little preoccupied though. He asked about you."

"Really? Straight-forward asked, no hedging?"

"Yeah. I told you before he was interested."

"True, but talks have never struck me as more than just polite conversation and vague interest."

"I am just relaying a message."

"Which was?"

"Please tell Paige I asked about her." Lady Menagerie chuckled.

"Oh. What did he ask you specifically?"

There was a slight pause. "He just wanted to know if I'd spoken to you since you'd arrived in Chicago."

"Oh."

"Is there something you haven't shared?"

Paige sighed. "Brandon asked me to a movie when I get back in town."

"Just you?"

"Yes."

"And you said?"

"Yes."

"Okay."

"Okay? What do you mean by 'okay'?"

Lady Menagerie laughed. "Sweetie, all of life is not a mystery. 'Okay' is 'okay'."

"You aren't going to ask me why I accepted?"

The chuckle came again. "If you don't know why you accepted, you definitely need to put in some prayer time to get to know yourself better."

Paige considered her answer for a moment. She was on her own. "So you're taking off the training wheels, huh."

"Yes, you've been flying without them for a while, but if it looks like you are going into a dead spin, I may through you a line."

"Much appreciated."

But still, Paige wondered if she was heading in the right direction where either one of them was concerned and was there yet a third road that had neither one of them on it?

*   *   *

Paige sat next to Vivian's bed, opposite of Mason. Sleep had been elusive, and she didn't know what was pounding harder: her head or her heart. She had thought of many different scenarios in regards to how Vivian would take the news, and it all had to do with presentation.

Mason was going to have to begin, due to the fact that he and Rachael had been told that Vivian's mother had died in childbirth and had shared that same information with Vivian when letting her know she'd been adopted.

"Is something wrong?" Vivian asked, feeling the tension in the room. "Have you changed your mind?" She turned to Paige.

Paige moved quickly to assuage her fears. "No, sweetie. I have not changed my mind. We just have something to tell you and though I think it is a good thing, I don't know if you find it good or bad news."

"Oh." Vivian said on a sigh. She stared expectantly at Paige.

Here it goes. Paige sighed.

"Remember, Viv, when your mother and I told you we chose you to be our daughter because your mother died after giving birth to you?" Mason began.

Vivian nodded, a frown knit between her brows.

"Well, I recently found out the hospital you were born in made a mistake."

"What kind of mistake?"

"I found out that your mother didn't die in childbirth. She is still alive."

Paige watched as the different expressions mirroring Vivian's emotions ran across her face. Excitement quickly extinguished by fear and trepidation ran the gambit through her expressive eyes. Her bottom lip began to quiver as her brows drew together. "Does she want me back? Does she want to take me away from you?"

Paige drew Vivian's attention by moving closer and taking her hand. "No sweetie. I don't want to take you away from your daddy. I just want to give you a kidney."

Paige watched, holding her breath, waiting for what she had just said to register with Vivian. When the child's eyes became wide, she knew it had clicked.

"You're my birth mother?" Vivian asked incredulously.

Paige nodded, not trusting herself to speak.

Paige watched as Vivian stared at her as if she were trying to commit her facial features to memory. The moment was so profound it pulled at Paige's chest.

Paige's breath caught in her throat. She worked at swallowing a few times to temper her emotions. She threw a glance at Mason briefly for comfort and he offered a smile of confirmation.

When Vivian finally spoke, Paige was moved to tears.

"If you give me your kidney, does it mean I have to go with you?"

Paige shook her head. "I am only here to make sure you can live a longer, happier life with your father. I would give you my kidney even if it meant I could never see you again."

Vivian was quiet for a long while. Paige was wondering what was going on in her head and how she was digesting the information.

"You don't want me?" Vivian's lower lip began working again.

"Why would you ask that?" Paige squeezed her hand.

"You gave me up when I was born and you aren't going to take me away now…"

Paige got up to rest gently on the edge of the bed and wrap her arms around Vivian. She just held her for a moment.

"I didn't know you were alive either. When you were born I was very young and there was some confusion. The nurse told me you had died. I thought you were in heaven until your dad came and told me about you." Paige leaned back to make sure Vivian understood. When the child calmed, she continued.

"I would like to have the chance to get to know you, but I will let that be your decision. Your father and I just thought you should know. Nothing will change unless you want it to."

Vivian turned towards her father. Paige watched the interaction between the two. The unspoken communication between the two was something she envied. She had seen it with her sister and Gladys as well. She had given up so much, missed so much.

She moved back to her chair as Mason moved onto the bed on Vivian's other side and engulfed her in a hug. Paige noticed the tears spiking his lashes and was shaken by the depth of his emotion.

He whispered something in Vivian's ear, but it came to Paige as a murmur. She bowed her head to give him privacy with his child. When she heard Vivian giggle she looked up curious as to what caused the sound. Mason was planting sloppy kisses all over her face.

"Ewww, Daddy, that's too wet," Vivian complained between laughter, trying to evade her dad's lips, covering her face with her hands anywhere she thought would be her dad's next target.

Finally he stopped to let her catch her breath, but he did not leave the bed.

Paige felt, once again, like the odd man out in her own children's lives. This, she resolved, was the price she was meant to pay for the anger she had let consume her those many years. She wondered if the Lord would redeem the time for her. She knew He could, but would He?

By the time Vivian and Mason looked back at her, she'd made sure none of her inner turmoil was mirrored in her expression.

"I would like to get to know you better too," Vivian said shyly. "Do I have to call you mom?"

Paige shook her head. "No, but I can't have you calling me Ms. Morganson either. How about Paige?"

"How about Ms. Paige? My dad said it isn't proper to call adults without a title."

Paige shrugged. "Ms. Paige it is. I would like that very much as well. Whenever you like, I am available for us to start to get to know each other."

Vivian's face broke into a hesitant smile. "How about now?"

Paige took another deep breath. "If you think you can take it. I have another surprise for you." She opened her purse to take out the picture of another child that looked just like the one that had just turned to her with a look of expectation.

*   *   *

Paige lay in her hospital bed later that evening after being checked in and going through a number of tests as part of her pre-op. She slowly recounted her time with Vivian and Mason. She was proud of her daughter's intellect though she knew she couldn't claim credit for it.

Vivian's ability to grasp the information and ask direct questions did not evolve from her parenting. The only other, truly uncomfortable moment for Paige was when Vivian asked her if she was married at the time she had Paige and her sister Gladys.

"No, I wasn't married," Paige shook her head, wondering how much she should elaborate. She decided to wait until she was asked point blank... and she didn't have long.

"You weren't married. Where was my father? Did he know you were pregnant?"

Paige swallowed hard. "Mmmm..." Paige tried not to glance over at Mason. It wasn't as if he could be much help anyway since she had not shared with him the details surrounding the twin's conception.

"Your biological father was in the military and was stationed somewhere else. He didn't find out about my pregnancy until after I delivered." Matter of fact, he didn't find out about the pregnancy until a few years later when his aunt confronted him during one of his leaves. The drama that tore through the family as he tried to contact her left a frisson between the two immediate families that remained still to this day.

"Where is he now?" Vivian asked quietly, her chin resting on her knees that had been brought up to her chest several minutes before. Paige recognized the position as one of comfort.

"He passed away almost two months ago."

Vivian was quiet and still for a long time before she spoke again. "So he never knew I was alive," she said more as a statement and Paige shook her head in confirmation.

"Did he ever see my sister?"

"No, but he saw a picture of her."

Vivian suddenly looked up at Paige, her eyes bright with moisture.

"Do you think he was hoping to see me when he got to heaven?"

Paige thought about the question for a moment, then answered as truthfully as she could.

"I think he may have, but was probably very happy to learn that you weren't there yet. It meant that you get to live a full life." Vivian, though she didn't respond verbally, did give a hesitant smile.

"Did you love him?"

Paige, momentarily thrown by the question, recovered and found that she was able to be honest and happy with her answer for the first time in a long time.

"Not always, but I did before he passed away, and I do now," she stated emphatically.

Vivian nodded. "Enough to marry?"

Paige shook her head. "Never that much, but enough."

"Do you think you will ever marry?"

Paige shrugged, wondering how they had gotten to this line of questioning and how long it would last.

"I hope so...one day."

"Do you want more children?"

Paige looked from Vivian to Mason, who had been as quiet as a statue, and then back again.

"Mmmm...if he wanted children, then yes. Yes, I would have more children. I missed some good parts, like your first words, first steps, first laugh, first bath...but if you allow it, I can still experience some of your great moments."

"Like what?"

"Graduation, your first fancy dress dance, your first day in high school, your first crush..." She finished in hushed tones.

Vivian giggled. Mason frowned. Paige laughed.

*   *   *

"What's that funny smile on your face?" Paige turned to see her sister poking her head through the door. Her smile brightened.

"Hey Mel, you're early. It's good to see you."

"You are looking bright and cheery. How are you feeling? How did the rest of the tests and pre-op go?" Mel came in, glancing around and laying her purse on a chair by the door.

Before Paige could even answer the first questions, Mel commented. "Well at least it looks better than the last one you were in." She shrugged then plopped down into the chair next to Paige's bed.

Paige watched her sister for a moment. She knew she was nervous and concerned. She always rambled at the mouth when she felt anxious about something.

"It's going to be fine, Mel. There is nothing to worry about. It is a common enough procedure. I will be up and walking around in a couple of weeks."

Mel met her eyes. Taking a deep breath, she let it out slowly. "I didn't come here for you to assuage my fears–I came to support you. I will get my act together, but I need to know how you truly feel. Aren't you just a little bit scared?"

Paige thought for a moment. She decided to be as honest as she could. "Yes, scared, but not fearful. I've never been through anything like this before. I wonder how I will handle the pain. If I will recover really quickly or have a lot of soreness for a while, but those things pale in comparison to what Vivian is going to go through.

I can't just dwell on my pain. My main concern is that her body doesn't reject the kidney, nor there be any infection."

Mel nodded. "So, she really looks just like Gladys, huh?"

Paige chuckled. "They are identical twins. But of course there are some differences. Vivian is just a little quieter, but I think that is more because she doesn't know me as well. She is sharp, really sharp, and just as straight forward and inquisitive as Gladys."

"The apple doesn't fall too far from the tree, Paige. You are just the same."

Paige shrugged it off.

"How is the father?"

Paige regarded her sister for a moment wondering if she should open this can of worms with her. She thought better of it.

"He is a nice man. I am happy Vivian was placed in a loving home. I see she is very much devoted to him, and he adores her." Not taking her eyes off of her sister, she adjusted her bedding around her. "I not only feel fortunate to have another chance to be in my children's lives, I am honored to be able to do this for her and him."

Mel nodded knowingly. "It must be really hard on him to have lost his wife, and facing all of this alone with his daughter," Mel stated, referring back to some of the information Paige shared with her the night before. Paige only nodded.

Paige had left out some of her more recent misgivings regarding her reactions to him. If her sister smelled even the most remote possibility of attraction between Paige and a man, she was all teeth and talons and could not be removed until she had every detail.

Just then the door opened with Mason sticking his head in, concern creasing his brows but easing slightly with surprise to see that Paige had a visitor.

"I'm sorry to interrupt. I was on my way out and just wanted to stop in to make sure you were comfortable and had everything you needed."

Paige quelled a groan as she watched Mel's expression.

281

She had turned at his voice, and Paige could tell from her profile that she was almost startled by his looks. Paige knew that if it were any other man, she might find this amusing since Mel's and her tastes in men ran the opposite ends of the spectrum.

It took Paige a moment to realize that she had not responded, but when Mel turned back to face her, she tried hard to get back on track.

"No need to apologize, Mr. Jenson. I have everything I need. My sister will take care of me."

Then she gestured towards her sister. "Mel, this is Mason Jenson, Vivian's father." She watched as Mel's eyes widened just the tiniest bit.

"Mr. Jenson, this is my sister, Melanie Miller."

Mason came into the room, his hand extended. "Nice to meet you. Please call me Mason." He glanced quickly at Paige and back to her sister. "Paige used to, and since we are practically family, I don't see the need for the formality."

Mel, regaining her composure, stood up and took Mason's hand. "I am in full agreement. Would you like to join us?"

Mason waved his hand, cutting off anything else she may have said. "No, as I said, I was on my way out and I just wanted to make sure Paige was comfortable. I feel better knowing she has someone here to look after her." He leaned closer to Mel as if conspiring against her. "Do you notice how she tends to take over and try to control situations?"

Paige stiffened at the obvious tease. It was too familiar.

"Yeah…only since she was three. Do you know how hard it is to play Barbie Dolls with someone who claims that Ken should be dressed in the apron because Barbie has to work late and since she had the better job, he needed to stay home and take care of the kids? It totally killed the fantasy for me since it always made Ken seem like a bit of a pushover. I had always thought of him more of a man's man myself." She finished with a laugh.

"Thank you, Melanie. That explains a lot."

"It's Mel, and you are very welcome."

Paige gave an unladylike snort. "If you two are done insulting me, I would like to know how Vivian is doing."

Mason's lips twitched on the sides as he tried to reign in his smile. "She is doing well. I haven't seen her this spirited in a long time. I'm glad I took your advice. I do believe this strengthened her will. She is excited about meeting her sister."

Paige leveled a warning look at Mel to behave.

She wasn't comfortable with her sister sharing information about their childhood, and even less comfortable with Mason sharing any newfound information he had of her. She didn't know how close she wanted these two to become, especially since they were so intimately linked to her.

What if things turned sour between her and Mason? She needed to keep a relative distance from him so that they could at least stay civil towards each other for Vivian's sake. She didn't need the complication.

She didn't need the look Mel was giving her right now either.

Mel ignored her.

"Well, I have some things to do before visiting hours are over. I will see you in the morning?" He waited for Paige to acknowledge him. She inclined her head.

Looking back at Mel, "Again, it was a pleasure to meet you and I am looking forward to sharing more stories on our girls… and Paige with you." He wiggled his eyebrows, causing Mel to giggle.

Paige's breath caught, a warning flag waved in front of her eyes. She didn't like this side of Mason. He was too carefree, charming, witty, and way too beguiling.

"The pleasure was mine, Mason, anytime."

Paige looked back at Mel, astounded. Her sister was flirting.

Had she just been dropped into the twilight zone? Was there a camera hidden somewhere catching all of her expressions. She let her eyes roam around the room without turning her head so as not to draw any attention to herself.

She watched her sister watch Mason until he reached the door to turn and wave. She then turned to him, lifting her chin in response to his "goodbye."

She kept her eyes on the door long after it closed, not looking forward to what would be a long list of questions from her sister.

The room was quiet and Paige's curiosity finally got the better of her. She glanced at her sister who just stared at her with what she could only describe as a stupid grin on her face.

"So where were we? Oh yes…" Mel said with the flare of a diva.

"So…how is the father?"

Paige stalled trying to collect herself. Mel was like a bee sensing pollen. She could also sense fear.

Paige glanced over Mel's shoulder at the door behind her, and then returned her gaze. Taking a deep breath, she answered.

"Trouble."

Mel's initial frown slowly morphed into a smile as she studied Paige's agitated expression.

Paige watched as her sister folded her arms and propped her feet up on the lowered bed railing, making herself as comfortable as possible. She glanced at the clock on the wall. Two hours until visiting hours were over.

She looked back at her sister then slumped her shoulders in defeat, leaned back on her pillows and got ready for 120 minutes of interrogation, Mel-style.

CHAPTER 40

"Your test results look good, Mr. Tatum," Dr. Connor began as he sifted through some of the papers in a manila envelope.

Brandon expelled the breath he didn't realize he had been holding. He heard a similar sound from across the room where Dominy sat.

Dominy had gotten back in town a few days before. *The guard is back at his post,* Brandon thought ruefully.

"Your blood work looks promising; all the levels are within a healthy range. I am going to request a CT Scan for later this month, but I don't see why we shouldn't see some changes for the better." Dr. Connor took off his bifocals and looked Brandon squarely in the eye.

"How are you feeling? Pain, fatigue, nausea?"

Brandon felt pinned to a wall. "The side-effects were a little stronger this time, but I believe I faired pretty well during the first cycle."

Dr. Connor then looked to Dominy for confirmation. Dominy only nodded.

"Do you need any anti-nausea medicine?" He asked, turning back to Brandon.

"No-" Brandon began.

"Yes," Dominy said, interrupting him.

The room was quiet.

Dr. Connor looked between Brandon and Dominy for a brief moment then spoke. "Dominy, would you mind giving us a moment of privacy?" He kept his eyes on Brandon as he spoke.

"My pleasure," Dominy breathed as he got up and exited the room.

"What's on your mind, Brandon?"

Brandon leaned forward, clasping his hands in his lap. He looked down, trying to think of the best way to work things in his favor.

"I need to go to Chicago."

"That isn't a smart idea." Dr. Connor leaned forward as well.

"I wasn't asking for your opinion. I wouldn't do it unless it was absolutely necessary and it is necessary for my peace of mind."

The doctor did not reply. He just continued to regard him with a slight frown.

"Look, I know it's risky: filtered air, close quarters, the trip itself...but I will only be there a couple of days at the most. I will do whatever it takes to make sure that my immune system is as strong as possible. I would build a fortress around it if I could.

I have a friend that I need to make sure is alright. Once I do that, I will go back to fully concentrating on my healing."

"Couldn't Dominy go for you?"

"No. I need to do this myself."

"Does Dominy know what you are going to do? Even if I don't try and stop you, he may."

"Once I tell him why, he won't stop me," Brandon said emphatically.

The doctor heaved a heavy sigh, wrote something down on a sheet of paper, and handed it to Brandon.

"I want to see you a week after you get back. No later, Brandon." His tone was non-negotiable.

Brandon nodded.

"I hope she's worth it."

Surprise flitted across Brandon's features before he could school them.

"It could be a family member."

"Is it?" Dr. Connor countered.

Brandon smiled sheepishly. "No."

Dr. Connor inclined his head, a small smile transforming his features, causing him to look a decade younger than his 56 years.

"Anything else?" Dr. Connor spied him, making him feel like an eight-year-old in his father's study, asking to go somewhere he had no true hope in getting permission to go.

"Well, there is just one more thing..."

*   *   *

Brandon was full of nervous energy. He stared out of the window of the cab, seeing nothing. His knee bobbed up and down almost as fast as a shiver, as his body tried in vain to use up the excess energy he was creating with his anxious thoughts.

Paige had not picked up her phone, nor had she come back into town in the week and a half since they'd last spoken. Unable to get a response in what he deemed a timely manner, Brandon called Pastor Lawrence to see if he'd heard anything from Paige or her family.

A few hours later, Pastor Lawrence returned Brandon's call with sketchy-at-best information on Paige.

She'd gone ahead with the procedure and, initially, everything seemed fine. The young girl's body seemed receptive to the new kidney, but Paige's vitals were slowly declining. Paige's sister explained as best she could that there may have been a mishap during surgery that caused Paige to bleed internally. The puncture was so small it took hours for the doctors to diagnose it. Once they'd gone back in and found the source of the slow bleed, she was very weak and had been placed in ICU for much more than the original few hours of her initial recovery.

Mel, whose concern was only magnified by her daughter's anxiety and her inability to comfort her while her sister lay fighting for her life, was close to breaking down.

Brandon immediately volunteered to visit Paige. He still had his Chaplain's card, not to mention his elder's license. Plus, he would call in a favor from one of his father's friends that had many affiliations with the director over the Chaplains serving that HMO. Begrudgingly, Pastor Lawrence gave his permission after questioning Brandon's health for more than a half hour.

Questions raced in a cycle through his mind. What would he find? Would she be awake? If she was, would she want to see him? Was she in a lot of pain? How much longer would she have to be there?

He looked through the front windshield, passed the divider separating him from the front seat. He could see the hospital looming a few blocks ahead. Its 25th floor seemed to touch the cloud-filled sky. Handing the driver a bill as he exited quickly, he made his way through the doors and up to front desk to check in and receive directions to the elevators that would take him to the ICU.

Once he reached the nurse's desk, after he identified himself and stated who he was visiting, he was told that Paige had been moved just that morning to DOU, the Direct Observation Unit one level down of recovery from ICU. Slightly unnerved, but nonetheless relieved that she was doing well enough to be placed out of the Intensive Care Unit, he boarded the elevator to Paige's floor and made a beeline for the room number he was given.

When he reached the door, he was a mass of nerves and knew it wouldn't be fair to her to take it in the room with him. He took a deep breath to regain his hold on the peace he needed to surround himself in before pushing it open.

He scanned the first empty bed then crossed the cloth divider. His heart stopped momentarily at the sight of Paige: pale, fragile-looking, with tubes running from her nose, arm and hand.

He stood there for a moment, unmoving. He couldn't seem to galvanize his legs into the action needed to carry him to the other side of her bed.

"Oh, Paige…what have you done to yourself?" His voice, a ragged whisper, sounded loud in the silence of the room. His throat worked hard to swallow the lump he felt rising up with excess emotion. He fought to keep it in check, even as the back of his eyes began to burn.

Unfamiliar with the intensity of his feelings, he turned his attention towards trying to bring logic to his reaction to her. How could it be so strong, his care for her? How could it have sprung up so quickly, like a weed after a day of rain? He didn't know how much he'd missed her until he had gotten off of the plane and his heartbeat doubled in anticipation of seeing her.

He didn't regret witnessing her in this state. It was even worth this image of her being branded into his memory just to see her at this moment.

Taking a deep breath, he walked to the far side of her bed to where her right hand lay, free of tubes and binding. He needed to touch her and prove to himself she was still alive, to see if she was warmer than she looked.

He quietly picked up the chair in the corner, placing it next to the bed. He sat down and very slowly and tenderly picked up her hand, held it between the two of his and without taking his eyes off of her face, he began praying.

It was in that position that Mel found him when she entered the room. He glanced toward her, registering her surprise, then watched as she glanced at his name tag with the Chaplain pin attached.

A soft sigh of relief escaped her lips as she smiled. "I am so glad you are here." She spoke in hushed tones. "It is wonderful to know that this hospital caters to the whole man. How did you know she was clergy and would be receptive?" He could tell she had mistaken him for the in-house Chaplain, but he was hard-pressed to correct her.

He laid Paige's hand back down as he thought about his answer. He could tell that the woman was a relative because of their shared features. He decided to be honest.

"I'm Elder Brandon Tatum. I'm part of the clergy of Skylight Temple, Elder Morganson's home church." He watched her eyes widen then a warm smile touched her lips as she slowly moved towards him with her hand outstretched.

"I'm Melanie Miller, Paige's sister. How very thoughtful and generous, I might add. Pastor Lawrence said I shouldn't be surprised if Paige had a visitor from the Sick Committee. I thought he was talking about a member of the sister church, New Horizon. They aren't too far from here."

Brandon shook the pretty woman's hand, noting the hazel eyes and full lips, a lot like Paige's, but somehow Paige's eyes shown brighter and her lips appeared softer.

"How long have you been a member of Skylight Temple, Elder Tatum?" Mel continued after a pause long enough for her to do a head-to-toe physical assessment of her own.

"A few months."

"Do you and Paige work closely on the committee?"

"No. In fact, I am over the Men's Ministry. I used to work in this capacity at my former church and offered to step in while she was away."

He saw the slight narrowing of Mel's eyes and could almost see her working her puzzle of him in her mind. "Do you have other business or family in the city?" She watched him with a sharpness he found a little disconcerting.

He cleared his throat that had suddenly become very dry.

"No." He didn't elaborate.

"You came just to see Paige?"

Brandon just nodded.

"How long will you be in town?"

"Just for a couple of days." He placed his hands in his pockets.

She looked at him for a moment. He expected more questions. Instead she said, "She was moved this morning, but hasn't regained consciousness." She shifted her gaze to Paige's sleeping form. "The doctors said she is in stable condition now though. I can't tell you the scare it all gave me."

"I can understand," he said with more emotion than intended.

Her eyes riveted back to him. "Can you?"

"Yes," he responded on an exhaled breath.

"Have a seat, Elder Tatum. I think it would be nice if you and I got to know each other better."

Brandon's brow rose as he ushered her towards his chair and moved to sit across from her. "You first."

*   *   *

"Hey Dom."

"Brandon, how's it going? How is Paige?"

Brandon placed his feet on the ottoman in front of the small recliner in his hotel room.

"She is resting, but she hasn't regained consciousness since I've been here." He blew out a deep breath, removing his clergy collar, name tag, and pin.

"Have you been there all this time?" Dominy's concern could be heard through the phone.

"Yes, but I didn't overdo it. When I came to visit with Paige, her sister was there. We got to know each other, or should I say she got to know me."

"Really? What's she like?"

Brandon began to chuckle. "Inquisitive. I honestly believe if I didn't answer all of her questions to her satisfaction, she wouldn't have let me stay there, even knowing I had come from out of town and was there to pray for her sister."

"She sounds like a regular guard dog."

"Don't get me wrong. She seems really sweet, but she is very protective and, considering things didn't go as smoothly as Paige tried to assure everyone they would, she has reason to be protective. I don't know Paige even half as well and I feel just as protective. We sat and talked for quite a while. She even showed me pictures of her family."

There was a pause in the line.

"You know, Brandon, I know I encouraged this relationship between you and Paige, but I don't want you getting in over your head."

"Are you telling me to stop pursuing her or cut and run because she is going through a difficult time?"

"No. Not at all. I just want you to consider your own health in all of this. You know Dr. Connor was less than thrilled about you visiting Paige in a hospital."

Brandon shrugged as if Dominy could see him. "Yeah."

He could hear the exasperation through the phone. "Are you still set to come back tomorrow?"

"Yes. Remember my flight gets in late. I am taking the last one out of here. Dom, I need to call Pastor and give him an update. I will talk to you later, okay?"

"Alright, Brandon. If she wakes up, let her know I am thinking about her. I'm sure it will do a great deal towards her healing."

"I'm sure. See you tomorrow, Dom."

*   *   *

Later that night Brandon lay in bed trying to reconcile the laughing, smiling Paige to the one he saw earlier that day. More than hoping, he knew in his spirit she would recover but it was hard swallowing passed the helplessness he felt.

Was that how his family felt about him during his last bout with cancer? He knew that was some of the reason for his hesitancy to inform them of him coming out of remission. He allowed himself to ask the question that had been hovering in his mind. What if he didn't get better?

Sure, he'd listened to the hopeful voice and news of his doctor and he would hold on to that, but what if he wasn't meant to have the "Happy Ending" with Paige. Could he walk away so she didn't have to go through what he was going through now, but with no hope for recovery?

I'm in deep, Lord. What I feel for her I have never felt for anyone else. I know I should have considered coming to You sooner regarding her, but I was sure I could handle my feelings for her, whether I stayed or walked away. She has become intrinsically important to me. It is as if each smile, laugh, and the conversation has fused itself in my mind and become a continual part of my thought process. Even as I talk to people or watch television or read an article, I wonder how she would react or what she would think of it. There is so much I want to share with her, but if it is not a part of your perfect will, God, please assure me of it. I've been guarding my heart, Lord. I've lived without these feelings this long. I think I can let her go if that is what You want, but You will have to tell me soon because too much longer and I will not be able to turn away. Not without leaving a part of me with her.

He continued to lay there, forcing himself to go quiet. It was 2:35 am, almost four hours later, when he received his answer and the peaceful release that allowed him to go to sleep.

*   *   *

It was late morning by the time Brandon exited the elevator leading to the nurse's station on Paige's floor. He checked himself in while greeting the nurses. "Good morning. Happy Thursday to you." He smiled at each of the nurses individually.

He engaged them in a short conversation about the weather and the city. He also asked if there were any specific needs they had. As he was dutifully jotting down prayer requests, he missed the greetings given to the gentleman that had stopped briefly in the direction of Paige's room.

When Brandon was done, he inquired about Mel and was told she was already in the room, but he missed the glances between the nurses and the inquiring looks as he left to walk down the hall to Paige's room.

Brandon was aware of voices as he pushed the door open. His ears perked up at the sound of the male voice responding to Paige's sister. He stepped in the room, curious, walking around the partition.

Mel saw him first, her eyes brightened then became cautious. "Hello Elder Tatum. Good to see you this morning."

"Good morning, Melanie," he returned her greeting, glancing over at the gentleman standing close to Paige's bed.

"Elder Tatum, this is Mr. Mason Jenson, the father of the little girl who received Paige's kidney."

He let out a breath. His shoulders sagged slightly in relief. He reached out, taking the man's hand in a firm handshake.

"Congratulations. Mel tells me that your daughter is recovering well and isn't showing any signs of rejection. The miracles of modern medicine."

He watched something flash through Mason's eyes, but was unable to identify it. "Is medicine a miracle?"

He could hear the slight challenge in the man's voice and wondered if it was his collar he was responding to, or him.

"I think the ability to obtain and retain the knowledge to diagnose and the wisdom to perform life-saving operations is a miracle. How else can you describe it when man gets to hold the heart or another vital organ in their hand, place it back into an orifice and have it work?"

Mason nodded, not agreeing or disagreeing.

Brandon turned his attention towards Mel. "Has there been any change?"

Mel's face had lost some of its glow when she shook her head. "Not so far, but she has been resting well, so the doctor says. It all looks like sleep to me."

"I guess, as long as her body gets the opportunity it needs to rejuvenate itself."

There was a pregnant silence for a couple of seconds.

"So how do you know Paige?" Mason asked.

"Oh, I am sorry." Mel broke in. "I didn't finish the introduction. Elder Brandon Tatum is a Chaplain and part of the clergy at Paige's church."

Mason's brow rose slightly. "Does your church make it a practice to visit the sick out of state as well?"

Brandon eyed him seriously. "Only when there are special circumstances."

"Oh? And what is Paige's special circumstance?"

"Paige herself is the special circumstance." Brandon didn't think he could make himself any more clear without just coming out and stating it.

Mason rocked back on his heels for a moment, absorbing the information.

Brandon could feel Melanie's tension and chastised himself for his behavior. What was wrong with him? Why did he feel threatened by this man's interest, let alone his presence? Wouldn't he feel compelled to visit the woman who lay in a precarious state of health due to helping his daughter? He was trying to think of a way to change the subject when Mason spoke.

"So you pray for everyone right?"

Brandon forced his face to remain impassive. "Of course. I've been praying for ... Vivian?"

Mason nodded.

"Right, along with Paige. Do you mind if I meet her?"

"I was just about to ask you the same thing. I would be honored."

Brandon saw Mel visibly stiffen. He looked over. "Are you alright?"

"Oh, yeah. My back is just a little stiff from sitting so much and I spent the night on one of those little cots. If I do it again, I may have to be admitted myself." Her overly bright smile was not lost on Brandon.

"Do you mind if I go with Mason to visit Vivian for a bit?"

Mel shook her head, her bottom lip caught between her teeth.

Brandon got the feeling she wanted to say something, but was unable to due to their company.

"I'll be back soon."

She just nodded in response.

He glanced down at Paige once more before leaving the room behind Mason.

"So Elder Tatum, are you full-time clergy?" Mason asked him as they walked towards the elevators.

"No. I work for a pharmaceutical company," Brandon answered in monotone.

"Do you do a lot of traveling?" Mason pressed the down button, looking over at him as they waited.

"Not anymore. The novelty of living out of suitcases, hotel beds, and cold room service wore off pretty quickly." He offered a smile, working on his compassion towards the man whose daughter still lay in a hospital bed, even if she was faring better than Paige right now. "May I ask what you do for a living?"

"I'm an architect. I'd taken a leave of absence a few years ago. I just recently went back to work full-time."

Brandon recalled Mel mentioning that Mason's wife had died two years before, but didn't think Mason would be comfortable with his sympathy.

"How long have you known Paige?" Mason's question brought his thoughts back as the doors closed them in and the elevator began its ascent.

"Only a few months, but we have worked closely and the elders are a pretty tight-knit group. Paige was the first person I met beside the pastor and his wife. She has such an open and giving nature, it didn't surprise me when she told me of her intentions to donate a kidney to a complete stranger. If only the world had more people like Paige Morganson, we all might be better off."

Mason nodded, his eyes becoming a bit hooded. Brandon watched as Mason stared at each digit illuminating above the doors. Silence loomed around them.

Brandon cleared his throat hoping his next words helped more than hurt.

"I can't even begin to understand what it is like to have a child in the hospital. I have nieces and nephews, but still I don't think I have even a vague understanding." He turned to Mason. "Is there anything I can do for you?"

Mason looked at Brandon for a long moment. The wariness that was obvious when Brandon began to speak suddenly cleared. A tentative smile moved across Mason's lips. "You mean that, don't you."

Brandon frowned, wondering what had been the cause of such distrust. Since they'd not had much interaction, he suspected it had more to do with his collar.

"Yes."

Mason shook his head slightly then took a deep breath before speaking. "Mel is awfully proud of her family. Did she share pictures with you as well?"

Brandon, momentarily unsettled by the abrupt change in subjects, tried to regroup before answering.

"Yes. She showed me pictures of her daughter, husband, Paige, and herself. I didn't know digital keychains could hold so many pictures." He chuckled, hoping his attempt at brevity would lighten the tension he felt flowing around them.

Mason shared in his laughter. "I know, Mel and Paige are very close. You feel the love and pride they have in each other when they speak of each other." He touched Brandon's arm to slow his progress as they exited the elevator. "Thank you. I really appreciate the offer of help and your sincerity. So much so that I am going to give you a piece of advice that I hope you take. Keep an open mind."

"About what?" Brandon asked trying to quench rising feelings of unease.

"You'll see." Mason's cryptic statement hung between them as Brandon followed him to his daughter's room.

"Hi honey, how are you feeling?" Mason walked through the door, striding over to a pretty little girl sitting up in bed. Brandon was few steps behind so he didn't see her face until Mason had pulled back from their hug.

"I'm feeling a whole lot better today. Is Ms. Paige doing…" Her voice trailed off when she noticed he was not alone.

Mason turned around to Brandon, eyeing him thoughtfully before he made the introduction.

Brandon was for all accounts and purposes perplexed. Upon first glance the child looked familiar, but as he got closer, he began to focus on her hair and startling eyes that looked exactly like the child in one of Mel's digital pictures.

"Elder Tatum, I would like you to meet my daughter, Vivian Jenson. Hon, this is Elder Brandon Tatum, a friend of Ms. Paige's, visiting from Los Angeles."

The shy smile upon first eye contact brightened into one of hope and expectancy. "Does this mean she is awake? When can I go see her?"

Mason began shaking his head slowly even as the words began to pour from his mouth. "No sweetheart, she is not awake yet."

Still trying to work through the dimming fog of a puzzle that refused to come together, Brandon stood back as Mason soothed his daughter.

Catching her attention once again, Vivian slowly held her hand out to Brandon. "It is a pleasure to meet you, Elder. Is that like a pastor or a priest?"

He shook her small hand gently, inclining his head in answer. "It is more like a pastor's servant with authority to lead funerals, weddings, baptisms, things like that. Really I am merely a servant that is able to help the pastor by doing more for him."

Vivian cocked her head to the side in deep thought. She looked back and forth between her father and him as if trying to decide something.

"Are you Ms. Paige's boyfriend?"

"Vivian, I don't believe that is any of our business."

"I don't understand why not. After all she is..."

"Vivian Leigh." Her father, saying both of her names with such a tone of finality, broke off what she was about to say. She gave a pout but obediently clamped her mouth shut.

"Not to overstep your father, but no, I am not her boyfriend. We are only good friends and I came as a favor to my church and pastor to pray for her."

"Couldn't you pray for her where you were?" Vivian asked before she remembered she was supposed to be quiet.

"Yes, that is true," Brandon replied sheepishly, "Okay, also to make sure she was doing alright. We hadn't heard from her and were beginning to get worried. She is a very special person, but then I believe you already know that." He bestowed one of his brightest smiles on her, finally coming out of his stupor.

"Could you pray for me? My mom used to pray for me all the time before she got sick. I believe she still does, but she does it from heaven now." Brandon could see how Mason shifted back and forth uncomfortably. He didn't know what bothered him more: the mention of his deceased wife or Vivian asking a stranger to pray for her.

"That is one of the reasons why I am here. One is to meet the beautiful and extremely blessed child who God gave another chance at life to and to pray for you. Not only will I pray for you now, I will pray for you every day from now on."

"Now?" She asked as if he was about to hand her a new present. She was precious and something about her child-like faith and excitement reminded him so much of Paige. In that instance, he knew it wasn't just an uncanny coincidence. They were relatives.

"Now." He placed one hand on Vivian's shoulder and held out his other to clasp Mason's, who hesitated for a few seconds then joined them.

An hour and a half later Brandon found himself back at Paige's door full of more questions than he left with. Mel must have gone to get some coffee because Paige was alone. He assumed the same position as the day before, claiming her hand once again.

After an hour of sitting in the same position while nurses came in to check her vitals and make notes then leave, he flexed the muscles in his neck and shoulders, continuing the slight movements to his toes to relax some of the tension.

"Come on, baby. I am going to have to leave soon. I was hoping to see your beautiful eyes before I left. I know you need your rest, but you can't blame me for being selfish. Please wake up. Give me a little smile I can take with me. Let me know you are alright."

He kept talking in quiet whispers, leaning closer and closer to her ear. His heart was desperate to see any movement. He became so intent in watching he almost missed Mel as she slipped through the door. He looked up to greet her, seeing signs of strain around her mouth, but his attention was quickly averted when he felt the slightest tension at his hand.

He looked down to see Paige's fingers tighten around his hand. He gasped, not quite sure if he was imagining it.

He glanced up at her eyes as he stood so he could lean closer. Her lids were still for a moment as he continued to tighten then release his own hold on hers slowly, feeling every so often the response of hers.

Her lids began to flutter slowly then more quickly. He watched, holding his breath, marking the exact moment her lids raised to reveal those dazzling eyes. He expelled the breath, feeling his lungs give a sigh of relief.

"Hi there," he said in greeting, feeling the intensity of her gaze like a boulder coming at his gut full speed. She looked more like a woman waking from a long nap than a person regaining consciousness in a hospital bed. He almost expected her to stretch.

She looked at him, not seeming to wonder at all at his being there, then her lips curved into a smile that shattered the rest of his reserve, and sent his heart flying. *I hope I heard you correctly God because it is too late now,* he thought to himself.

"Hi." Paige's response was scratchy and barely audible, but it was beautiful to his ears.

Mel came around so that she was also in Paige's line of sight.

"Hello, sleepyhead," Mel teased.

Paige gave her a ghost of a smile before frowning in discomfort at the effort it took to swallow.

"I'm going to get you some water, then I will call for the nurse," Mel quickly responded.

Brandon couldn't seem to drag his gaze away from Paige. He didn't even notice he was still holding her hand until she squeezed involuntarily while raising her head enough to sip on the straw Mel had presented to her.

Right as the door closed behind Mel, Paige whispered, "Heard you."

Brandon leaned closer to see if there was any more to the sentence. She only repeated herself a little louder.

"Heard you."

He stared at her as realization came to him. "You heard me? You heard me while you were sleeping?"

She nodded then closed her eyes briefly, a smile coming to her lips. "You like me."

Brandon froze for a moment, stunned by her words.

She opened her eyes and he could see she was teasing him.

He shrugged his shoulder nonchalantly. "Aaaaaa," he said dragging out the short 'a'.

She watched him, her eyes sobering.

"Okay, maybe just a little." He punctuated the statement by placing his forefinger and thumb parallel to each other, half an inch apart.

She smiled again, then as if she just remembered something, a look of alarm came over her face. "Vivian."

Before he could answer, the nurse came in with Mel fast on her heels.

Brandon stepped away, releasing her hand as the nurse began to check her vitals.

"Well, Ms. Morganson, you gave us quite a scare there. How are you feeling?"

"Raw."

"Your throat is going to be scratchy and raw for a moment, but that should fade soon. Are you feeling any other pain?"

Paige nodded.

"How bad is it, 1-10?"

"Six," Paige responded after a brief pause.

"Okay. I will let the doctor know that you are awake and responding, and I will get you something for the pain. I'm sure you will be happy to know that Vivian is responding well to her new kidney. She is healing fast. All she talks about is how worried she is about you and meeting her twin sister. And I'm sure Auntie is more than thrilled to see you come around…" The nurse went on for a few seconds more, not realizing how the level of tension shot up.

Brandon watched Paige and Mel's eyes meet, and apprehension caused the hairs on the back of his neck to stand up. Paige had twins? Surely he'd heard wrong, but when Paige's eyes met his he knew just as sure as if she'd said it herself. She obviously wasn't everything she made herself out to be.

He wanted to get alone with her, hear her deny it or explain why she didn't speak of them, let alone take care of them herself. And who was Mason? Was he the biological father? Was there history there, or worse yet, a possibility of reconciliation?

He could have laughed at himself, coming across as if he had a right to stake any claim to Paige. He seemed to be the odd man out.

The room suddenly felt very close. He needed to get some air. He stepped forward to the bed after the nurse made her leave, but he remained out of arm's reach.

He met Paige's searching gaze. He could tell she was worried. She opened her mouth then closed it again, unable to form the words. He felt as if a heavy weight was placed on his shoulders.

"I am going to have to leave. I have a plane to catch in a few hours and it is the last one of the day. I am glad that I got to see you while you were awake. I will let Pastor know how you are doing, and you know we will continue to pray for you."

He turned to Mel and held out his hand. "Melanie, it was a pleasure meeting you. Maybe I will see you if you come to visit Sky Light Temple." Mel nodded as if she were dumbstruck.

He looked back at Paige one more time. Her eyes were suspiciously bright. "Take care of yourself, okay?"

She nodded. "See you."

"Brandon, let me walk you out." Mel said, placing her hand briefly on Brandon's forearm. He nodded and obediently followed behind her.

*   *   *

"She has twins?" Dominy sat back on the sofa in Brandon's apartment watching him pace back and forth. The words spoken were the same ones that had gone around and around in Brandon's head on the long flight home.

"What kind of woman has twins but doesn't take care of either one? Do you think she was on drugs at the time?"

Brandon stopped his pacing as he thought about the question. "I don't think so. From what her sister quickly explained, Paige wasn't even aware of Vivian until she met her a couple of days before the procedure."

"Wait, how is that possible?"

"I asked the same thing. Melanie said they all were told that Vivian was stillborn, but she wouldn't share why she was raising the other twin, Gladys. She said I would have to discuss that with Paige."

Brandon went on to share everything that Melanie told him once they exited Paige's room. Dominy sat there slack-jawed for most of the rendering.

"So, what are you going to do now? She has a lot more baggage than we first thought. Do you think you will have the strength to pursue a deeper relationship with her *and* deal with the drama in her life? After all you are a very private person that is pretty possessive of his peace."

Brandon sat there listening and pondering Dominy's diatribe. Could he, in good conscience, cultivate a more meaningful relationship with Paige knowing what was already on her shoulders? She not only had a demanding career, but needed time to recover and begin to nurture her relationship with her other daughter. Did she even want to make time for him and, if she did, what if he didn't recover, and this time his battle with cancer didn't end in remission?

He believed he'd heard correctly the night he spent in Chicago in prayer. The Lord had reminded him also of the dreams he'd had when they'd first met. His heart had begun to beat with new emotions from the moment he'd heard her trying to wiggle out of their introduction, and he was not in a hurry to have it stop any time soon.

He studied his hands as he came to the realization: he loved Paige and, try as he might to keep it from happening, he was a goner.

He lifted his eyes to Dominy's waiting stare.

"It's too late. To leave her is not an option. I just hope what I feel and want for her is enough because I get a distinct feeling that Vivian's father may want to share more than just Vivian with Paige."

Dominy raised an eyebrow. "Really?"

Brandon nodded, explaining some of his conversation and time spent with the man and his daughter. "But I may have the advantage."

"And what is that advantage?" Dominy probed.

Brandon looked at Dominy. Feeling a deep conviction in his spirit, he answered, "God and my relationship with Him."

CHAPTER 41

"Are you sure?" Victoria listened intently at what the investigator was saying on the other end of the line, "I need more than just your word. I need paperwork and I need the contact information for Grace Morganson. I will be looking forward to proof by tomorrow."

Once assured that she would have what she'd been seeking in her hand, she disconnected the call.

Victoria had watched along the sidelines as Vivian made a slow recovery while the Morganson woman's health began to slip. She'd remained hopeful that the procedure would go off without a hitch and all parties would go their separate ways within a couple of weeks of the surgery. Fate, she believed was laughing at her initially, but one never to give in especially when she could manipulate circumstances to work in her favor, she'd decided to work the woman's almost-fatal outcome to her favor.

Knowing the Morganson woman had recently regained consciousness but was still weak, she decided to pay her a visit. The information she'd gained would go a long way to cajoling the woman into doing her bidding regarding Vivian.

Sure, the woman was like a shiny new toy to Vivian, which was why Victoria had done nothing to discourage the child's fascination with her biological mother. In the end, it would magnify the blow of finding out that the Morganson woman had no intentions of bringing her pregnancy to term.

Victoria wasn't completely without heart though. She would run the information by Mason for good measure first, since he looked as though he was falling under the wiles of the woman. One thing she definitely did not need was for Paige and Mason to form a bond. The results of their union could prove catastrophic to her plans to win custody of Vivian.

Besides, if her sources were correct, there was another man waiting in the wings for the Morganson woman. He had visited her for a couple of days under the guise of a chaplain from her church. Were these people so gullible that they would not question a man flying thousands of miles to a woman's bedside, just to pray for her and let her know people were thinking of her?

He would ultimately make up Victoria's mind as to whether she would share the information with her granddaughter.

Life could be cruel and Vivian wasn't so young that she hadn't been affected by the darker side of it. But this time Victoria would be there to mend, nurture, and mold the child in the ways she believed she should grow.

*   *   *

Victoria knocked briefly then stepped into Ms. Morganson's room. She advanced to the middle of the room, peeking around the divider.

"Good morning, Ms. Morganson. How are you feeling today?"

Victoria registered the startled expression on the woman's face before she answered in a voice now as smooth as gravel.

"Mmmm. Are they giving you something for your throat? I know an excellent throat and vocal cord specialist. If things aren't back to normal soon, I could give him a call for you?"

The woman nodded.

Victoria had to give it to her; Paige looked only a little worse for wear, considering the harrowing experience her body had just gone through.

Her sister had braided her hair in intricate rows that crossed over one another all headed towards the back left side of her neck. Once there they were pulled into a ponytail that rested over her shoulder, the hair ending at her heart, squared off with black rubber bands.

Though she was still pale in comparison to the healthy bronze glow she'd flaunted when they first met and the area underneath her eyes hinted at dark smudges, she was still a beauty. It galled Victoria to no end that women with her color could wait until well in their 40's before having to don makeup.

She placed what she hoped was a compassionate smile on her face and asked if she could sit with her for a while. The woman complied.

Never one to mix words, Victoria, once seated, worked the conversation up to the subject she wanted to cover.

"I know you and I don't know each other well, Ms. Morganson…"

"Please call me Paige. I would think we were well past formalities at this point."

"Yes… well…like I was saying. We haven't gotten a chance to interact with one another, what with your misfortune." She watched the woman's eyes darken slightly, but no other reaction could be read. This woman, although compassionate, was sharp.

"I'm glad you are feeling better. Did the doctors give you a time table for when you would be released?" She looked down smoothing her skirt. She knew no such thing could be assessed so quickly, but she wanted the woman to know that she had no intention of sharing Vivian with her longer than necessary.

"Not yet…too soon," came the raspy response.

"Ms. Morganson, I came here for a specific reason today. In light of the fact that you are entering our family at what some would call the 'middle of the story', I thought it would be only fair to share some of our family history."

The woman's eyes narrowed slightly. "Why, when you can't even call me by my first name?"

Victoria shifted in her chair at the intense stare the woman was giving her.

"Alright then, Paige…" The name tasted bitter in her mouth. "Would you like to hear the 'ins and outs' of the Branchett/Jenson clan?"

At the woman's nod, she took a deep breath and pressed forward. She began with the acquisition of her land and how she'd built it up to the small dynasty it was today.

She shared snippets of her relationship with her daughter, Rachael, and what she considered, at best, a strained relationship with her son-in-law.

She continued on to explain the tension that had sprung up due to their relationship and what she considered Mason's manipulative manner within their relationship. She spoke of her selfless act of helping the couple find and adopt Vivian, then regarded Paige carefully when she told her of her knowledge of Paige's original intent to abort the twins.

To her surprise and consternation, Paige didn't flinch. The only proof that she'd heard her was the slight rise of Paige's chin and the coolness that swept over her features, only to disappear in mere seconds. As much as it pained her to do so, she admired the woman's strength.

Victoria pressed forward, revealing her intentions on gaining sole-custody of Vivian. There were quite a few things she'd left out, just in case Paige had a hand or two to play. She wanted to make sure there were a few cards left off of the table.

She watched intently as she delivered the next line, assessing the woman's reaction, even as the words flowed from her lips. She wanted to know what moved this woman. She had a feeling she wasn't easily offended and thus far wasn't given to bouts of religious rhetoric. To Victoria she was a bit of an anomaly; not fitting into any one category.

"I have met people like you. They claim to be God's right-hand man…or woman, but if you open their closet you find more skeletons than Disney's Haunted Mansion." She took a breath, composing herself, dawning the cool shroud of contempt that would allow her to release the aggression and frustration that had begun to form from the day she'd first heard of Paige Morganson.

"I'm not sure what your motive is; whether it is to assuage a guilty conscious or a need to get to know the daughter you never knew – not that this relationship should be any different than with the one you gave away."

She watched as Paige's mouth opened, only to close again without a word uttered. She watched as her jaws clenched then went slack with the force Paige made to resume her more serene façade.

Hmmm. Obviously she wasn't as calm as she was portraying, but she wasn't sharing either. Why didn't she defend herself?

"I will not have you getting my granddaughter's hopes up about any type of relationship you may have with her. She may appear to be well adjusted, but she is in a very fragile state right now and I am trying to build an environment of stability around her. I would prefer it if you didn't disrupt the delicate balance that has been established."

No answer came from Paige. Her eyes were only slightly brighter. Victoria decided to drive her point home.

"To be completely honest with you, I would rather you had as little contact with Vivian as possible. It's obvious you didn't want her to begin with. There is no need to cause any more upheaval with this sad attempt at regaining any nominations you may have lost along the way for Mother-of-the-Year."

Paige's eyes closed. Victoria was sure the effort it was taking to remain silent was weighing heavy on her. *Just one more score,* she thought to herself.

Victoria adjusted herself in her seat so that she was facing Paige head on. She didn't want to miss a single blink.

"I would hate for Vivian to have to find out that not only did you go to the hospital with the intent to have her killed in your womb, when you delivered her you found the thought of her so heinous you pretended she was dead and paid the nurse to give her away." She sat back with a ghost of a smile playing upon her lips, belying the malicious intent of her sentence.

Paige's eyes widened and her nostrils flared in surprise. "That's not true." Her voice was a mere whisper with a trace of incredulity. "I was told she was dead."

Victoria sat back watching the expressions steal across her face. Well...well...well... "You play the victim well. And the Oscar goes to – Elder Paige Morganson for Best Actress starring in 'A Messed Up Life.' Did you even ask to hold your children? No," she replied for Paige, her face contouring into a nasty grin, "You could barely look at them, otherwise you would have known that both babies were more than healthy."

"Didn't know...I was told she was dead." She watched as Paige laid her head back on her pillow, her throat working furiously as she tried to swallow back the tears.

"Would it have mattered if you did? You gave up your other daughter almost as quick as you delivered her. Twins would have been a little too much, even for your sister – saint that she is."

"How...h-how do you know?" Paige breathed in deep, trying to get the sentence passed her throat. "How do you know all this?" She finished with halting clarity.

Victoria leaned forward, her face only a couple of inches from Paige's. "It was bad enough that after your plans of abortion were thwarted, you didn't just allow your children to be taken in and nurtured by loving families," Victoria sneered, "You couldn't leave well enough alone. I would think you'd just go back to your life, such as it was. One would think you'd have the decency to feel some shame. I know I would have been all too happy to disappear and chalk it all up to one big mistake. Most people wouldn't take the chance of being caught with their pants down, publicized." She watched as what color that was left in Paige's face, fled.

"You didn't think I wouldn't investigate you, did you? You and your mother were amateurs."

Paige's brows came together. "What...my mother? What does my mother have to do with this?"

Victoria leaned back, folding her arms across her chest, almost preening with the havoc she saw roaming the woman's face. She shrugged her shoulders, refusing to answer. Now this woman would know Victoria was not a force to be reckoned with. This woman's character would not stand up in any court and she wanted her to know she knew it.

She would wait now and see if the woman would take the bait and come clean about her part in her mother's attempt to blackmail her. How could she not know? It was true that she was young, but no one's mother could be that wicked. People didn't just go around selling their grandchildren.

Even with her own family's flaws, she knew her parents only wanted what was best for her. It didn't matter that her and their ideas of what would make her happy were worlds apart.

Paige's slight shift brought Victoria back from her thoughts. She watched as Paige's eyes opened and leveled on her. He voice, rough with emotion, was barely audible.

"My mother and I have been estranged for quite some time. What did she do?"

Victoria's confidence in her assessment wavered a little as she continued to watch the gambit of emotions wash over Paige's face, her breathing becoming more shallow.

Wanting to know if there was a possibility that Paige didn't know what she was referring to, she ignored Paige's question, deciding to ask another of her own.

"When did you first discover that Vivian wasn't a stillbirth?" she surveyed Paige's every action.

"When Mason came to see me in New York. If I hadn't seen Vivian with my own eyes, I still may not have fully believed him – picture or no picture."

What a conundrum. She would still check this girl's answer, but it was becoming clearer that Paige may not have been involved in her mother's scheme to finagle tens of thousands of dollars from her.

"What did my mother do?"

"You won't get any more from me. If you really don't know, you will have to find out for yourself."

Paige's eyes lit up like fireworks against a black sky. She was visibly shaking with pent up emotion. She closed her eyes, but not before Victoria saw the flash of anger and betrayal.

She was still for a long time. Victoria could only register a slight change in her breathing.

The door opened, drawing Victoria's gaze away from Paige.

The nurse that stepped around the divide came over to the other side of Paige's bed, pressing buttons on the monitor, checking her vitals over the past few minutes.

"There's been a lot of activity." She said surveying the screen. She then settled a wary glance on Victoria. "Are you in pain?" She addressed Paige.

Paige, her eyes still closed, shook her head slowly, silently answering in the negative.

"Are you sure? There is no need to try and suffer through it. It will only get worse and you will do yourself more harm by not getting the rest you need." She stayed at her bedside until Paige opened her eyes.

"No. I am fine." As if knowing her answer wouldn't appease the nurse, she tried again. "Please. Just 15 minutes and I will sleep."

The nurse studied her for a moment, contemplating her plea.

"I will be back in 10 minutes." She speared Victoria with a look. "Not a minute more."

Both Paige and Victoria nodded. The nurse hesitated for a moment more, then left the room.

After what seemed like many minutes, Paige spoke. Though halting, her words were clear. "You are…too beautiful a woman…to carry such hurt."

At first Victoria thought she'd heard wrong, but her brain couldn't come up with an alternative for the words spoken. Stunned into silence, Victoria had no comeback. Paige went on.

"Vivian sincerely loves you. There's no need to blackmail your way into her heart." She breathed in and out heavily. "You have a lot to offer her. Your strength is commendable…even if it is sometimes misplaced."

Victoria, still stuck on speechless, was growing more uncomfortable by the second.

"Anger, hate, and shame almost killed my babies through me. I won't try to hide it because …" She breathed deeply, beads of sweat breaking out on her upper lip. "Because I won't live in shame anymore. I now have more love to give than hate. That is what I want to share. What I will fight to share…not custody."

The words struck Victoria forcefully. They echoed in her ears, like waves continuously pounding against the side of a mountain, not allowing for any other thoughts to intervene.

"Vivian loves you. She needs you because you are part of her mother. A part that can never be replaced or lost, but it can be tainted if you let it."

A steely-eyed gaze pinned Victoria and she noted Paige was not one easily intimidated because she didn't have anything to hide.

"I've spent time with Vivian. She is gorgeous inside and out. I even see some of you in her. It will only hurt her if you tell her something that is now irrelevant. Think about it…how would you feel if your mother told you that you were supposed to be aborted?" Paige tried to change her position and grimaced at the pain. Her breathing became labored and honestly, it startled Victoria. She rose out of her seat going for the call button.

"Let me call the nurse back in."

Paige shook her head then brought her hand up to grasp Victoria's.

"Not yet."

Victoria watched as Paige struggled to slow her breathing. After a minute she opened her eyes, the pain still evident in the dilation of her pupils and the perspiration on her forehead. She held on to Victoria's hand with a vice-like grip.

"Let her love you...it isn't going anywhere. You have another chance, just like me. Take it! That's all that's worth fighting for."

Paige's features contorted with the level of her pain. Victoria released Paige's hand and fumbled with the remote at her side.

"Sssssh. I have it. I will press the button. You rest. I'm sorry. You rest." She pressed the button repeatedly until the nurse walked in. Paige clasped her hand again and Victoria gave Paige all of her attention.

Long after the pain medicine was administered, Paige held on to Victoria's hand and Victoria let her. When she thought Paige had fallen asleep she disengaged her hand and stepped back to collect her purse. She was still shaken from their conversation, and she needed to regroup.

She was halfway to the door when she heard Paige.

"Victoria..." She turned and stood at the end of the bed. "We aren't done. Will you come back tomorrow?"

Victoria's first thought was *absolutely not*. The last thing she needed was to get close to this sprite of a woman that made her lose focus but what came out of her mouth was a clear "Yes."

Paige nodded then closed her eyes. She was breathing deeply and evenly before Victoria reached the door.

Victoria was consumed by emotions she'd set away for a long time. She worked to guard herself against the compassion and admiration she'd felt toward the woman with an unbelievable tenacity for life. She still wasn't sure she could put to rest the feelings of distrust and animosity towards her. The two, warring emotions were causing her head to pound, so she gave in to the one that usually won.

She would reserve right to keep her anger and distrust for Paige until she was able to check her story against Mason's. She'd been meaning to speak to him about going against her wishes and approaching Paige. This would serve a two-fold purpose.

Victoria decided against visiting Vivian that day. Instead, she headed back to her apartment. On the way, her mind drifted over her confrontation with Paige, every now and then highlighting on an expression or phrasing Paige had used. She became more and more agitated.

She thought about her Rachael and the rare moments of peace and camaraderie they'd found with each other, especially after Rachael had accepted Jesus Christ in her heart.

Victoria had never really begrudged Rachael her beliefs and the happiness she'd found in embracing her faith. She just wanted to keep Rachael grounded. Many others didn't think like she did – inside and outside the church.

Rachael had always jumped head-long into things she believed in. She would allow herself to be totally consumed by it, she was so passionate. She'd gotten that trait from her father.

To be honest, she'd only tried to discourage her daughter's penchant for religion because she was afraid of her being taken advantage of by the same clergy who she'd been abused by herself.

The more Victoria allowed herself to consider what Rachael was really expressing, the more she understood that Rachael's love for God outshined any adoration she may have had for the leadership. She realized too late He was who Rachael drew her strength from. A strength that she herself still failed to obtain.

Darn that woman for making her remember, for making her feel anything besides the anger and hatred she'd built up as a fortress around her heart. She would have to reinforce it before she came anywhere near Paige again.

Upon entering her apartment she headed straight for the phone, dialing Mason's number. It rang four times before going to voicemail. "Mason, this is Victoria. I know you may be tempted to ignore this call, but I think it would be to your best interest if you called me back ASAP." She disconnected the call. No greeting or salutation was needed. They were long passed being sociable. She was hard-pressed to be civil towards him. He didn't deserve the adoration her granddaughter bestowed upon him.

All it would take was time.

CHAPTER 42

Mason whistled an unrecognizable tune as he made his way down the hall to Paige's room.

The sun had awakened him early that morning and the vision of a woman's face who owned the most beautiful pair of fire-inspired eyes danced before him even before he could form a complete, coherent thought.

His day was off to a wonderful start. It had been almost two weeks since Paige regained consciousness. Upon his first visit, Mason had been hesitant, not knowing how he was going to be accepted. Would she blame him for the unforeseen pain and continued disruption in her life? After all, he did approach her with what could have been misconstrued as an opportunity that would have been impossible to ignore. But as soon as he poked his head around the divider and saw her smile widen just for him, he knew he had worried in vain.

What he couldn't ignore, though, was Mel's reluctance to leave Paige while he was in the room. At first, he thought he had misread the looks between them, but upon his second visit Paige almost had to threaten her into leaving so that she could tend to the much-needed errands while he was still there.

Once Mel had left, he voiced his assumption and offered to leave, but she assured him that Mel's wariness wasn't so much directed at him, as it was towards Victoria and any dealing she may have with his family.

She went on to share parts of her visit from Victoria, but he had a feeling there was something she wasn't telling him. He didn't know her well, but her eyes were almost as expressive as Vivian's and he always knew when she wasn't telling him the whole story.

He wondered if it had anything to do with the call he received from Victoria. Even their conversation did little to infringe upon his great mood. She'd called him, angry that he'd gone to New York in spite of her request to keep away from Paige.

He'd informed her that Paige had a right to be told that Vivian was her daughter and it was inhumane to keep the information from her even as they looked to her for help. They went through what had become their usual dialogue regarding Vivian, but this time she was somewhat civil.

He shrugged the conversation off, thinking it was just Victoria's way of keeping herself in the forefront of his mind. Not like he could forget. Victoria was as inconspicuous as a machete sticking out of the sides of a person's head.

During the last Halloween he'd seen a teenager dressed in all black with a prop of a machete going through his head. It instantly reminded him of Victoria. He wanted Paige to trust him. He wanted her to feel comfortable in placing her confidence in him. Why? Why did he think rabbits were cute? Why was he most at peace when he was drafting floor plans or working new angles on reconstruction work? He just did. He wanted to get to know Paige, and for the first time in a very long time he wanted a woman to get to know him. Not Mason the dad or Mason the widower, but Mason the man.

So for the last few days he'd made it a part of his daily schedule to visit Paige after coming from work and visiting with his daughter.

His visits were short; no more than fifteen minutes, especially when Mel was in the room. But last evening he'd stayed for more than an hour and they'd conversed on many subjects, smoothly transitioning from school experiences and teachers to whose words and attention had an impact on their lives still to that day.

They spoke of the different career paths they'd wanted to take when they were young, only to be discouraged by family's opinions, peer-pressure, or by the work they found out it would take to achieve a job in that career. Mason was surprised to learn that Paige had at one time considered changing her major to Business Management and Marketing.

"What made you consider that route?" He asked, watching a sheepish look come over her features.

"The professor that taught Introduction to Advertising and Marketing was extremely animated and passionate. I believe one-third of the class was ready to change their major by the middle of the semester," she finished with a chuckle.

"What changed your mind?"

"When we got into statistics and his wife, an advertising representative for one of the major firms in the city, was a guest lecturer for Networking right before finals. All the females were crushed to find out that he was married, moi included." She finished with self-deprecation, a smile playing at the corners of her mouth but never deepening.

He thought there might have been something there, but wasn't willing to ask.

"And in all of this time, you didn't see your daughter?"

She hesitated for a moment before answering. Her eyes were imploring. "I wasn't ready to acknowledge her as my child because I didn't want to confront all of the emotions that went with that. They were neatly packed away and I could be just like every other 19 to 21-year-old, college sophomore, whatever that meant. I didn't have responsibilities beyond myself, my grades and miniscule thoughts of my future, and honestly I wasn't willing to take on any more than that. I know it was selfish, but I was stubborn and wouldn't consider dealing with a child."

"And your sister was alright with that?"

She shrugged. "My sister is very protective, if you couldn't tell."

"Yeah," Mason interrupted her, "In the beginning I thought we hit it off, but the last few days it's been as if she doesn't want to leave you in my presence."

"She is a little piqued with me. I told her I wanted to do my rehabilitation at a nearby facility instead of finishing my recuperation at her home. She doesn't understand that I need to be 100% as soon as possible and I need someone that will push me more than coddle me. And then there is the opportunity to get to know Vivian better while I am out here, if that is still alright with you."

He nodded, not sure that if he could keep the elation out of his voice if he spoke. Paige went on, none-the-wiser, trying to explain her sister's need to take care of her. "Mel, being quite older than I am, took it upon herself to raise Gladys because she was more stable than I was in a lot of ways. In a lot of ways, she was more of a mother to me than my own. She believed one day I would regret it if I'd given Gladys away to someone outside of the family."

"Is she right?" Paige was quiet for a moment then looked at Mason, never flinching.

"Yes. She is right. I can't imagine the regret I would feel if I never had the chance to get to know my girls."

"What about other types of relationships?"

"Are you asking me if I dated in college?" She threw him a sly look.

He shrugged and nodded, all of a sudden feeling uncomfortable with her answer. He didn't know what he was expecting, but it wasn't the answer she gave.

"No. I didn't date in college. I'd had a pretty active social life my first couple of years in high school. I was going for 'heartbreaker of the decade'." She shrugged.

"I know now it was a cry for help, but at the time I was looking for a way to escape the pain and anger. My drug of choice? Boys."

He was surprised she shared such a personal part of her life with him. "You were in high school? I'm having a hard time wrapping my mind around that. Where was your dad?"

"See it from my point of view. By 15, I had been pregnant with twins, delivered them, estranged from my mother, and angry with a world I was convinced I had been born into to be used. My thinking may have been flawed, but it is how I survived. 'Keep your heart safe by doing to men first what they would have done to you later.' That was my mantra. My dad worked so much, I found time to do my dirt and be home before he missed me. My stepmom wasn't doing too much better herself, so we had an understanding. If I stayed out of her business, she would stay out of mine."

"Really?" was all he could say. He sat there trying to absorb this new information.

"Sorry," he said after a moment of just staring at her, "I'm having a hard time thinking of you like that."

"Believe me, I was the girl you didn't want hanging out with your daughter…or mine." She took a deep breath. "I'm glad that doesn't show on me anymore. I am not that person. That Paige was broken and hurting, and in turn, hurt others because she was trying hard to portray herself as something she wasn't."

"What was that?"

"A person that knew herself and what she wanted. A person with a healthy psyche and a healthy self-image."

"Why didn't you have those things?" He really wanted to know what began it all. He'd felt she had been skirting around the answer at every turn.

She became still. He wasn't even sure she was breathing. It was as if she were standing on some type of precipice that she was deciding on whether or not to step off.

All of a sudden, she inhaled deeply, holding it and letting it out slowly. He thought she was in pain and asked her if she needed the nurse. She waved it off.

"It was only a matter of time. What I am about to tell you is not a sad story or a tragedy because I am the victor. Okay?"

Not truly understanding what she was saying, he only nodded.

She began by giving him a small history of her family. How they moved around a bit due to her father's job transferring him rather frequently. She was an introvert as a child and chose to entertain herself rather than seek friends, which made it hard in school when she did start to want to befriend girls in her class. She wasn't sure how to approach them and found herself eating alone at lunch a lot of the time.

When she was nine, they'd moved to a small suburb in Atlanta. Her mom was particularly happy because she was now close to her sister and her family but a few months after they moved her mother and father separated, and they found themselves spending more and more time with her aunt, uncle, and their five children.

The youngest, by the name of Stone, was a book warm and seemed very shy but always had plenty to talk about when Paige was around, so they talked about books and cartoons. He even showed her some of his poetry and used that as a lure to get her by herself. She was honored that a 15-year-old would want to hang out with her, even if he was just her cousin. She had finally found someone that she could confide in…until the first time he touched her in a way that made her feel uncomfortable.

Mason sat there unmoving, listening intently, sitting on the edge of his chair not because he was riveted by her story, but because he couldn't decide whether remaining still as a statue or bolting out the door would aid him in maintaining his dignity.

What type of animal preyed on lonely children? He tried to continue to listen to her story, but was seeing less and less how it could end in anything but tragedy.

When she shared how she'd conceived the twins only to be carted off to abort them, he was hastily wiping away tears of anger, frustration and hopelessness. Hopelessness for the woman/child that she'd been that had no hero or heroine to rescue her or come to her aid. She struggled through pregnancy at the tender age of 14.

But if none of these things happened he wouldn't have Vivian; the love of his life, his very reason for breathing. He found himself torn between thanking her for carrying them to term, even as he cursed the very soul of the man that placed his seed in her womb.

He remained seated by sheer will, swallowing against the nausea. He didn't want to hear anymore, but was desperately hoping for that victory she said she could claim.

He was pulled from his tumultuous thoughts by Paige calling his name. He didn't know how many times she'd called him before it registered.

"Mason."

"Yes."

"You look like you are having a hard time over there."

He took notice of his stance and found that he was slightly out of his chair, hands fisted at his sides. He relaxed his hands and sat back in the chair.

"Mason."

"Yes?"

"Come here." Paige patted the bed next to her legs.

He stared at her, not sure he'd heard her correctly.

"Please."

He rose slowly, not very confident in his legs remaining under him let alone carrying him the few steps it would take to get to her bedside. He took a deep, fortifying breath, moved forward and sat down.

Paige adjusted herself, raising herself straighter in her seated position then placed her hand on his.

It registered somewhere in the back of his mind that this little slip of a woman, who was sharing her nightmare was trying to console him instead of asking for him to console her. He was shaken even more by this event than the story itself. Was it possible to heal this fully?

"The road itself wasn't pretty and the journey was even rougher but there were two treasures that came from it, along with many moments that shine brighter than any jewels I could possess. It took some time to find me," she pointed to her chest, "that I love in all of this. But once I did, it allowed me to see my children the way God had always seen them and intended I see them."

She leaned closer, pinning him down with her gaze.

"I can love Vivian the way you love Vivian, and I can see her the way you see her. I can see the beautiful, vibrant, precious child with the sweet soul instead of a thing that just reminds me of what was so violently taken from me. This is not a story of woe, Mason, but of victory because that is the way I chose to end it."

She looked down, seeing his hand in hers, and seemed to remember herself. She unclasped his fingers and moved her hand away. He felt the loss immediately.

"A few months before Stone died he called and asked me to eulogize him. He knew he was dying and had written it in his will for me to officiate the service. In August of this year, I had the honor of eulogizing his funeral."

He sat there unmoving. He couldn't imagine. What had it taken for her to do something like that? What type of gall must a person have to even ask someone they caused so much pain, to perform such a service?

As if reading his mind, Paige continued. "I forgave him." She shrugged then went on to tell him of Stone's call and his apology.

"See, this is a story with a happy ending: I chose to dwell on the things I have gained because in the end they are all that count. I have a relationship with God I cannot deny, nor ever will. I not only have one gorgeous child I get to know, but two, and Gladys has a sister she can get to know if you'll permit it. I have met you and your family. I got to return some of the favor of you being a wonderful father by gifting Vivian with a kidney, and Stone accepted Jesus Christ before he died and now has eternal life with the Father."

He was quiet for a moment, processing what she said.

"How…but aren't you angry at all for what he took?"

"For a long time I was, but all it did was take more from me. It took the place of my healing for a long time because all I was looking for was people to feel my pain but no one could, not really. It took the place of me looking for love in the right place and in the right face, because I couldn't even look myself in the mirror without feeling rage. So instead of having a healthy relationship, I went for the guys that wanted what I was used to men wanting from me and what I figured wasn't valuable anymore anyway.

By the middle of my junior year of high school, I was more than out of control. I was spiraling with no place to go but further down. Thankfully, right before I bottomed out I took a friend up on her invitation to bible study. She had been hounding me since the beginning of the semester and I could see a definite change in her. She seemed happier; not giggly, but content. I'd thought she'd fallen in love or something because we didn't hang as much as the year before, and she had been worse than me.

Anyway, the night I decided to go, I was all ready to give up. I'd been stealing valium from my stepmom. Just a little at a time so she wouldn't notice. I'd decided if I still didn't have answers that night after church, I was calling it quits. I couldn't handle the pain anymore."

"Did you get your answer?" Mason's curiosity was piqued.

"Not in the traditional 'yes' or 'no' sense. My question wasn't just 'Is there a God?' It was more like 'Where was He when I needed Him? Why wasn't I worth saving?'

I don't think I was in that sanctuary more than two minutes when a little church mother came up to me and asked if she could give me a hug. I let her and she held on, hugging me tighter and tighter until I began to hug her back. At first I was a little uncomfortable, wondering if this was something she did with everyone then she whispered in my ear. 'Baby, God's been waiting for you. He says He is going to prove to you, you are worth it.'" She paused for a moment, shaking her head slightly then looked back up at him, her eyes shining with moisture.

"I remember those words like it was yesterday. I pulled back and asked her, 'Worth what?' She just looked at me for a moment and smiled. She smiled like she had just won the lottery or something. I looked over at my friend thinking the woman might be a little touched, but my friend just nodded. I looked back at her and she said, "Worth His Son dying on the cross."

For a moment, I just stood there confused. I know there was a big question mark stamped on my forehead. She pulled me back in for another hug and whispered, "His Son died on the cross, baby, so that you don't have to." My head started spinning because I couldn't believe what she had just said. She laid all my business out right in front of me.

I almost wanted to ask her if she knew my stepmom, but I kept quiet and let her continue to tell me about myself. After a few more sentences I was convinced that there was no way she could have known all of this unless God told her.

When she told me that life could be so much sweeter than I ever knew, I started to cry because I wanted that but I was so tired I didn't even want the hope she was giving me.

She took me to one of their prayer rooms and she talked while I cried some more. I was there the whole time Bible Study was in session, but she stayed with me, talking and praying, and calling me 'precious' and 'valuable'. Though I wasn't completely convinced by the time I had to go home, I figured it would be a shame if I let all her time go to waste by killing myself.

A part of me definitely believed she was telling the truth though, because I went to church that Sunday and bible study every Wednesday there until I went to college."

Mason was fascinated. He sat there contemplating the ramifications of everything Paige had just shared with him. There were so many reasons why his daughter shouldn't be alive right now. If just one thing was done differently in Paige's life he wouldn't have the love of his, but was it for his benefit as well as his daughter's? Had God been trying to get his attention or was it just that his daughter was a jewel of His like Rachael?

"Sure enough," Paige continued, "the more I attended, the more I began to understand that the one person I was missing in my life was the same One with the answers to all of my questions. But you must already know this because your wife had a wonderful relationship with God. Your daughter talks about it, and she shares one with Him as well."

Mason looked at his hand lying on her blanket: cold, still, and alone. Exactly how he felt, he knew at that moment that he'd missed it. All the times his daughter had pleaded with him to listen, to feel...it was too late.

He shook his head, not wanting to see the condemnation in her eyes or worse yet the pity, because he refused God when He had tried to speak to him once when he was a boy then through his wife, and again through his daughter.

"It's not too late," she said softly, placing her hand back over his. He didn't respond, neither did he look up to meet her eyes.

He heard her inhale deeply and let it go quickly, sending a small gust at him. He finally looked up and saw her eyes alight. "You know, one of my biggest questions was 'Why?' Why did it happen to me?"

He was almost afraid to know, but he wanted to...so badly. "Did you ever get the answer?"

She kept her eyes steady on his, nodding.

Before he could ask her what, she said. "He said it is for such a time as this."

He worked the sentence over in his head, trying to extract the true meaning.

"Just for this." She reached up and poked his chest.

In just that moment, he swore all the air escaped from his lungs. The thought was too huge to embrace. He watched her watching him, but for the life of him couldn't think of a thing to say or do.

After a few moments, she sat back and seemed to shake herself. "It is not a puzzle to be analyzed, Mason. It just is. You are worth everything I went through, if it could help you realize how much He loves you."

He didn't know what to say. How was he supposed to receive that? What would she think of him if he didn't accept it? Would she walk out of his life? He began to panic.

Paige must have seen it in his eyes because she changed the conversation, laughing to herself.

"My sister is just crazy about games: board games, card games, word puzzles; you name it, she has it. Do you want to play? I used to be the Spades champion in our class student union. "

Not quite ready to leave her but desperately happy she was ready to change the subject, he agreed, and they enjoyed the next half hour like they had enjoyed the first.

He made sure to stay away from any questions that would bring about any heavy subjects, and she encouraged him to tell her how he'd met Rachael.

In all it had gone a long way to lighten the atmosphere, and allow them to share likes and dislikes. They found they had a lot more in common, and as the night drew to a close he found himself longing to spend more time with her.

He knocked briefly before entering her room and called out, so as to make his presence known before he peeked around the divider.

She was sitting up in bed, some papers in her hand and spread all over the bed.

"Hello," she greeted, a smile lighting up her face.

He noticed the smudges under her eyes was less noticeable and her voice, which originally reminded him of velvet against his ears, was a little less raspy.

"How are you feeling today?" He pulled up a chair next to the bed, only then spying the bouquets of flowers against the windowsill.

"I'm having a good day. Less pain and the doctor says that my recovery, so far, has been expeditive."

His raised his eyebrows. "Expeditive?"

"Okay…maybe not expeditive, but quick enough for him to be pleasantly surprised. My apologies, I'm working on my vocabulary today. It's how I keep words that I don't normally use kind of close in my mind so I don't have to stop as often in mid-sentence while writing to look one up in a thesaurus. How is Vivian doing?"

"She is healing well. One might say she is also healing quickly, rapidly; making a speedy recovery. Fast…fast may also work."

Paige quirked a brow at him. "Oh…you've got jokes…"

"No. Just using some of my words so during our next conversation you may use words I can understand."

She chuckled. "Touche`."

"Nice flowers," inclining his head in the direction of the windowsill. The array of colors coming from the daisies, sunflowers, black-eyed Susans, and reed-long flowers with purple blossoms he didn't know the name of, brought cheer to the room. It made him feel just a little guilty about not thinking of bringing her some as well.

He peered around him and noticed two more bouquets sitting on a back table, along with cards standing open. Squinting his eyes, he was able to read the outward greeting of one and his heart dropped. He didn't know.

He got up without turning to her and walked over to one of the bouquets of pink roses, fingering one of the petals while he got a closer look at the cards. Most were birthday cards, with a few "Get Well's" mixed in.

"Happy Birthday! Why didn't you say anything?" He finally turned to her, feeling low.

Paige took a deep breath, letting it out in a huff, impatience riddling her features.

"Because it is not my birthday," she replied sardonically.

Huh?

He walked back over to his chair and sat down.

Before he could ask, Paige explained.

"It's a gag gift from the Visitation Committee I belong to. They know I don't like people making a big deal over me, but they got wind of my extended hospital stay from a 'big-mouth elder' so instead of sending 'Get Well' cards they sent 'Happy Birthday' cards." She shook her head.

Mason laughed; a rumble that started deep in his chest and came out in a guffaw. The look on her face was priceless. She actually sounded perturbed to be getting flowers. The ridiculousness of it all made him laugh harder as the moments ticked by. He was delighted by the refreshing nature of this woman.

"You should have seen your face." He tried hard to explain his laughter, noting the curious look on her face between chuckles as he gained control of his mirth.

A smile played at her lips, and even though he could tell she was struggling to keep her lips straight, she was failing.

He leaned back sighing, allowing his stomach muscles to relax.

"You and I, we are becoming friends, right?" He watched as she thought it over.

"I hope so, at least for Vivian's sake."

What about my sake?

He tried to stay on track with his line of thinking.

"Could I ask you a personal question?"

She crossed her right arm over her, the hand coming to rest on her left shoulder; meant to look like comfortable position, but purely meant to protect.

"Sure," she quipped despite the defensive move.

He took a deep breath and looked her squarely in the eye.

"When is your birthday?"

He saw the look of surprise cross her face as the question registered, then she laughed loudly, realizing he was teasing her.

He may not remember flowers, but he could make her laugh.

"April 17th," she stated almost shyly after catching her breath, "But we are not close enough for you to ask me what year."

"From what you told me last night, I already know what year. My vocabulary may need a little upgrading, but my math skills are just fine."

He watched as her cheeks tinted red. This woman was a contradiction. One moment she would openly share the most intimate and what he considered painful details of her life, but held fast to information he could easily find out with a phone or computer.

"Don't worry. I won't share your secret."

"Which one?" The sly wit was back. He watched her eyes flashed mischievously.

"The one where you seem almost too young to have achieved so much. When I grow up, I want to be just like you."

Her eyes widened at the unexpected compliment. The color heightened under her cheeks even more. At first, he didn't think she was going to respond as she stared back at him but before he could begin to feel uncomfortable she replied.

"Well, you better not. I'd hate to have to sue you for breach of confidentiality."

He shook his head, trying for a sober expression. He lifted his right hand as if he were going to recite a pledge. "I Swanny."

"What?" she laughed.

"Bugs Bunny... 'I Swanny' instead of I swear." He wondered what had brought the cartoon to mind.

She gave him an appraising look that he mistook for judgment for him quoting Bugs Bunny.

"I have a twelve-year-old and since I can hardly understand the cartoons today. I'd rather we watch something I know isn't teaching her violence, sex or drug use, together." He allowed his lifted shoulders to finish off the sentence.

"Defensive aren't we. I was going to say, 'I guess I missed that episode, but I am a fan'."

"Really? What's a favorite?"

"When Bugs ends up on an island and pretends to be a native to trick them into letting him go. He begins speaking another language and when the subtitles pop up they don't look like they match what he is saying at all."

He nodded his approval.

"I see today's conversations are going to be very intellectually challenging." She wiggled her eyebrows at him as she shifted to a more comfortable position.

They kept the light banter up for a while then he brought up the subject he'd been thinking of since he'd met her in New York.

His hands were clammy. "So, since you are going to remain in Chicago for a little longer once you are admitted in the rehabilitation center, would it be alright if Vivian and I take you out to eat on occasion?"

"Absolutely. I would enjoy that. I think I might be a little offended if you left me there to suffer through all those meals alone."

"And what if I wanted to take you out to dinner, just the two of us?" He watched her intently.

"Like as a date?" She didn't take her eyes from his.

Like as any occasion that would allow you to let me take you to dinner, was what he wanted to say but had a feeling, with Paige, that was the swiftest way to a 'No.'

"No. Paige I just enjoy spending time with you, getting to know you, like right now. But you have to agree this place leaves a lot to be desired."

He tried to keep his voice impassive so as not to give away his true desire. He shrugged nonchalantly.

She cocked her head to the side quizzically.

"Why?"

He paused, looking her square in the eye, even though he could sense her looking right through him. He tried for light-heartedness.

Suddenly, it was very important to know that they would have a chance to spend some time together outside of these walls that made him feel all but indebted to her; an atmosphere where they could just be two individuals spending time together just because they wanted to.

He wasn't prepared to find out why his feelings were all of a sudden so intense, so he tried to bury it as swift as it came so he could deal with it another time…hopefully in the distant future.

"Look, I have tried, but I can never seem to get the chef here to prepare my steak medium rare. As much as I enjoy our visits, I can't help but feel that you have been cheated. From your words, the few times you have touched down in Chicago have been a little more than layovers caught in a weather 'black hole'. We Chicagoans are very sensitive about out how people perceive our town, our sports teams and our history."

He saw her sigh. "Okay, at least I am, but I think the least I can do is introduce you to other experiences in Chicago besides delayed flights,

322

scratchy sheets, hospital foods, monitor beeps for music and the occasional slumber that you wake up from with one less organ."

He finished with a shrug. "I'm just sayin'… I love Chicago and would love to give you another chance to see it the way I do."

"Well, when you put it like that, how can I refuse?"

She leaned forward conspiratorially, placing her hand up next to her mouth. "Besides, the monitor beeps aren't that bad."

Mason reared back, clutching his heart in feigned hurt.

"Aww, you have mortally wounded my city's pride, but I am up to the challenge. I will champion my home's reputation and I will diligently work to get you to change your mind." *If I don't I'll never get you to come back and visit.*

"Is that what having a twelve-year-old does to you?"

"What?"

"Makes you corny?" she smiled, her brows coming together slightly.

He laughed out loud, working hard to get himself under control.

"Touché."

He was about to tell her how good she was for his ego when the sound of the door opening drew his attention away and shut his mouth.

Thinking it was a nurse coming in to take Paige's vitals, Mason was surprised to see Victoria walk around the divider as if she was expected.

He noticed the surprise on her face that was quickly replaced by cool indifference.

Now that's something new.

"Mason." The one-word greeting was clipped with an edge as sharp as picked ice.

Never mind.

He reciprocated the greeting, not bothering to get up.

"Good afternoon, Paige. How are you feeling today?"

"Wonderful, Victoria." Paige smiled openly. "I told Mason when he came in that today was a good day. I really feel like I am on the road to recovery."

"That's good news." Victoria walked over to a seat close to the window. Not bothering to move it closer she deposited her purse on the windowsill, next to the flowers.

When conversation didn't begin immediately upon her being seated, she stated. "Oh, don't let me interrupt." She made a gesture with her hand that they were to resume.

There's that machete.

"Well, I am going to get going. I am glad you are feeling better." He stood up, placing his hands in his pockets. He smiled down at her, lingering a little, hating to leave her presence.

He didn't promise to see Paige the next day because he had a feeling if he did, Victoria would be there waiting for him. And what was she doing there anyway? Last he knew, she wouldn't refer to Paige as anything but the "Morganson woman".

"Victoria." He regarded her, his voice void of emotion.

Before she could finish inclining her head in return, he turned back to Paige dismissing her.

Paige's features showed her discomfort in the level of tension between them. And for that reason, he turned back to Victoria.

"Did you just come from visiting Vivian?" Victoria stared at him so long, at first he didn't think she would answer him.

"Yes." No attempt to elaborate.

Just evil.

He took a deep breath, turning back to Paige who now wore an apologetic, one-sided grin.

He shrugged. "Have a good night."

"You too. Thanks for stopping by."

Her sweet smile mesmerized him, pushing all other thoughts out of his mind. He walked out of the room the same way he walked in – whistling.

CHAPTER 43

Paige vacillated between enjoying the serene environment of the rehabilitation center and longing to be surrounded by her own belongings.

She missed her apartment. She missed the spiritual peace and well-being that enveloped her as she walked through the door. She missed her desk by the picture window, her chef's kitchen, but even more so she missed her bed. She didn't think she'd had a full, undisturbed, night's sleep since she'd left for Chicago almost a month ago.

She was itching to have her full independence back. She was experiencing less and less pain, and her gait was less halting. She hadn't realized until she was on her feet just how much of her health she had taken for granted.

It was kind of frustrating to be out of breath and sporting a healthy sheen from the effort it took to cover the six feet from the bed to the bathroom. But that was still a dignifying step up from the catheter she'd worn upon waking up from surgery five days later than she'd expected.

This pain she wouldn't wish upon anyone. It seemed to be all over and then would escalate and focus on that one, fine point through her, edging its way to her back near her spine. She couldn't tell where it began, but it literally took her breath away, until she was able to administer the almost debilitating drug that would bring relief at the press of a button.

True, she had visited many people with health issues varying from a broken limb to a terminal illness and though she had treated each person with loving concern and a sympathetic ear, it was definitely different being able to empathize.

She may not have desired all of the attention in the beginning, but as the hours stretched on, many of the days she found herself hoping that someone would come through the door that she could speak to.

It was amazing what being left with one's thoughts, days on end, could do. In the beginning she embraced the peaceful environment, spending hours enveloping herself in prayer and fully devoting herself to meditating on her God. She sang and hummed, encouraged herself with scripture and read a couple of the books she'd brought with her but had yet to touch.

When she finally felt peaceful enough to do so, she allowed herself to ponder the last few weeks. She knew in order to listen to how the Holy Spirit would guide her through each decision, she needed to be objective. Her emotions had been claiming a lot of her attention lately, and she wanted to get her body and soul under submission before she made a wrong move.

Her work kept her somewhat busy, but when she longed for human conversations the interaction between the characters in her books ran a distant second next to real life. Thankfully, Carmen had been able to reschedule and create a few signing dates towards the end of her stay in Chicago. As it was, she wasn't scheduled to go back home until the beginning of November. It only made for good strategizing, with Paige already staying in Chicago.

Truthfully, she conceded, the medal for keeping her sane belonged to Mason, Vivian, and surprisingly enough, Victoria. She could admit that her first run-in with Victoria was nothing nice. It took stepping outside of herself to be able to see the woman as her granddaughter saw her.

The anger and hate that poured forth out of that woman was so vile it actually left a bitter taste in Paige's mouth. When the woman began to rant and rave, accusing her of being the most heinous of women, she just wanted her to disappear. She'd imagined a bus driving through the hospital room and taking the woman with her – quickly.

The pain that had begun as a low ebb was quickly escalating, and she didn't want to show the woman any weakness that she could prey upon. She'd thought about opening her mouth a couple of times to scream for the woman to leave or to press the button to call the nurse, but considered doing something no one else in the woman's family seemed to have done.

She listened to the woman's voice instead of the words and beyond the anger, she felt the sadness and desperation. It called to that compassionate place in her and all she could think of for a moment was what she could say to ease some of this woman's pain. It was only by the grace of God that she was able to keep her focus when the woman started talking about her mother.

She was momentarily dazed by hearing this stranger refer to her mom, the woman – even she couldn't find loving words for. *If this woman had any dealings with my mom and has survived it well enough to speak about it, she is one strong person.*

She didn't think about her mother often – on purpose. Grace Morganson-Dillard was one huge reminder of her failures. Her failure to have a loving bond with the woman that birthed her, failing to do anything that would elicit even a feeling of pride let alone compassion and nurturing from the woman. Failing to win the fight they'd had in regards to her going to the hospital for an abortion.

She'd thanked God profusely everyday for seeing both of her children delivered and in good health since Mason had informed her of Vivian's existence.

Most of all, she was ashamed that she had failed to find a redeeming factor in her mother, besides the fact that she was human and thus had the opportunity to one day become a child of God.

Paige knew that she needed to deal with her unforgiveness towards her mother. At first she'd thought it odd that she could forgive her cousin, whose very presence in her life brought enough pain and sorrow to fill many lifetimes, but still fail to forgive her mother.

It was only after much self-examination that she realized she was able to rationalize his actions as a response to weakness, sickness, or demonic oppression; whereas she regarded her mother's reaction as a form of betrayal.

It wasn't as if she didn't attempt to forgive her. She'd participated in three-day revivals, all-night prayer and deliverance services. She had gone through Christian counseling and conferences of healing and being set free, but the ability to forgive her mother taunted her.

She'd thought she'd let go a couple of times, but knew even as the thought of her mother came to the forefront of her mind, she still harbored a great deal of resentment towards her. Grace had a knack for showing up – at least, her works – at the most inopportune time and as much as Paige had worked to refrain from rendering judgment over her, she always found herself grimly reminiscing.

It was an unspoken rule between her sister and herself that neither would bring up her mother in conversation. While she'd stayed with her sister immediately after being released from the hospital, her sister had tried to convince her that her mother's actions were done more out of concern for Paige because having to raise a baby at 14 may have been more than she could bear, not to mention the constant memory of the way the child was conceived.

Paige, after hearing this argument one too many times, asked her sister the questions she had formed so many other times in her head in regards to the subject of her mother.

"I wonder, Mel, if she was so concerned about my future, why she didn't do or say anything to show me she believed me when I told her I was raped by her nephew. Why the words 'I will help you raise them' never came out of her mouth and why even adoption wasn't an issue. The first and the last words were 'we need to fix this', like I had the flu or contracted some other contagious disease and the only solution was to blot it out. Mel, it happened to me. I went through the hurt, pain and shame, only to carry the fruit of that shame and I still never considered killing them.

I'm not saying that I am any better than someone who would have, but I never expected my mother to treat me like I single-handedly brought this on myself."

"But you didn't tell her. You must have been hesitant for some reason."

Paige remembered lifting hurt-filled eyes to her sister. "We both know mom is somewhat given to drama, and she can be as protective as a pit bull. I didn't tell her because I was afraid for Aunt Faye and what she would do to Stone. Never once did I think she wasn't going to believe me or worse yet, try to hide what happened by killing someone who grew inside of me. I am alright with you taking Gladys, but not if you ever consider allowing mom to take care of her."

"You don't have to worry about that," Mel explained ruefully, "She said as long as I have Gladys, she wouldn't be a part of my life."

With guilt compounding the hurt, shame, and anger every time she looked upon her child or into her sister's eyes, Paige soon went to live with her father and his new wife.

Though he never approached her about her falling-out with her mother after their first conversation, she had a feeling that her father knew more than he let on. She was just too much of a coward to share it. He was all she had left; the only place she could find separation from the anger that had seemed to control every waking emotion.

Over the years, Grace would pop up at certain family events, playing the doting role of "mother of the wayward child". Once in college, Paige declined most invitations to family functions, citing too much homework or lack of funds for the trip.

The last she'd heard, Grace was in Seattle, Washington. Paige hadn't cared enough to inquire about what she was doing there. It had been enough to know she wasn't close enough to bump into.

Knowing all of this, she was sure she caught her sister off guard when she'd mentioned her a couple of days before Mel left Chicago.

"Mel, I need to know if you heard from Grace, when Gladys was around six-years-old."

Mel had been flipping through the channels of the television she'd been half-paying attention to, when she slowly put down the remote. "Huh?" Mel looked at her as if she'd grown another head.

"Did Grace try to contact you when Gladys was six?" Paige thought Mel hadn't heard her since her voice was still very raspy.

"Maybe…" Mel looked at Paige expectantly.

"What do you mean 'maybe'?" Paige became very still. How much did her sister know? Was it true?

"Mom and I don't share the same type of relationship as the two of you do." Mel was holding the magazine so tight it was taking on a new form, but Paige didn't interrupt her. She would ride out this new part of her nightmare as if she were watching it on the television.

Mel continued. "She called me a couple of years after you left to go live with Dad. She wanted to talk to you, but I let her know you were already gone. She even said she tried to reach you at your father's, but you wouldn't return her calls." Mel looked at Paige, beseechingly. "I know there is a great deal of hurt and pain between the two of you. I know we agreed not to talk about her and I have respected that for 12 years, but just because you didn't wish to have a relationship with her didn't mean I had to pretend she was dead to me too."

Paige finally spoke, trying to undo some of the damage she knew she'd inflicted upon her sister when she asked her to take care of Gladys. "Why do you think I left?" she began quietly. "When you told me Grace wouldn't come to see you or talk to you while I was there, I felt guilty. I'd come between you and your relationship with her. I wasn't so selfish that I could completely forsake your need or love for her but I just couldn't stand to see the condemnation in her eyes when she looked at me, especially when I was still dealing with the guilt and shame of it all."

"I just wasn't strong enough to fight her. I was so hurt and angry that she would think that of me but I should have been prepared in some way…it wasn't like we were ever close…There were many nights I laid in bed wondering if I could have done things differently; first on that day when Stone attacked me, and next with you." She silenced Mel by placing her hand over hers when Mel opened her mouth to interrupt.

"Please let me say this. It has been a long time coming." Paige took a breath as she tried to organize her thoughts. She watched as the magazine slowly unwound in Mel's hand.

She looked up into Mel's big, clear brown eyes. "I didn't know how to be strong enough for everyone in the family. I didn't know how to work through what happened without bringing shame to the family. I just wanted everything to go away, so I went away and tried to pretend it didn't happen."

She took another deep breath, expelling it slowly, watching as she ran her hand over her sister's. Ten years spanned between them in age, but to look at them you couldn't tell it. Even Mel's hands, a slightly lighter shade than Paige's, were wrinkle-free.

"In a way, that only made it worse because I missed some of the most precious parts of my baby's life and I left you to pick up the pieces with mom and the family." Paige paused when emotion left a lump in her throat too large for her to talk around. She squeezed Mel's hand, silently relaying that she wasn't done. "I thank you for being there though. If you weren't I probably would have lost both of my children that day."

Paige met Mel's gaze once again. "I'm sorry I did that to you. I took advantage of your maturity and age, but I am glad you never gave up on me."

Mel, whose eyes were just as wet as Paige's, patted her hand, tsking. "We have been through this before and as much I wished it could have happened differently, Marc and I are more blessed than you know by Gladys.

It may take a few years for all of us to heal and make Gladys as comfortable with you as she is with us, but I love how you have embraced life now. Mother or not, I wouldn't allow you around Gladys if I didn't think she needed you and could learn from you as well."

Holding hands was no longer enough to convey their love for one another. They embraced each other in a fierce hug, faces wet, and murmuring endearments.

Taking a few cleansing breaths and laughing at each other as they tried to compose themselves only to dissolve into more tears and laughter, they finally gave up and just held each other in a loose hug. Years of guilt, fear, resentment and questions were shared and relinquished over the next hour as they openly spoke on the subject that even as of that morning was taboo.

"I think...I think Grace may have tried to blackmail Vivian's grandmother," Paige whispered, finally approaching the loathed subject.

Mel's eyes grew round. "Why...how...what?"

Paige followed Mel's line of thought, even if she couldn't get the full sentences out.

"I think Grace knew about Vivian not being stillborn." Even as the words came out of her mouth her eyes filled with tears of outrage and anger again. She had been trying to piece together the conversation with

Victoria for a couple of days now and always ended up with one, nagging thought. If her mother found Victoria's information then she must have known that Vivian wasn't dead and if she knew Vivian wasn't dead, how did she get her out of there without the nurses, Paige and Mel becoming the wiser?

"When we thought my other child was stillborn, what did you do?"

Mel just sat there looking dumbfounded for a moment, then she looked down as if she couldn't look at Paige.

"I was busy holding Gladys. She was so small and she looked at me with those huge eyes…just looking at me like she was trusting me to take care of her. I barely noticed when you delivered Vivian, and when the nurse said there were complications, mom said she would take care of everything. You were so nonresponsive by then, I took it upon myself to take care of Gladys. I wasn't paying attention."

"I'll have none of that." Paige took the hand closest to her. "It wasn't your fault. We've been through this." Paige sighed. "I'll just have to get to the bottom of this myself. I have used you as a buffer long enough. If you will give me mom's information, I think it is about time we had a talk."

Mel just nodded. The reconciliation between the two was still too fragile to challenge. Paige counted on this because she didn't want what she had to say to her mother to come back on her sister in any way, shape or form. Mel had been her human shield for too long.

"Some help I am," Mel said with a self-deprecating grin, "I wasn't even here when the Wicked Witch of the Midwest came at you. Is she the reason why you have been so quiet the last day and a half?" Mel fumed, her mouth drawn in a tight line.

Paige nodded. "Not so much quiet as thoughtful. Believe me, it has been awfully loud in here." Paige pointed to her head, smirking.

"What did she say exactly?"

"She accused me of being in on some type of blackmailing scheme with Grace. Mel, I wouldn't be surprised if something poisonous ended up in my I.V., that woman was so vicious. She actually scared me and after Grace Morganson-Dillard, that is saying a lot."

Paige went on to tell Mel about the conversation she shared with Victoria. She wasn't surprised when Mel attached herself to Paige from then until it was time for her to go back to Atlanta. She was even going to try and get another extension from work, but Paige wouldn't hear of it. Mel still called her twice a day, but that was still better than having to explain to any visitors why they weren't trusted to be in the room alone with her. It had been downright embarrassing, and a little more than annoying.

Mel gave over Grace's information, but Paige was hesitant to make contact with the woman that with two words could make her feel smaller than a millipede. She also didn't know how to maneuver the conversation quickly towards the answers she wanted, given the fact that it had been twelve years since they'd last spoken. Her answers would have to wait, but she already knew she couldn't put it passed Grace to have attempted what Victoria accused them of.

Paige knew from past experiences that Grace was capable of such deceitfulness. What really concerned Paige was whether or not she could be objective to recognize the truth regarding Victoria's claim.

It was a good thing Victoria decided to keep her distance for a while. At first Paige thought Mel had confronted the woman and warned her away but when she did appear at Paige's door again a couple of weeks later, she seemed far removed from the hate-slinging banshee ranting and raving in front of her only a couple of days after she'd awaken.

She'd walked in the room hesitantly, carrying a couple of smoothies, going on and on about how she didn't know what Paige liked or was allergic to but chose for her what Vivian liked because after all, Paige was her mother. Warily, Paige accepted the drink, but after a few minutes of holding it she set it down on the table in front of her, untouched.

She saw the quick look of hurt cross Victoria's eyes, but she wouldn't feel guilty about not trusting her or accepting the peace offering. Really of all things, food was the last thing she would accept from the woman right now.

She sat there and just waited for Victoria to tell her why she was really there. She motioned for Victoria to take the seat next to her bed but after a few seconds of staring at the seat, Victoria declined and said she couldn't stay long. Paige merely nodded, seeing the woman was on edge. She decided to share something that had been going on in her head since sharing their first conversation with her sister.

"I owe you an apology." She saw Victoria's eyes narrow and knew she needed to explain quickly.

"I am sorry for the pain I inadvertently caused you. When you came in here a couple of weeks ago, I saw the anger and pain my mother had caused you and though I don't have all the answers yet, I want to know if you could forgive me for my role in it."

"If you didn't know what was going on, how could you be at fault?"

"By creating the environment for it in the first place. I'm not going to get into all my history with my mother, but suffice it to say we aren't terribly close. Some of that is my fault, and our relationship opened some doors for treachery to be done whereby you became an unsuspecting victim. For that, I am sorry."

She was met with quiet.

When Victoria finally spoke, her voice was almost as low as a whisper but edged with steel.

"Answer me truthfully. Did you know about the blackmail attempt?" As Paige watched the woman, her spine seemed to become as stiff as a rod. Her posture and demeanor transformed right before her eyes.

Not knowing how else to convince her, Paige let the one sentence be her full answer. "No. Like I said, my mother and I haven't been on speaking terms for a while."

Victoria stared at her, her eyes seemed to pierce her very soul. Paige saw what it was that board members, ranch hands and any other person under Victoria's hand went through. She was more than happy to know that her livelihood was not held in this woman's grasp.

"Are you telling me that you haven't talked to your mother in more than six years?"

"No. I am telling you that I haven't talked to my mother since I gave birth to Gladys and Vivian."

"How is that possible when you were only fourteen yourself?"

"It is complicated and nothing I wish to talk about at this time. Will you respect that?"

Victoria never took her eyes off of Paige. It didn't take much to see that she was sizing Paige up. After a few moments, Victoria shrugged. "I have enough of my own dysfunctional family drama. I am not looking for anymore. Do what you want."

Paige, disregarding the notion to check her emotions at the door, allowed her impatience to surface. "What are you doing here?"

Victoria bristled slightly then as the seconds ticked by she relaxed and a ghost of a smile crossed her lips.

Paige got the feeling that Victoria had gotten exactly what she'd been looking for – a rise out of her.

Paige counted down from 20 before repeating her question. She had gotten to 3 by the time Victoria decided to speak.

"I just came by to apologize for my behavior a couple of weeks ago. It was wrong of me to take advantage of you in the state you were in. I should have waited until you were feeling better to state my concerns regarding you being in my granddaughter's life."

Paige waited expectantly for a few moments but upon realizing that this was all Victoria felt the need to apologize for, she nodded again not quite sure how else to let her know her apology was accepted. Soon after that, Victoria said her goodbye and left, leaving Paige both slightly amused and bewildered.

Honestly, Paige didn't know how Victoria would react to the words of love she'd been led to give in response to Victoria's scathing diatribe, but obviously her conscience had been dealing with her. Well that, and the prayers she'd been sending up on her behalf.

Victoria showed up again the next day towards the end of Mason's visit, and the tension between the two was enough to make Paige question how Vivian dealt with them. She silently pleaded for Mason to at least make an attempt at being civil. He conceded but Victoria barely budged.

So when he'd left, Paige told Victoria that her room was a neutral zone, one she needed to remain peaceful and serene.

"I don't want you to feel that you are not welcome, but I will not get in the middle of this little feud you have going on with Mason. If the two of you can't squash your differences even for Vivian's sake, then I feel for her.

You are not only cheating yourself, but you are cheating her of having a happy family environment. I know there is a great deal of history there, but I am not willing to lend myself as a war zone for you and Mason to try and gain ground over." The only indication she gave that she had heard Paige was a slight nod.

From that moment on they shared an agreeable, albeit questionable, camaraderie. Victoria would come in, always baring some type of small gift and sit next to Paige's bed. There were days when they didn't share more than four sentences between them. It was just comfortable. This went on for almost two weeks before Victoria began holding conversations that consisted of more than a paragraph with Paige.

Paige had just come from physical therapy and was in more pain than she'd remembered being in since the first week after she'd regained consciousness. She was exhausted and relished the thought of placing her head on her pillow and not being disturbed for at least four hours.

When Victoria walked in toting a gift bag, Paige spied her warily. She watched as Victoria placed the bag on the side table and sat down in her chair. Paige didn't say anything even when Victoria picked up the remote and began surfing channels on her television but when she began to straighten Paige's bedclothes around her, Paige clasped her narrow wrist in her hand. Victoria looked up at Paige, finally noting the creases at the edges of Paige's eyes, her dilated pupils, and the furrow between her brows, registering her obvious pain.

"Oh, I'm sorry. Can I get you anything? Have they come and given you anything for the pain yet?"

"No."

Victoria was thoughtful for a moment. "Do you want me to leave?"

Paige let out a heavy sigh. If she said, "Yes," she would hurt the woman's feelings and only God knew what she would do next. She'd learned quickly that people around Victoria could hurt – emotionally or physically – and Victoria would stick by them. But if she was hurt, she would strike out like a wounded animal with a wall at his back. And don't be the cause for her pain...

"No. Please stay, but I hope you don't mind if I doze a little."

"No. Not at all."

Paige nodded and lay on her side trying to breathe shallowly. She looked at Victoria's profile, studying it for the first time. It was evident that Victoria was once a raving beauty, but the sour look that seemed engraved on her face had added at least ten years. She felt a physical ache for her and what she'd lost. Paige recognized that Victoria could have been a clear, spiritual portrait of Paige in a few years if she had not allowed God to work in her life, alleviating her of years of rage. She vowed right then that she would do whatever it was He wanted her to do in order to help this woman let go of some of the pain and embrace His love.

"So what's in the bag?"

Victoria shifted in her chair to face Paige, the lines suddenly relaxing in her face. Paige was caught off guard momentarily by transformation. "I brought you something. It isn't new, but I think you will like it all the same."

She reached behind her for the bag and pulled out a platinum-lined hourglass. The particles in the bottom tubing glistened too brilliantly to be sand. Paige's breath caught in her throat. She took it from Victoria's hand slowly, bringing it close so that she could discern what they were.

Her eyes grew wide. Just as she'd feared, it was shaved gold. It was too exquisite a gift. She was sure Victoria wouldn't be too happy with her turning it down but she just couldn't accept anything so expensive.

She looked at Victoria trying for what she hoped was an appreciative smile. "Victoria. Thank you so much, but..."

"It wasn't as expensive as you think, and I thought it would be a perfect symbol for what you have given Vivian. Time is more precious than gold and that is what you have given her. There is nothing we can do to repay you for that."

Paige took a deep breath to calm her heart, which had taken off at a gallop at hearing Victoria's words.

"I didn't do this for any other reason but to allow Vivian to have a halfway decent life. That is all I could have asked or hoped for." Dare she finish with her true desire of playing an intricate part in her daughter's life?

Victoria was quiet for a moment. She had turned back towards the television, but Paige stared at her profile as water collected at the corner of her eye.

Paige's mouth dropped open for a second in horror. *Lord, please don't let this woman start crying. I don't know if I can handle this today. I just don't have the strength.* Paige clenched her teeth hard. She knew she was being selfish but the inner tantrum she was having would not lend itself to compromise. *Augh!. This is so unfair. Why do I always have to be the one that exhibits Your qualities. Just once… just once I want to be able to quietly lick my wounds.*

But just as soon as the thought entered her mind, it was quickly followed by an impression of an answer.

*And…the church mother you would call in the middle of the night, crying, who quietly struggled through arthritis in her knees, but would still kneel and pray for you…*Paige felt sufficiently chastised. "The gift is beautiful. I really appreciate it. Thank you."

Victoria offered Paige a smile. She gently patted Paige on her leg, pulling herself up to what Paige had come to refer to as her 'stiff-as-a-board posture'.

"Well, I need to go. I want to take Vivian to get some school clothes before she starts on Monday. She is so excited. It is all she talks about." Victoria rolled her eyes feigning exasperation but allowed just enough of a smile to show that she secretly loved it.

"Bye," Paige called after her. She mused at the thought of Victoria not showing this side of herself to anyone else. Before she left Chicago she would have to have a heartfelt talk with her about how she treated her family. She was not looking forward to it, but the constant prompting she received from the Holy Spirit was causing her unrest and a deep conviction.

She would speak to her with as much love as possible, and take her time to hear exactly what it was God wanted to convey to this woman that could soften her heart towards her family. She knew Victoria was hurting and extremely lonely. She also knew that she was a proud, stubborn and resourceful woman, which spelled trouble if Paige wasn't careful with her wording. She saw what Victoria had been putting Mason through, not that he didn't provoke her, but Paige didn't have any interest in being her next bull's eye for target practice.

The thought of Mason was a whole other point of contention. He had begun visiting her when she was still in the hospital, and she'd begun looking forward to their visits more and more. He made her laugh and it felt so good to laugh and have someone to banter with.

They freely conversed about all things Vivian, his work, places they'd traveled and their hobbies. She shared information on some of her characters in her new book, and even put together tentative plans to join him and Vivian when they traveled to California around Thanksgiving. Mason had been promising Vivian a trip to Disneyland.

In the beginning, she found that she compared their conversations and interaction with those she'd had with Brandon. But the more time she spent with Mason and the longer she went without hearing from Brandon, her practice of comparing them passed.

The only thing they didn't talk about open and comfortably was God and that, for her, was like not discussing an elephant that had come to sit next to them. He was there and she wasn't willing to ignore Him for Mason's sake.

This was the cause of a few uncomfortable moments because she wasn't willing to keep Him out of her conversations and Mason wasn't too keen on acknowledging Him in the places of his life that he would share with her, even when it was so glaringly obvious to her that God was working second by patient second to pull him closer.

The physical attraction was also a source of unease. Though she worked not to give Mason a clue to how he affected her, it was apparent that he wouldn't reject the notion of their fledgling relationship taking on a deeper role.

She was fighting it with everything she could. So much so that the day before when he had stopped by to bring her an individual, Chicago-style pizza, she went out of her way to ignore the energy that passed between them, especially when their fingers touched as he handed her the box. She could tell that he wanted to hold her gaze to see if she had also felt the current, but she refused and, after thanking him, she made an excuse of being too busy with last minute plans for the book signing, to spend more than a few minutes with him.

She saw the disappointment momentarily alight his features, but she couldn't encourage more than they shared. It would only complicate things and set them both up for pain.

She'd prayed to God, wondering why they even shared this chemistry when it was obvious to her that the element she could not live without in any relationship she would have with a man, was missing. That was a shared love and understanding of God.

From day to day, at the end of each of their visits, a light wave of tension would pass between them. She hoped he would keep the salutation brief, accompanied with no more than a pat on the hand or shoulder, or an equally brief hug. He would always lengthen the physical contact just long enough to make her break away first.

Often times she would lay there praying afterwards, sometimes asking and other times pleading for God to take away this attraction she had to this man that caused her to wonder if the skin at his cheek was as smooth as it looked, if he always smelled as good or if all of his hair felt as silky as the strands at his collar that touched her arms a couple of times she'd lost the battle against hugging him a little too tightly, for her sake.

Most of the time she would argue that he wasn't hers, and therefore the very thoughts she had for him that went beyond friendly admiration were wrong and not to be indulged. But though Mason may never have had an inkling that she worked so hard to seem unaffected, his constant presence was wearing at her nerves.

During her last week in the hospital, Vivian, now fully recovered, was able to go home. Sometimes she would come and visit with her father; before she was discharged, she would come down and visit by herself.

Paige was motherly proud of her beauty, intelligence and humility. She was passionate about God and they would discuss stories from the Bible; Esther was Vivian's favorite woman of the Bible while Deborah, for this season, was Paige's.

They talked about the places Vivian wanted to visit. During her sixth grade year, she'd become enamored with castles which were one of the reasons she wanted to go to Disneyland. Paige smiled at her innocence and suggested that she ask her father to take her to tour Hearst Castle while they were in California. Paige couldn't stifle the grin at Vivian's reaction to finding out she might be able to go in a "real live castle," as she called it.

Paige found that they did have a lot in common including their dislike for ketchup, sour cream, blueberries, and curry. Paige was delighted to find that they shared a love for spinach, gardening, and earth tones.

They talked about Vivian's expectations for the school year, and though she'd been a straight-A student the previous year, she was very doubtful that she would be able to catch up on the month she'd missed. Mason had hired a tutor after conferring with her teachers, and had begun bringing some of her work to her so that she wouldn't be so far behind that she would be left back.

Paige asked Vivian about her mother, Rachael, and Vivian's eyes lit up with the love she had for her mother. She talked about the big and the small things she and her mom used to do, like praying together, going on 'mother/daughter dates' which could be anything from dinner and a movie sometimes after church, to just stopping off for ice cream on the weeknights Mason worked late. They went on weekly trips to museums and parks, which she now did with her father. She shared with Paige some of her mother's hobbies, and how she missed going to church with her.

"Does your dad ever take you to church?"

Vivian shook her head in the negative. "He just drops me off at my friend, Pam's, house or lets me stay over Saturday nights so that I can go to church with her and her family."

Paige was thoughtful. "Well, I can't promise anything regarding your father taking you to church but when you come to California I would love for you to visit my church, and when I leave Chicago I would enjoy it if we could pray with each other every day."

Vivian let out a little squeal. "Could we really?"

"Yep. I could call you either every morning before you go to school or right before you are ready to go to bed. This way if anything comes up in the day we can have fewer interruptions. How's that?"

Paige couldn't hold back the emotion threatening to pull her heart from her chest. She was full of joy as her daughter jumped up and hugged her tight. It hurt a little but it was the best pain she'd felt in a while.

Her surprise visit the day before she was transferred from the hospital to the rehabilitation facility came in the form of Richard Branchett.

Never meeting the man but hearing him referred to briefly by Vivian and Mason, she was more than curious.

He knocked before entering. When she answered, he walked in, introducing himself as Victoria's husband and Vivian's grandfather. Paige's eyes went wide. She couldn't help but stare at him. He was nothing like she'd imagined, nor was he what she would have pictured for Victoria's spouse.

"I am sorry it has taken me this long to come and share my gratitude for what you have done for my Vivian."

Paige was having a hard time focusing enough to form words, so she just nodded.

"But I guess you would have done it anyway," he continued, "with or without accolades. She means so very much to me…to us. Do you mind if I sit down?" He gestured toward the chair.

Finally finding her voice, Paige replied. "No, I don't mind. Please sit down. I am sorry for being rude. You being here just surprised me. Vivian mentioned that you were out of the country." She watched as he settled himself, unfolding his long legs in front of him.

He was a handsome man with skin the color of toffee that contrasted nicely with his chocolate brown eyes and even darker hair. If it weren't for the liberal amount of gray at his temples and at his crown, she would have placed him in his mid to upper forties. She wondered how many of his features Rachael inherited. Judging from some of the conversations she'd had with Mason, Rachael had definitely shared his easy smile that warmed you with its welcome.

Noticing he had not spoken, Paige decided to ask one of the many questions that came to her upon his introduction.

"How long have you been in the country?" She straightened her sheet around her legs.

"A few days. I will be flying back out tomorrow. I have been spending most of my time with Vivian and Mason. She is looking so much better. It is a miracle."

His last sentence caught her by surprise. "Yes, it is. One I believe you have been praying for?" Her lips slowly curved into a wide smile.

He inclined his head, grinning sheepishly, the action causing him to look even younger.

"So, how are you feeling? You look to be recovering well. I heard it was a little touch and go there for a few days."

She cocked her head to the side, watching him intensely. "Did Victoria tell you this?"

A shadow of something akin to hurt crossed his features very briefly. "No." He cleared his throat. "Mason called me soon after the procedure. My colleagues and I have been praying nonstop for you and your family. How are they taking all of this?"

"Mmmm. Better than I expected, considering all that we have learned in the last month." She folded her hands in her lap.

"I'm sure...I'm sure." His voice seemed to drift off with his thoughts.

"Vivian told me you have been doing some missionary work. Where have you been?"

"We've been helping mostly in the surrounding villages of Kampala, the capital of Uganda. We split our time between the outlying villages of Kampala. Some of them have names, ranging between 2 to 3 kilometers. Most of them, however, are as big as the biggest building, orphanage or farmland with sparse housing or lean-tos.

When I get back I will be spending a few weeks at Hope Village, an orphanage about 30 kilometers outside of Kampala, and Kiteezi Village, whose residents have been dealing with a malaria and diarrhea outbreak, and deteriorating living conditions due to the landfill near their town. One of my partners told me that a few days ago things took a turn for the better, and the stench that used to overtake the village has eased along with the attack of mosquitoes and green flies that used the landfill as their breeding ground."

"Is your work dangerous?" Paige was intrigued.

"Not necessarily. We try to adhere to the rules of the government and culture. We travel with a guide, native to each town so that we can be more of a help than a hindrance. Though many of the people were introduced to the Islamic religion hundreds of years ago, many are now Christian. Uganda is considered one of the friendlier countries, not to mention beautiful and regal. Her mountains are majestic and the vibrant colors we don't have here in the terrain are so overwhelming. The first few days, all you want to do is just sit and take in the magnificence of what God created. I could do nothing but thank Him for allowing me to experience such unadulterated beauty."

Paige was silent as he continued to share some the experiences of his latest trip with her. After another fifteen minutes he suddenly stopped, and she stared at him quizzically.

"What?"

"I didn't mean to come in here and ramble on like this. I just merely wanted to see how you were doing and to introduce myself."

Paige assured him that his stories sounded like anything but rambling. "Has Victoria ever gone with you?"

Richard gave a look that indicated that she knew better but he obliged her. "Victoria is not the type to spend her days handing out food, cleaning up after anyone, or taking care of sick or healthy orphans."

"Have you asked her?"

Richard was thoughtful for a moment then shook his head. "No. No I haven't. Victoria and I have been at odds lately." His voice grew somber, but just as quickly as the clouds covered his eyes, it lifted. He took a deep breath and squared his shoulders.

"Tell me about yourself, Paige. My granddaughter raves about you. She says you're an elder at your church? What do you do?"

Paige began to share pieces of her ministry, her career and some of the ways God drew her to Him and her church home. Richard asked her question after question about her beliefs and about her church's history as well as denomination.

They spoke amicably and passionately about experiences in ministry that changed their lives, as well as certain aspirations.

Paige found that she liked Richard Branchett. For a man of such wealth, he was very unassuming and humble. Surely, any man that could live with Victoria day in and day out had to be close to sainthood. She wondered if she had always been that way but before she could voice her query, he answered it for her.

"You know Victoria wasn't always like the way she is now. She used to be warm, affectionate, and almost generous to a fault. If I hadn't streamlined some of her more charitable undertakings, she would have given away everything."

He chuckled then looked at Paige. "Don't get me wrong. I would have let her, but I know her parents would have had a field day with her. They didn't support her taking her grandparent's farm. They had more ostentatious aspirations for her. You know like marrying a blue blood...throwing parties..." He began chuckling again and Paige joined him, but it faded when his smile left.

"What happened?" She asked.

"Challenges of life." He shrugged his shoulders.

"Disappointments, disagreements, tragedies..." He took a deep breath. "She didn't, what you could say, bounce back. Instead of looking for answers that could help her heal, she sat and waited for the next thing that would go wrong. Sometimes I wonder if she thinks she is being punished for going against her parent's wishes."

"Have you talked to her about this?"

"Many, many times."

"Did you ask her about her parents?"

"You don't ask Victoria about her parents unless you want to suffer her wrath. I'm not afraid of her. I used to be the only one that could get her to open up, but since Rachael died…" His voice faded off again.

Paige pressed. "Since Rachael died…?"

He looked up from his hands to judge her features. She hoped he could see the concern in her eyes and not mistake it for gaining information to gossip. After a few more seconds, he decided to continue.

"She got angry, very angry – at Mason, at me, and probably herself. It is anger that I can't even speak to. It's like she feeds on it for strength, but it's also eating at the woman that I fell in love with. I hardly recognize her." His voice caught and it seemed to alert him as to how deep he'd let Paige see into his emotions. He cleared his throat again.

"It sounds like she and Mason have quite a bit in common," Paige murmured.

Richard stared at Paige for what seemed like minutes. She could tell she'd said too much and busied herself adjusting her pillows. When she turned back to face him, he placed a hand on her shoulder.

"No. Mason has his own story. One that is better left to him sharing with you. All I am going to say is his struggle comes more from running than trying to find someone to blame. When he quits running, he will be an amazing and powerful man of God."

"Do you think he will stop running?" He stared at her for a long time and just when she didn't think he was going to answer her, he replied with a question of his own.

"What do you think? I have the feeling you can hear God just as well, if not better, than I can."

Paige didn't know what to make of his cryptic sentence. Was it really any of her business? She shook off the thought just as quickly as it had come.

Thankfully after that Richard changed the subject and they conversed until the nurse came in to change her bandage.

"Mr. Branchett, it was an honor to meet you."

"It is Richard and Elder Morganson, the honor is mine. I hope to see you again in a less…sterile environment."

She laughed. "The name is Paige, and I hope it is too. I am looking forward to it. Meanwhile I will be praying for your safe passage to your destination and an equally pleasant return. May the Lord continue to watch over you, and I pray He keeps his hedge of protection around you, your loved ones, and your colleagues. May his angels encamp round about you, and may you find favor where others found closed doors. In Jesus' name, Amen."

"Amen," he repeated after lifting his head.

"Thank you, Paige…for everything."

"Likewise," she said, trading the sentiment and inclining her head.

After one last wave, he left and she felt just a little more alone. Instead of indulging in the dark thoughts, she concentrated on the nurse and her ministrations, trying at small talk until all she could do was pray silently.

*   *   *

Paige was pulled from her musing when the phone rang. Glancing at the caller I.D., she noted Lady Menagerie's number.

She had weekly phone conversations with Lady Menagerie, which for the most part left her encouraged and lighthearted. She missed her church family greatly and was hungry to hear anything and everything that was going on.

"Hello."

"Good Afternoon," came Menagerie's melodic greeting. "Have you started the countdown?"

"Yes. Today marks one week before I can kiss this place goodbye. Remember, I won't be back right away because I have a couple of book signings lined up before leaving Chicago."

"I remember. Are you sure you aren't jumping the gun? I know you will be sitting during most of it, but you should be resting and taking it easy. You may feel great but your body is still recovering from the procedure and the shock from the complications."

"How about I make you a deal? I will do the two book signings and when I get home you can restrict me to bed rest for the first week."

"I don't make deals. Just take care of yourself."

Paige chuckled. "Yes, Lady Menagerie."

"Don't get smart with me," Menagerie quipped over the line. "You are still small enough for me to take you over my knee."

Paige laughed. "Well with all the weight I've lost you could probably blow on me and I would topple over."

"I see…dieting the hard way." She could hear the smile in the older woman's voice as she teased. "Well you better not come back looking too different. Brandon won't be able to recognize you and he's been, dare I say, anxiously waiting for your return."

Paige gasped quietly. She paused for a moment then sucked her teeth. "Really? I couldn't tell. I haven't gotten a call from him since before he left."

Paige wondered why the only communication she received from Elder Tatum after his visit were short, impersonal notes with scripture on his monogrammed stationary and the occasional, encouraging text message, also of an impersonal nature.

She would have understood if he had not contacted her at all after finding out about her twins. Disappointed, but she would have understood.

What she didn't...couldn't comprehend was why send notes and texts when he didn't want to have anything to do with her?

True, it wasn't as if they had any type of understanding, but from what phone calls they shared and interaction they had before her going into the hospital, she thought they were headed towards some very positive territory.

Then there was the fact that he flew to Chicago to see how she was doing and to wish her well. Who does that? Mel had explained that he didn't just happen to be there on business and from what she gathered from her conversation with Lady Menagerie, Brandon had requested to visit her.

She explained all of this to Lady Menagerie, hoping she would be able to shed some light on the subject and assure her that she wasn't reading too much into his verbal silence.

"You know I asked Elder Tatum why he'd not spoken to you since leaving Chicago when he inquired on how you were doing a few days ago. He said he didn't want to intrude and that you seemed to have your hands full with family and trying to recover. He said he didn't want to be in the way."

Paige was quiet while she considered what Lady Menagerie told her then voiced her conclusion. "I think that is a bunch of malarkey."

"So if that isn't the truth, what do you think it is?"

Paige began slowly. "I think my life, well, my family drama scared him."

"Mmmm. You have to admit. It is pretty fantastic even for the imagination. When you two began talking, to him, you were Elder Paige Morganson: single, lover of God, and author.

In Chicago, he watched you suffer from the complications of your operation. He found out that you were not only a mother, but to twins that you don't even have custody of. Then there is Mason, and though he only discussed meeting the man and praying with his daughter, I definitely detected a trace of curiosity.

I think he has every right to be wary. He may be reacting cautiously, but he hasn't been able to hide his interest the few times your name has been mentioned in conversation."

Paige sighed, releasing some of the unease she felt at Lady Menagerie's words.

Before she could verbalize what she was feeling, Lady Menagerie spoke. "Speaking of Mason, how is that going?"

"What 'that'?"

"Whatever you want to label your relationship with him."

"We are parents to Vivian, respectively, and we enjoy each other's company. He has taken me to out, along with Vivian, a couple of times to introduce me to 'his Chicago', as I mentioned before."

"How's the 'everything else' between you two?"

Paige shrugged her shoulders before she realized that Lady Menagerie couldn't see her.

"Tense."

"With the physical attraction you shared with me regarding you and Mason, could there be anything else besides just the physical attraction?"

"I don't understand." Paige wasn't playing coy, she just wanted to make sure she understood exactly what Lady Menagerie was asking.

"Beyond the intense physical attraction, do you have feelings for him?"

After thirty seconds of silence, Lady Menagerie spoke again. "Okay…so I believe you have some things to consider. I will get back to you on this."

"It isn't that serious. I have had time to do a lot of introspection. Lying on your back does that. Just because your body isn't moving doesn't mean your mind isn't still going a mile a minute."

"So why the long pause?"

"I do care for him, but I don't know how much of those feelings are in direct correlation with my admiration for the father he is to Vivian or gratefulness for allowing me to be a part of her life. There is also the fact that we will always share a bond through her.

It has been a dream of mine to be an integral part of my children's lives for a long time. Even with all of this, his distance from the Lord is a huge drawback. How can I even consider a relationship beyond what we have when I can't freely share my world with him?"

"Believe it or not, Paige, people do it all the time. Sometimes neither spouse is a believer when they get married, or one is and the other eventually comes to love the Lord."

"I know, but I know better than that. I believe I should be able to share my love for God freely with my partner. I thought you would encourage my decision." She was having a hard time keeping the defensive tone out of her voice.

"Don't get me wrong. I'm not asking you to travel the harder road, just the one God has for you," Lady Menagerie placated.

"Spiritually we aren't equally yoked and though I know he can overcome it, he is so angry and bitter. He still blames God for some of the things that have happened in his life. If his late wife and daughter, who truly love the Lord, could not encourage him to have a healthy relationship with God, what chance would I have?"

"Is this still Paige I am speaking to?" Lady Menagerie's voice held an edge Paige only heard when she was being chastised. "Why does it sound like you are using these reasons to build a wall to defend yourself against him?"

"What do you mean? They are biblically-based as well as what you have taught me to consider." Paige could feel her frustration growing with the conversation.

"True, but as I said before, be open while guarding your heart. If God wants to use you to draw him closer, be open to it. If you stay on the defense regarding your feelings towards him, you may miss the opportunity for God to work through you in ways you can't imagine.

It's your love for God that draws people, Paige. It is a light that shines brightly, attracting those hurt and surrounded by the darkness of their thoughts. Don't inadvertently cover it up for fear of him drawing closer to you, until he recognizes who is truly drawing him."

"I don't want to lead him on," Paige whined with impatience.

"Then don't, but at the same time, don't stop being his friend or allowing God to use you to convey to him something he could not receive from his family.

In other words, don't push him away because you're uncomfortable with the feelings he provokes in you."

"I'll consider what you have said."

"I know you will, honey, and I want you to do the same for Brandon. You know, just because he meets certain criteria on your list doesn't mean that he's the one for you either. You already know you can't judge a person by their title or what comes out of their mouth. I trust that you will continue to seek God in both of these relationships. So now that we have gotten through that, I want to know if you are going to be back home in time for our Thanksgiving event?"

"Definitely before then. I actually should be back in time to participate in the committee again this year." Paige was only too happy to follow the change of subject.

They talked for another twenty minutes before disconnecting the call. Paige picked up her laptop and did some research for her book. It was always an easy way to lose track of time and thoughts of anything else while researching reference material online. If she wasn't careful, hours could go by while she maneuvered through the pages that guided her from one reference point to another.

This day would serve its purpose because the last thing she wanted to think about was Mason and the outing she'd agreed to go on with him at the end of the week.

CHAPTER 44

Victoria opened her laptop at the desk in the living room. She'd been up since before dawn trying to trace the sense of foreboding that seemed to have attached itself to her earlier in the week.

She waited for it to boot up as she sipped at her coffee, glancing out the window for what seemed the 80th time in the last hour. She was restless and that never sat well with her. She usually equated restlessness with a lack of mobility in any project or stage in life.

She wasn't getting as far as she'd hoped with Paige. The woman was somewhat of an enigma. She never reacted the way Victoria assumed she would and it made Victoria uneasy, at best.

She couldn't help admiring the young woman. If they'd met across a conference room table, Victoria wouldn't have let the work day come to a close without offering the woman a position. Her uncanny ability to assess the motive of her opponent coupled with her self-control was to be commended.

Victoria replayed their first encounter again. She noticed the woman's surprise upon her greeting but as she revealed glimpses of her purpose for visiting, Paige became still. She'd expected any emotions from fear to a cool, calculating impassiveness. The intensely sharp gaze, though, was disquieting. The more Victoria pressed, the more still the woman became until she lay there looking like a statue. True, she acted as if she had no clue about her mother's dealings. Victoria expected that. Who would admit to such a scheme as to use blackmail to take back a child?

Even still, it didn't prepare Victoria for what came out of the woman's mouth next or her reaction to those words. Victoria wasn't new to the manipulations of "religious-minded" people who weren't below using the Word of God to criticize, belittle or condemn those who weren't acting in accordance with their beliefs.

Paige's title said it all. One didn't reach that station in the church overnight and, usually by the time they'd achieved the title, they had long since forgotten what and who had wooed them to the church in the first place. The memories of who they were before accepting Christ had been discretely filed away and forgotten. Along with the memories went the compassion that would allow them to love people.

Oh, she had been there once upon a time and it wasn't a world she longed to rejoin any time soon. She would continue to try and protect her granddaughter from the same fate she'd suffered.

Victoria typed in her password and navigated to her email where she'd stored photos. She opened the folder and perused the gallery of pictures she'd received from Rachael over her last few years. Some were just of Vivian, and others were of both Rachael and Vivian. The pictures including Mason were sparse and she liked it that way.

There was one in particular Victoria looked for whenever she gave herself permission to open this folder. She pressed the button forwarding from one picture to the next until what she was looking for filled the screen. It was a picture of the three of them: Rachael, Vivian and herself. It was taken on Vivian's fifth birthday by Mason, something she chose to forget whenever she looked at this particular photo.

Rachael stood next to Victoria with Vivian in front of them looking not at the camera, but at Victoria, who had just promised to let her help feed the cows the following morning because she was now a 'big girl'.

The child had held onto her coattails all day, never letting her out of her sight. Rachael had been beside herself with worry when later that evening, she'd gone in to check on Vivian only to find her gone from her bed. They searched around the house then outside, only to find her in the barn on a bale of hay under a blanket, fast asleep. Later, when asked what she had been thinking by going to the barn alone, Vivian said in a matter-of-fact-voice that she didn't want to be late feeding the cows and she wanted to make sure she would be there early. No one could chastise her because they were too busy trying not to laugh.

That was the last time they would be at the farm before Rachael's diagnosis and that woman would threaten to take away her granddaughter. It was the happiest memory she had been able to hold on to. She tried not to compare it to this day but couldn't keep the thoughts away. Two years ago today was the last time she would hear her daughter's voice. If she'd known at the time she wouldn't make it to the hospital on time, she would have recorded their conversation.

Two years and what did she have to show for it but more chasms in her relationships. She'd not seen nor heard from Richard in almost a month and she'd heard from Vivian that he'd come to visit her at her father's house.

Victoria exited out of the picture, its folder, and the program used to house them. She would lock it away until another bout of weakness forced her back into it.

Victoria got up and set the kettle on to heat the water for her tea. She sifted through the mail Martha sent her. So far nothing was terribly urgent that it couldn't wait until she got back home next week.

Home...

She'd reached the second to the last envelope when her hands froze. It had arrived. The 12X9 envelope marked confidential with no return address that she was sure housed information, including the whereabouts of Grace Morganson-Dillard. She was happy she'd put one of her men on it as soon as she'd heard about Paige. Whereas Paige's life seemed to be an open book, Grace lived in the shadows.

Did the woman even know that her daughter almost lost her life on an operating table in order to procure better health for the daughter Grace had hidden? It wasn't for Victoria to speculate on anymore. She now had the information she'd been waiting for. She'd even gone to Paige's hospital room under the guise of making amends, just to see if the woman showed up or called. Not a word.

After three weeks of visits, enduring a half hour to an hour of the poor excuse for television and the occasional conversation, Paige reluctantly admitted to being estranged from her mother. Victoria begrudgingly came to the conclusion that Paige was not only unaware of Grace's scheme, she hadn't been in contact with her in a very long time.

Not that Victoria had allowed herself to grow terribly fond of the woman/child, but there was a peace that surrounded her that drew Victoria time and time again. It was like a long forgotten dream that would come upon her in waves of feelings, overriding her senses for a moment, then dissipate before she could make a conscious effort to capture it and turn it into rational thought.

Victoria used the excuse of dropping in unannounced at all hours of the day to make sure Grace wasn't in her life, but Paige's quiet acceptance of her company and her lame excuse for an apology continued to confound her. The background she'd done on Paige's church didn't unfold any cult-like characteristics, but it did seem if Paige were the norm, that they groomed their people to appear humble and meek. The only evidence that she had of the fire in Paige was the spark in her eye when she'd accused her of blackmail but still she didn't retaliate as most would have.

More and more she was coming to the realization that Paige was truly a lover of people. It was something she could use to her advantage, but she would have to be very careful because it could surely backfire on her.

The whistle of the kettle pulled her from her thoughts. She made herself the tea and sat back down to go over the contents in the envelope that would help her construct her formula for Grace Morganson-Dillard's day of reckoning. For Paige's sake and the sake of her granddaughter, she would try to keep her out of the path of destruction.

She went over the pictures of Grace, Melanie, Paige, and Stewart Morganson. She noted that Paige had received her defiantly strong chin and jaw from Grace; the same chin and jaw she'd passed down to Vivian. The eyes, cheekbones and nose, however, were compliments of her father, who had been a very handsome and distinguished gentleman.

She read through the file, noting the divorce due to irreconcilable differences after 22 years of marriage. She and Richard had been married for 33. Would their marriage suffer the same fate?

She knew Richard wouldn't approve of what she was planning, but Richard hadn't cared enough to try and contact her, so that was a moot point.

In fact, he had just reinforced her belief that happiness and peace were fleeting, fragile and unpredictable – but anger and pain, they were ever present and could be used to strengthen her resolve when all other emotions failed. Yes, she would use her hate to fuel her because she couldn't afford to feel anything but anger right now. A lesser emotion would break her resolve and the fortress she'd wrapped around her heart.

She refocused, going through Grace's work history, places she'd lived and that she'd remarried five years ago, only to be widowed in less than three. She now lived in Seattle, Washington, alone.

Victoria wondered idly what she could do to this woman that hadn't already happened. She seemed to be estranged from her family and now lived up in some dreary town where it rained almost 300 out of the 365 days of the year.

A slow smile crept upon her lips. She would find the woman's weakness and, when she did she would snatch it, dangle it in front of her and pretend to give it to her then destroy it, all while the woman watched.

At one time, Victoria thought to use Paige, but the woman's absence even at Paige's near-death told her volumes. This was no "Mother of the Year." She would find it, that she was certain of.

She looked up at the clock over the stove. Meanwhile, she would get dressed and ready for her day. There were a lot of things to prepare for.

CHAPTER 45

Paige was nervous.

The agitation in her voice and constant smiles throughout dinner were a telltale sign. At first, Mason thought it was it was the fact that it was just the two of them, but as the late afternoon moved into night, she only seemed to grow more restless.

They began with lunch at a restaurant known for its American home-style cuisine. They talked about the different areas of Chicago. Paige admitted that she hadn't taken much of an interest due to its infamous 'Hawk' weather patterns and the challenges of getting a flight out.

He'd led her on a tour through several streets in the Lincoln Park district, sharing pieces of their history and information on their architects. She asked a lot of questions as they walked through The Theurer-Wrigley House, stared up at the Francis J. Dewes House, remarking on their structure and the genius of the architects and builders of that era in being able to construct such time-honored 'stone art'. They finished off their tour of Lincoln Park with the Conservatory and Botanical Gardens situated just west of Lake Shore Drive. He watched her grow quiet as she stared through the ceiling of the glass building that had been constructed to house tropical foliage as well. They rode through the Old Town Triangle Historic District which sat on the edge of the North side. He'd shown her a number of older buildings, now landmarks that fueled his passion for architecture. The stone and brick structures spoke of a mastery that he held in reverence. They walked along the street after parking near the John Hancock Observatory which he promised to show her near sunset. The street was crowded and he took her hand to help guide her through the crowd a number of times. After a while, he didn't let go.

It felt good to be able to share his love of this city with someone; to be able to look at it through the eyes of someone seeing it for the first time. He was glad the weather had held up; it made it easier for them to walk the leaf-lined streets, observing Chicago in what was one of his favorite seasons. The multicolored leaves carpeting the ground in front of him made it look as though nature had gone all out to help him convince her that Chicago was a city worth getting to know better. If he was lucky, she would come and visit more often.

They'd made it up to the top of the John Hancock Observatory when he decided to ask her the question that had been rolling through his mind all day. He'd watched while Paige slowly walked around the observation deck, taking in the 360-degree view of Lake Michigan and the night cityscape. When she finally turned to him, she had stars in her eyes and a huge smile on her face.

"This is absolutely breathtaking. Thank you for showing me this." She looked back out of one of the many floor-to-ceiling windows. "The water is so beautiful at this time of day. It looks so vibrant and full of life." The last of the sentence she spoke more to herself than to him. He stepped closer so that they were sharing the same window. She looked over at him without saying anything more. She just stared at him.

"Yes?" He leaned against the framing of one of the windows, folding his arms across his chest.

Paige opened her mouth then closed it, opening it again, only to close it again and look back out the window.

"You don't say," he quipped, trying to bring levity to what she seemed to be having a hard time saying.

A smile lifted the side of her lips closest to him and he congratulated himself on his victory.

"Chicago is beautiful," she finally said. Her voice no longer held reverence, but sadness.

"What's the matter?" he asked, concerned.

"It has been such a beautiful day and you have been so gracious in introducing me to your city. I've enjoyed it more than I know how to express…" Her voice faded once again.

"You're lying, Paige."

She whipped around to face him, stunned. Her mouth formed the word 'what' but no sound came out.

"You have been nervous all day. I don't see how that equates to enjoyable."

She looked down sheepishly, taking a deep breath.

"Is it me? Are you not comfortable being with me?" he asked.

"No. That isn't it…well, maybe just a little bit before."

"Before what?" he encouraged.

"Before I got to know you better, but not today." She still didn't look up at him.

"Then what is it?"

She began wringing her hands together and he took them, pulling them apart. A warmth stole over him that he hadn't felt in a long time. It was peaceful and inviting, if one feeling could do all of that.

He used her hands to turn her toward him. She finally looked up and he saw confusion and hesitancy in her eyes.

"I just don't... I just don't understand."

"Paige, I am really going to need you to finish your sentences. I am a single father to a twelve-year-old, not a miracle worker."

"Everything you showed me today. Every piece of stone, board of wood, every flower and body of water you have shown me that makes your city unique is beautiful to me because of who made it." She pulled her hands from his. "There was a time when I didn't know, let alone acknowledged, the Creator of all of the most gorgeous treasures we have been given dominion over. You may think me a fanatic in my beliefs, but my need to acknowledge and give thanks to God for all of the wonderful things I have experienced today is essential to me. Being able to thank Him is what makes the turning of the leaves, colors of the different stone structures, the sunset and your lake that more glorious to me.

It is because I know Who to thank. It's humbling and awe-inspiring. It makes me feel complete in knowing that I belong to all of this. I am part of a creation that I find peace, enlightenment, beauty and pride in. I'm not saying you can't enjoy these things without acknowledging Him, but to me it's important to know that I am a part of this." Her hand spanned the view of the lake. "That I am not alone or separated by this skin."

She looked back up at him and what he saw in the moisture of her eyes he wanted to, but couldn't even think of how he would begin to tell her. He needed time to get his thoughts together because she was making him feel and search for things he'd long since let go of.

Could he ever feel that way? Could he feel that he belonged to something else, something bigger than him? He, who had created a comfortable life for himself and his daughter? True, it wasn't void of drama. Victoria made sure of that, but it was safe for the most part. He knew what he could control and what he couldn't control, and he invested only in the things he believed would yield more comfort and joy – until Paige.

She was a variable he couldn't control. He thought about her all of the time. He had to fight himself not to call her several times a day or to just sit and stare when he was with her. There was a light and strength in her that reminded him of Rachael, but that was where the similarities ended...

Where Rachael's beliefs and love for God sometimes made him feel left out or convicted because he wasn't ready to surrender the anger that had helped motivate and keep him focused as he built this life, Paige's love for God was a testament to that surrender. Her love for Him was so sweet, it was almost contagious. And her ability to trust Him and see His promised victory in her life, even when she had every reason not to, caused him to wonder if he couldn't also obtain such peace.

She was looking down at her shoes again and he wanted so much to know what she was thinking. He placed his forefinger under her chin to lift her face to his searching gaze. He saw her eyes go wide, startled by his action, and for a split second he saw awareness cross her features. She was looking at him like he'd dreamed on the nights he was unsuccessful in exorcising her from his thoughts. It was the look she gave him just before he bent his head to brush his lips to hers. He wondered if they would taste the same as in his dreams.

He didn't know he was leaning forward and bending closer until her features changed to fright, and she side-stepped him while turning her head.

"I'm sorry. I didn't mean to," he explained in haste, then wished he could have called back the words.

Her brows came together as she passed him an accusatory look then her features relaxed. "You're lying," she said, throwing his words back at him.

He shrugged, relieved that he hadn't ruined the day with his lack of self-control.

"Okay... a little," he said, sheepishly, "but that wasn't my intention. I just wanted to see what you were thinking." He placed his hands in his pockets because he was itching to touch her again. "I never said you couldn't talk about God or share how you feel about Him."

She huffed. "You may not have verbalized it, but it was implied. Every time you shifted uncomfortably, tensed, or quickly changed the subject, you told me in your own way that you didn't want to hear about Him. Now here we are, more than a month of seeing each other almost every day, and you still don't know my world. Not because I didn't want to share it with you, but because you didn't want to hear me. Why are you so angry when you have so many reasons – from what I see – to be happy? Why are you so lonely when you have people that love you in your life? Why?"

Normally, he would have been twenty paces away from anyone that had the nerve to ask him those questions because they were usually dripping with condemnation or condescension, but he could tell that Paige really wanted to know where his turning point was.

He glanced at her, out the window, then back at her. "Come on. We can talk about it over dinner."

He escorted her to the elevators then down the street to a Cheesecake Factory not too far up the street. It was a little crowded, but having made reservations in advance, they were shown to their table almost immediately. It was a small two-seater, towards the back of the restaurant, which afforded them some privacy.

Once seated, their drink order was taken expeditiously and they were free to talk until their food order was taken. Only, now that they were seated across from one another, Mason wasn't sure how to begin.

Finally, he took a deep breath and told her the story of his childhood, which wasn't much different than any other until he was twelve. He shared with her the day he and his mom discovered that his father had another family. It may not have been so devastating if his mother wasn't second in line, and thus not legally married to his father and left without any means to keep a roof over their heads or food on the table.

His mother, who basically shut down after the funeral, was deemed unable to care for him after two months of not raising up from her bed. He'd continued to go to school, eat lunch, which became his one meal of the day, and pocket what he didn't eat so that he could take it home to his mother.

He'd thought maybe they had a chance after waking up one morning to find his mother sitting at the kitchen table. She asked him questions about school and he thought she was on her way to recovering.

He'd raced home that day, thinking she would be hungrier than usual because she was now moving around, but when he got home he found her on the floor of the bathroom, barely breathing. He called 911and from there things only got worse. His mother was committed and he was passed from relative to relative for the next couple of years.

When it was obvious that she was not going to be released soon, his relatives were no longer willing to take care of him, and he was placed in the foster care system.

He paused to give the waitress Paige's and his order.

"The kicker was, my father was the reason my mom and I were in church every Sunday. He would tell me that when he or my mother weren't able to take care of me, God would be there. That I could really only trust in God and that He was loving and kind and stood on the side of right."

357

He paused for a moment. "You know, he would use the fact that God was all-knowing as a form of discipline. He would tell me 'I might not always see you and your mother may not always see you, but God sees everything.'" His laugh was hollow. "Too bad I didn't think to ask God to share with me what my dad was doing the weeks he would travel, so that I could have been a little prepared.

At twelve-years-old, the same age Vivian is now, I was left without a father, then a mother. It isn't that I don't want you to talk about God; I am just having a harder time forgiving Him. I still can barely understand how you were able to get around that trust issue with Him. If He is all knowing, why would He allow someone to do such terrible things to an innocent woman or child?"

Paige splayed her fingers out on the table. She wondered if the answer she'd been given when she'd asked God the same question would mean anything to Mason.

She would try.

"For me, the answer was as simple as, 'free will.' We are all given free will; we have the ability to love and hate, but choose one or the other. We have the ability to help or harm, choosing again to do one or the other. I can't explain why some choose to destroy instead of build or cause pain instead of heal. Everyone has a story and reasons for what they do, but if I learned nothing else, it was that I was given the gift to choose because I had free will. I could choose to allow what my cousin did to me to dictate my actions for the rest of my life and buy into the lie that I was not responsible for my actions, and thus a victim of that same lie that I no longer had a choice.

When God sent His only begotten Son to die on the cross for me, I was given the gift and responsibility to choose. I had the gift of knowing that I had free will and the responsibility to use that will to show others that they too have the free will to choose life over death, to love instead of hate, to hold on to peace instead of anger."

She watched him frown in consternation over what she'd said and decided to bring it closer to home. "Would it mean the same to you if Vivian loved you because it was programmed into her upon the signing of her adoption papers?"

He thought about her question for a full minute and a half before answering. "No. I would rather her love me because she wanted to."

"Even if it meant taking the chance that she could also someday hate you?"

"Yes, but I would try not to do anything to warrant that hate. God knew what would happen. He knew my father was a liar and a cheater. He knew how I would feel about Him, how angry I would be…but it didn't mean enough to Him to keep it from happening."

Paige's shoulders slumped momentarily in what looked like defeat, then she took a deep breath and looked back at him with sadness in her eyes. Nothing more was said because their food arrived and what had started out as a hope of them getting closer came to a bitter-tasting stalemate.

The rest of dinner was spent in quiet thought. Nothing more was said until they were settled in the car.

Paige glanced at him from the corner of her eye. She took a deep breath so she could deliver the next few words with less of a sting. She cleared her throat. "Mason, I know I don't know everything about you, but I am going to have to say this now because of just that reason. You can accept it or not, but I do hope you listen first and react later." She watched him until he took his eyes off the road long enough to nod at her.

"I believe the reason you have such a hard time relating to God is because you've been playing 'savior' too long." He turned to look at her sharply then back to the road.

"Please listen to what I am trying to say, and not entirely on its delivery. It is not my intention to make you upset so please forgive me if I do. As it is in any home, there can only be one Alpha male. If you believe, as you have for so many years, that everything you have has come to you by your hand, what is the purpose in seeking a relationship with someone you think has not much more to offer you than you can acquire yourself? If I may be so bold, I feel that you are arrogant and self-centered about your life and your relationship with your daughter and, if you keep going this way, you will end up alone. But worse than all of that when you die, you are going to hell and you will never see your wife or your daughter again because they will be spending eternity with God in heaven.

This whole time, you have been watching and judging God for what you believe He has done to you, your mother, your daughter and your wife. You have been waiting for Him to give you what you believe He owes you, but you haven't even acknowledged, let alone thanked Him for everything He has given you. Let me just touch on the two obvious ones. Your wife's relationship with God allowed Him to express His love for you through her. She loved you very much, but she was able to love you with a more perfect love because she endeavored to love you as God does. Your daughter shares that same relationship with God because your wife planted that seed in her. She loves you and she prays for you, but she wouldn't have even existed if life were perfect and rosy. If one dynamic had changed, you would not have even known her."

Page paused; she was surprised and encouraged that he had allowed her to go this long without interrupting her. "What I am trying to say, in a nutshell, is God has been trying to give you the very thing you haven't been able to obtain on your own; the one thing that you have been secretly longing for but violently and openly denying. He's been trying to give you peace."

Mason turned away from this woman, this witch, this enchantress that caused him to think he was coming back to life, but all the while was plotting and scheming while she delved into his mind and sat at the door of his heart. He was just another assignment to her. Well, she had delivered what 'God wanted her to say' and he would be damned if he was going to let her know how much her words had affected him. He watched the cars on the freeway. Raindrops that began falling on the window came in and out of focus as he fought to keep his anger at bay.

"Mason?" Paige inquired.

Before she could say anymore he retorted, just a little sharper than he wanted, "I heard you."

The rest of the ride was done in silence, each person caught up in their own emotional cyclone. The moment he pulled up to the hotel she'd checked into that morning, Mason came around and opened the door for her. Understanding that he wanted out of her presence, she murmured a hasty 'Thank you" and got out. Paige wouldn't have had the chance to take back anything if she wanted to, which she didn't, but she was hoping harder than she wanted that he would be able to take what she had to say and know that she only wanted what was best for him.

She watched as he got back in the car and rolled down the passenger window. "Go inside, Paige. You're getting soaked." She had not even noticed the rain.

She turned and walked the few steps to the front door. She had only stepped over the threshold when she heard his car take off. It was as if he couldn't get away from her fast enough. She walked through the lobby and into a waiting elevator.

"Lord, he didn't take it so well. I was really hoping he would have though. I think we could have been friends." She was cut off in mid-thought. How would you have taken being called an arrogant, self-centered male with delusions of grandeur?

She froze. But that wasn't what she was trying to focus on. *That was merely a fact*, she thought about it a moment longer as she pressed the button for her floor, *a fact that I would have been less than pleased to have pointed out to me also. Boy, did I make a sham out of this one...*

But everything she said was true.... this was really getting complicated. She saw now that rushing or helping God in this situation was only going to make it worse if she hadn't already killed it with her mouth.

On the slow trip up, Paige went over and over in her head what she said to Mason and each time it sounded worse. By the time she walked into her room, she was anxious to make right what she had done.

She opened the drapes and sat down at the small table holding her laptop. She picked up her cell phone and was just about to dial when panic hit her. What if she did it again? She sat there staring at the phone in her hand for 15 minutes before she got up enough courage to press the buttons that would dial Mason's number. She listened as it rang on the other side. First nervous, then as the phone continued to ring she began to breath more deeply. Finally, right before the voicemail came on she sighed with relief.

"Um, Mason...This is Paige, Paige Morganson. Uh, I just dropped you off. Oh this is not going well... I called to tell you I am sorry for how I talked to you in the car. I...uh...I..." She should have gone with her first thought to write something down and just recite it over the phone. "I am just really sorry. I get in front of myself sometimes and I keep talking without understanding how my words sound all of the time. I had time to think of it on the way to the hotel and..." She was cut off by a beep signaling the end of this voicemail. She took the phone away from her ear and stared at it for a moment. It read 'Disconnected' after a couple of seconds. That was it.

Good job, Paige. Good job. She threw the phone on the bed, stood up, and turned to stare out of the ceiling to floor length window to the street below.

*　　　　　　*　　　　　　*

Mason was sitting on the edge of his bed when his phone began to ring. He walked over to it as it lit up revealing the caller.

Paige.

This woman just didn't know when to quit. He balled his hands into fists to keep from reaching for the phone. He let it go to voicemail and

361

twenty seconds later was not at all surprised to hear the tone alerting him to a message being left for him. *Tomorrow.* Tomorrow was soon enough to have to deal with her.

Meanwhile, a very strong drink would help numb some of the pain he was feeling.

CHAPTER 46

"Did you call her?"

"No."

"Why haven't you talked to her? Did you change your mind?" Dominy looked over at Brandon, repeating the same question he did almost every day. It was causing Brandon to finally give his plan pause. Not to second guess himself, but give it pause nonetheless.

"No."

"Are you trying to make her think you don't care as much as you do?"

"No. Aren't you getting tired of asking me these questions?" Brandon said, restlessly shifting in his chair.

"Aren't you?" Dominy responded, pinning him with a stare. Brandon went still.

"Is that it? You're trying to wear me down?"

"No. I'm trying to, for the last time, talk some sense into you before I resort to beating it into you."

"Dom, I know what I am doing."

"So do I. You are letting her slip through your fingers by convincing her that you don't care enough to even call her."

"No, I am not," Brandon grumbled, trying to relay, yet again, that he was not in the mood for this conversation.

"Really? Because that is what I would think if I were in her shoes."

"As I said before, I've sent messages and texted her."

Dominy looked at him as if he'd never seen him before.

"Well I hope she's smarter than I am or at least able to read minds."

"What are you trying to say, Dom?"

"Straight up? You're messing up."

"Why? Because I haven't called her ten times a day?"

"No, because you haven't called her at all." Dominy peered at him across the breakfast bar. "What is really going on? Are you having second thoughts again?"

"No."

"Then you have me baffled because I don't see what avoiding the woman you like will do for your chances with her."

"I told you what God said..."

Dominy interrupted him. "Are you telling me that you are leaving this relationship up to God to manipulate?" His question was met with silence. "You can't be that messed up."

"I didn't say that, but what if I did?"

"It is called a relationship for a reason, I don't care what God told you. You relating to her and communicating with her is still a big part of the equation. Right now, all you have is what you always had: one very strong relationship with God. Although I don't really know how strong that could be with you acting like this. He is probably trying to decide if a bolt of lightning might knock some sense into you. Even with God's blessing, you need to work. He won't just hand it to you."

"I know that."

"Then what is going on?" Dominy began talking with his hands, showing his agitation.

"Nothing."

"True, but why?"

"I'm giving her some time." Brandon shrugged.

"To what? Change her mind?"

"Dominy!" Brandon sighed, showing his exasperation.

"What?!" Dominy said, mimicking Brandon.

"Stop."

"Why? You have me miffed man. I don't get it." He took a deep breath, lowering his voice and trying to approach the subject from another angle. "I could understand it if you changed your mind after finding out about the twins and extended family. No one would blame you for backing away from all of that."

"That's not it. What Paige did was commendable. I don't know what her history is, but what little her sister did share shed a lot of light on things. Enough to make me want her in my life even more."

"Then you have me stumped. Why haven't you at least called her so that she knows you're still interested?"

"Because."

Dominy waited for the rest of the explanation. It didn't come.

"Man, I am starting to lose my patience with you. What is it then?"

Brandon blew out a long breath as he organized his thoughts. He knew it was a long shot that Dominy would understand and an even longer shot that he would agree if he did, but he was just tired of the debate.

He waited another minute before answering to gird up his strength and resolve.

"I wanted her to be sure."

"Sure of what?"

"Her choice."

"What are you talking about?"

Brandon rubbed his hands together in an attempt to quell some of his emotions. As much as he and Dominy had shared in their life, he still wasn't ready to show him how vulnerable he really was at this moment. "When I was in Chicago, I got the feeling that Vivian's dad may also have feelings for her. So, I decided to be quiet so she could make up her mind."

"Make up her mind? Between what? A person who flies all the way to Chicago from L.A. to see her and make sure she is alright then doesn't call her and a man that is there day and night to show her how much he cares? I don't know what your plan was, but if I were her, I would choose him."

"Dom..." Brandon said in warning.

"What? I don't know how to say this man. Well on second thought, yes I do. You messed up." Dominy leaned back on the island in the kitchen. His hand moved slowly, then faster as he passionately brought his point to a conclusion. "When you find someone like Paige, you don't stand back and usher other men to your spot. You tell her how you feel and hope she either does or can feel the same way. You woo her, you court her. You don't leave her in a hospital room to recuperate with the attentions of another man, sending her the occasional text."

Brandon sucked his teeth in irritation.

"What is it?" Dominy's eyes narrowed.

"I just need her to be sure that she not missing something back in Chicago."

"Are you looking for a guarantee?"

"No. I just don't want her to have any regrets. I wanted her to know what she was doing. That she's sure."

"So… what if she decides she wants her child's father because she believes you aren't interested?"

Brandon shook his head. "The lack of interest of one doesn't automatically guarantee happiness with another."

Dominy shook his head in amazement. "Either this is the most thoughtful and selfless act you've ever committed or it's the dumbest." Brandon rolled his eyes in annoyance.

"Let me see what my meter says." Dominy bent an arm at the elbow with his palm facing himself. He placed the elbow on his other palm pretending the fingers were guiding along an invisible meter. He allowed his hand to waver for a moment, then let the arm fall to his left. "Beep, beep, beep. Definitely dumbest."

Brandon was not amused by his antics and tried to ignore him, but his next question came too close to the truth.

"Wait, are you hoping she picks the father of her child?"

Brandon didn't answer, nor did he give Dominy any indication that he'd heard him.

"That's it, isn't it?" He came away from the island to lean towards Brandon again. "You were hoping if you gave her some time, she would pick him and you could bow out gracefully and go to God with a clear conscious because she chose someone else."

Brandon remained quiet, giving Dominy all the confirmation he needed.

"I don't know who you are trying to fool, but if I figured it out I'm pretty sure God saw it coming a long way off. For all of your 'talking and drawing close to Him' I think you couldn't be further away right now. You're lying to yourself and claiming false modesty because you are too afraid to go for something you want." Dominy came out of the kitchen and started pacing. "The kicker is, He's already told you. You who have ministered to people, lived by example, been a messenger for those who were too loud to hear Him themselves – including me, by the way – and you knowingly disobey Him."

Brandon stared at Dominy, stunned.

"Don't look at me like that. Just because I have my own issues doesn't mean I'm not listening to you when you share your thoughts and how He uses you. Right now though, I can honestly say you are wrong. I hope you hear me."

"I didn't do anything," Brandon whispered.

"Exactly."

Brandon's head snapped up, his eyes piercing one second then beseeching the next.

Dominy raised his hand to stop the plea. "Man, don't even. You and I have been on this block before, only it was me making the excuses and you cutting them down."

Brandon stared back down at his clasped hands on the table.

"What if things don't work out?" Brandon let the question finally form on his lips.

Dominy was quiet. He looked up and what he saw made him flinch.

"What if God is wrong? Is that what you are asking me?"

"No." Brandon let out an exasperated breath. "You're talking about a woman who has dealt with a lot of death in her life. I don't want to add to that."

"Then don't," Dominy replied in matter-a-fact fashion, "Live."

"It isn't always that simple." Brandon thought hard to find the words to explain his distress. All he could think of was the scene of one of his former elders, whose wife of four years had died due to complications from a car accident. He was distraught, angry, and on one occasion after ranting, he'd broken down crying. At that moment, Brandon wondered if the pain was worth the five years they'd been together.

It stuck with him and he was thankful that his family didn't have to go through that on his behalf. It was just those thoughts that had kept him rooted to the spot he was right now.

"Why?" Dominy replied, pulling him out of his reverie.

"Why what?'

"Why isn't it that simple?"

He looked up at Dominy studying his features. "If Robin died tomorrow, would you still be happy you fell in love and married her?"

"Absolutely," Dominy responded without a moment's hesitation.

"You would be hurt though."

"Devastated."

"But you would still have done everything else. Fell in love, married her?"

"Yes," he said with conviction.

"What if you'd only had a couple of years with her?"

"Even then."

"Why?"

"She makes my life complete. I didn't know it until I met her, but afterwards I had a hard time remembering when she wasn't in my life. The love and everything else we share is a part of me, and if she were to die, then they would still be a part of me and I would rather have the memories than to never have been able to experience it."

Brandon was thoughtful.

"I have two words for you," Dominy said, holding up two fingers respectively.

Brandon quirked a brow, holding out little hope that they weren't the beginning of a repetitive debate he lost with Dominy every time.

"Barbara Collins."

Yep. It was time to send out an APB; all hope was lost. He groaned, but he wasn't giving in without some resistance.

"What?"

"Barbara Collins." Dominy repeated.

"Naw man." Brandon sucked his teeth.

"Yep." Dominy slowly nodded his head to the affirmative.

"Not even."

"Barbara Collins waited a whole semester in the 11th grade for you to ask her out and finally the day before she moved away she told you she wished you would have asked her, but she couldn't wait anymore."

"No she didn't." How many times had he given the same rebuttal? He was going to have to think of some better comebacks.

"I was standing right there. Barbara Collins, the girl that half the boys at Garwood High would have given their left eye and teeth just to sit next to in class, waited for you, mister. She wouldn't be interested in me. She only asks me questions because she had a hard time with chemistry."

Brandon shrugged. "It could have been true."

Dominy pierced him with an exasperated look. "Bran, she got higher scores than you did in chemistry."

Brandon opened his mouth to comment, but Dominy held up his hand in disgust, bowing his head. "Barbara Collins. Barbara Collins." Dominy just repeated, shaking his head.

"Will you stop with the Barbara Collins story? When will you ever let that go?"

"When you act like you learned from it."

"And what was it that I was supposed to learn?"

"Carpe Diem. Not to continue to let life pass you by. To take hold of things you want and that are for you. To catch hold of life and live it."

"I live."

Dominy just stared at Brandon for a moment. "We have just talked about it. You told me God told you – point blank – that Paige is for you. Do you know 85% of people would love to be able to hear God so clearly and confidently? And still, you don't move."

Brandon opened his mouth, but Dominy interrupted him.

"Call her, man. You know better than I do that no one is promised tomorrow. If it isn't a disease, it could just as easily be some type of accident, but if you are gifted with the chance to share your life with someone, do it."

"Yeah, but will she think it's worth it?" Brandon said under his breath.

Missing Brandon's last statement, Dominy started in on him again. "For your sake I hope God has favor on you, even with your foolishness.

If she comes back and by some miracle is still interested in you, I want you to stop speaking all this nonsense about you dying."

Brandon opened his mouth, but Dominy put up his hand.

"I mean it, Bran. Or I'm leaving in the next thing moving. I didn't come back to bury you, but to encourage you to live while you are giving up every reason to do so."

"I didn't give her up."

"Yeah? Prove it. Call her. Ask her how she is doing, feeling. Ask about her family. I don't know." Dominy threw up his hands. "Ask her about the weather. Just call her."

Dominy walked out, momentarily leaving Brandon in the living room to think about their conversation, no matter how convoluted. He placed his head in his hands. When had things become so confusing? He had only meant to give her a chance to assess her own feelings in all of this. Even though God had told him they would be together, he wasn't insensitive enough to assume that she didn't have a choice.

Dominy peeked his head back in the room. "By the way, do you know when she will be back?"

Brandon clenched his teeth, turning away from him. "No."

"Mmmm. I wonder, if you'd taken the time to talk to her, if she would have told you."

"You don't have to go to your room, but you do have to get out of this one," Brandon growled.

Dominy chuckled and went back down the hall.

Brandon took a deep breath. He picked up the cordless phone in the living room, dialing the number he had already done so many times during the past three weeks. This time though, he didn't hang up before it began to ring.

The weeks had dragged on like God had given permission to set back the clock a couple of hours a day. He missed her. He missed her warm smile, the passion that kept the fire lit in her eyes. He missed her eager laughter, not to mention her wit.

Another cycle of chemo and radiation had begun the past Wednesday. He had gone from waking, to prayer, to work, to chemo or radiation, to home with only the occasional bible study and outing with Dominy to break the monotony. He'd attended an elder's fellowship a couple of weeks back, but it only magnified Paige's absence. He'd flat out refused the next fellowship. It was too hard.

What if Dominy was right? What if he had inadvertently pushed her into another man's arms? The beep of the phone transferring him to Paige's voicemail brought his thoughts back to the present.

"Hey, Elder Morganson…Paige. It has been a long time. I hope you are doing well, I've been praying for a quick recovery on your behalf. Umm, well, I was just wondering how you were doing. If you get a moment, give me a call." He rattled off his phone number just in case she'd lost, forgotten it, or it didn't show up on her Caller I.D., then hung up the phone, feeling relieved from finally calling her. Nevertheless, he was also disappointed because she didn't answer and he knew it would be at least another few hours before he could give it another try.

Now that he had given himself permission to call her and think about her, the thought of her not calling back or him having to go another day without speaking to her was quickly dissolving his resolve to keep her at a safe distance from his heart. The wall he'd begun to erect over the past three weeks was leaning precariously. One more nice, hard shove and it would topple.

He shouldn't have listened to Dominy. He shouldn't have let him talk him into giving in.

CHAPTER 47

Paige was exhausted. She felt as if her life had been swept up in a whirlwind of signings, packing, traveling, making plans and catering to two families. Ruefully, she thought of Lady Menagerie's advice to take it easy. Now she wished she had. Her body ached, and even the luxury of being back home in her own bed was not enough to help rejuvenate her.

She'd tossed and turned, dreaming of lying in a hospital bed with a 360-degree view of Chicago, feeling the peaceful weightlessness for a few seconds as everything gave way from under her. She plummeted towards the water, strapped to the bed, wondering if she could somehow break free before claiming the water for her grave.

She woke up, heart beating wildly, with a fine sheen causing her gown to stick to her. She took long even breaths, willing her body to relax from its tense pose as it waited to hit the water.

She glanced at the clock. It was 4:06 am; 6:06 am in Chicago. Her body clock was still on Central Standard Time. It had only been four days since she'd arrived back in Los Angeles, but each one was full.

After making calls and resting on her first day, she'd tried in vain to combat the jet lag: going to sleep early and waking up late. She usually stayed up for at least 18 hours when flying from the East to force her body clock back to PST. Knowing she needed the rest if she was going to make it through the week, she'd tried the opposite approach – gaining more sleep than needed and waking up feeling sluggish.

She'd cleaned and dusted her second day back, talking to her plants and going through mail that Lady Menagerie had picked up for her with the mail key she'd left under the bowl on the table near the door. True to her word, Lady Menagerie had stopped by a couple of times a week while Paige was out of town to water her plants and collect her mail.

On Friday, she tried to take it easy, knowing Saturday was going to put her endurance to the test. Later that day Melanie, Gladys, Marc, Vivian, and Mason were to arrive in town and meet up for a meeting/reunion dinner. None of them would take her up on her offer to cook, so they'd decided to meet at her apartment at 6 o'clock that evening and caravan from there.

Things had moved so quickly her last week and a half in Chicago, she still wasn't sure she'd be able to journal it in any organized fashion.

After being released from the rehabilitation facility with glowing reports from her doctor upon her follow up, she'd been escorted to her hotel by Carmen, who'd come into town to make the final arrangements for her book signings. She would stay in a hotel on North State Parkway, near Old Town Triangle District. She'd picked that one specifically because it had reminded her of her day with Mason, which would have been perfect until she stuck not only her foot, but her leg, arms, and torso, into her mouth.

It had taken two days of constant calling before Mason returned her call. He'd been cool and nonresponsive at first and she couldn't blame him; she had overstepped her bounds. He'd tried to blow off her apology at first, but she stood her ground and nearly begged him to hear her out.

"I was wrong. Mason, I was wrong to say the things I did." Silence met her on the other side of the line.

When Mason did speak, his voice was barely a whisper. "You were wrong to tell me what you thought of me, or you were wrong in your thinking?"

Paige thought about his question, knowing it would set the stage for their relationship – whatever that would be.

"A little of both, so please let me explain before you interrupt or assume anything. I know that's what I did to you. I assumed and prejudged, but if you would allow me, I would like to get to know the real you." she almost tripped over her words in her haste to be heard.

"Okay. What parts did you assume and why?" Mason asked, still quiet.

She took a deep breath, relieved that he was willing to listen. Maybe she was really off the mark.

Letting it out slowly, she began to talk. "I shared with you some of my past in regards to my cousin and my girls. What I didn't share was the hurt and anger that took precedence. I had been betrayed and wronged on so many levels. I used those reasons to fuel and spur my anger and hatred because if I stayed angry and closed off my fortress of hate, I wouldn't have to worry about being hurt by anyone or anything.

For years I used people, abused people, and left relationships before they could begin because I was sure they were going to do the same to me. I managed to achieve quite a bit: high school, college, a job, but I was mean. Not overtly cruel, but I had no compassion or feeling for anyone. I went on like that until my dad died of a heart attack. I sat there in the church during the service, numb – I mean completely numb. It could have been a stranger being buried for all that I felt at that moment." Paige paused to organize the rest of her thoughts.

"It got my attention. My father was a good man." Her voice cracked, but she continued. "He was someone I never considered not trusting or believing. He was always there. He wasn't necessarily an affectionate man, but I never had to wonder if he loved me because it was always implied. Even after my parents' divorce, I knew he still loved me. After I'd had the twins, he allowed me to come live with him and his new wife of a few months without question.

It was obvious he knew what had gone on, but he never brought up the subject. I think he was waiting for me to bring it up, for me to be ready, but I never was. I wish I had. It may have made my healing process easier.

After all that he'd done for me, I sat in that church and felt nothing. I had hit an all-time low in regards to my emotions. I had finally achieved what I thought I wanted: I had successfully locked away my pain behind the anger. What scared me was the lack of feeling I had for my own father. I was emotionally dry." She went silent, but after a few moments she went on. "When you and I went to lunch, before I went into the hospital, we had a conversation about my issues with God and how I had to learn how to trust Him. You made a comment about your stance with God. Remember?"

"Yes." His reply was quiet and short.

"You got angry with me because you thought I pitied you." She was met with silence again. "I was so hurt for you at that moment. I remember that feeling well and I remember some of the places I still had to go before He was able to get my attention. The tears were due to frustration on my part because there wasn't a thing I could think of to say at that moment that could cause you to give up your seemingly life-long pledge of animosity and blame towards Him."

"Why would you feel the need to say something? Why would it bother you so much?" Mason asked.

"Because I was there and I'd heard who I called 'Jesus Freaks' at the time try and convince me that He knew about me and I wasn't alone, but that wasn't my problem with Him. I'd been taught in Sunday school that He was 'there' – where ever that was – but it only helped stack evidence against Him in my case. If He was there, why didn't He stop those things from happening to me? If He knew the struggle I was going to go through, why didn't He intervene before?"

Paige took a breath. She had rambled a little. "Was I completely off the mark?"

She heard Mason sigh. "No. Not completely."

"Well, that is what I thought that day as well, but I used that to assume that you were just as angry and leery of Him as I'd been and that was wrong of me. You may have been able to come to terms with your distrust in Him in a way that worked for you, or you just don't believe in the need for Him in your life at all, which people do every day." Paige huffed, becoming impatient with herself for going around and around. "I assumed you were as angry and hurt with God as I was, but in some way, shape or form, even deep down, wanted to reconcile." As she finished she could hear the hope in her heart coming through her words.

"Is that even possible?" she heard him ask, more to himself than to her.

"You are speaking to one who knows it's possible. I wasn't just a sinner: I had my own fan club. There is a book called <u>God Chasers</u> by Tommy Tenney. I could have written the book <u>God Haters</u> and felt I was justified."

"It's hard to imagine you being there. You seem like a poster child for Him." He said without malice.

"Therein lies my dilemma: if you can't imagine that I was where you are, how can you ever imagine being where I am?"

The phone line was quiet for so long, she was about to call his name to see if they were still connected. He spoke up slowly.

"What was your first step?"

"Considering the possibility that I was wrong, or that there was a part of the story I was missing. So... Mason...can you forgive me?"

"For what? Saying what you did on Friday?" His voice had lost all of its gruffness.

"Yeah and for assuming you believed He owed you something. I abused my title and relationship with Him by leading you to think that He wanted me to tell you about yourself. For that, I am sorry, more than you know, and it isn't just because I got dealt with because of it." She spoke softly.

"Dealt with, how?"

"He had a few choice words for me as well. First, about how I approached the subject with you, which was with condescension and condemnation; second, on how I didn't represent Him in my presentation because my job is to show His love, even when He uses me to chastise; and third, the fact that I thought to chastise you at all. By the time He was

374

done, I felt pretty low – not because He chastised me, but because I lost focus of what I was being used to do." She finished on a sigh.

"Which was?"

"To be an example of His love and what that love can do when it's not perverted."

"Do you mess up a lot?"

"Enough to be grateful that He still thinks I am worthy of being used. Only two, three, or four times…an hour."

Her joke was met with silence.

"I don't know how much… just enough never to forget that I am human and humbled by the fact that He would want to use me again."

"Mmmm."

"Mason?"

"Yeah?"

"I'm really sorry. Will you forgive me?"

"Yeah. I guess so."

"Thank you very much," she said and smiled, allowing a small giggle to escape. "So are we still on to meet up when you come to California? I talked Melanie into coming out with Marc and Gladys. I thought it would be great if Vivian and Gladys could spend some time together. Gladys told me they speak on the phone quite a bit."

"Yes. I made arrangements for us to stay at a hotel near Universal Studios the first two nights. It is a surprise for Vivian and from what I could see, it is closer to your place than a hotel near LAX. We get in Thursday evening and I will surprise her with a day at Universal Studios on Friday. We can meet you for dinner as originally planned, go to Disneyland Saturday, rest on Sunday and head north toward San Francisco on Monday."

"Wow, you won't be too tired? What about Vivian; don't you think it will be a lot for her?" She asked.

"The Universal Studios Tour is still mostly filled with tram rides and I looked up special services at both places. I reserved a wheelchair just in case at Universal, and two at Disneyland."

"I will be fine, though. I will not need a wheelchair. If I get tired, I will just make up an excuse like wanting to ride the Fantasy Land attractions over and over. Most of them are sit-down with short lines," she chuckled, only half-joking.

They talked a few minutes more, going over Friday night's dinner plans, flight itineraries, and directions she would send him via email. The conversation segued to the Thanksgiving holiday and their individual plans, as well as how they'd spent them in the past.

"I heard Vivian on the phone with you last night. Thank you for that. She really misses that with her mom."

Paige wanted to suggest that he could pray with her, but didn't want to compromise their fragile truce. "You're welcome. Hey, if you two aren't too tired, why don't you come to my church on Sunday? Service doesn't start until 11 am"

"I'll give it some consideration," he said, sounding distracted. "Paige, it looks like I have another call coming in. I will call you later this week okay?"

"Sure," she answered and, with that, he was gone.

The rest of the week went quicker than the previous two, hands down. She'd been surprised to see Victoria walk into the bookstore while she was giving a small reading at a book-signing. She sat in the back until it was time for her to sign, then went to get something to drink at the inside café until the line had dwindled to two.

Paige noted her movements with a small degree of amusement, a grin played on her lips even as she sighed in resignation. Far be it for Victoria to wait in any line.

She watched as Victoria strolled up to her. Out of the corner of her eye, she saw Carmen circle closer, giving the woman a wide berth, but allowing her presence to be known just the same.

Victoria glanced at Carmen, sized her up, and just as quickly dismissed her. Knowing this would raise Carmen's hackles, but not wanting to give Victoria the satisfaction of seeing Carmen's ire, she called her over.

She stood up to greet Victoria. "Hello Victoria."

"Hello Paige. You are looking well."

"Thank you. You are looking beautiful as usual."

Victoria inclined her head.

"Victoria Branchett, I would like for you to meet my manager, Carmen Menascal."

The women shook hands, exchanged pleasantries, then Carmen turned to Paige. "I am going to go speak to the store manager." She inclined her head towards Victoria. "Mrs. Branchett."

Victoria turned back to Paige. "I thought I would come and say hello. You had a really good turnout. Is it always like this?"

"Actually this was a little light, but it was almost last minute. I think it went well, considering."

She looked at Victoria expectantly, but Victoria stood there for a moment with her hand on her purse, then she eyed one of Paige's books. Fingering it, she turned it over, read the back then pushed it towards Paige.

"Will you sign this for me?"

Paige, momentarily startled, opened the front cover. "Will you read it?"

"Only if you say something nice." Victoria smiled tentatively.

For the first time since Victoria had started visiting Paige, she felt as if Victoria was being genuine. She smiled back and started to write.

To Victoria, I wish I could have gotten to know you better while I was here. I think I missed out on someone very special. Call me if you ever want to share yourself. Paige.

She scribbled her signature and closed the book back, handing it to Victoria.

Victoria watched Paige as she took the book, then opened the cover to read the inscription. Paige smirked, wanting to shake her head at the challenge in Victoria's eyes.

Victoria slowly put the cover back in place. "Will you have lunch with me tomorrow? I am only in town for a couple more days."

Paige wondered what she really wanted, but knew the only way to find out was to accept her offer. "Sure. Where do you want to meet?"

"I will pick you up, if that is alright. I can be at your hotel by 11:30 am."

Paige saw Carmen returning. "Alright, 11:30 is fine." She gave Victoria the name and address of her hotel. Victoria slightly nodded and then smiled one last time.

"I will see you tomorrow," she finished, just as Carmen stepped back to the table.

"Tomorrow."

Victoria and Carmen exchanged 'goodbyes' and Victoria went to the cashier, book in hand.

"Boy, she is some piece of work."

Paige didn't respond. She just watched Victoria make her exchange with the cashier and exit the building, thinking that the next day would be the true beginning or end of their relationship.

*   *   *

The morning came with a wind chill factor that made Paige shiver just looking at the numbers in the weather report. She was not looking forward to going out in that weather. She could not get back to Los Angeles fast enough.

As usual, she was early and decided to wait for Victoria in the small café attached to the hotel's lobby. She figured Victoria would call when she arrived. No one would get out of the car in this weather unless they absolutely had to.

As she sipped her tea, she forced herself to calm down and accept the peace as she prayed for guidance. Though the woman was almost old enough to be her grandmother, Victoria reminded her of herself before she accepted God's love in her life. She knew she couldn't share this with Victoria. It would only sound condescending to her. Paige just hoped she could say something that would help. Paige knew all too well where she was headed and desperately wanted to help divert her from this path of destruction.

She had just taken her last sip when she saw Victoria pull up outside. She organized her things and walked out through the lobby to the waiting car.

"Good morning," Paige greeted with a bright smile as she slipped into the passenger's seat.

"Good morning." Victoria's smile was less bright, but genuine nonetheless.

Paige sat back as Victoria maneuvered the car away from the curb and into the flow of traffic.

"Well, Paige, you have been in Chicago for quite a while. You must be getting a little anxious to head back home." Victoria didn't take her eyes off of the road.

"Yes, but I would say more excited than anxious. I miss my apartment and my bed."

"What about your friends? I know they must miss you a great deal by now."

"Yes and I miss them. My First Lady threatened to come out here a number of times, claiming that from the moment she arrived until she got on the plane she would coddle me to near insanity. I will enjoy seeing her again, but I have never felt comfortable being given a lot of attention."

"What about the young man who came to visit you? It must be hard being away from you for so long."

Paige turned to Victoria. "What young man?" Paige had a suspicion Vivian shared Elder Brandon's visit with Victoria.

"Vivian told me that a young elder from your church prayed for her when he came to visit you."

Suspicion resolved. *Note to self: Vivian can't hold water.*

"She said he was very handsome." Victoria slid a quick glance Paige's way to assess her reaction. Paige gave her nothing.

"Really? Vivian thinks Elder Tatum is handsome? That is interesting."

Inside, Paige smiled. *Well, the child has taste. He is handsome.*

"That's all you have to say? 'That is interesting'? Do you agree?" Victoria replied as she came to stop at a light.

Paige shrugged. "That Vivian finds Elder Tatum handsome?" she dodged the question.

Victoria went silent. Paige had to hand it to her. She didn't huff or accuse her of acting coy or obtuse. She just stopped digging, but Paige knew this was not the last on the subject of Elder Tatum.

It was only a few minutes before they pulled into the receiving area of a Four Seasons. They allowed the valet attendants to help them from the car and Paige waited for Victoria so that they could enter together.

Paige was on alert. She wondered if she was just being paranoid by the fact this was Victoria's turf and she had home court advantage. She tried to shake the thought; they weren't adversaries or rivals. In fact, she'd hoped they could become friends.

Her angst was only heightened by the formal, dining style of the restaurant.

She was thankful there was a doorman because she was almost afraid to touch the antique doorknob attached to the most beautiful stain glass door she'd ever seen. As much as she tried to prepare herself for the opulence of the Victorian style tea room that had been expanded for fine dining she was awestruck upon entering the establishment.

Rich burgundy and champagne colored the walls in an elegant show of wealth. Paige let her eyes roam around the room as inconspicuously as possible while she took in the plush carpet, panel style windows and chandeliers spaced throughout the dining area.

Once they were comfortably seated at a small table near one of the narrow floor-to-ceiling windows overlooking the lawns, Victoria asked if Paige wanted to sample any of the wines. Paige shook her head in the negative, and watched as Victoria declined the sommelier with the barest nod of her head.

Paige took a deep breath to steady herself for whatever Victoria had planned. She settled herself and looked up into Victoria's waiting gaze. After a few moments of silence, she decided to begin.

"I have to tell you that I find it refreshing that we can be in each other's presence and not feel the need to fill the silence with just anything. It makes the words you do speak all the more important."

"Really?" Victoria looked at her skeptically.

"No." Paige fidgeted with the pendant hanging from her necklace. "Not really. Actually I find it a little uncomfortable and slightly eerie, but I am guessing that was your intent. Do you want to share with me the other reason behind this meeting?"

Victoria continued to watch her then made an exaggerated effort to straighten her place setting.

"You continue to surprise me, Ms. Morganson."

Yep. Here it comes.

"Is that a good thing?" Paige asked, wondering if this was the moment of truth.

"I find it disconcerting."

"Oh."

"I have been watching you, since you walked into Vivian's hospital room."

"So that's what you've been doing? Watching me?" Paige interrupted.

"You seem to have a lot of facets." Victoria went on as if Paige had not spoken. "But what I find most fascinating is that you are direct and open. It isn't too often that I find people without something to hide, especially in your vocation and avocation, as a matter of fact."

"That's unfortunate. I would hope that I would be the norm and not the exception in my line of work."

Victoria peered at her. "Are you truly that naïve?"

"No, I am that hopeful. I am not deluding myself into thinking that people don't lie, no matter the occupation or ministry. I just hope that when I come across their path that we can meet at least on an open and honest level." She stared back at Victoria. "Let's take you and me for instance." She noticed Victoria stiffen as if ready to fend off an attack. *Very telling.* One part of her was chanting "Let her have it! Let her have it!" and the other part of her spoke softly, "What did you come here for?" The wind went out of her sails.

"I was hoping that today could be one of reckoning where we lay all of our cards on the table and you could let me know why you really kept coming to visit me when it was obvious that you were, at best, uncomfortable around me." Paige sat back, ready to listen and hoping Victoria would finally tell her the truth.

"Why would you placate me?"

Paige's grin didn't reach her eyes. "You know better than I that you would not allow me to placate you any more than I would try to preach to you. I would like to dispense with all of this bush-beating though, because I am getting a little dizzy."

The waiter came to take their order and Paige followed Victoria's lead, ordering a salad with grilled salmon.

"I am very particular about who my granddaughter is influenced by. You are in a perfect position to lead her in many different directions. I want to know what they are."

"And here I thought you and I had a problem. That's a load off of my mind. That's easy: I want what is best for Vivian. I want her to live a full and happy life without feeling oppressed or insecure about expressing herself. I am more than happy that she has a relationship with God. I believe it will go a long way in helping her to avoid certain pitfalls."

"Well, unlike you, I don't consider her choice of passion to be as harmless. There are too many variables; too many people who are walking around in sheep's clothing."

"But that is everywhere."

"Yes, but most people don't expect to see it in the church. That's why it is so much more dangerous."

Paige took a deep breath. "I'm not going to dissuade Vivian from continuing to seek a healthy relationship with God. It would be different if all she wanted to do was go to church because she wanted to be needed, but it is more than that. Her love for God is helping her to heal. She finds true peace with Him; something just going to an edifice and singing in it, won't do. She knows the difference, and in this day and age, that is a rare gift. I only hope she keeps it."

"Are you planning on deepening your relationship with my granddaughter?"

"Yes."

"Are you planning to continue to date my son-in-law?"

What? Where did that come from?

"Well, I can say this: you sure do like keeping people on their toes," Paige stalled as she decided whether or not to let Victoria in her business.

Victoria's lips became two thin lines, but that was the only shift in her features.

Paige sighed. "I think I will decline to answer that question."

"You just answered it for me."

"No I didn't and I don't appreciate you assuming anything about me." She lowered her voice, afraid her agitation was showing. "I have been forthright with you, not conniving, deceitful, or arrogant about what I could give Vivian that no one else could. I wasn't expectant of any type of gesture of appreciation and yet you still assume. What do you want?"

Just as she asked the question, a light bulb went off in her mind. Victoria was afraid she would match up with Mason against her. With Paige as the biological mother and Mason, the adoptive father, Victoria's fight for custody would lose even more ground. Victoria had more to lose than she ever did.

"I want you to go away and leave my granddaughter alone. I want you to put an end to any designs you may have on carving out a life with her and Mason and taking the place of my daughter."

Paige was struck dumb for a moment by the sheer desperation unveiled by the woman's words. She blinked, trying to think of something to say that could convince this woman that she only wanted to help, but alas it was obvious Victoria heard and believed only what she wanted to.

Paige sighed with resignation, placing the napkin that was in her lap, on the table.

So much for lunch.

"I won't go away. Promise to leave my granddaughter alone."

She could have denied seeing Mason, but she thought it was a lost cause. "I will be in Vivian's life for as long as she will have me."

"And Mason?" Victoria asked through barely opened lips.

"You want me to stay in Mason's life too?"

"You know that's not what I meant. Why are you being so obstinate all of a sudden?"

"Because love and compassion don't seem to work. You aren't capable of hearing me when I speak to you in loving concern, so I'm going to meet you where you are."

"Is this supposed to be some exercise out of your intervention 101 manual? Save Victoria from going to hell by showing her a reflection of herself?"

"No…but now that you brought it up, do you think it would work? Because I am all out of suggestions."

"Why do you try so hard? I've seen your face. There is no real love lost between us. What? Is there a special going on? Are they giving money for every soul won these days?"

"That's a good one. Maybe I'll tell my pastor about that; he is always urging us to reach souls at any cost – pardon the pun. He has tried just about every other way to encourage us to win souls…why not pay us for them?" Paige crossed her arms.

Victoria just stared at Paige as if she'd grown two heads.

"Mmmm. Well I see I finally got your attention." Paige finally gave in and decided to come to Victoria as straight as an arrow.

"You, Victoria, are not easy to like. Not because of anything you own or because of your looks, but because you don't want to be liked. Sadly, I have glimpsed a few times a beauty in you that makes me want to cry for its inability to break through. Don't get me wrong; I can tell the times you have been trying to use me to get information and the times when you just allow life to be and take in the peace that has been trying to make its way into your heart for a long time.

"I don't know what you have gone through to get to the point where your armor is so thick that not only can you not feel pain, you can't receive love either, but I do know that I have been there and there is a way out if you want it."

"Are you preaching to me?"

Paige interrupted whatever else she was going to say. "Not a chance. I wouldn't dare. I am only to tell you that He misses you and even though you have placed people, experiences and things between you and Him, He will always be closer than you think."

"Oh, so now you are trying to speak for Him. Have you no shame or fear of Him?"

"He doesn't need me to speak for Him. He does that all the time, but sometimes it may be easier for you to hear from a messenger. I am simply relaying the message. Whether you decide to receive it or reject it is completely up to you, though I sure hope you receive it because Vivian needs her grandmother, just like she needs her father and grandfather." Paige shrugged. "That's all. I will let it rest."

"Was this all a part of your assignment?" Victoria's disdain was apparent.

"I'm sorry if I gave you the impression that I was being less than genuine. To tell you the truth, I admire quite a few things about you. I wasn't lying when I talked about your beauty and strength. They are some of your most prominent assets. I could have learned a lot from you, but

I'm not willing to compromise the peace in my heart for it or trade it for a future with my daughter. I'm willing to walk away…or at least catch a cab if you want to cut this lunch short."

"No need for dramatics. Eat your lunch. The salmon here is the best."

Paige picked her napkin up and placed it back on her lap. She had delivered His message. Not the way she was sure He wished, but it had been done nonetheless. She would deal with the consequences later.

"I can honestly say that I have never met anyone like you, Paige. You're so transparent. Aren't you afraid I will use it against you?"

"You mistake me for someone with something to lose. I don't work for you, I am not indebted to you, and you don't have a hell to put me in."

"No, but I have been known to make people's lives a living hell."

"I don't doubt it, but I will still have peace, love for myself, and God. That is something you can't take away."

They sat in silence as their food was brought to them.

"So," Paige continued after taking a few bites of her salad. "When lunch is done today, should I lose your number?"

Victoria took her time, eating slowly as if Paige hadn't posed a question.

When she did answer a few minutes later, it was nonchalant. "I will let you know when I call you."

Oh brother…and she said I was dramatic.

"Eat your salmon before it gets cold."

"Yes ma'am," Paige replied obediently.

Coming out of her reverie, Paige rolled her eyes at the ceiling. *Really God, I know you know all of my weaknesses, but why do I keep getting the ones your people have messed over?* Already knowing the answer, she didn't wait to listen, but instead began to get ready for her first day back at church.

As she sifted through the clothes in her closet, she spied the Mickey Mouse Sunhat sitting on top of her hat box. Her thoughts immediately went back to earlier that day.

The excitement the girls exuded was contagious. She had gotten up earlier than needed, but was still surprised at how fast the time went. She was just putting on her sunscreen when Mason and Vivian arrived. She couldn't get into the car before Vivian began to expound upon her experiences from her visit at Universal Studios the day before.

Paige smiled over at Mason as Vivian went on, only pausing to take a much-needed breath. Paige was warmed by the happiness she saw on the child's face. During one of the few breaths Vivian took, Paige asked

Mason if he had a good time as well. He answered by mimicking Vivian, throwing his hands up in an exaggerated fashion to help explain what a wondrous time he'd had.

Vivian played at slapping him on the back, trying to get him to stop making fun of her. Paige laughed at their antics.

They met up with Melanie, Marc, and Gladys who'd been staying closer to Disneyland because they were visiting both parks.

As he'd promised, Mason had reserved a couple of wheelchairs, but Paige refused to get in it and so did Vivian.

The day was cool and slightly overcast, which made it perfect for a day in the park. Vivian had everything mapped out from what part of the park they should start in, what rides they should go on first, to where they should be inside the park at lunchtime. Everything was organized so well that they were strategically placed for each parade and meal. Paige asked Vivian if she'd ever thought about becoming an event planner. When Vivian looked at her curiously, she explained that people were paid well for the same thing Vivian had done for them that day. Vivian thought about it for a moment then looked at Mason.

"Hear that, Dad? I should be paid for what I did today, but don't worry I can take my payment in candy."

"Oh really…" Mason responded, throwing Paige a look.

Paige struggled not to laugh and turned to Mel, trying to hide her face.

"You know, hon, Paige seems to know so much about event coordinators, she would know better than anyone how valuable the work is that you've done today. I think you two should negotiate a deal."

Paige opened her mouth to challenge Mason, but quickly closed it after seeing the look of expectation on Vivian's face. His steps slowed as she tried to come up with something to say.

"Welcome to motherhood," Mel whispered as she passed her, smiling.

Marc, overhearing the exchange, laughed out loud, taking Mel's hand and swinging it back and forth.

"What about my gifts?" Gladys said with a look of expectation. "I showed Vivian how to dress to be Princess Jasmine. I helped fix her hair and everything cause the makeup artist was too busy to help everyone."

"How about you and Vivian spend the night with me and we can see your skills tonight."

"Are you sure?" Mel looked at Paige with concern in her eyes. "It might be too much."

Paige waved her hand. "A mani/pedi and facials shouldn't be too hard on me. May they stay?" Paige turned to look at Mason for approval. He shrugged.

Vivian and Gladys jumped up and down, happy to have something else to look forward to.

The rest of the day went quicker than she would have liked. She was going to miss spending time with her girls and the rest of her family. Since coming back from Chicago, her apartment was a little quieter than she remembered.

Paige walked through the apartment and looked in on a slumbering Vivian and Gladys once again. This day was one she would remember for many years to come. They'd taken plenty of pictures. It was a cushion to soften the blow of seeing Vivian leave tomorrow.

As she walked back, she noticed that she had a message. She went back to her bedroom and picked up the line, dialing in her passcode. She listened, surprised at hearing Elder Tatum's voice after such a long time. She was even more surprised at the feelings his words evoked. Happiness, warmth, and elation joined the curiosity that had been the main emotion towards Brandon.

She smiled as she climbed between the sheets of her bed. Tomorrow, she would find some of the answers to the questions that had been roaming around in her head.

*   *   *

"You came! Wow...I thought you might be too tired after yesterday," she said to Mason over Vivian's head, as he hugged his daughter to him. She placed her arm around Vivian, hugging her back to her after he'd released her, using the moment to collect her thoughts.

She released her and looked up at her father. "I'm glad you could make it, Mr. Jenson," she nodded.

"Please, once again, call me Mason," he said, looking a little more than uncomfortable, his hands in his pockets.

"Dad needs a hug too," Vivian said, excitement in her voice at being in a new place.

"Oh. Well then...while I am giving them out." Awkwardly, Paige leaned forward, wrapping her arms around his shoulders. She gave a short squeeze and released him.

"So...I see you found your way here pretty easily?"

"Disneyland was great, Dad. Thank you again. I liked Fantasy Land the best! All the pretty dresses…" Her sentence faded as she recalled the day.

Paige and Mason exchanged looks and smiles.

"And then last night, Gladys and Mati and I had a great girl's night. This is the most awesome vacation ever!"

Paige stopped Vivian. "Who is Mati, Vivian?"

"You are," Vivian answered.

Paige looked at her quizzically, waiting for an explanation. When it didn't come, she looked at Mason for help.

He was no better. He just shrugged.

"What does 'Mati' mean?"

Vivian lifted her shoulder looking down. "Gladys and I agree that we don't want to call you what everyone else calls you, but that "Mommy" might be too…weird." She blew out a breath, peeking at Paige through her lashes to gauge her reaction.

"Mati means 'mom' in Slovenian. We looked at a whole list online and we like that one. Is it okay?"

The back of Paige's eyes began to burn and, since her heart was now in her throat, all she could do was nod.

Vivian gave her a quick, firm hug then let her go.

It was all worth it. If she could break out in a song and not be put away, she would. If she could only sing…

"Well, come on inside and have a seat," Paige said, watching as Mason shifted from his right foot to his left foot.

"It's alright, we can find our own." Mason looked almost embarrassed.

"Why? I am not on duty today and Marc, Melanie, and Gladys are already seated. We can sit with them."

"Are you sure? We don't want to stir up anything."

Paige looked back at Vivian, curiosity plainly written on her face. Vivian just rolled her eyes dramatically. Paige had to work hard to stifle the laugh that came up.

Inside the sanctuary, they were greeted by an usher who'd met Gladys on one of her previous visits with Melanie. She did a double take when she saw Vivian. She turned quickly spying Gladys sitting in the pew she'd escorted her to, then turned back around.

"Welcome to Skylight Temple," she said, handing Vivian and Mason a bulletin and then looked at Paige.

"We will join the rest of the family," Paige informed her, while giving her a quick hug. They turned and began to walk down the aisle to the pew where Marc, Gladys, and Melanie sat.

Vivian moved around Paige in her excitement to get to Gladys, Paige held back to allow Mason to sit next to Vivian. Melanie and Marc greeted Vivian and Mason, and Gladys stretched to shake hands with Mason.

As they sat down, Mason gave Paige a look of apology.

Paige smiled back, but was too aware of the closeness.

Paige looked over at Melanie silently asking for strength. Melanie's sympathetic look changed as she looked passed Paige's shoulder.

Paige turned and saw Dominy coming into the pew. She released the breath that had momentarily seized in her lungs.

"Do you mind? Brandon is on duty today. Is someone sitting here?"

"Hi Dominy!" Paige relaxed, flashing a genuine smile. "Nope. Take a seat. How are you? I didn't know you were still in town?"

"I actually left for a little while." He leaned closer in a conspiratorial manner. "Honey Dos. I had to go back and see about the wife. You must have been gone a while if you didn't notice my absence. I can't believe it. Is that allowed?" He wiggled his eyebrows, making her giggle.

"It feels like forever. Let me introduced you to my family."

She began at the furthest point. "Down there is my brother-in-law Marc Miller, and my sister, Melanie. This here is Mr. Mason Jenson, and the two in the middle are our twins, Gladys and Vivian." She turned back to look at Dominy quickly then turned back to everyone else. "Everyone, this is Dominy Harteman." They all waved back to Dominy.

Paige looked back at him. Dominy was good. His eyes were slightly wider, but he took it all in stride, though she could tell underneath he was extremely curious.

"How are you feeling?" Dominy asked looking at Paige, his features growing serious.

Paige smiled stiffly, "Someone has a big mouth." She'd only shared the severity of her situation with Lady Menagerie, only giving her permission to share the information with the Elder's Council. As a 'favor', Lady Menagerie had conceded. Brandon, of course, knew because he'd seen it first-hand.

"Not really. I am the only one he told outside of the Elder's Council, and you are not supposed to know I know so please-"

"How could you betray him like that?" She turned towards him.

"I like you better right now," he said in a whisper.

Paige laughed. "You are absolutely incorrigible. I now understand why he treats you so badly. You ask for it."

"It is all a part of my master plan."

"Huh? What plan?" Paige leaned closer so that she could hear him better.

"My plan is to get him to have a little fun in life."

"Psh, good luck with that plan. Let me know how it goes."

He was going to say something else but the organist had begun playing and the procession of the Pastor and First Lady, along with the ministers and elders, began.

Paige noticed Brandon as soon as he passed their row. He didn't acknowledge any of them, which didn't faze her; you weren't allowed to greet people during the procession. What did strike her as odd was the icy stare he gave Dominy once he had reached his position.

"What was that?" Paige asked quietly

"Oh, you saw that?" Dominy looked at her quickly then looked away. "Maybe he is afraid I will say something I am not supposed to... too late."

Paige bowed her head, trying to quell her laughter. She only managed to silence the emotion, but the tears still came.

Just then the choir began singing, ending the conversation.

Service went forward. Paige could see that the girls were enjoying themselves. Mason, still a little tense, was at least a great deal more comfortable. She didn't even look at Melanie and Marc. They had come to visit before and loved her church almost as much she did.

The only time she saw Mason visibly stiffen was when the visitors were asked to stand. The whole row stood under her coaxing.

Melanie introduced herself, representing Marc, Gladys and their church family in Atlanta. Mason took his cue from Melanie and introduced himself and Vivian.

Just before they all sat down, Pastor Lawrence stood up and asked Paige to stand. She got hot as she usually did when she was called out and given special attention to, publicly.

"Is one of these lovely young ladies the one you donated a kidney to?"

"Yes. Vivian." She wouldn't give anymore, not unless he forced her to and she really hoped he wouldn't.

"It is wonderful to meet all of you. I do hope you will fellowship with us after service." Then he went back and sat down to allow service to continue.

Paige sat down trying to calm herself. She took deep breaths and let them out slowly.

"Do your ears do that a lot?" She looked over at Mason and the small composure she had gained was gone.

She nodded at him, her ears growing uncomfortably hotter by the second.

"That could be embarrassing."

"You don't know the half of it," she mumbled

She heard Dominy cover his laugh with a cough.

"Sssh," she said to him turning slightly, trying to display the sternest face she could. It did no good. His shoulders just began to shake in quiet laughter.

Paige looked up to see if Brandon had caught the exchange. His face was a mix of emotions, but the furrow between his eyebrows showed a bit of impatience towards Dominy.

"Oooooh you are in trouble now. You better behave yourself otherwise Brandon is going to get you," she whispered.

After service, Paige asked Dominy if he would join them. He accepted, but it was contingent upon what Brandon wanted to do.

"I'll meet you up there if it is alright."

She nodded then turned to Mason. "I know we are scheduled to go to lunch, but if you would be willing to go up to the fellowship hall for 20 minutes, then I will not have to endure two months of questions."

He shrugged and nodded.

As they all walked into the hall, Paige came face to face with Brandon.

"Good afternoon, Elder Tatum." There were so many questions she wanted to ask him, but now wasn't the time. After getting his message last night, she thought he would be more pleasant or at least a little less reserved. She was just confused.

"Good afternoon, Elder Morganson. How are you feeling?"

"Very well, thank you. I think you remember my family." She turned to Mason. "This is Melanie's husband, Marc Miller. You've met Mason and Vivian, and here is Gladys."

Brandon shook Mason's hand, and Melanie and Marc's, but his smile brightened when he came to Vivian. She reached up and hugged him, and Gladys followed her example and hugged him as well.

"You are looking very well, Ms. Vivian. How are you feeling?"

"More than 100%." She stood up straight.

"Awww. I see you got the memo."

"Yep," she stage-whispered an explanation to Gladys. "Elder Tatum prayed for me when I was in the hospital. He said that he would continue to pray for a speedy recovery and that I would be better than 100%." She smiled back at Elder Tatum.

Paige was floored. Well, he didn't seem uncomfortable with the girls. Maybe it was just with her.

"It's a pleasure," he said to everyone.

Dominy sidled up to him. "So are you all going to be together for Thanksgiving?"

"No. Melanie, Marc and Gladys are staying, but Vivian and Mason are headed up north."

Dominy just nodded his head. "Well, it was a pleasure to meet everyone. I hope you have a safe trip."

She looked up at Brandon, hoping to see anything that would relay what he was feeling.

"Are you sure you're alright?" Brandon's question was innocent enough but the open concern in his eyes felt a little more intimate, making her feel slightly uncomfortable.

She nodded. "I feel almost as good as Vivian." She pasted on a bright smile for everyone. "How's your family?"

Brandon looked startled for a second, but answered. "They are all doing very well."

"Good to hear." She nodded then turned to see the pastor signaling to her.

"We will see you later. I am sure Pastor Lawrence's patience won't last too much longer." He then turned to everyone else, waving goodbye, and turned to go to the opposite side of the hall.

She was only a few steps away when she overheard Dominy talking to Brandon. "You won't know until you ask her."

Paige chanced a sly look back, but Brandon had pressed his head close to Dominy's to get him to lower his voice.

Paige stood next to Lady Menagerie, eyeing some of the food on the long table used to serve as a light snack during the fellowship hour. She'd brought her family members forward, going through the introductions again. Lady Menagerie listened with interest as Vivian and Gladys regaled her about their experiences the day before, finishing each other's sentences in their haste to relive their favorite parts.

Every now and then, she would glance at Paige and smile. She was also touched by their new name for Paige and said as much. Paige, try as she might, couldn't seem to stop watching Brandon who seemed to be all over the room. She would look up to watch the myriad of expressions flowing across the twins' faces, only to catch sight of Brandon speaking to one elder or another. He looked good – maybe a little thinner – but he was even more handsome than she remembered.

He had been a beautiful sight when she'd finally fully awakened in the hospital. It was his voice that pulled her from the dark cool place that held nothing. No fear, no time, no pain, but also offered no link to thought. It was his voice, muffled at first then smooth and unchanging. It flowed through and around her like a lifeline that she was finally able to grab a hold of and follow out of that place of nothingness.

The concern and urgent pleas were what finally got her attention, urging her to respond otherwise she would have lingered right on the edge of consciousness, happily swimming in the soothing sound that enveloped her.

She'd struggled a few times to surface enough to use her eyes or hands, but it took so much energy just trying to remain cognizant of the sound, she didn't have the strength to push further.

She hovered there for what seemed like forever until it became insistent that she push and, alas, there was a hint of light, but more so came the feeling of a constant squeeze. It was light at first but grew stronger until she realized that the almost rhythmic movement wasn't getting tighter, she was just becoming more focused upon it until she was able to mimic it.

That's when she was pushed head-long into brighter lights, distant and closer sounds, and the deep, warm voice that she could finally identify as Brandon's. Nothing had ever sounded so sweet.

"Paige, did you?" Paige came back to the present with a start. Everyone was looking at her with expectant expressions. Glad they couldn't read her thoughts, she sat up in her chair straighter and addressed Pastor Lawrence.

"I'm sorry Pastor, I…was…somewhere…thinking…sorry. What was the question?"

A hint of a smile crossed his lips as if he knew exactly what she was thinking. "I asked if it even entered your mind the possibility of this moment with these two beautiful, young women."

"Not in my wildest dreams…but eyes have not seen, ears have not heard, nor has it entered into the hearts of men what God has for them," she finished in explanation. A few others at the table nodded their heads in agreement.

They were heading out the door when she felt a hand on her elbow. She looked up as Brandon leaned close to whisper. The breath on her ear was distracting. "May I call you later?"

Unable to do more, she nodded.

"What time?"

She swallowed, hoping her voice didn't relay everything she was feeling. "6 o'clock tonight?"

He nodded, smiled, and was gone just as quick as he'd shown up.

After lunch, Paige invited her family back to her apartment to relax. They decided to watch a movie and Paige made sundaes for everyone. Her sister joined her not only to help, but to get an explanation.

"Was it my imagination or were there sparks today?"

"What are you talking about?" Paige tried to dance around the subject.

"Elder Brandon Tatum. He couldn't keep his eyes off of you and you him for that matter."

"I don't know what you are talking about." Paige leaned further into the freezer to hide her expression.

"You are such a bad liar, even when you are trying to hide your face. Even Pastor Lawrence caught you daydreaming."

"What do you mean? I was just thinking about how nice it was to have my family with me, and how grateful I was for the second chances I saw around me."

"Nice try, Sis. You may have been thinking that at some point in the day, but not at that moment. No...the far off place you were visiting when Pastor Lawrence was trying to get your attention had your eyes soft, lips parted, and breath slow and deep. Not to mention the goofy look on your face."

"There was not!" Paige interrupted with indignation and embarrassment. She could feel herself blushing.

Mel laughed as she continued to tease her sister. Paige tried to push her out of the kitchen, but she wasn't budging. That was how Marc found them.

He leaned against the wall, watching as Paige armed herself with the can of whipped cream, aiming it at Mel. "You wouldn't dare."

Mel retreated slowly and Paige began to stalk forward. "Then you don't know me very well."

Mel glanced around the counter and spying the open container of fudge, picked it up only to have Marc come from behind and snatch it from her.

393

"Hey…what…?" Mel, startled by the interruption, turned around looking at Marc.

Before she could continue he leaned in and stage-whispered. "I can't just stand by and watch you waste a perfectly good jar of fudge, especially after St. Thomas."

Mel opened her mouth then closed it. Her complexion darkened with a flush as a smile tugged reluctantly from her lips.

"St. Thomas? What happened in St. Thomas?" Paige said before the meaning began to dawn on her.

"None of your business!" Mel blurted out in her haste to stop the conversation before it began.

"Hon, why don't I sit with you in the living room," he continued, "It looks like Paige has it all covered in here."

Marc placed the fudge back on the counter, sending Paige a conspiring look before he exited in front of Mel.

Paige couldn't contain the smile, but looked up innocently when Mel threw her a threatening look. "We aren't done, Paige."

"What…I can't even remember what we were talking about?"

Mel lifted two fingers, pointing them to her eyes then Paige's twice, gesturing that she saw through her little ruse before Marc pulled her completely from the kitchen.

Paige's laughter could be heard clear to the living room over the movie.

Mason walked around to the driver's side after Paige hugged Vivian for what seemed like the twentieth time in the ten minutes they stood out in front of Paige's apartment complex, exchanging goodbyes.

"Do you have one left for me?"

"What?" Paige cocked her head to the side.

"A hug."

"Sure." She leaned in, wrapping her arms around him to give him a farewell embrace. She squeezed then release, ready to put some space between them but he held on for just a second longer. He set her back, but not completely out of his embrace.

"I am going to miss you." The sincerity in his eyes caught her off guard.

"Thank you." *Thank you…Thank you?*

"I'll call you when we get back to Chicago."

Paige nodded, beginning to feel a little uncomfortable.

He let her go. She wrapped her arms around herself, unconsciously rubbing away the tingles in her them.

"Paige?"

"Yes."

"Have you…would you ever consider a long distance relationship?"

Paige was speechless. "Uh…um…I honestly don't know. I haven't given it much thought?" She stepped back a couple of paces.

"Have you given it any thought?"

She wasn't dumb. They had been playing around this subject since he'd asked to show her his Chicago. She would be as honest as possible.

"Yes it did cross my mind, but I think it's best if our relationship remains focused around Vivian." Her heart stuttered at the look of disappointment that crossed his features.

He opened his car door then looked back once again.

"Are you sure?" he asked, standing between the car and the door.

Paige nodded. "I'm sure. The distance between our worlds right now is a lot further than Los Angeles and Chicago." She smiled ruefully.

He seemed to consider this for a moment then nodded in agreement. "I guess it could be seen that way. Goodbye, Paige."

She raised a hand as she watched him slide into the driver's seat. He started up the engine and rolled down the window, a smile on his lips that didn't quite reach his eyes.

Just at that moment, something came over her and she knew she had to say what had just been whispered in her heart. She stepped forward, reaching through the window to stay his hand on the wheel.

"Mason, if from this whole thing with me being chosen as Vivian's donor, meeting you, Victoria – from the drama and secrets, to the complications with the procedure – if all of that was so He could get you to possibly consider Him and be open to Him…it was definitely worth it. You are definitely worth it. I see value in you, worth more than 24 karat gold." She squeezed his arm then patted it before stepping back.

She watched as he struggled to express himself, his eyes showing his gratitude and something she couldn't quite make out. His lips lifted slowly into a smile that brightened his whole face, causing his eyes to sparkle in such a way it brought moisture to hers.

With one last nod between the two of them and a parting wave to Vivian, Paige watched as they drove off. She sighed deeply before turning back towards the apartment.

She walked up the stairs, entering her apartment as her phone was ringing. She closed the door and walked the few steps that would take her to the phone, when it went silent. She glanced at the clock on the wall: 6:15 pm. She had forgotten about Brandon's call.

CHAPTER 48

Dominy sat on the couch in Brandon's living room after lunch on Sunday, not paying any particular interest to the made-for-television movie. Brandon could feel his eyes on him, but chose to ignore the looks coming his way, until Dominy started making indescribable noises. After the fourth time Dominy sucked his teeth, Brandon turned off the television and faced him.

Dominy turned to him. "I was watching that."

"No you weren't," Brandon replied sardonically.

Dominy just looked back at him.

"What Dominy? And don't say 'nothing,' because you have been glaring at me and making remarks under your breath for the last hour and a half."

"Are you sure you want to hear this?"

"No, but I'd rather hear coherent words come out of your mouth rather than whatever else you have been saying."

"It's about Paige."

"When is it not?"

Dominy just shrugged. "As much as it pains me to say it this time, I am going to have to tell you, 'I told you so'."

"Please, don't put yourself through any discomfort on my behalf. Just keep it to yourself," Brandon dead-panned.

"You know while I was sitting next to Paige and that Mason guy, I could feel a different type of energy." He started looking uncomfortable.

"What kind of energy?" Brandon asked against his better judgment.

"The kind of energy that draws awareness to an attraction between two people."

Brandon was quiet for a moment. He couldn't deny that he was curious about the relationship Paige and Mason shared. The fact that Mason had shown up with Vivian in the church had thrown him for a loop. He'd watched them sitting in the pew looking uncomfortable, Paige trying to keep her attention on Dominy and Mason on Vivian, but they were doing too good a job.

Besides that, though, there was little that one could see from their outward appearances that would cause a person to think that their relationship was passed friendship.

"So what are you saying, Dominy?"

"If you are still considering pursuing her, you better do it as soon as possible. I still believe you made a big mistake by giving her all that time, but that is water under the bridge. Call the woman, let her know how you feel and be direct about it. No hinting or paving the way for her to guess how you feel; no waiting for God to send a sign or a beam of light with a message in it for her to see you as 'the one'. Just tell her...but there is something else you have to do first."

Brandon listened quietly as Dominy's suggestion whirled into a tirade and only quirked his brow at the additional command.

"Call your family."

Brandon couldn't keep the scowl from forming on his forehead.

"Let them know what's going on. You said you would talk to them after the first cycle was over, but you are now halfway through the second set and you have yet to let them know anything."

When Brandon still didn't answer, he breathed a heavy sigh. "I don't know what you are thinking so you are going to have to tell me."

"I haven't told the family because the doctor said the last report was promising. No need to upset them for nothing. That is why I said I would wait in the first place. In regards to Elder Morganson, I am scheduled to call her at 6 o'clock." Brandon continued to hold his gaze, happy to have answers that he was sure would pacify Dominy for the time being.

"Hmmph," was Dominy's only reply.

Refusing to show his level of exasperation with Dominy, Brandon turned back to the television and turned it on, deciding to ignore Dominy and his lack of enthusiasm.

"You know what I think?" Dominy began.

"I couldn't even begin to fathom what is going on in that puzzle of a mind you have," Brandon shot back.

"Hey, respect the relationship. I haven't steered you wrong."

Brandon threw him a challenging look.

"Oookay, I haven't steered you wrong in the last year."

"How about minute... if I wait at least 50 seconds." He checked his watch.

"Six months," Dominy volleyed.

"Hour."

"Month," Dominy countered yet again.

"Day." A light crept into Brandon's eyes.

"Week."

Brandon let his stare answer his question.

"Alright, today I haven't steered you wrong, so pick up that phone and call your Dad."

"Dad?" Brandon felt panic seize him. His hands grew clammy.

"Don't worry. I got your back."

"I am not calling my dad," Brandon said stubbornly.

"Alright, then your sister."

Brandon was anything but anxious to tell his sister about coming out of remission, but it was much better than calling his dad, who would no doubt hop on the next plane to come and see for himself how his son was doing, and then try and force him to go back with him.

No one's prayer was as good as his father's. No one could take care of the family better than his dad and no one, including himself, could receive healing unless his father was on the frontline to help administer the laying on of hands, send up the petition or war against the principalities that were holding his healing hostage.

When Brandon was young, he would sit and listen in awe of his father praying. Sometimes he would go to the small chapel after school and sit in the back and listen. Other times, when his dad would pray silently, he would talk to God himself: tell Him how His day went, what he was feeling, and what he was hoping for.

As he got older, he became aware of the some of the struggles his father was facing, like the never-ending battle for more money to upgrade, fix or maintain the chapel, the house, the cars, clothes, etc. The prayers were still for the sick, dying, lost and broken.

Reverend Elias Tatum; larger than life and held up higher than he should have been in Brandon's eyes. He still held him in high esteem, but was constantly held at arm's length when it came to sharing affection or emotion.

Anyone who witnessed Reverend Elias and First Lady Ava's relationship were left with little doubt of their love and devotion for one another. Their eyes would tell it all and if that weren't enough, the opening lines of his sermons that spoke of his gratitude and to God for bringing her into his life – which was said with sincerity each time – confirmed it.

The relationship between father and children were different. Brandon didn't know if it was the fear of getting too close to his children, especially after the untimely death of Peyton – their fifth child and Brandon's older sister by 18 months.

Peyton, the most boisterous, willful, and happiest of the Tatum children was never seen without a smile on her face. She seemed to wake up with her mind made up to be happy, no matter what. Brandon, who often felt eclipsed by her larger-than-life personality, loved and worshipped her. She could do no wrong in his eyes. He followed her everywhere and may have followed her to her watery grave, if he had not been spending the weekend with his godparents at the time of her accident.

The scene that he had come home to that Saturday night was dark and void of any of the warmth he'd come to expect in the household. It took seeing everyone's face except Peyton's to know immediately that something was terribly wrong. He questioned his siblings, but only Marjorie would answer him. She took him into the room he shared with his older brother, Elias Jr., sat him on the bed, and tried to explain in a way that a five-year-old could understand that he would never see Peyton again.

There was a pond at the edge of their property, usually gated to keep the younger children from entering without the supervision of an adult. Peyton, taking advantage of her mother's distraction with last minute details for the Annual Church Picnic to be held the next day, snuck out of the house with Royal, the family's golden retriever, to the pond.

By the time the dog was able to draw enough attention to himself, Ava, with the youngest, Makayla, still on her hip, noticed that Peyton was missing. Marjorie told him that their mother ran faster than she had ever seen her move. All of the children, seeing her run out of the house, followed only to catch up as she pulled Peyton's lifeless body out of the water.

Marjorie helped administer CPR while E.J. was sent to call an ambulance, but Peyton never regained consciousness. Marjorie, eyes full of tears, told him she had never heard their mother scream like she did when the EMTs weren't able to resuscitate her either, and never wanted to hear it again.

Brandon felt the loss profoundly. It was as if the sun had been extinguished in his world. He couldn't understand how something like that could happen to a man such as his father who was so devoted to God and his family; but beyond that, he couldn't understand how his father could still pray and serve God as he had in the past.

He remembered the small, closed casket sitting in the front of the church during her funeral. He cried until he made himself sick; not so much because he missed her, but because he wanted to see inside the casket to assure himself that she wasn't in there and that she was with the

Lord as his mother had promised him. It was the only solace he could find as a five-year-old; if she was with God, then it meant he would see her again and nothing meant more to him at that moment than seeing his favorite sister and best friend again.

For months he would hear his mother walking down the hall in the middle of the night, looking in on all of them – two, three, even four times – but never let on just how much of a void Peyton had left in her life or how hard it was to watch him and her other children grow, knowing that Peyton would never have that opportunity. He didn't know any of this until she stayed with him for a week after a session of chemo. It was funny what people could share when they thought time was short.

After a few months, his father began accepting speaking engagements. At first, his father went up a few notches in his eyes. As he began traveling and accepting speaking engagements, the money began to come in and it seemed that the prayers sent up for so long were finally being answered.

It seemed though that the more his father traveled, the more of a stranger he became to his children, until Brandon knew more of his father second-hand than from anyone–on–one time. To feel closer to his father, he began going to the chapel and praying as he remembered seeing his father do many times in the past.

One Thursday evening he was praying when his father came upon him in the chapel, asking him what he was doing. When Brandon told him that he was filling in for him with prayer, his father told him to get up and out. Prayer was not a game or a job. Brandon tried to explain that he was not playing and that he was told by the Lord to pray, but his father wouldn't listen.

Once again deflated and discouraged, Brandon left his father's presence. Instead of embracing prayer as something they could do together, it was made clear to Brandon that this was another place in his father's life that he was not welcomed.

The older he became, the further apart they became, until he stopped sitting in on his father's prayer or preparation for Sunday sermons. He found his own prayer closet sitting on his made-up bed. He prayed silently most of the time. Having been filled with the Holy Spirit at twelve he also prayed in tongues, never forgetting to remind God of the one promise he'd asked for, even at five: that he would see his sister one day.

"Brandon." Dominy's voice shook him out of his musing.

"Humm?" Slowly pulling himself out of the daydream, Brandon looked over at his friend.

"Are you going to call Marjorie, or am I going to have to do it?"

"No, Dominy I will do it." Brandon sighed in exasperation at Dominy's persistence.

"When?"

"Right now," he replied, because he knew Dominy wouldn't take any other answer.

Dominy didn't move.

Brandon got up and retrieved the cordless phone, then looked pointedly at Dominy.

"Could I have some privacy?"

Dominy stared at Brandon for a full minute before he got up and walked out of the room.

He sat there for a full five minutes before he even dialed her number. He hated having to share this news with his sister, but she was the only one he would consider telling. She had been the voice of reason during his last bout with cancer almost eight years ago. She didn't scream or cry, not in front of him anyway. She didn't pity him or let him pity himself. She treated his cancer like the illness it was – something he would heal from.

The only difference this time was that he wasn't as sure that his healing would come before he left this earth, but he wouldn't share that with her. He pressed the numbers that would connect him to Marjorie Sanders and waited until she picked up the phone.

*   *   *

"Now it's 1 to 5. Brandon where's your game?" Dominy called out after side-stepping Brandon and taking the ball to the hoop again.

"Just check the ball," Brandon said, ignoring his taunt. He tried to concentrate as he ran the ball down the half court they were playing, to set himself up for a lay-up. He faked and threw, but it was still blocked by Dominy. The failed shot seemed to take more energy out of him than if he'd made it. He stopped, placing his hands on his thighs, trying to catch his breath.

"Do you want to call it a game?"

"Psh, and listen to you gloat all the way home? No thank you."

"Sorry brother, but if you keep playing like this you would hear me gloating anyway."

Dominy threw him the ball and he threw it back then went to work playing defense. They played for another ten minutes in silence until

Brandon sent an elbow to Dominy's ribs, causing him to lose breath and lose focus as he advanced to the net.

"What was that foul all about?" Dominy whirled on him, surprised by the unsportsmanlike conduct.

Brandon shrugged. "If you can't take the heat…"

Dominy walked over to the bleachers surrounding the park's court to retrieve his bottle of water. He sat down, making it clear that he was through.

"What is this about?" Brandon demanded as he walked off the court.

"I'm not in the mood to be your punching bag today," he replied just before tipping the bottle up to his mouth.

Brandon joined him on the bench, grabbing his own water bottle. He nodded his head to the next group of men waiting to use the court, giving them permission to take it over.

"I take it things didn't go so well regarding your conversation with Marjorie?"

Brandon exhaled a long breath. That was the understatement of the year. "Nope." He took a swig.

"Care to elaborate?" Dominy said after it was clear Brandon wouldn't.

"Nope."

"Why are you being so stubborn about this? It isn't like you."

"Why are you on my case? You were on me like white-on-rice until I called her and when I do, you want a play-by-play."

"I'm your friend. I care about you."

"You're nosey."

Brandon's retort was met with silence. Well, almost silence. He could hear Dominy counting under his breath.

"Brandon. I know we are tight, but you need your family's support. I don't care how close we are, there are only so many hugs I am going to give you."

Brandon tried hard to suppress the smile working at his lips. He wasn't successful so he shook his head to hide it. He wanted to be mad at Dominy; mad at him for convincing him to call Marjorie and Paige. Neither conversation did anything to dispel his disquieting emotions.

Marjorie took the news hard and barely managed to stifle the sobs in her voice. It tore at his heart to hear her pain, not only for him, but because he hadn't told her sooner. They spoke for more than an hour, with him trying to placate her by promising to keep her informed and follow the doctor's orders to the 'T'. She wanted to call everyone immediately and have the family band together for his sake, but he begged her to give him a little more time. He hated the thought of his mother finding out the news from anyone but him.

"You have 48 hours to tell mom, then I'm going to."

"Marjorie…"

"Don't 'Marjorie' me," she said, mimicking his whine. "You have 48 hours to call mom and tell her, otherwise I'm doing it."

"Fine."

After they hung up he looked at the time, noting that it was a quarter after 6 o'clock. Not really in the mood for idle chit-chat, he called Paige more out of obligation than desire.

After his call was redirected to her voicemail, he breathed a sigh of relief and hung up without leaving a message.

He knew she had Caller I.D., but it was now a day later, and she hadn't called him back.

Maybe she didn't want to talk to him. Maybe she had decided to go after the ready-made family. He shook his head, trying to expel the morose thoughts before they took over.

"You know how much I hate causing my family pain. I would do anything to keep them from going through what they did eight years ago."

"I understand, Bran, but don't you think it's unfair to you and them by keeping it from them? No…never mind. We've already been through this. I think it is unfair and selfish of you to go through this without letting them know what's going on."

"You are more than welcome to your opinion." Brandon shrugged.

"So…did you call Paige?" Dominy asked as a way to change the subject.

"Yep. She didn't answer the phone and she hasn't called back." Brandon added, answering Dominy's next question before he could open his mouth.

Dominy picked up his gym bag and stood up from the bleachers. "Come on, I'm starved. Let's get something to eat."

Relieved that the conversation was over – at least for the time being – Brandon collected his things and followed Dominy to the car. His appetite had waned the week before, but was back with a vengeance now that the light nausea that had accompanied his last round of chemo had abated.

*   *   *

Brandon laid across his bed, glancing at the clock, trying to decide whether he would give her another day to call back, or if he would call before his eight-thirty p.m. courtesy curfew.

He sat up in bed, reaching for the phone just as it rang.

"Hello?"

"Brandon?"

"Hi, Paige." He tried to keep the excitement out of his voice.

"Did I interrupt you?"

"No, not at all." Maybe he'd tried a little too hard. *Relax man. It is only a call. ...Yeah. One I have been waiting for since...forever.*

"You sound a little distracted. Are you sure you don't want me to call back later?"

"I'm sure. How are you doing?"

"Well...very well. I feel good, getting plenty of rest thanks to Lady Menagerie, who has been acting more like my warden than my friend."

He heard the smile in her voice and it struck him then how much he missed it, how much he missed her.

"I hate to sound like a looping background, but you should take it easy."

"Yeah, yeah, yeah. So I won't go out and run a few miles or go to the gym."

"You don't go to the gym anyway."

"See then, what is the big deal?"

He was relieved that they could fall into the same light bantering as before. It made all the days they hadn't spoken melt away.

"Maybe I couldn't put a word in for you with Lady Menagerie?"

"You would probably convince her that I needed more rest. Stay away from Lady Menagerie. Ya' heard me?"

"I hears you, Boss Lady," he said, chuckling.

"Hmmm. Now that's more like it." She started giggling. "How have you been, Brandon? Visit anywhere interesting lately?"

He could tell she was dancing around the more serious subjects, but they would come. It was inevitable.

"Not unless you call Tarzana interesting. I had to drop off some paperwork at someone's house. Boy, you can really get lost up in those suburbs. It seems like all the streets are dead ends."

"Yeah, quite a few streets are like that. It encourages privacy."

"Duly noted."

They spoke for a few more minutes about the San Fernando Valley and the outlining areas that were the best to raise a family and hide out from the media. The conversation transitioned to her career and her anonymity, then her next travel dates and to her family.

"Vivian really seemed to take to you," Paige stated. She verbalized her curiosity regarding the girl's reaction to him on Sunday.

"When I was Chicago her father asked if I could go up and pray for her." He started by way of explanation. "She is precious. I know she didn't grow up knowing you, but I see a lot of you in her, especially her zest for life."

Paige was momentarily speechless. She wouldn't have believed that Mason asked Brandon to pray for Vivian if she'd heard it from someone else. She wanted to ask how it came about, but instead commented on the latter part of his sentence.

"Thank you. That means a lot to hear you say that. She is refreshing, like a ray of hope. She is so on fire for the Lord, and at such a young age. She is inspiring."

"You have a beautiful family, Paige. You should be proud."

"I am, and I'm grateful. They are a gift I never expected. What about your family? Is everyone well?"

"Oh yeah. In fact, I wouldn't be surprised if they came to visit before the end of the year." *Actually I'd bet on it.*

"I can't tell by your voice; is that a good or a bad thing?"

"For the first few days it's good. After the third day, it isn't as good. By the 5th day, good isn't even in the running as a word I would use to describe their visit. Don't get me wrong, I adore my family. But I also love my privacy and with my family, there is no such thing."

"Well, I don't think I need to explain my sister to you. She is the same with everyone: protectively loving…or is it lovingly protective. Whichever sounds the best. You pick."

The conversation went on for a while longer, and just before he was going to end the call, Paige interrupted him.

"Brandon?"

Here it comes. "Yes?"

"I need to know something."

"Okay."

"Why did you stop calling me after you visited? Was it because you found out about my family, my twins, Mason?"

"Yes and no," he answered with very little thought.

"Oh."

"I have to be honest: finding out that you have twins was a shock, but probably not nearly as much as it was for you."

"How did you know? ...Melanie." She finished more to herself than him. "Did you keep in touch with Melanie?"

He paused, not sure if he would be betraying her sister's trust. "Mmm...maybe you should ask your sister."

"Your answer was a bit ambiguous. Could you elaborate?" she asked quietly.

"I figured things were complicated enough without me adding to the mix."

"Why would your continuing to stay in contact with me complicate things more? I thought we were becoming good friends, especially after you came to visit me...prayed for me...talked me through the darkness."

"How much did you hear?" Brandon's heart began beating rapidly. He'd known he'd crossed the line of friendship with some of his endearments, but he had so desperately wanted her to wake up while he was there. He wanted to see her look at him with those golden eyes, to make sure she was going to be alright. Who was he fooling; he crossed the line as soon as he stepped on the plane to go see her.

"Mostly just your voice, at first I couldn't make out anything, I just heard the warm timbre of it calling to me, as if it were a rope pulling me away from the darkness. I could sense you pleading and that is what caused me to surface. You sounded anxious and it got my attention. I didn't want you to feel that way because of me."

"Why not for you?" he asked, curious about her response.

"Because either way, I was going to be alright."

If he didn't know for certain that she was the one for him before, he would have had a hard time convincing himself otherwise after that last statement. Her confidence in the Lord was like a colorful garment that only enhanced her beauty the more, both on the inside and out.

He chose to sidestep her question for now.

"You know before you left, you accepted my offer to take you to a matinee. Would you still like to go?"

"Why didn't you answer my question?"

"How about I answer your question after the movie, say... on Saturday?" he wagered, stalling for time.

"How about you tell me why you thought staying in touch would make things more complicated, then I will consider going to the movies with you on Saturday."

He started laughing. He'd forgotten about the more willful side of her personality, but then, he ventured, she may not have survived without it.

"Alright you win, but I would prefer you withhold judgment until I am done with my explanation."

"Fair enough," she answered easily.

He took a deep breath wondering if there was yet a way to answer her question and keep his feelings to himself. After a few moments he shrugged, deciding to be open and honest.

"I didn't know what your relationship was with Vivian's father and so I chose to step back and give you some time to grow accustomed to... your new family."

"Well...it's going to take more than a few weeks to...how did you say...*grow accustomed* to being the mother of twins and bonding with their families. Are you sure you want to wait that long before we continue with our friendship?"

"I guess that would depend on the type of relationship you are considering with Mr. Jenson."

"Ah, now we are getting somewhere. If you wanted to know, Brandon, why didn't you just ask?"

"I didn't want you to think I was assuming anything..."

"I would say you assumed a lot more because you didn't ask me," she said, interrupting him. The line was quiet for a moment.

"Are you upset?"

He heard her sigh. "No. Just a little disappointed. It would have been nice talking to you while I was in rehab, twiddling my thumbs."

He felt two inches tall. He wanted to make it up to her. "If you are available on Saturday, I would like to take you to the movies and an early supper. Will you go with me?"

"Is this a date?"

"Ummm...not necessarily," Brandon said, backtracking.

"So you still would have asked me to go to the movies with you if I told you that I'd decided to form a more significant relationship with Mason than mother of his daughter?"

"Well that's pretty significant, don't you think?"

"Yes, but you didn't answer my question...again."

"Mmmm...no, I wouldn't have asked. I don't want to give Mason any cause to be jealous."

"You think he's so insecure that he would be jealous of my friendship with you?"

"Not so much insecure as smart, but enough about Mason. Will you go out with me on Saturday?" He started chuckling at the ridiculousness of the situation.

"My sister, Marc and Gladys won't be leaving until Sunday morning. Would it be alright if they came along? It will be a while before they come back this way."

Brandon didn't quite know what to make of her request, but she had been more than forthcoming, so he didn't see any reason why she would feel the need to hide behind her family. "Sure."

"Then I would be happy to go the movies and dinner with you. Oh, by the way, what are you doing for Thanksgiving?"

"I was invited to Pastor's Lawrence's house, since I won't be going home and Dominy is going back for a while to spend time with his wife."

"Good, then I'll see you then as well. I thought it would be nice to have my immediate and church family together for Thanksgiving."

"You are very fortunate."

"Yes I am."

"Paige?"

"Yes."

"Thank you for agreeing to go out with me."

"Ah, that's what friends are for."

He was quiet. He wanted to ask her if that was all she saw in him, but he knew he hadn't given her reason enough to see more. He would.

*   *   *

Thanksgiving was a festive affair. Brandon couldn't remember the last time he laughed so hard. Between childhood stories, college hi-jinks, and Pastor's and Lady Menagerie's own wedding ceremony that almost wasn't due to a misunderstanding, his stomach ached.

Brandon was surprised to find that his pastor had almost allowed his pride to come between him and Lady Menagerie, but the fact that he'd placed that same pride aside and took it one step further by suggesting that they reaffirm their love by restating their vows every year caused Brandon to reassess his recent behavior regarding Paige. What would be so bad about Paige knowing how he felt?

"What do you think keeps your marriage so strong?" Paige asked Pastor Lawrence.

"No matter how angry or frustrated I may get with her, I consider what life would be like without her; how many things I would miss. Like her smile, when it's on full-blast, because of something I was able to do for her. When I look at my beautiful daughter. There is a peace I feel when I walk into my home; the fact that if I don't get a hug or a kind word from anyone else that day, she will give me one, and knowing beyond a shadow of a doubt that she is the one God has given me to love and cherish. There is also the fact that she has my back, she makes a mean German chocolate cake and she can put a smile on my face with one word or action." He took Lady Menagerie's hand and kissed it, looking deep into her eyes during the last of his answer.

Brandon could have sworn that if they all left the table, the two wouldn't have noticed. Dana cleared her throat noisily. "Elder Paige, we have learned not to ask them questions like that when there is company because they get lost in their own little world."

"That's alright. I think it's wonderful after so many years to be that in love."

"Well, I would rather just have it implied."

"Dana, your father and I would have thought you would be more than used to it by now."

"I am, but it's still embarrassing when we have company."

"Well I say more power to you and congratulations on a healthy marriage," Marc called out.

Paige, who'd been seated opposite of Brandon, looked up to catch Brandon eyeing her. He couldn't seem to take his eyes off of her, but if he didn't get a hold of himself soon, she may think he'd gone stalker on her.

He forced himself to look away and not look back until she said or did something that would warrant his gaze. Thirty seconds later, she asked if he could pass her the bowl of mashed potatoes and he was right back where he started. He tried to concentrate on the conversations going on around him, but nothing held his attention greater than how delicately she ate.

Awww, Lord, help me out! Make her ugly for a moment or make her do something unattractive so that she is not such a distraction. This is ridiculous. By the end of the night, she is going to think there is something seriously wrong with me and the pastor will never invite me to another holiday meal again.

"Brandon." Brandon pulled himself from his petition as Pastor Lawrence addressed him. "Will you be spending Christmas with your family this year?"

"Yes. It looks like they've all decided to convene here."

Lady Menagerie's eyes went wide as what he said sunk in. "All of them?"

Brandon nodded. "Aaaaalll of them."

"Wow," Lady Menagerie whispered on a breath.

"Why, how many are there in your family?" Paige asked.

Brandon took a breath. "There is my mother and father, Reverend Elias and Ava Tatum. There is Elias Jr., Sara Tatum-Connor, her husband, Samuel, and their three boys and girl, Samuel or S.J., Ryan, Philip, and Sarah. There is Theodore Tatum, his wife, Everzie, and their little girl, Reina. Next is Marjorie Tatum-Brown, her husband, Paul, and their two girls Brianna and Sydney, myself and last but definitely not least, Makayla Tatum.

"Wow," Paige exclaimed more to her sister, Melanie, than to him, "It must have been nice to be part of such a big family."

"Yes…It had its good and challenging points."

"What is a good one?" Paige asked.

"You never had to worry about people not showing up to your birthday party."

His remark elicited a laugh from the table.

"Challenging?" Melanie inquired.

"Sometimes you could get lost in everything that was going on."

"Did you get lost?" Paige asked, her voice soft and comforting even before he answered.

"No, not really. I kind of kept to myself."

"How did they let you?"

Brandon shrugged, not wanting to put a damper on the night by bringing up his sister, Peyton. "I liked to read and study, something that was usually done alone."

Everyone nodded their head and went into a quiet reverie except Pastor Lawrence, who seemed to know what he was feeling. Brandon didn't doubt it since he and his father had been friends for so long. Pastor Lawrence winked at him and he smiled back.

After dinner, they all retreated to the back, closed-in porch. The house, situated on a hill, boasted a view of downtown Los Angeles on a clear night, and this evening allowed them a view of the Coliseum and some of the taller buildings in the downtown skyline.

Dana broke out the board games and the rest of the evening was spent in the emotional high of winning or low of losing, but always with a great deal of laughter, teasing, and cajoling.

I am home, was what continued to go around and around in his head.

Just before he left, he asked Pastor Lawrence if he could talk to him in private. Following him into his study, he sat in one of the wingback chairs facing the man he'd come to welcome as a surrogate father.

"I would like to start seeing Paige. I wanted to know if you had anything to say about that."

"In what way?" Pastor Lawrence said, steepling his fingers together.

Brandon shrugged. "Deeper than a friendship."

Pastor Lawrence was quiet for a moment. "How are you feeling?"

"Good."

"How were your last test results?"

"The doctor says it looks promising. I don't think I would consider starting anything with Paige, no matter how much I would like to, if my last test came back negative."

"Why not?"

"I don't think it would be right. I wouldn't want to develop anything with her, only to hurt her." Brandon was sure this was Pastor Lawrence's same concern.

Pastor Lawrence leaned forward, watching Brandon with such intensity he began to squirm.

"You know, your father and I found ourselves talking a few years ago about Peyton. He told me of his love for her and how he cherished her, then of the heartbreak of losing her so young. I asked him if he would have rather not had her than to hurt the way he still obviously was. He didn't even think before he told me 'no'. He said losing Peyton was devastating, but there were things that she brought his life in that short time that caused him to look at life differently and do things differently.

The reason I share this with you is to show you that you can't allow your presumptions about tomorrow to dictate what you do today. No one knows and no one is promised, but they don't allow that to keep them from loving and living. Don't let it be any different for you. I am happy you are taking this step."

"Thank you."

"I also know that I don't have to remind you that Paige is like a daughter to me."

"No sir." Brandon met his level gaze

Pastor Lawrence's stern features softened as his face transformed into a smile. "See that it stays that way."

Brandon nodded.

*   *   *

It didn't matter that he'd been awakened with his spirit praying at five-thirty a.m. Saturday, the morning still went by in a blur. Every now and then, he berated himself for being so anxious, and would force himself to slow down.

The excitement racing through his veins wouldn't allow him to keep still for too long, so by the time 9:00 am came around, he had cleaned the floors of the apartment, finished four loads of laundry, changed the bedding in the two bedrooms, showered, dressed and changed twice.

Finally exhausted, he sat on the couch to catch his breath, and dozed off until his phone woke him up ten minutes before he was to leave.

"Hello!"

"Are you alright?"

"Yeah….yeah…uh…what time is it?"

"Ten 'til eleven."

"Awwww man…phew." Brandon got up slowly, placing his hand over his heart as if that could slow down its frantic beating.

"What's the matter? Are you alright?" Dominy repeated, concern in his voice.

"I dozed off and thought I'd over-slept. It would have been a disastrous way to start a first date. I can't tell you how happy I am that you called."

"Hey, not a problem. You know I had to at least call you and see if you were one big, walking nerve."

"Ha…ha, I can always count on you to take advantage of a situation. How's Robin? Has she gotten tired of you yet?"

"Touché…she is doing well. She actually misses you and wanted me to let you know that she will be out there as soon as you make time for her. She was a little hurt to find out that she was no longer your number-one girl."

"I knew I kept you around for a reason, even if it is only because your wife is so smart. Tell her she will always be my number-one girl, no matter what."

"Whatever…so have you decided on where you are going to take her for dinner?"

"Well, this is her sister, brother-in-law, and daughter's last day in town, so we are making it a family outing."

"Wow. You work fast. You went right past courting Paige, to courting her family."

"And now I know why it has been so peaceful around here. Bye, Dom. I will tell Paige you said 'Hi'."

He could still hear Dominy's laughter as he hung up.

He checked himself in the mirror in the hall, picked up his keys, and walked out the door.

Two and a half hours, one movie, one hug and a stomach-cramping set of laughs later, he found himself sitting next to Paige at a family-style restaurant that served American cuisine.

He concentrated on getting to know her family and answering questions about his family, his job and his work at Sky Light Temple. He was as open as he could be and, once the initial barrage of questions was answered, he relaxed enough to observe the dynamics of their relationship with one another.

Paige seemed content to allow Melanie to lead the direction of the conversation. Topics ranged from some of the characters in the movie they watched and how well they portrayed some of the gospel pioneers, to comparisons of the Pentecostal churches in the early 1900s and those at the end of the century. He watched how she sat back listening to the discussion, participating every now and then but mostly enjoying the banter between Melanie, Marc, and himself, especially when it came to their comparisons of the spiritual power wielded by the church mother during the 1930s through 1980s. Each had their opinion of what would help fill in the gap left in the church by the last generations of mothers, but they all agreed on the need for more teaching of the spiritual gifts.

She was different than the bold, opinionated, independent woman she exhibited during services and with the elders. She was contemplative, softer in some ways, but her presence was no less demanding of attention. If anything his attention was drawn even more to the serene creature that shied away from acknowledgments, but whose very life demanded that people take notice of the spiritual boldness she exuded with each hour of service, mentoring, and prayer.

He knew it might be early to think of such things, but he wanted her to meet his family. He wanted to see the expression on his dad's face when he introduced him to a woman who took so much joy in life and God.

Once he pulled up to her apartment building, he exited the car to give Marc, Melanie, and Gladys a hug and to pray for a safe return. They, in turn, expressed their appreciation in being included in the day and their delight in meeting him. They reminded him of how much he missed his family.

Paige hung back as the rest of her family walked in the building. She turned to him, her arms crossed in defense against the wind that had picked up.

"You should go on inside, Paige. I don't want you to catch a cold." He was reluctant to relinquish her for the evening, but didn't want to watch her shiver.

She shrugged her shoulder slightly. "It was only a breeze."

He shook his head at her stubbornness.

"You know, your stubbornness is one the first things I noticed about you."

She looked at the ground for a moment then back up at him. "I am not quite sure how to take that." She hugged herself tighter.

He instantly wished he could take it back. He hadn't meant to make her feel uncomfortable.

"It's just a fact. You just reminded me of our first meeting." *This wasn't happening.* It seemed that each time he opened his mouth, he made it worse. He really just wanted her to go inside.

She stared at him as if she were expecting him to elaborate. When he didn't, a puzzled look settled on her features.

"Okay… well…then…" She slowly started taking steps toward the building.

"Paige?"

"Yep?"

"I had a really good time with you and your family today."

She looked at him, cocking her head to the side. "Really? So did I." She paused and he was about to speak when she continued, "Until about thirty seconds ago."

"Oh." He looked down, trying hard to think of what to say to undo his faux pas. "Do you want to know what the second thing was that I noticed about you?"

Her eyes narrowed briefly. "Mmmm...I don't know, but if it is that I am spoiled or selfish, we can end this conversation. I don't know how much more facts about myself I would care to hear."

"It was your eyes. They were like looking into liquid gold. I've never seen anything so beautiful."

He watched as the pensive expression on her face was replaced with one that was more thoughtful.

"So I am a stubborn woman with beautiful eyes." She watched his color darken by his flush. She expected an apology, but it never came.

He shrugged. "See it from my point of view. I walk into a hallway only to hear you tell your pastor that you don't want to meet me. Then you tell me that you are sorry, not for not wanting to meet me but because you got caught trying to ditch the introduction. Not really the best first impression."

He saw her grimace. "Did I hurt you a lot?"

He lifted his shoulders and kept his hands in his pockets. "Not enough to keep me from wanting to be your friend." He wasn't about to tell her about the dreams that had kept her on his mind that first week.

"Why?"

"You don't want to be my friend?"

Her shoulders shook with laughter. "You know you have an annoying habit of answering a question with a question when you don't want to answer."

"And yet, you still insist on me answering."

"Blame it on the stubborn streak in me. Why?" she pressed again.

"I figured Pastor Lawrence knew what he was doing by trying to get you to show me around a new city. He probably knew I wouldn't have to worry about you trying to take advantage of me or corrupting me, so I thought I would give you the chance to redeem yourself."

Paige interrupted him. "Are you always so arrogant?" She placed her hands on her hips, her eyes turning a shade darker.

"Only when I'm teasing."

He watched as she took a step closer, searching his eyes for a sign that he was doing just that. After a few seconds, she leaned back and a smile lit her face. "You had me going there for a moment. I was about to start wondering how my discernment was so off. Not just mine, but my pastor's as well."

She watched as he rocked back on his heels, but offered no more than a quirky smile.

"You're not going to tell me why, huh?"

He hesitated for a moment. "If I told you that something in you touched me, would you take that as my answer?" He held her gaze, hoping she would relent.

"If it's the truth ...for now," she said saucily. She turned to go inside.

"Paige," he called after her. He really wasn't ready for her to go yet.

She turned back around, having only to take a step. "Yes?"

"I really did have a great time with you today."

"So did I. I wasn't too sure you were having such a good time at first. I haven't learned to read you yet."

He immediately picked up on the 'yet'. Did that mean she wanted to?

"Your family is fun. Do you always joke and laugh like that?"

"They downplayed it a little because they didn't know how you would react. I know they weren't what you expected, but I thank you for being so gracious about including them." She smiled shyly.

"I expected at the very least to share a movie and a meal with you and your family, and my expectations were exceeded by great conversation and the opportunity to see you in a different environment. If you allow me to, I would like to have another chance to do so."

A gleam entered her eyes. "Well I don't know…" She began to shake her head. "My family is leaving. It may be a while before we can all get together."

"I'm willing to take my chances with it just being the two of us." He put his hands in his pocket to still the nervousness in them while trying to appear nonchalant.

She laughed. "Alright then, you are on. I will go out with you again."

"How about tomorrow at four? There is this place I want to show you."

She hesitated for a moment. He wondered if she thought seeing him two days in a row was moving too fast.

"Okay, but not for too long. I need to put in a few hours at the computer."

"Tomorrow is Sunday," he said, reminding her that it wasn't really a work day.

"My writing isn't work; it is more like ministry. It gives back to me and I have put it off all week with my family visiting."

He nodded his head in acquiescence. "Good night, Paige."

"Good night, Brandon." With that, she turned and walked up the few shallow steps to her apartment building. He watched her until she disappeared inside.

He wanted to pump his fists. Not only had this day gone well, but he was also going to see her again tomorrow. He knew he was pushing things by asking to see Paige a third time within a week, but his next round of chemo was due to start on Wednesday, effectively ending any socializing for a few days.

He was almost giddy enough not to fear calling his mom later. Marjorie had given him some additional time, nearly ecstatic when he had called to tell her about Paige and her family. He knew it was wrong, but

417

he was desperately in need of the time to think of some way to break the news.

*   *   *

"How did it go?"

"Good morning to you too."

"Don't give me that. You didn't call me, so I am calling you."

"Early, I might add."

"Not over here."

Brandon turned onto his back so that he didn't have to put as much effort into speaking.

"So how did it go? What did your mom say?"

"She was upset that I didn't tell her sooner."

"Mmmhmm, and?"

"She wasn't convinced with my doctor's report. She wants to see for herself."

"Are you going to continue to make this harder than pulling teeth?"

"Why should I make it easy for you?"

"Because I am your only friend," Dominy said, matter-of-factly.

"No you aren't. Paige and I are becoming fast friends."

"Really? That's nice. Have you told her yet?"

He walked straight into that one. He had no good answer so he kept quiet.

"I take that as a 'no'," Dominy hinted.

"Take it any way you want to."

"No need to get nasty. I was just wondering."

"No, you were meddling and trying to make a point..."

"Are you going to tell her?"

"Eventually."

"Sooner or later?"

"I don't know but I will make sure you are the last to know."

"Okay, alright. Boy are you grouchy..."

"Forgive me, but hurting my mother doesn't usually incite feelings of euphoria. She put up a good front though. She didn't cry once while we were on the line. She just kept repeating that if God healed me once, he could do it again like it was her new mantra."

"Don't be that way, Brandon. That's what she may need to hold onto in order to get through this."

"I am not faulting her for her faithfulness in God, but what if He chooses not to heal me in this life? I don't need her to have a reason to doubt Him."

"Not saying that I believe for one moment that you won't get through this, but Mother Ava has lost a child before and she still loves God."

"Yeah, but two children?"

"Let's hope she never has to deal with that."

"When is your family coming out? I want to make sure I'm not there when they are. They will skin me alive for keeping your secret."

"Mom is coming in the second Friday in December and staying through Christmas. The rest of the family will be coming in the beginning that next Monday, up until that Friday."

"Where are they all going to be staying?"

"They are staying in hotels. Mom and dad will be staying with me."

"Wonderful. I think I will stay here for the holidays."

"You were going to do that anyway."

"Yes, but this way I don't have to feel guilty."

"Yeah well, thank you for helping me start out my day on such a light note. With that, I guess I will get ready for work."

"Wait just a minute. You didn't tell me how your date went with Paige?"

"It was not a date. We just went to a shelter that was serving a special Sunday dinner for the holiday, and then had coffee at a nearby café."

"Did you have a nice time?"

"Yes."

"Did she have a nice time?"

"I think so. We talked for almost two hours but then she had to go home and put in some time on her book."

"Did she tell you what it was about?"

"Yes. It's a fictional novel revolving around the life of her cousin and continual denial of God's love, some of the places and situations he found himself in, and why he was unable to accept God's gift in the first place."

"Did she share with you their past?"

"No. I don't think she's ready and to tell you the truth, I don't know if I am either. I can't imagine…" He started to breath deeper to keep down the wave of nausea that hit him.

"Yeah…well…so you had a nice time?" Dominy struggled to change the subject so they could end the call on a lighter note.

"Yes. She is so vibrant and intelligent. She loves what she does so much, you should see her glow when she talks about it. Her eyes light up like fireworks in the night sky. You can't help but be enamored."

"Thank you for the heads up. I'll make sure to never to ask her about work. Robin would never forgive me if I became enamored of someone else."

"I dare say I would help her take you out."

"Funny man. Are you going out again?"

"Maybe Saturday. Hopefully the side effects of my treatment on Wednesday won't be too harrowing."

"Have you thought of kissing her?"

"No," he answered too quickly. Dominy started laughing on the other end.

"Liar. Well…my work here is done. I will leave you with that thought for the day." He continued to chuckle.

"Satan, get thee behind me."

"I keep telling you, the name is Dominy. I don't go by Satan anymore."

Dummy. "Goodbye Dom." He hung up once again to Dominy's laughter ringing through the receiver.

CHAPTER 49

Victoria strolled through the house minutes before dawn, slowly reacquainting herself with all the downstairs rooms between the stairs, leading to the atrium and to the kitchen. She could smell the coffee already brewing and for the first time since arriving back home, a small smile crept around her lips.

She felt a calm she hadn't known since before...she couldn't remember. This feeling was so much better than any of the ones from the last few days. It was amazing what it did to realize and resolve one's self to just holding on to things you could control.

Today was the beginning of days she could do something about. She had a farm to oversee and an annual gala to prepare for.

The Wing Cup Annual gala was a charity event used to raise funds for several, non-profit organizations. It helped fund the local offices and social networks as well as research facilities for muscular dystrophy, leukemia, breast cancer, and this year, acute renal failure due to accidents and the National Living Kidney Donation Foundation.

Since it was an annual event, she only needed to make sure the vendors were still lined up and checked for any changes in their protocol, charges or personnel. As usual, Victoria liked working close to everyone involved with every event she coordinated.

Today would be full of checking in with all managers, superintendents, and farm-hands. Since it was getting close to the Christmas holiday and bonus time, she needed to update her list of employees since her last visit three months before.

Her mind strayed to Paige as she continued to walk from the main dining hall to one of the ballrooms. She wondered if Paige would take her up on her offer to have her visit for a few days. The initial look that crossed Paige's face was priceless. Victoria knew she was hesitant and didn't want to hurt her feelings, but Victoria was serious. What Paige had said during their last lunch together had resonated throughout her mind over the following days and week.

Paige didn't mention it during their conversation two days prior, but Victoria wasn't going to bring it up again for at least another few calls if Paige failed to do so.

She knew Paige was still hesitant about their relationship. She didn't know quite what to expect herself, but she was going to put forth a bit more effort than normal to see if the peace that came with talking with Paige, as of late, would last. She didn't know how much she'd missed not being angry until she was able to listen to Paige talk about her time with Vivian before she'd left without jealousy, bitterness or resentment, for not being able to share that with her daughter.

She began to think about the different relationships in her life, wondering how much was truly under her control and what she might be able to do immediately to make life easier on herself. One thought that stayed in the forefronts of her mind was the pending court date that would begin her custody battle for Vivian.

For some reason, she wasn't as invigorated at the thought of stealing Vivian away from Mason. Sure, she wanted her grandchild to have the best of everything. She wanted her to live a life of privilege, but something Paige said during one of their conversations had her considering another scenario that would cause Vivian more pain than good.

Later that day she would call her attorney and have him drop the case. She had more important things to deal with in the immediate future. She wasn't ready to go all 'Brady Bunch' on anyone and make nice. She just figured she could do more for Vivian when she wasn't so desperate to remain with her father. The late teens were hard years. If she played her cards right, Vivian may come to live with her for a few of them. Hopefully by then, whatever had crawled up Richard's behind would have died and her husband would come back to his senses.

The nights were getting longer and it was getting harder to ignore Richard's office downstairs or the chair in the sitting room off of the bedroom they used to share. Her fourth night home she found herself laying in his chair, just so she could feel close enough to him to fall asleep. Night five and six were pretty much the same.

Day seven she decided to spend a few days at a spa just so she wasn't in the house at night, and now she was back.

She walked into the kitchen, poured herself a cup of coffee, and continued to the sunroom to watch the sun come up over the back 40. Later that day she would talk to the caretaker about the soil health of the unplanted acres, since the 280 acres of crops on the east side of the house were harvested on a seven-year rotation cycle.

She sat down on one of the high-back chairs, facing the windows that spanned the length of the western wall. The colors were even more brilliant than the day before. She began reminiscing on her and Richard's first few years at the house. She couldn't remember ever being so happy. Renovating the house and working the land until it began to produce again had been a hard haul, but it was something they'd worked on together.

Richard was the one person that believed she could turn her grandparent's vision into the success it was today. They'd been through so much together. Her mother's and father's accidental deaths had angered her because she felt she had been cheated out of being able to prove that she could do what they said she couldn't. She had slowly come to terms with the loss, made easier by the news that she was going to be a mother again but a few months later, a small fall in the wrong place at the wrong time ended that pregnancy.

She shifted her musings to the view before her, struggling to stay in the present. The past held too many sad thoughts, and today she'd vowed to only deal with the things she could do something about.

Never one to leave her bedroom unless she was fully dressed, Victoria finished her coffee just as the sun fully crested the back hill. She would go from here to visit the foreman and ride through the back ridge.

From complete darkness to light took 20 minutes and, by the time she walked from the room, she felt as if she had already moved through most of her day. She just hoped that she would be tired enough by the time she came back tonight to sleep.

*   *   *

Two weeks later, Victoria dragged herself up to her bedroom. She was too tired to have dinner in the dining room, and had already made arrangements for Martha to have dinner brought to her room. An errand, though, crossed her mind as she passed through the sitting room. Still unable to sleep, she'd spent more time in there than in her bed.

The days had continued to drag on, but she'd kept herself busy with the gala and playing a more participatory role in the lives of her workers. It was uncomfortable at first, to say the least. She wasn't aware of the new employees that worked the acres that Richard usually oversaw. They held tobacco, a crop she wasn't too fond of, but this had been his baby and whether he was here or not she would still have to communicate with the workers.

No one asked her questions about Richard; no one asked her questions, period. She sat in the jeep next to Pasqual and allowed him to give her a rundown of each section, day by day.

She would take in the information but as time went on, Richard's absence from the farm and lack of calls became a lump in the pit of her stomach that weighed heavily on the peace she'd been able to carve out for herself when she first came home.

The passion at which she went about her days and the pride that she had once seen in her land waned. She needed to get away.

She picked up the phone, dialing Francis, her pilot, only to find that he wouldn't be back in the office until the next day. She called Paige, wanting to hear some of those encouraging words that seemed to just drip from Paige's mouth, but after four rings the call transferred over to her voicemail.

Victoria ate her dinner in Richard's chair and watched the fire she'd had Mr. Daniel make lick at the wood until a peaceful slumber finally overtook her.

The next morning, she woke to a vaguely familiar scent. She was hesitant to move, knowing that her muscles would scream in protest to her sleeping in the chair all night. As the haze of sleep receded, she began to take notice of the position of her body. She was in bed. When had she gone to bed? She searched her memory but kept coming up blank. The scent passed by her again, like a breeze at the end of summer. It was warm and elicited warm memories of...

Richard! Her mind became instantly alert. She opened her eyes, but there wasn't anything that looked different from the night before. She trained her ears for any foreign sounds but none came to her in the few seconds she'd sat rod still. Finally she allowed her body to relax, working to keep the morose thoughts at bay.

She got up out of bed and walked over to the window. Her breath misted the pane as one tear escaped unheeded. A knock at the door drew her attention away from the poinsettias lining the front walk. She didn't turn, expecting Martha since it was way past her normal breakfast hour.

She'd noted the lateness by the position of the sun – something she had done a lot lately. She was grateful that her mind had rested long enough to allow her the reprieve. The clearing of a male throat caused her to turn quickly and her breath caught at the sight of Richard standing in the doorway.

Her eyes roamed his features, clothes, and statue in one sweep. If this was a hallucination, it was the best one yet. She was too afraid to move forward, lest he disappear. If it was really him he would speak, wouldn't he? She blinked rapidly but he was still there each time. Her breath started coming quickly, almost keeping pace with her heart as it started to race.

"Hello Victoria." The sound met her ears just as her legs gave way from under her.

CHAPTER 50

Mason paced the floor in his room. He had been home for two hours and felt like a caged animal. He'd called Paige earlier that day, but it had gone straight to her voicemail.

They'd talked almost daily since he'd left California with Vivian. He'd worked not to allow their parting conversation to ruin his time in the Bay Area with his daughter.

They had come home and reestablished their father and daughter pattern. Their lives revolved around his work, her classes, and nightly conversations over takeout.

There was only one difference: Paige. She was the first thing they both thought of in the morning since her and Vivian's prayer time had been relegated to the mornings.

He could hear Vivian giggling, talking and praying with Paige before she got ready for school. Sometimes he would listen at the door as they prayed for him, Victoria, Elder Tatum, and any of her classmates that had solicited prayer after finding out that she would pray for anyone. Most of the time, they would come away with an answer they could understand. For the first time in his relationship with his daughter, he felt like he was walking the sidelines of her life.

It was nothing that Vivian or Paige said that caused him to feel ostracized; it was the bond that was growing and strengthening between them. It was like they'd spent the last 12 years in each other's lives and were closer than most mothers and daughters. He couldn't quite understand how it was happening but it made him uncomfortable.

Would Vivian begin to wish she could spend more time with Paige? Oh how he wished against it. The very thought caused his heart rate to spike, so he started taking his showers during their morning devotion and prayer, get dressed, then on occasion would ask Vivian to pass him the phone before she hung up.

Most of the conversations they had were light and pleasant. He would ask her about her book, any new signing dates, how Gladys, Carmen, Melanie, and Pastor Lawrence and Lady Menagerie were doing. He even inquired about Victoria, after learning of their continued communication, but never Brandon. He was the unspoken taboo and she followed his lead.

He didn't want to know if they were seeing each other; if they were developing a relationship deeper than what he witnessed that Sunday. He didn't want to consider her choosing Brandon over him. Brandon was what he couldn't be.

The day Brandon had walked into Paige's hospital room and he saw the expression he'd quickly tried to disguise as he looked at her, Mason knew. He knew it was only a matter of time before Brandon would make his intentions clear. He wondered if the Pastor looked down on fellow clergy getting involved. He could only hope.

He had tried to make his feelings known and draw her closer while she was in Chicago, but Paige had this uncanny way of keeping him at a safe distance. He knew she felt the magnetic energy between them and he had seen the awareness of attraction in her eyes more than once, right before they went from a warm, sizzling amber to a cool topaz, void of emotion.

He missed her. There was such a peace that surrounded her; it caused him to gravitate towards her. It didn't matter that they were thousands of miles apart. He could even sense when she was on the phone. That was usually when he would go take his shower, trying to drown out any thoughts of the discussions she and his daughter were having about God, heaven, hell, the Holy Spirit, or any other part of the biblical realm.

He'd recently had a debate over the need for Vivian to continue to attend church without him. Each Saturday night she would ask if he would accompany her, and each Sunday morning he couldn't seem to envision himself walking through the heavy wooden doors he would drop her off in front of. He hadn't entered those doors since Rachael's funeral. He wasn't ready to let go.

This was the same thing he told Paige when she'd asked him why he wouldn't attend church with his daughter. "Do you want to be ready?"

"Are you suggesting that I enjoy seeing my daughter walk alone through those doors?"

"No, I'm not suggesting that you enjoy it, but what are you doing about it?"

"I'm letting time handle some of it. Every day, I believe things are getting a little bit better."

"Well that's good, but what are you investing in that time that is going by?"

"What?" He tried not to get annoyed.

"Time can act as a buffer or a band-aid, but only what you do with that time can actually help you to heal. Sure, if you give it enough time, anything can find its way under enough thoughts to lay dormant for a while but it will rear its head sooner or later and you will have to deal with it one way or another."

"Don't beat the bush, Paige, it's already dead. You have my permission for this lecture."

"Do I? Would you listen to me if I told you that the very threshold you can't cross is the one that is keeping you right where you are?"

"And where is that?" he asked, sarcasm dripping from his voice.

Paige ignored it. "Feeling alone."

"I am not alone."

"No, but you feel alone, and you are far from it."

"What are you saying?"

"Just that there are many around you that love you."

"Including you?"

"Of course including me, but that is beside the point."

"Why can't it be the point?"

"Because that's just not how it is."

"You can't deny that there is a physical attraction between us." He could hear her sigh.

"I would be lying if I did, but what does that have to do with anything?"

He was silent for a long time.

"Mason, I have never experienced this electricity that seems to buzz about when we are close and I would be lying if I told you I haven't been tempted to see where it could go." He knew there was a denial coming, but held on to her admission for all that it was worth until she continued.

"But I can't be moved by what feels right physically. I need to know that it is also a wise decision all around, and it isn't."

"Why would you say that?"

"Because I need more."

"I'm not asking you to have a relationship based just on our physical attraction. We have fun together and have plenty in common, including love and equal hope for the well-being of our child."

She quietly reiterated, "I need more."

"What more is there?"

"My spirit man needs the same attention you would give my body and my mind. I won't deny Him."

"I am not even going to admit to understanding what that means because I don't. What would I have to do with your spirit man? Isn't that God's territory?"

"My love for God is essential to any relationship I would have with you. I can't love you wholly without my love and adoration for Him. There are things that I would miss and overlook regarding you as a man; a triune man that you would need. Whether you wish to acknowledge it or not, I believe man is made up of three distinct parts: body, soul (which includes the will, emotions, and intellect), and spirit. It's hard for me to show you love for a part of you that you deny, and it is impossible for you to love me with that part that you don't believe you have."

"So, that's it?" he sighed. "No consideration for the future? Anything could happen, you know."

"Believe me, I know more than most that anything can happen, but I am not going to give you false hope or lead you on."

"If Brandon wasn't in the picture would your decision be as quick?"

"Honestly, I don't know. I might have been so spooked by my reaction to you that I would have held you even further away."

"Why?" It was as if she was speaking a language like English, but the words didn't make sense when they were strung together.

He heard her tapping something in the background. "I won't subject myself to the pain I've witnessed by two, unequally-yoked people trying to 'make it work'. I need to be able to trust the man I am with."

"Do you think I would be unfaithful to you?" He felt as if he'd been slapped in the face.

"It's more than any physical thing you would do, though I wouldn't think that you would do anything like that or hurt me intentionally. It has to do with the love of my life, being able to share Him with you and knowing without a shadow of a doubt where you get your guidance from.

I need to be able to allow my partner to protect me, but how can I trust you to protect me when we hear from two different sources?"

"Are you saying that if I were to reestablish my relationship with God that you would be open to taking our relationship to the next level?" Would he consider it if she said 'yes'?

"No."

"Then what are you saying?"

"I'm saying 'no' right now to any type of relationship outside of sharing Vivian and friendship. It doesn't matter how badly I want you to develop a relationship with God, if it isn't for the right reasons it isn't going to work. You have to do it for yourself because you want to, not for me."

Was there no hope for them? Was that what she was getting at? He didn't need to be hit with a brick – no more than twice, anyway.

"Well… I guess there is nothing more to say on the subject. You seem pretty set in your decision."

"It doesn't mean it wasn't a hard one, but it is for the best."

"For who?"

"For everyone involved. I am being honest with you. I do want you as a friend."

"While you're being honest, tell me: are you considering becoming more than friends with Elder Tatum?" He had broken his rule not to mention him. It hurt to think that he'd lost out to God's man. He was human. It wasn't like he was the spawn of Satan even though he felt like God treated him like that every now and then.

"That's really none of your business."

"Why not? You are the mother of my daughter. If you are going to be a permanent part of her life, I should be made aware of relationships that may have an effect on your interaction with her."

"I disagree. If I decide to deepen my relationship with Elder Tatum, it is not in direct correlation with me not going beyond friendship with you. I am not choosing him over you. It was never between the two of you. If he's not what God wants for me, the discussion would be the same."

"I think everything has been said."

"I don't want to end our call like this."

Too bad. "I didn't either but I don't see anywhere to go with this."

"Oh… I don't know, it could be worse."

"Mmm. I doubt that."

"You could be having this conversation with Victoria."

Ugh. That's true. "I might be a glutton for punishment, but I am not suicidal."

"True. Would it make it any better if I told you I really value your friendship?"

"No."

"How about…I am grateful that Vivian was adopted by you?"

"Now you're just blowing smoke up dark places," he said sardonically.

She giggled. "Thank you, Mason, for allowing me to be in Vivian's life and in your life, whatever the capacity. I don't take it lightly."

Mason huffed, releasing the next breath in a long, slow measure. "You are welcome, Paige. I have a few things to take care of for work. I will talk to you later?"

"Yes. Later is alright."

He'd hung up the phone wanting nothing more than to wipe his desk clean with one swipe of his hand. The frustration was overwhelming, but the heartbreak was devastating. In a few weeks, Paige had come to mean more to him than just his daughter's mother. She had come to symbolize life. He could feel something other than anger for the first time in a long time and he didn't want to lose it.

*   *   *

He'd gone over their conversation in his head for almost a week, and he finally thought he'd gained some understanding of what she was trying to say. Now he needed to find a way to explain it to her so that she could understand that he wasn't talking about a light affair. He wanted something meaningful and lasting, even if it meant going back to church and getting to know her world.

Yeah...he was ready...mostly.

Now if she would just call him back, he could tell her.

CHAPTER 51

She wasn't going to call him back.

It was for the best that she gave them some space. The last conversation they'd had hurt too much. She had hung up the phone with Mason, her heart feeling battered and bruised. She couldn't keep the tears from falling. It seemed that every other time she opened her mouth during their talk, she was causing him pain and the worst part was that he couldn't understand why. She would give it a couple of weeks, unless Vivian handed him the phone after they prayed and then she would have to come up with some quick excuse as to why she desperately had to get off of the phone.

She knew she was being a coward with the avoidance, but she wasn't strong enough to keep having these conversations and not give in – even if she could give him a little happiness for a moment. The day of reckoning would come on swift wings and what would she have on her hands then? The blood of the man who may have one day come to God, if she had only been strong enough to continue to deny him... She would not be the one. She would not answer his calls and she would not return them until she was sure he understood that there couldn't be any more between them than friendship and Vivian.

Then there was Brandon, Mr. Enigma himself. They had been out about half a dozen times and she still wasn't quite sure what to make of him. He seemed to like her company. He kept asking her to accompany him places. When he wasn't on duty, he would sit next to her in church and the last two Elder fellowship outings, he was very attentive and quite jovial. She just didn't know if he was just taking Pastor Lawrence up on his advice to get to know her and allow her to show him around the area or if he was interested in her as more than a friend.

It wasn't like she was in any position to be in a relationship. She was still getting to know her girls and making strides to re-acclimate herself to the work on the Visitation Committee. The deadline for her book was coming up fast, and she was being pressed by her publisher. After she finished, there would only be a small reprieve before she began traveling again. When was she supposed to make time for a relationship?

Even as she considered it, her lips rose at the corners. She would make time. The last couple of times they went out she'd really enjoyed herself. Whether it was going for walks around Santa Monica Pier, Universal Board Walk, the movies, lunch or dinner, they never ran out of things to talk about. The sky was the limit and it was so comfortable being in his presence, she would forget the small, anxious moments she would have while getting ready.

Her mind would work overtime, trying to concentrate on what she would wear, if he would say something this time that would clue her in to what his expectations were, and if she would accept it. He seemed to be in the forefront of her prayers. She didn't know whether her desires to have a deeper relationship with him than friendship or past fears were clouding her ability to hear God's answer clearly. She knew that the feelings of peace that rested upon her when praying for or about Brandon were vastly different than any feeling she received about Mason.

She'd spoken to Lady Menagerie the night before and, though she had hinted that Brandon did have feelings for her that extended passed friendship, she refused to say any more.

She did, however, ask Paige what her feelings were concerning him. She admitted her desire and hesitation to move forward without a clear answer from God.

"Are you looking for an audible answer or a knowing in your spirit?"

"Either one will be fine."

"I know you haven't been down this road in a long time, but I am advising you to live in the moment. It is pretty much understood that we don't date, but we court, so that much is a given. The rest will take care of itself as long as you continue to live in the moment.

Don't introduce any scenarios or challenges that aren't present. Enjoy yourself, but most of all trust that you and your relationship with God will continue to grow stronger in this relationship, as it would without it."

"How do you know?"

"You are my other daughter. I've seen you grow since you walked into the church. You have never done anything to cause me to think differently. Also, the more anxious you become while waiting for an answer from the Lord, the harder it will be to hear Him."

"Yeah...I know that." Paige sighed. She was getting ahead of herself.

It was the first week in December and the street-lights were dressed in red, green, and silver tinsel. Paige took a walk just to clear her head. The last chapter had taken a lot out of her emotionally. When she'd embarked on this journey to redeem her cousin in fiction, she didn't know what the Lord would do through her writing for her and for those who read it. She'd discovered long ago that the talent she used as a hobby and a tool to exorcize her over-abundance of emotion also ministered to her.

She often found that a meandering thought would take her through a scene that would cause her to pause, reflect, meditate and ultimately, praise God for the direction He'd led her. By the time she'd reached the middle chapters, she was enraptured in a healing process that exposed and helped her relinquish hurts and scars that she had grown used to and tried to identify herself by.

This book was working her emotions into overtime. As much as she wanted to see the finished work, she desired to continue in the deliverance that left her feeling lighter and more in charge of herself.

This morning she'd cried through a whole box of tissue. The heaviness that had awakened her drew her to her desk. It remained as she wrote until she found herself face down on the floor, in a prostrate position, arms spread wide, heaving around racking sobs. Some of the things that were purged from her soul were revealed to her right away. Others she knew would show themselves in dreams and her interaction with others.

She sighed heavily, knowing that she was pretty much done writing for the day. She took her time, letting her senses soak up the sweet smell of the leaves still falling from the trees, the warmth of the low-hanging sun on her face and arms and the sound of a piece of paper picked up by a breeze that swept around her tunic top. She was in the perfect place and therefore not at all surprised when the answer that seemed to have been eluding her came upon her as an impression.

Now all she had to do was wait…patiently.

Paige walked into her apartment as the phone rang. She hastened her steps so that she could reach it before her voicemail picked up.

"Hello?"

"Hi. Are you alright? You sound out of breath."

Brandon's voice wrapped around her like a blanket, causing a smile to come to her face. "I am good. I just came in from getting some fresh air."

"Do you want me to call you after you've had a chance to settle in?"

She locked her door then went back to flop on the couch. "No. I am all good. How are you?"

"Better now."

"Oh? Why is that?" She hedged, her smile growing wider.

"Because I get to hear your voice."

"That's a wonderful thing to say, but didn't I talk to you yesterday?"

"Yep and that is what made my day so great yesterday."

"Wow. You are a charmer when you want to be," she flirted.

"Mmmm."

"What?"

"I must be out of practice. I thought I was always charming."

"Well…you have always been a gentleman, but it seemed that you just put forth special effort to be charming right now," she said, back-peddling.

"It's alright. I am just going to have to be more deliberate with my expressions."

"Well it could be worse; people could accuse you of being too straight-forward." She dangled her legs over the arm of the sofa.

"I don't know…can one be accused of being too honest?"

"Not necessarily too honest, but I have been accused of being brutally honest or extremely straight-forward. I don't believe in mixing words."

"That's a good thing. People don't ever have to wonder what you think about them or if you are being deceitful."

"That's true. I normally don't make people wait to find out what I am thinking, but I am not too transparent."

"I bet I could read you."

"I am going to hold you to that."

"What would I get if I guess right?"

She sat up, her full attention engaged. "Oh, you are a gambling man?"

"I would rather call it a gift for doing what I say I can do."

"Okay, you pick, but understand that I am going to want a gift if I prove you wrong."

There was a moment of silence on the other end.

"Are you still there?"

"Yes."

"Are you busy? Could I show you something?"

"Umm…not really." She looked around, wondering how quickly she could make herself presentable. "When?"

"Is a half hour too soon? I want to let you see it before all of the light is gone."

"Okay, half an hour it is." She hung up and made a mad dash for the bedroom and master bath.

What he wanted to show her ended up being a dog park with a huge pond and a circumference stretching a mile wide. The trees were still full for December, but that was not rare in Southern California, which held many trees that bloomed year-around or were slow-moving into the mild winter season.

It was quiet on this side of the water, since most of the larger areas of grass were easily accessible from the west side of the pond. They walked for a while, but when he led her to a bench she was more than content to sit and watch the occasional jogger or gaze at the pond whose glassy surface rippled occasionally with disturbances from the atmosphere above or life beneath.

She had forgotten her gloves so she sat on her hands, allowing her body to rock back and forth slowly calming her heart. She turned to look at him. His eyes were darker than she remembered. They were warmer too. She could be safe there, right in the middle of that soft warmth.

"Paige?"

"Hmmm?"

"What are you thinking?"

"That you have truly found something amazing and I am very honored that you would share it with me. It's so peaceful here. I could write here." She allowed her gaze to roam about her again.

"I have a random question for you."

She looked back at him. "Okay."

"Is there anything that you fear?"

Yep, it was random. She looked down, trying to think of something that truly made her uneasy, something she feared and just when she was going to give up, the very situation she was in came to mind. The uncertainty of so much in their future made her very uneasy, but how do you explain that to the person you are in the situation with?

"My fear comes more from doing new things, stepping into situations where I don't have at least a semblance of control."

"But you can't control life," he responded almost too quickly.

"Mmmm…No, but I can control where I go, who I go there with and why."

"When was the last time you dated?"

She didn't see that coming. She watched him, wanting to see his reaction to her answer. "Maybe five, six years."

He just nodded, giving nothing away.

"And you?"

"Quite a bit longer."

"You're not going to tell me?"

"Eventually."

"How do you ask someone a question you don't intend to answer yourself?"

He shrugged. "All answers are optional."

She rolled her eyes. "Now you tell me. I see you have a bit of a stubborn streak in you too."

"I plead the fifth."

She feigned a yawn. "I plead boredom."

He rocked his body so that his shoulder shoved hers. She playfully pushed back harder. He didn't retaliate and, after a moment, they went back to admiring their surroundings.

She placed her hands on either side of her thighs, clutching at the bench they were sitting on, swaying lightly back and forth.

"This place is beautiful. I can't believe I've never been here before. It's funny how when you are new in town you are able to see things that people who have been here for years overlook every day."

Today was different somehow. Their usually easy and lighthearted conversation was slightly stilted and all over the place. She could tell he was a little uneasy but couldn't for the world figure out why.

She spied two birds fighting over a twig, probably for one of their nests. They became so focused on shooing the other away, neither saw the squirrel that was watching and took advantage of the moment to steal the twig from both.

Paige let out a healthy guffaw. "That was classic." Her robust laugh was joined by Brandon's deep rumble of a laugh that gradually grew to overshadow hers. She couldn't remember him laughing so hard or with so much abandon. It almost stunned her.

He caught her looking at him before she could gather her thoughts. "What?"

"You have a beautiful laugh. Why don't you do it more often?"

"Are you saying I am too serious?"

"I am not saying anything. I am merely making an observation. You have a beautiful laugh, but just now it amazed me that in the time we have spent together this was the first time I could remember you laughing so freely."

"Are you not happy?"

The question seemed to catch him so off guard. He just stared at her for a moment then blurted out, "I laugh."

"I'm sorry. I didn't mean it to be an accusation. I just wondered why you didn't do it more often." She shrugged matter-of-factly.

"I will work on it," he said, a smile pulling at the corners of his mouth. He wiggled his eyebrows at her and she giggled.

"So how's Dominy?" she asked, wanting to change the subject.

"He's doing well. He is always happy when he can pester someone. Right now, I am happy to say it is Robin getting all of his attention."

She laughed out loud.

"You two are so funny. Anyone can see that you are the best of friends, but you treat each other with such disdain sometimes. I don't understand it."

Brandon smiled sheepishly. "Dominy has a way of bringing that out in people. Besides, there's only so much male bonding. Truthfully though, Dominy is the best friend anyone could ask for. If it weren't for him, I might not be here today. He has given me more than any other human could ask for in a friend, in a brother. He came into my life at eight and filled in the gaps."

It was quiet for a moment as Paige took in the information. Anyone could tell that they were very close friends but from what Brandon just told her, Dominy was a very rare find. Many people didn't have that type of relationship in any part of their life.

"To say you are fortunate sounds like an understatement. You are blessed greater than many. If even half the world had Dominys, life would be so much safer."

"You know I said that same thing a few years ago and I do believe there are, but they just didn't have the fortitude, knowledge, teaching, or understanding to step up to the plate."

Paige nodded. She was a little overwhelmed by the depth of this human being sitting next to her. The peek into his soul he'd just given her made her contemplate her own ability and depth to love. She'd never met a man who was able to express himself, let alone feel that way about a friend of the same sex. It moved her profoundly. She was glad to know him and let that and the other feeling resonate within her.

"I kind of wish he was coming back before the New Year," Brandon said, pulling her from her thoughts. "My family is coming to town in a couple of weeks and Dominy is good at running inference."

"Don't you get along with your family?" Now that she thought about it he didn't say much about his family. She only learned he had six siblings at the Thanksgiving dinner.

"Oh, yeah, we get along famously. It's just that I am one of the younger ones and you never get old enough to outgrow being the baby."

"Do you get coddled a lot?" She couldn't imagine this big man being handled like a child.

"Not so much coddled as given an immense amount of attention. Anyway, Dominy is always able to come up with something clever to draw their attention or ease the tension when I get frustrated with all of the hovering hens."

"They love you, and they just sound affectionate."

He shrugged then raised his hand, gesturing for her to come from the bench. She got up and when he held his hand out, she took it. Her hand was swallowed up in his palm, it was so big. *Hmmm, baby of the family. I wonder what the oldest son looks like. Probably a bear.*

They followed the path around the pond, holding hands, talking about some of the events he had planned for his family during the holiday. They had been quiet for a moment when she looked up to watch a squirrel run the length of a tree, sprinting around it and stop, becoming like a statue.

She'd often thought this before and found herself just as thankful as she had come full circle in this cycle.

She was happy she was no other creature but a human being, and even more so that she was Paige Rosen Morganson right here at this very moment in time. She wasn't aware of the smile that had come upon her face until he called it to her attention.

"Would you be willing to share that thought? I'm curious to know what causes smiles like that one."

She turned back to him, surprised at the comment. It seemed to be more than just a request for information. She watched his features but they seemed light and friendly.

"I was just thinking that I was perfectly happy being who I am in this moment right now." She didn't take her eyes away from his.

"I used to do this thing when I was particularly happy to be in a certain place at a time. I usually saw an animal or another person that was doing or going somewhere different and I thanked God that I wasn't them because I was right where I wanted to be." She sat back on the bench diverting her eyes, knowing she was about to share an intimate part of herself with him but unwilling to stop.

"The first time I can remember doing it was when I was headed to Magic Mountain as a young child. It seems that each time I took it upon myself to acknowledge how happy I was in that moment, the memory stayed. Now I have a new one to add."

"Why?" He wanted to hear her say the words straight out.

"I'm glad to know you, Elder Brandon Tatum. You are a gift to my day."

"You stun me when you speak like that."

Paige shrugged. "I'm paid to be able to express myself. Sometimes it is a struggle and other times, like now, it comes with ease. I love it when the words from my heart have an accompanying word in the English language. Some expressions I want to make with my heart don't have good enough words in the English language to describe them and I am stuck with a less than satisfactory substitution."

Brandon chuckled. "I see you don't converse with men much. Most would have considered you intimidating about five sentences ago."

Paige laughed but sobered quickly. "And you? Are you intimidated?"

"No, impressed, fascinated, intrigued... Curious, but not intimidated."

"Come on let's walk over there." He pointed to a walkway up a small hill from the lake.

They had walked a short way in silence before he spoke.

"How do you do it? How do you live life with such fervor?"

She thought about the question, trying to think of the best way to answer. "Life itself doesn't hold any special meaning for me. If it weren't for God, I doubt I would still be here. I would have ended my life long ago, if not by my hand then indirectly by someone else. My passion for life is in my relationship with God. He makes it beautiful, something to look forward to. He is the love of my life. I wake up to seek Him, commune with Him, and be used by Him."

"Why?" his voice was barely a whisper.

"I didn't have the best childhood, but certainly not the worst. I didn't have a lot of time to just be a child. He gave that back to me. He taught me how to love myself. He convinced me that I was worth saving, that I wasn't someone just placed on this earth to be someone's foot-stool."

"Do you mind talking about it? Your childhood, what happened?"

She looked up, eyes clear. "Nope. I don't mind. What do you want to know?"

"You have twelve-year-old twin girls and you are...how old?"

"Twenty-six."

"I am not quite sure how to ask delicately how you came by twins at that age," he said apologetically.

"I don't think there is a delicate way to ask." She shrugged then continued. "I was painfully shy as a child. I didn't have any friends in school. I was too afraid they wouldn't like me, so I didn't even try. I just stayed in the world of my books. My cousin, Stone, became my best friend. We moved to California when I was nine, and my cousins were...different. They accepted me, bookworm that I was, but Stone always took it one step further, encouraging me to play with the rest of the kids in the family. I felt like I belonged somewhere."

She went on to tell him about how uncomfortable their relationship had become and how he'd cornered her the day he'd come home from Boot Camp. She was going to continue when she stole another glance at Brandon, his jaw was clenched and his shoulders were hunched.

"Maybe I should stop now," she said, stopping to turn to him.

"No. I am okay."

"Really? Because you look like you are going to stroke out. I am no longer pained when I talk about this. I have received my healing, but I'm not sure if I should continue." She watched him shake his head in denial.

"He...he...raped you?" The words sounded like they were grounded out through his teeth.

"Yes," she said solemnly, not moving forward, still watching the expressions on his face. He went pale and she became frightened. She wouldn't be able to pick him up if he passed out. He looked up, his eyes were frantic, searching for something then he was taking long strides towards the closest trash bin. He leaned over it, heaving and retching. Paige was so surprised she was momentarily glued to the ground then as he heaved again, she ran over to rub his back. "Sssshhhh. It's alright, it's okay, I'm alright now. I'm fine, better than fine now. Shhhh."

This reaction was new to her. She didn't quite know what to make of it.

He was breathing hard. She reached in her bag, pulling out some tissue, staying behind him to give him some privacy, reaching the tissue around him. He took it, apologizing.

"No need to be sorry. It isn't an easy thing to stomach – no pun intended. Mmmm then again..."

She saw his shoulders shake. He was laughing now. *Good sign.*

She turned around to look back down the walk, giving him just a little more space and time to compose himself. She was studying etchings, small markings people had made, and overall cracks in the cemented walk when he came up to her a few moments later. She glanced up at him from the corner of her eye, his hands were back in his pockets but his posture was more relaxed.

"I'm sorry about that back there," he said, looking forward.

"Don't mention it." She tried to quickly dismiss the subject, but he didn't seem ready to move on no matter how humiliated he could have been by his body's reaction to her news.

"If you don't mind, I would like to hear the rest."

She stopped and turned to him. "Why?" She couldn't understand. It seemed to upset him a great deal, so why would he want her to continue?

She began to shake her head. "I don't think that is such a good-"

"I'm fine. If you don't believe me, we can go to that bench and sit while you tell me the rest. I probably won't be sick again."

"If it repulses you so much why..." he interrupted her again.

"I'm not repulsed so much by the story as I am of the thought of it happening to you."

She remained silent as she thought of his reply.

"Look," he stopped, turning to her in the middle of the walkway. "I'm going to tell you something, but I hope you're not going to hold it against me." He took a deep breath squaring his shoulders, but still it was a few moments before he said anything. It was as if he was trying to will the thoughts to her just so that he wouldn't have to confess.

"I don't know when my feelings for you grew stronger than friendship, but they did, and long before today or even before you went to Chicago." He stopped. He seemed to be searching for the right thoughts amongst the leaves on the ground and then finally, he looked up holding her with the intensity of his gaze.

"I...um... feel very protective of you. I know that is not something you want to hear." He rushed on before she could interrupt.

"I am only telling you this so that you understand that my reaction wasn't because I was disgusted by what happened but more on the fact that I couldn't do anything to stop it from happening, and that it happened to you. I know it is not rational, and I am working on this overreaction my body has to the thought of you being in any type of pain."

"So... the feelings you have for me that go beyond friendship are that you feel very protective of me?"

He looked taken aback by the question then recovered and shook his head, a sardonic smile coming across his lips. "No. Those are absolutely two different subjects. I can't believe I messed it up that bad." The last statement was barely audible and was said more to himself as he looked at his hands for an answer.

"Could you just continue for now and I will explain the rest later?"

"Why, if you...react so strongly towards the thought of me experiencing pain, do you want me to continue with this story?"

"I want to know." His eyes were clear and determined.

She looked at him for a moment longer, unsure about sharing what happened next in her life but maybe he would take this better.

Ten minutes later, she'd shared with him her experience with her mother and her intention to have an abortion. She looked over at him to survey his reaction to all of this. He looked a little uncomfortable, but didn't say anything, so she continued.

She didn't go into detail with the labor, just giving him the same story she'd been given at the time.

She took a deep breath before going on to the next phase of her life. Though the memories no longer hurt as much, she did find it slightly embarrassing sharing such personal feelings with him one-on-one.

She told him about her anger and hatred for herself, her mother, cousin, and the child she knew had survived; the agreement she made with her sister in regards to keeping Gladys and the path of self-destruction she got on, trying to find a way to relieve the pain, even if it was temporarily.

She glanced at him from out of the corner of her eye, not quite able to turn fully to him, and saw that his expression was stony. She continued on quickly so that she didn't lose her nerve.

"I had a friend in high school. She was always inviting me to come to her church but even after three years of counseling, I was angry and..." She took a deep breath, "suicidal." Still feeling some of the shame of almost giving up everything she had gained, she looked down trying to gather her courage to continue.

"The night I accepted her invitation was the night I was going to kill myself. I figured if I couldn't get the answers I needed from there, it was hopeless."

"So you got the answers because you were there?"

"Not necessarily that night, but I got something I'd been missing until then."

"What?"

"Proof that my existence wasn't a mistake and though I had no true understanding of how important I was to God at the time, a Mother in the church stayed with me until I at least had an inkling. It was enough to get me to doubt that I was right in thinking that I was put on this earth just to be abused. That doubt was enough to get me through the night and back to church that Sunday."

By the end of the month I'd not only joined the church, but was filled with the Holy Spirit."

A wistful expression came upon her face as she remembered the women who stayed with her until she received the Holy Spirit and the first few weeks she floated on air, having peace for the first time she could remember. She looked at him, then, a dazzling smile changed her whole countenance.

"It didn't stay easy. The peace wasn't always enough to keep me from battling with depression, but I at least had a way to fight it when I remembered I didn't have to succumb to it. But then people started coming into my life, like my spiritual mother, and they mentored me and led me on a path towards a personal and intimate relationship with God. Little by little, I gave Him my anger and excuses for staying where I was in life and He gave me reasons to hope and love myself."

Tears started to cloud her vision, but she didn't mind sharing this part with him.

"It wasn't a fast process, but what I thought was a sacrifice in the beginning, was junk I didn't want by the time I truly understood what I was gaining in Him. I was happy, truly happy, and somewhere in the midst of it I was able to see things with an objectivity I wasn't able to before, which allowed me to forgive my cousin, my mom, myself, and any other person I was holding a grudge against for 'ruining my life'." She smiled sheepishly, realizing that she had gotten lost in her thoughts for a moment, but she continued.

"I let go of certain relationships and let Him be my everything. Some people thought I was living in a fantasy world and that my relationship with God was irrational; that maybe I was too radical and had lost a grip with reality. But I was happy and I was nice to people, whereas before I was mean and just didn't care because I thought that was the easiest way to survive.

After college I got a job as an assistant project coordinator with a non-profit that helped pregnant and new mothers gain resources, and helped network with other organizations to give them the tools to share those resources with their members. It was a lot of work, but I loved the thought that what I was doing really helped people.

It was the job that brought me to Skylight Temple six years ago, because I'd moved into this area. There you go…most of my life story." She threw her hands out as if she were finishing a magic act but got no reaction. The more time that transpired, the more anxious she became. When she couldn't take it anymore, she asked, "Are you alright?"

His head snapped up as though he were being called from a far off place.

"Sorry, it's quite a bit of information. I didn't know…I was just processing everything," he said, letting his voice trail off. "So…how are you now? I mean your relationship with your…cousin and your mom…how is that?" He asked with obvious curiosity but seemed unsure how to ask his question.

"My cousin died in August of this year. I eulogized his home-going service. He'd accepted Jesus Christ on his sick bed and called me to ask if I would do his funeral and make amends, but by the time he apologized for everything, he could no longer speak. His nurse was able to relay what he wanted to say, though. When I arrived a few days later, he was already gone. Now that I look back I think it was best that way."

It was quiet once again. She looked up to find him watching her intently as though he could glean more from her expressions than what she wasn't saying.

"And your mother?" he reminded her.

"A work in progress." She smiled bleakly. He took her hand again, giving it a comforting squeeze and his lips curved into a smile that warmed her.

Bolstered by this, she took courage in her next breath and asked him to explain his remarks from earlier.

He came to stand in front of her. He was so close she had to tip her head back to look at him.

He took both of her hands, stepped back far enough for her not to strain her neck.

"I do feel protective of you. That I cannot help, but that is *because* my feelings for you are stronger than friendship, though I cherish that too, and will continue to even if your answer to my next question is 'no'."

Her respiration quickened suddenly. Her hands felt clammy and she hoped he didn't feel it. Was he saying what she thought he was saying? She really hadn't seen the signs. He was always so calm and cool...she shook herself out of her musing so she could pay attention to what he was saying.

"I would like to date..." he stalled for a moment then started again, "I would like to court you, Paige."

She stood there trying to look as still as possible, as the little girl in her head did the happy dance.

"Paige?"

"Yes."

He looked at her expectantly.

"That wasn't a question."

His brows knit together as he went back over what he said. His eyes remained serious. "Paige Morganson, will you allow me to court you?"

"Yes, Elder Tatum, I would," she replied with little hesitation.

"You can call me 'Brandon'." She laughed at his attempt at humor while accepting his hug. She was so happy her insides were buzzing. She probably sounded like an electric razor if you got up close.

They soon headed back to his car since the park closed at dusk, and because neither was eager to part company, they went to a nearby cafe and talked until she started yawning.

It was the most glorious day of her life. The whole walk was worth it. She was flying so high, her feet didn't touch the ground as he walked her back to her apartment. At the door, he gave her a slightly lingering hug that chased the chill of the outside away, and she left him with the promise to see him that Friday.

She walked into her apartment, slowly closing the door behind her. She placed her feet in front of her until she reached the bedroom. She made purposeful movements while she concentrated solely on the task of preparing for bed.

It wasn't until she climbed beneath the covers that she let the day run through her mind over and over again, each time slowing it down until she screamed, kicking the covers and flailing her arms, no longer able to keep her happiness bound. She jumped up out of bed and began doing the same dance the little girl did in her head earlier, giggling and laughing all the while.

Thank you, Lord. Thank you for stepping into time to rescue me. Thank you for never letting me go. You are my #1 love, the reason my soul sings and my spirit sighs. You are my healer, my comforter, my best friend, my father. You are my rescuer. Thank you for the gift of Elder Brandon Tatum. I will cherish him in today and if you give it to me, I will cherish him in tomorrow. Thank you...thank you...thank you...thank you...thank you.

The tears were flowing heavily but as each one fell, her soul and voice lifted higher.

Bless your name, Lord. Bless Your Holy name. I magnify you, Father. There is no one greater than You, Lord. There is no one that can do the things you do. Bless your name, Lord. I glorify you, Father. The Glory is all Yours, Lord. I live to worship you, Lord. For you are God, and next to You there is no other. Hallelujah! Hallelujah!

EPILOGUE

Victoria woke up slowly to the feeling of wet warmth on her forehead. It moved to her cheek, then on to her neck. She tried to recall the dream that had taken her back under. Working through the fog and mist shrouding her consciousness, she felt the movement again, only this time it was on her chest. As quick as light piercing the darkness, it all came back to her.

Richard, Richard was there. It wasn't a dream...

She didn't know she had spoken the word out loud until she heard the familiar voice respond, "I'm here, Victoria."

She opened her eyes and waited for them to adjust to the light and the man leaning over her.

"How do you feel?"

Her throat was dry, making it hard to swallow. "Better...much better." She didn't know whether to smile or hide her elation in the fact that he had come back to her. She watched his reaction, looking for any sign of what he was thinking.

"You scared me there for a moment. Did my presence shock you that much?" He leaned back, allowing her to take in the light stubble on his jaws, which were thinner than she remembered, his broad shoulders that barely filled out an old t-shirt, and his jean-clad legs.

"No...it's just that I have been waiting...when I didn't hear from you I thought..." She couldn't seem to finish a sentence. There was so much she wanted to say, so much she wanted to do. "I missed you," she finished lamely, but her eyes never left his.

She saw an expression cross his features, but it was so quick she couldn't decipher it.

"I missed you too." The back of his hand grazed her cheek and she grasped it, holding on and making sure she wasn't still caught up in a dream. She pressed her lips to the calloused palm, reveling in the scent of him. They remained like that for a few seconds before he disengaged his hand.

She watched as a shadow came over his eyes. "We need to talk and it's best if we do it away from the house. It is getting late for breakfast. Would you like to go to brunch with me?"

447

She nodded eagerly. She would have agreed to anything that would keep him close, keep him there.

"Good." He stood up, patting her on the shoulder. "I am going to take a shower and shave the last 18 hours from my face, and I'll meet you downstairs." He walked to the door, glancing back right before he closed it. He gave her a tentative smile, which she returned whole-heartedly.

She sat up quickly, then checked to make sure that the room stayed straight. Feeling stable, she went to her drawers, pulling out necessary items. Her heart was lighter than she could remember. Richard was back. She quickly made her way to the bathroom, closing the door behind her.

She prepared herself as she waited for the shower water to warm. As an afterthought, she decided to use Richard's favorite body wash scent. She remembered storing extra in her closet. She wrapped herself in a robe and walked back out of the bathroom, only to find Richard at her desk near the window with papers in his hand.

She watched his shoulder's sag. His expression was guarded, causing the hairs on the back of her neck to stand up. She walked towards him, curiosity erasing thoughts of her errand from her mind.

"What's that?" She inclined her head towards the papers.

Richard didn't respond immediately, but took a deep breath as though he were gearing up for battle. "I wanted to be here...I was going to wait but..."

Victoria raised her hand, gesturing for him to hand over the papers.

He slowly placed them in her hand. Icy fingers raised down her back as she focused on the words of the title page:

PETITION FOR DISSOLUTION OF MARRIAGE

*   *   *

Mason sat on the edge of the pew next to Vivian. He adjusted his tie for the umpteenth time, struggling for air to fill his lungs. He felt a small hand on top of his. He looked down into his daughter's eyes that seemed to see too much. He managed a crooked smile because only one side of his face seemed to be listening to him.

Vivian returned the smile then patted his hand. "It's almost over," she whispered.

He nodded his head and returned his attention toward the pastor. He watched as the pastor retrieved a cup of covered water from where one of the elders had placed it under the podium. His thoughts took him to Skylight Temple and how the elders worked the service. He never thought he would have enough experience with churches to be able to compare services.

He continued to half listen to the sermon as his mind wandered back and forth between the past and present until he felt his hand being squeezed. He looked over again at his daughter and followed her eyes to the front of the church, where the pastor was now giving the invitation to those who wanted to accept Jesus Christ as their Lord and Savior, those who wanted to rededicate themselves and those who were in need of prayer.

He looked back to his daughter, whose eyes were now pleading. An indescribable feeling came over him. The closest he could come to deciphering it was to call it a mixture of fear and dread. "I'm sorry, Viv. I'm not ready." His heart nearly broke at her expression. Her lower lip started trembling, but she nodded her head in acquiescence. He squeezed her hand in assurance but when he looked up he spied the pastor looking at him.

"Is that you, Brother Jenson? It is good to see you in church this morning. It has been a long time." Mason nodded in acknowledgment, feeling all the eyes of the people in front of him now giving their full attention to him. He felt sweat break out on his upper lip.

"Why don't you come down here and allow us to pray for you?" The pastor gestured with his hand for him to come forward. He looked down at Vivian whose head was also down, but hanging suspiciously low.

*   *   *

Melanie walked in the back door of the house heading straight for the kitchen, her bags of groceries held precariously in her hands. Just as she reached the counter, one of the bags fell forward, its contents spilling out onto the granite top.

"Phew…" She sighed, grateful for the bag waiting until that moment to come undone. "Gladys, I'm home!" she called out. After a few seconds of quiet, she called out again. "Gladys, come down so you can help me put away these groceries." Not hearing a reply, she righted the items and turned to go search for her daughter.

She made it to the doorway of the living room when Gladys rounded the opposite door, her breath coming in short gasps.

"Mom, mom! You will never guess who came to visit!"

Melanie looked up but there was no one behind Gladys. She glanced around the living room, eyeing a set of luggage near the door.

"You know you aren't supposed to let anyone in while I and your father are gone. Who is here?"

"I'm certain that doesn't apply to family."

The voice reached her before the small-framed woman rounded the corner into the living room.

Melanie worked hard to keep the surprise out of her voice, knowing that was exactly what the woman wanted. She stood still, regarding the woman with little more than an impassionate expression.

"Don't you have a hug for your mother?"

As she walked towards the woman all she could think was, *This does not bode well for Paige.*

Not knowing if Paige's call had prompted the visit, she knew she would have to warn her that their mother had resurfaced.

*   *   *

"So... you think you can read me well..."

If he'd been watching the storm come over her eyes instead of being distracted by her lower lip caught between her teeth, he would have already had his answer.

Instead he was taken by surprise as those lips came closer. His eyes flew up to hers with fleeting hope.

He was transfixed by the darkness swirling in them, mesmerized by the color – now close to caramel – that seemed to reach out and hold him hostage.

He felt her palm cup his jaw. Her hand was incredibly small and soft, her fingertips fanning along the side of his face, just short of his ear. He felt each one like a hot poker emblazoning itself upon his skin, branding him to her. He was utterly lost in the sensations of her.

Her face blurred as she came closer, and he had to close his eyes to keep the overwhelming feelings from swallowing him whole.

He wasn't aware of how many seconds passed by as they shared breaths, but, belatedly, he realized she wasn't continuing to close the space between them.

He raised his lashes slowly, daring not to move, lest he break the spell, but as she came back into focus he saw her smiling and the world turned on its axis catching him beneath it.

The shutter that went through him threatened to jar his teeth. He wanted to reach out for her and pull her to him to finish what this stupid bet began. He wanted it so much he could feel his body vibrate towards her, even as he used every ounce of will power to stay rooted.

"I win." He heard her say with that smile in her voice, and it struck him like a bullet.

He took one step back and then another, forcing her to break contact with him. He looked down, guarding his eyes as he attempted to get his emotions under control.

Of all the idiotic things he'd done, this by far was the dumbest. He swallowed against the disappointment once then twice. By the third time, his heartbeat was beginning to slow, but he still didn't have the courage to look up. He didn't trust her with what she would find in his eyes.

He turned around, not intending to go too far, just lengthening the distance enough to take a deep breath of air not tainted by her scent.

"Brandon?"

He lifted his hand with his palm facing her, signaling for her to stay.

"Brandon…I'm sorry…"

"Don't worry. It's okay."

She touched the hand he'd held up and it surprised him so, he yanked his hand back as if she'd actually burned him. He met her gaze unmasked for half a second, allowing her to see the tumultuous feelings he was trying to gain control over.

He heard her gasp in recognition and was sorry for it.

"Too far…I was mistaken…" He stopped, knowing that he didn't make any sense and that he was giving too much away. He knew better than to bet against her; she, who had caused him to feel things he never had before.

Paige stood where she was. The pain on his face was so unexpected it shocked her into immobility. She knew she had been playing with fire getting close to him, but she had so wanted to wipe that smug look off of his face and see if the walls of his forever-present reserve could be shaken.

Even though it had taken more energy than she had first thought to keep from actually moving the last few inches it would take to bring their mouths together, she was elated to find that she was able to resist the temptation. Not only had she considered it a long-awaited triumph, but she was also happy that the years of prayer, shut-ins, altar visits, deliverance and discipline she had been exercising had given her the strength and confidence in her understanding her makeup.

She had been so concerned about her self-control when it came to men she was attracted to. She wouldn't even entertain the thought, let alone get close enough to them emotionally and physically to be tried like this.

This victory had almost been as heady as those few, immeasurable moments when she held his cheek in her hand, mixed breath with him, watched the passion erupt in his eyes knowing beyond a shadow of a doubt that the power of their kiss was in her hand.

She weighed that second. That second she decided she was strong enough to resist him. It was in the length of the space between them and the decision of whether or not to rise up on the balls of her feet, pull his face towards her and touch those full, beveled, beautiful lips to hers.

She wanted that now though, and she wanted it bad. That was why when he moved back and turned away she found herself following after him; she had made her decision. She chose him. In that heartbeat when he'd moved away she tried to get his attention and explain her behavior in hopes that he would give her another glimpse of the emotions roaring beneath the surface of his cool exterior. Only when he looked back it wasn't passion but pain, and her elation deflated.

She watched while his shoulders rose slightly as he breathed in deeply. By the time he'd turned back around the cool reserve was back in place, and she found herself disappointed and wishing that he was still as affected as she was.

There was a sheepish smile on his lips now that turned into a sardonic lift on one side. He motioned with his head, cocking it to the side, and sending it back sharply in the direction of the bench. He turned back, walking to it and sitting down at one edge.

She followed his lead and sat down at the other edge giving him more time and distance.

She watched him shake his head ruefully, chuckling to himself. His hands clasped together.

"Sorry about my behavior back there. It was a stupid idea and just plain wrong for me to try and tempt you that way, but I see you are truly one well in control of her thoughts and emotions. You win, I will keep my promise." He didn't dare look at her, otherwise he wouldn't be able to get out the next sentence.

"Whatever you want. If you wish to leave now, I will take you home."

"May I speak now?"

He only nodded.

"Mmmmm. So, I may have anything I wish?"

He nodded again, still not looking at her.

She slid a couple of inches closer to him.

"Such reserve and resignation. Are you used to martyring yourself?"

She watched as his face turned to her sharply, his eyes searching hers for mockery but then they lost their glow and the hooded sadness came back. She had hurt him deeper than she first realized. She would make it up to him.

He didn't answer her. He just kept watching her, wariness taking place of the sadness.

"I'm going to try to explain something to you, but if you interrupt me I may not have the courage to finish. So please, I ask you to just listen. Okay?"

He nodded.

She took a deep breath, using the time to organize her thoughts.

"I am not sorry on a whole about what just happened, though I am sorry about how it has affected you."

She saw him frown and she raised an eyebrow. He remained quiet.

"I just gained something I have been searching for a long time and I want to share it with you. I need to share it with you." She rested herself on the back of the bench, keeping her eyes on him.

"I know you think I am afraid of men or at least being alone with men and it is true, to a certain extent. I let you believe it was the men I was afraid of, but in fact it is me or my reaction to them. Mind you it has been a while since I have allowed myself to feel any more than a distant respect for men. It was all I could chance.

I became very promiscuous towards the end of my teens. I was looking for someone that would accept me and my luggage but I settled for the ones that paid attention. There were one or two that I let in, but those relationships lasted just long enough for me to find a way to convince them that I wasn't worth it because I didn't think I was worth that type of love. I was just hoping they would see through my insecurities, jealousy, frustration with me and anger for being afraid in the first place. It was a tall order. I knew that, but I was hoping they were willing to love me past all of that even though I couldn't."

She had broken his gaze somewhere in the middle of her statement, her eyes watching some of the leaves swaying on the branch just behind him.

"I did a lot of things I never thought I would do with a lot of men I'd never have looked twice at but I began to use the attraction that lured them to try to keep them. I mistook the sex for intimacy, and moans and half-hearted endearments as declarations. I wasn't aware that even as I asserted my power over them I was losing control to the same urges I continuously gave into." She looked back at him, trying to see if he was disgusted but his expression was unreadable.

"When I rededicated my life to Christ, I received a promise that this was not all there was. That I could ask for forgiveness, put away my old ways, place my past into the sea forgetfulness and forgive myself. I had a chance to start over and I took it. Whatever it was going to take, I was up for it. I wanted to love myself and what I did. I wanted to find value in myself and my relationship with Christ allowed that. He convinced me that I was not only worth saving but that I had a purpose. My life wasn't behind me and my usefulness wasn't behind me either.

It's amazing how a purpose appreciates you in your own eyes. I found that I wouldn't put myself in places or situations that would compromise that purpose or the love I have found in myself. But I was so intent on avoiding certain situations, I didn't think of what I was going to do when they presented themselves." She had to look away so that she could finish.

"Not until I decided to be friends with you, did I have any care to explore it. I've watched people and myself long enough to know that avoiding a situation doesn't necessarily mean you are delivered. What would happen if I found myself in a situation where I had to practice what I preached? I needed to know what part of me was louder and even more important, what part of me I would inevitably listen to. I didn't know for certain until just a few minutes ago how much stronger my love for God and the spiritual strength I have in Him was than my flesh. It's nice to know I could resist you."

She saw him move and looked back at him. The frown was back.

"What I am about to tell you I am going to ask you not to use it against me. Okay?" She watched his eyebrows rise in surprise, but he lifted his hand as a promise.

"Now I can see that you are gifted in the area of restraint. Until the day of the bet I wasn't even sure you had feelings beyond friendship and a mild attraction for me. You seemed so cool and aloof, I felt a little ashamed sometimes of the thoughts I had of you." She watched as his eyes widened further. She could feel the heat of a blush come up her neck, her ears would be bright red in a moment.

"I would rather you not take me home right now. I am enjoying the day with you." She looked away, unable to say what she needed and look into his eyes at the same time. She was almost…no she was embarrassed, but it was no less true or humbling than what she'd just put him through.

"I would like to change my request on my side of this bet, if I may." Still wide-eyed, he nodded his acceptance.

"Maybe not just now, because it would feel more like me asking and it doesn't really fit with my romantic sensibilities, but before you drop me home today would you kiss me? Not as part of a pretense or game, but because you want to." She looked him straight in the eye and watched the myriad of changes sweep across his face. The second to last one was so intense it made her stomach knot up. Her hand fluttered to her abdomen, unheeded. Watching the movement, his features finally settled around a small smile.

She was the most surprising woman he had ever met. Who would have thought? He didn't think his life had room for this gift. The gift of her, Paige, this wonderful woman as unpredictable as any woman could be. He was amazingly blessed and for the first time in months he was more than content. He was sincerely grateful to be who he was in this moment.

He also wondered what would be an appropriate amount of time to wait before he kissed her. This was like giving a child a gift certificate to a candy store, taking him into that candy store but telling him to wait to actually pick something out.

So much made sense now, but he would have time to think about that later. Right now he was going to have to find things to talk about as far away from kisses as possible. Who was he kidding? Kisses, lips, breathing, hands and faces were all off the board as far as conversation was concerned.

"I saw First Lady Menagerie Wednesday night. She asked me about you."

"Really? What did she say?" She sounded on edge.

"Not much because she was on her way to a meeting. She wanted to know if I'd seen you recently, you know, as a part of the Visitation Committee. She was concerned about how you were feeling."

She rolled her eyes. "That seems to be the million dollar question lately." Her frown puzzled him.

"People are concerned for you. They want to make sure you are healthy and if you aren't, they want to know if they can do anything for you. You are surrounded by people who love you, really love you. The kind of love that would cause them to really miss you if you were gone."

He saw a creep of red come to her ears as she looked down and away from him.

"It's not that I mind the concern. I am blessed and I know it. I love my church. They truly are family to me. I am just not used to all of the attention. I am grateful. It could be so much worse, but I am healthy so I don't think that they should be spending time visiting me when there are so many others that would love to get that attention and visitation."

He watched her while she spoke, mystified by the reluctance she still had in accepting help. He really didn't know as much about her as he first thought. Surprisingly it wasn't disenchanting but alluring. He wanted to know everything there was to know about her and be on the inside of all of the jokes. He wanted to know what pleased her so he could do it before she knew how to ask for it and know what she didn't like so that he wouldn't do it. He wanted it to be memorable.

"Want to take a walk?" He asked as he watched her trying to blend in with the bench.

She looked up at him with surprised pleasure. "Yeah, sure."

"What's your favorite color?"

"We are down to colors? No more questions about my dreams and aspirations, how I want to change the world and press my mark to the very center of it by being used by God in every way?"

He shook his head, taking her hand in his as she began to walk next to him. Her fingers were cold so he wrapped her arm through his and stuck both hands in the pocket of his coat. He caught her sideways glance but didn't acknowledge it. "I already know the answers to those questions. Now I want to know what your favorite color is." She laughed her contagious laugh. He couldn't help but smile.

Since he'd asked to court her three weeks ago, they'd at least talked every day. They spent most of their weekends and early evenings together whether it was walking in the park, grabbing dessert, looking at the Christmas lights or going Christmas shopping.

He had been able to get away from the family for a few hours today to spend time with her alone at their favorite park so he could tell her about the cancer, but things were definitely not going in the direction he'd planned. He didn't know where he was going to get the strength from but he would have to tell her before she met his family tomorrow. He couldn't take the chance of her finding out from one of them.

"It kind of depends. I don't have just one favorite. It is the one on that particular day, month, or season that I am partial to; that makes me feel better. But to answer your question, today my favorite color is somewhere between the reddish-orange and yellow that tree leaves turn in the fall. No one gets it right better than God. Even when I see the fake ones in the stores all I see are slightly faded copies of the real thing." She let the sentence fade but the wistful smile told him she was away in a memory.

He pulled her back with his next question. "What is your favorite name?"

She looked up at him quizzically. "Paige?"

He almost laughed but then saw that she misunderstood the question. "What is your favorite name for a male or female?" She did laugh then.

"Mmmm." She looked up at the trees as she thought it over. A couple of seconds later she answered, "Alexander for male; Elizabeth for a female."

"I'm a little surprised by how quickly you answered." He stopped to face her, hoping her answer to his next question would be 'No'. "Are you saving these names for your children?"

She looked up at him. He didn't know he was holding his breath until she started shaking her head.

He turned them so they could continue to walk forward on the path lined by Black Cottonwood, White Adler and Sycamore trees. He started down a long line of questions that she answered about her favorite clothing, gems, months, books, people, singers, movies and food, which brought him to a question he had been thinking about for a while.

"Remember the first Elder's fellowship I attended?" He watched her incline her head. "You mentioned something to me when I told you what my favorite dish was at Ming's. It was the Sweet and Sour Chicken and you called me a ..."

"'A Sweet and Sour Man.'"

"Yes, exactly. What is the story behind that?"

"Why does there have to be a story?" He looked over at her but she was faced forward with a too innocent expression.

"First Lady said the same thing when I spoke to her a few days later. I asked her what it meant and she told me I would have to ask you, so I am asking you. Will you please tell me?"

She disengaged her hand from his and slid it out of his pocket. She kept her arm around his though and kept walking forward. He was having a great deal of fun watching her work at not blushing and it was only heightened by her failure at it.

"Could I decline to answer that one?" She finally turned to look up at him, squinting in the setting sun. The colors moving through the trees played in her hair and at that moment he couldn't think of any more questions.

"Um, yes..." he cleared his throat. "For now." His voice was still husky. He stopped walking. They were now shaded by a row of trees at the end of the walkway. There was a small breeze flowing through and he saw her shiver next to him.

Paige had kept track of the pathway. She watched the changing of the leaves from tree to tree as they walked along, playing interrogation.

She had given him an opening back there at the bench, and though she had said "Not right now", they were now a good hour away from that moment. Was he really going to wait until he dropped her home? Maybe she was mistaken by what she saw in his eyes. She wasn't used to men who were able to practice such a degree of self-control around her. Wait a second...he didn't give any indication that he intended to give her what she asked for as a reward for winning the bet. Maybe all of these questions were to distract her? She was beginning to feel really embarrassed. The sun was beginning to set and soon they would have to leave, and he was still asking questions. She was beginning to feel flushed with humiliation. She had shared some very personal information with him. Was she wrong in her choice?

Then he asked her about the "Sweet and Sour Man" comment she had made when they were in the parking lot of the restaurant, and she was done...done giving away information...giving away glimpses of her soul, so she asked to decline to answer.

Well now, they were at the edge of the trees and it was getting cold. A small wind blew right through her clothes and walked up her spine. The chill shook her and she was ready to concede to the evening and tell him she was ready to go home.

He turned to her, looking her squarely in the face. "Are you cold?"

"Yes," she nodded.

He took off his coat and held it out for her to slip into. It smelled like vanilla and sweet musk. She was never going to get used to the smell of him. It always made her mouth water. He pulled the oversized coat around her and rolled back the sleeves at her wrists. "Is that better?" She could only imagine what she looked like now – a little girl playing in her father's wardrobe. She felt dejected. She looked down at the smoothed over cement slabs and nodded again.

She was surprised when he reached out and placed his forefinger under her chin in order to raise her face. She wouldn't raise her eyes at first. "Paige, please look at me." His voice sounded slightly raspy, but when she looked into his eyes she saw concern.

"Did I do something?"

She shook her head. "No." *He had done nothing.*

"May I?"

His finger still under her chin was now accompanied by his thumb which held her in place. Her heartbeat quickened instantly, as if a gun had gone off at the races. She couldn't keep her eyes from widening in surprise and she knew he'd read it on her face when his mouth took on an easy smile. He stepped closer and three of her five senses picked up every minute detail.

She swallowed, trying to remember how to breathe. It felt like time was moving very slowly, and she was thankful because she wanted to be able to recall every moment of this.

He brought his other hand up to trace his fingertips along the edge of her brow to the hollow underneath her jaw, his eyes following them. He turned his hand over, allowing the back of it to run along the side of her neck.

She couldn't help the shiver that ran through her nor the heat that swam up to the tips of her ears.

"I like this thing your ears do. It is quite charming." He smiled, his eyes growing so warm they reminded her of black coffee. Not able to find her voice, she smiled sardonically. She'd always considered it a nuisance.

His gaze locked with hers and she found she could do nothing but watch as his face descended towards hers. As his eyes went out of focus she caught his mouth just before it lowered out of view. She looked up one last time to watch his lashes fan out along his cheeks, and then his lips touched hers. She didn't know what to expect, but she could not have imagined the warmth that budded and blossomed in her core.

The kiss started out slowly, softly. The movement of his lips on hers felt like he was trying to burn the feel of them into his memory.

She felt wrapped in a cocoon of warmth, the sensation filling her thoughts, spilling over into each one of her senses. She could feel his hands coming up to cup both sides of her face, as his lips molded themselves around hers. She could smell vanilla mixed with peppermint, and hear the roaring sound of blood rushing in her ears.

Her limbs were losing their solidity. She was melting into liquid warmth and she liked it. She began moving her lips with his, seeking something she didn't yet know the name of. But it was there, just slightly out of reach, causing her to move in closer. Even as she did, he began to lighten the pressure of the kiss, pulling back slowly, turning the one kiss into many small ones.

And then they were gone. Her mind screamed. It was over too quickly. She could still feel his hands on her face but the cool air between them let her know that he had moved away.

She opened her eyes to see him smiling at her, but the intense burning in his eyes belied what the rest of his features were displaying.

"That one was for you..." His voice was just a rough whisper.

Her breath caught in her throat.

"This one is for me." She watched as his head descended again, those beautiful lips coming back. Her heart started pounding in her chest now. The closer he came, the surer she was that he could hear it. From the moment his lips met hers, she knew it was different. There was an intensity to it that demanded a response this time. His hands rotated while his fingers splaying and moving to the back of her neck, holding her there as he pressed his lips more firmly to hers.

Like I was going to try to get away.

His lips moved back and forth in a hypnotic rhythm that ignited something deep within her. Where the first kiss had invited and welcomed, this one subdued and conquered. There wasn't a movement, sound, or feeling she wasn't aware of as the onslaught on her senses continued.

The rubbery languished feeling in her limbs was replaced by a deep heat that seemed to be flowing towards the pit of her stomach, and she wanted to see where it would lead.

She never remembered being kissed like this before.

She raised herself up on her toes, turning her head to the side in order to deepen the kiss. Straining to get closer, she reached up placing her hands on his shoulders for leverage. The groan that came from the back of his throat only encouraged her, pushing her past reason, seeking, searching, yearning...her lips parted under the pressure of his, and she sighed.

Then his lips moved from hers and she could hear his ragged breaths near her ear. His hands were on her back, she could feel the heat through his coat as he hugged her to him. She could feel his body heaving as his lungs struggled to take in enough oxygen. She wasn't doing too much better, her breaths coming in short gasps.

And then she was pushed away. At first she didn't know what had happened; there was a foggy haze that refused to clear from her mind.

She opened her eyes, noting that she would have fallen forward if his hands weren't on her shoulders holding her steady.

His head was down, but the deep crease between his brows did not escape her observation.

Great. She had made him angry. "S-sorry," she finally got out.

His head whipped up, startling her. He stared at her, eyes still blazing. "Why...are you apologizing?"

"I-I...thought I....You have a scowl on your face," she resorted to saying.

He finally took a deep breath and let it out slowly, removing his hands from her shoulders.

"That was directed at me, not you." He shook his head. "I know better than that."

She watched him quietly for a moment, going through what happened, and could only come up with one conclusion.

"Do you regret what happened?" She looked away, suddenly feeling very cold and very vulnerable.

"No. Not at all. I am just used to handling things with more control than that but I am beginning to understand that life with you is full of surprises. I should have known better than play with the tenuous grasp I had on my self-control. I am the one that is sorry."

She listened in silence, not interrupting while he berated himself.

"When you say you are sorry, does that mean you won't kiss me like that again?"

His eyes went wide. "You're not upset or offended?

She cocked her head to the side, confused. "Should I be?"

He stared at her for a few moments, then shook his head some more. He lifted his shoulders once and then let them fall in defeat.

"You are an enigma. I can't seem to figure you out. I thought a while ago when you were telling me about your little victory it meant you were happy about your restraint and ability to resist me. It pricked my ego a little, but I was willing to go along if it was what you wanted. No man, no matter the reason, likes to hear that he is resistible."

"I was intent on not pressing the issue, but then you responded so...and I wanted to know if it was to me or if you were just a really good kisser. By the time I figured it out I was perilously close to the edge. It was all I could do to make my hands set you away from me." The brightness was back in his eyes.

She watched the expressions sweep across his face, and then an impish grin crossed her lips. "You didn't answer my question. Does that mean you won't kiss me like that again?"

He groaned. She was going to test his reserve for sure.

461

"I honestly don't know if I have the strength to resist you."

"I don't understand. You are always the picture of restraint and cool reserve."

"On the surface, but underneath you have been hacking away at it from the first moment I saw your face. Each smile, each wide-eyed look, each laugh has taken its toll on my self-control, where you are concerned. If I were you I'd get one of your friends to chaperon us when we go out from now on."

"Really? Do you mind if I test that theory?" she said, taking a step closer. The glint in her eyes actually scared him and he backed away, hands up in surrender.

"Please, Paige, I'm serious."

"So am I. I find this news fascinating. What a very pleasant surprise." She took another step towards him.

"Ah come on, Paige, play nice." His back came up against the fence.

His back was ramrod stiff as she closed the gap between them, slowly moving like a predator about to pounce on its prey.

He watched her eyes as they danced then glowed, and then she was standing close enough to touch him. He saw her hand lift towards him and he clenched his teeth, resigned to stay immobile.

She placed her palm flat against his chest over his heart, but moved no closer. She watched his eyes, her gaze shifting back and forth between them looking for something, but he didn't know what it was. The feeling of déjà vu was almost eerie.

"I choose you. I choose this." Her hand patted the place above his heart.

The elation he felt was overwhelming. "Are you sure?" he asked in a quiet whisper, afraid the intensity of his emotion would choke him.

She nodded. "Yes."

The elation wavered slightly with the doubt that swept through him with the next thought. He had to tell her. She needed to know.

He placed his hand over hers, squeezing the fingers tightly for a couple of seconds as he bolstered himself with the courage to speak the words that could just as quickly have her reneging on the declaration she'd voiced only moments before.

He stared into eyes that held a whisper of promise for him.

One more minute, just one more, he promised himself as he watched her gaze turn from one of acquiescence to curious expectancy. He took a deep breath, closing his eyes briefly to lock away the memory of her expression in this instant so that he could pull it up later if she changed her mind.

The air seemed to still. He no longer heard the rustling of leaves, the squawking of birds, or the movement of smaller creatures. It truly seemed as if nature was holding its breath as it waited for him to get in one accord with it.

"Paige, you have been one of the greatest surprises of my life and I am deeply humbled by you." He swallowed hard.

"I need to tell you something…" He dared to look back into her eyes as he formed his next words.

"Okay, I understand, but…could we just wait right here? It seems that I have traveled so long to get to this moment right here. She reached up, drawing his attention from his thoughts. She traced her fingertips upon his dark brows, lightly skimming down the center of his face to the bridge of his nose.

She watched as he went still, allowing her to explorer his features by touch. He closed his eyes and she took in the beauty of his thick, black lashes, feeling the shine of them on her fingertips. She was grateful and wonderfully blessed to witness the beauty of this man whose features were becoming more and more exquisite with each glance.

She traced his cheekbones, skimming along to his jawline and chin. She took a deep breath as she tore her eyes away from his lips to return them to his eyes, which were now open and watching her. She smiled shyly, extremely happy to share this moment with him, no matter how long it would last. She wasn't in a hurry to do anything else but revel in the warmth of his gaze.

The expression on her face, poignant and clear as shards of glass, cut through his mind, pushing away the latter memory of her happiness, and flinging him into a sea of guilt for not being able to keep his own promise never to hurt her.

She'd chosen him, but did they have a future together?

One more kiss and he would tell her. One more kiss would prepare him for whatever answer she gave him. He had this one last moment of euphoria in the light of her eyes. No matter what, it was more than enough to know that she'd chosen him just like the Lord had said she would.

This is the end of this book, but the story continues

"My Oil of Joy For Your Mourning" the second book in the Promises to Zion Series. Keep reading for an excerpt.

My Oil of Joy For Your Mourning

Now Available

Join Paige, Brandon, Mason, Victoria and Richard in the next installment of the Promises to Zion Series, My Oil of Joy For Your Mourning. The story continues and new twists and turns reveal secrets kept for too long.

www.amazon.com/Your-Mourning-Promises-Zion-Book-ebook/dp/B00Q4CKOZO/

Excerpt From My Oil of Joy For Your Mourning

One month. She kept thinking. *One month... less than that; three weeks, two days, six hours, and a measly 22 minutes.* That was how much time she'd had to be blissfully happy – happier than she could ever remember being with a person. With no expectations of ill of fate caused by bad decisions, she hadn't seen it coming. She pondered back and forth as her eyes danced from one end of the carpet to the other, mimicking the racing thoughts in her head.

"Where did I go wrong? I know I heard You. It was just as clear as the blossoming love I feel for him. Augh! Why? Why am I continually denied? What is it about my life that thwarts, even repels, happiness? Why can't I have it? There are so many who never even experienced a moment of physical pain or illness. Why can't that be him?"

In the cool of the dark room, she waited... waited for an overwhelming feeling of peace; that feeling of calm and unexplainable rightness that would tell her that everything was going to work in her favor.

She waited for the feeling, and a word telling her that there was nothing to be concerned about. She waited...and waited...until she could no longer hold back the feelings of anxiousness and dread. She stopped waiting and gave into the dimming feeling of fear, letting the pain of another dream lost, wash over her.

A sob reverberated off the walls, causing her to start at the unfamiliar sound. She held her breath listening for the sound again, before realizing it had come from her. She then wrapped her arms around her body, hugging herself tightly. She girded herself with a shadow of strength, making one last effort to stave off the gut-wrenching heartache she feared would swallow her whole.

Not even making an attempt to crawl into her bedroom, she leaned over, laid her head on the sofa cushion, and pulled her knees up to her chest. She rocked herself back and forth until she fell into a restless sleep.

"I dreamed about you," he said, maneuvering into the right lane. In that fleeting moment his somber expression caused a knot to form in her stomach.

"What? When? Was it good or bad?" Paige turned towards him from where she sat in the passenger's seat. She could sense a restlessness within him, like he was struggling with a decision.

"The night after we met… well actually, the whole week after we first met." He glanced away from the tree-lined street he was driving them down. She didn't know how to digest this new information, so she tried wit.

"Wow. I must have made some impression on you." She watched as a hesitant smile passed over his lips, and it made her uneasy. "What were they about?" she asked, not quite sure she wanted to know.

They pulled up to a stop sign as he began relaying the series of dreams that had progressed a little further each night – the first being the one revealing him as a statue. The dream started at the beginning each night, only to advance just a little bit further than the evening before, until the last night when he was fully brought to life by her surrendering her heart over to him.

She found herself enthralled by the turn of events, wondering what it meant. She asked him if they'd spoken in his dream. He quickly glanced her way then back to the road, taking a deep breath. She was curious as to why he was having such a hard time telling her about a dream that he'd brought up in the first place.

"It fits."

She blinked after a moment, realizing that there was no more coming forth. "I don't understand."

"You laid your hand on the place where my heart should have been and gave me yours. It fit." He pulled into a parking space near her apartment building, turning off the ignition.

He turned so that he could fully face her. "'It fits' is what you said before you turned to stone."

She sat there trying to calm her heart that had just taken off at a gallop. Was he saying they were meant to be together? Had he taken the dreams as a sign that she was his? ...*But then there was the turning to stone thing.* Were they not destined to be together? She shook her head, working to stay in the present.

"What do you think it meant?"

She watched him shrug as he looked down at the gear shift between them. "At first I thought it was just my subconscious trying to get my attention. I was very focused on what I came to Los Angeles to do, which was advance in my job and take on a position at Skylight Temple. Getting involved with anyone was nowhere in my plans."

"And after?" she asked, trying to wrangle a reason from him.

"By the time the week was over I was...curious."

"Just curious?"

He smiled sheepishly.

Dear Reader,

It never gets old. These books are my heart beating on a page. The words speak to me sometimes way before they reach paper or just before and I am blessed.

It's hard to express the gratitude I feel for you choosing to spend your time in my world so I will just say thank you and ask that you would take a moment and leave a review. I really am interested in what you thought, what touched your heart and even what didn't.

Please send your questions or thoughts to me at authortraci@gmail.com

You can also visit my website at www.tawcarlisle.com and follow me at www.twitter.com/traciwcarlisle and www.facebook.com/traciwoodencarlisle

I am working on my next book because my characters just won't leave me alone and my crew-of-a-few are diligently combing the pages to make sure I didn't leave out any important details…

Until next time,

Keep reading and expand your dreams

Traci Wooden-Carlisle

About the Author

Traci Wooden-Carlisle lives in San Diego with her husband. She works as a church office manager and writes whenever she can find five quiet minutes. She's a former graphic artist by trade and still uses it as a creative outlet. She loves her coffee in the morning and fuzzy slippers at night. She loves to read anything romantic – the more inspirational the better. For fun she dances and teaches the occasional fitness class.

MY BOOKS

Promises of Zion series

My Beauty For Your Ashes

My Oil of Joy For Your Mourning

My Garment of Praise for Your Spirit of Heaviness

Next in the series:

Promises Fulfilled

Chances Series

Chances Are...

Chandler County Series

Missing Destiny

Missing Us

Missing the Gift

Made in United States
Orlando, FL
16 July 2023

35185742R00261